ALL MY MOST MEMORABLE TIMES HAVE BEEN IMAGINED

by

John P Devaney

The original versions of some of these tales first appeared on my blog, 'Anatomy Of A Madness', at http://jaypeedee.blogspot.com/.

Cataloguing-in-Publication data:

All My Most Memorable Times Have Been Imagined

ISBN 978-0-9556897-6-5

1. Fiction/Biography
2. Australia/England
I. Devaney, John.

Contents

For Laura, with love

December 2023.
Catherine and Rod,
with much love,
Laura. xx

The butterfly, a cabbage-white
(His honest idiocy of flight)
Will never now, it is too late,
Master the art of flying straight,
Yet has - who knows as well as I? -
A just sense of how not to fly;
He lurches here and here by guess
And God and hope and hopelessness.
Even the aerobatic swift
Has not his flying crooked gift.

- Robert Graves

Queen Victoria ..... felt that her true life had ceased with her husband's, and that the remainder of her days upon earth was of a twilight nature - an epilogue to a drama that was done.

- Lytton Strachey, 'Queen Victoria'

PART ONE:

FRAGMENTS OF A LIFE AFTER DEATH

1970 to 2009

1st May 2009

All my most memorable times have been imagined, but no less real for that ....

4th April 2009

It's possible to love with passion for so long that you forget what it was that captivated you in the first place but you're unable to stop loving because the passion has acquired an impetus all its own that hurtles you onwards into spaces that only exist because the things in which you used to believe have disintegrated, leaving a gap that needs to be filled. The loved object becomes entirely irrelevant, other than in the theoretical sense of fuelling a distraction, of helping you forget - indeed, when all is said and done, of keeping you alive.

And no, you never or seldom get anything meaningful or encouraging back from the loved object, which if it had a personality and/or a will would almost certainly actively despise you anyway.

18th March 2009

Trudging home from Tesco's, desiccated leaves crunching underfoot like wasted lives, I overheard clamorous shouts emanating from a distant rugby match, its participants presumably immersed, if briefly, in a shared reality even more surreal than mine.

In mine, escape is something purely theoretical, like equal rights for all, or the existence of extra-terrestrial life.

And yet, beyond all else, and in straight defiance of both empirical logic and experience, escape is everything I seek, and perhaps, when all the chaff is abandoned, the only thing worth seeking.

28th November 2008

A bald, emaciated caterpillar strains at something not quite reachable, totters semi-transfixed within an endless nanosecond of confused belief. Then falls, forever.

I too was once a coiled spring of pregnant possibility, my outward form contorted into a shape suggestive of supplication, horror or surrender. I crawled inside an empty, disused drainpipe that had somehow been provided, or forgotten, and was thus enabled to escape the kind of scrutiny we all must sometimes face, if only in our half-remembered dreams.

In mine there was a girl whose hair might fleetingly caress my naked skin if only I forgot to understand, if only I was innocent.

But too much comprehension made me penitential, and so I haplessly emerged to accept my sentence.

Suffocated into dysfunction then by terrors too incoherent and frenzied to be named, I sat examining that same bare skin in the feeble hope that I might somehow miraculously transcend it. I wished, with silent earnestness, for another life, another me, outside the constant cycle of confused regret, beyond the omnipresent disarray of my desires, ambitions and beliefs.

Sometimes, summoned up from deep within, another me in fact does emerge, intent on a spurious kind of resistance or self-protection, and I am forced to stand back in dumb acquiescence, complicit in a different type of fatalism to that which normally constrains me. Were I to intervene, the whole house of cards would tumble irretrievably down, and even the last vestiges of my sanity and solace would be lost.

And so, instead, I merely sit, and try to watch, a victim as much as an agent of my bemused, importunate rememberings.

2nd August 2008

Life is a forlorn, forsaken wildebeest being steadfastly devoured by unseen jaws. It is a gob of spittle, cursorily vented from the mouth of god, which glistens briefly, frail and unconnected, then dissolves. It is a disguise, which no-one will ever penetrate. It is a succulent piece of fruit, which falls untasted from fumbling fingers, and is consumed by oceanic silence.

And yes, it is, of course, an idiot's mindless rant, the ear-splitting sound of which can all too easily obscure its lack of substance.

It is all of this, and more besides - an unintelligible surfeit of sensory data, an infinitude of wrong answers to an impossible sum, an old man with a harelip drooling in remembrance of the breast, a joke that boasts a different punch-line every time it is told, the corpse of a unicorn presented in bite-sized chunks to a woman without a mouth.

A pitcher plant.

8th July 2008

The difference between lust and love is that the former ends up staring at you, shrew-like, on the corner of the street you once knew, supercilious pout exhaling smoke from half remembered embers as you pull your hat down low across your shaded, shameful face; whereas the latter is a series of dances with someone ever different, someone wholly unexpected and unique, who makes you feel believable.

20th May 2008

It is one of those bright sunny summer's days when everything is exposed: all the mesmerizing hope and frantic yearning, all the beauty, pain and ugliness. Shimmering facades concealing maggots.

Mostly out of guilt I venture out, confronted by the flagrant sun and my own, suddenly incontrovertible decrepitude, imprisoned in my bloated, fetid, seemingly omnipresent flesh.

A man with a moustache walks by, bewildering me. A young mother with angelic arms, and a tattoo that metamorphoses into a belt buckle, presses against her destiny.

I cross the road, anxious to at least endeavour to escape the inevitable despair, the feelings of regret that sometimes seem to represent my whole existence.

Skin, I realise, is just a metaphor for the importunate inevitability of the grave, which I sometimes think might not be quite the consolation I imagine, as I meander, not quite aimlessly, through Walton Cemetery, amused by all the meaningless headstones. ***'Here lies Albert Fraser Langley, born 1956, died 1970, and Rose Jennifer Langley, wife of the above, born 1956, died 2040 - Reunited in the arms of the Saviour.'***

Millions of years of evolution, and still we lack the courage to confront things as they are.

I go back home. Too much exposure can disable. The blazing, iridescent sun, though not quite forgotten, can briefly be ignored, and I can don my loose fitting trousers again as though my flesh, and insight, have once more shrunk to manageable dimensions.

25th March 2008

Once words are committed to the page they become fixed and immutable in a way that no human life ever can be. Thus, anyone who tries to infer a coherent and viable moral framework from any written source is at best a fool, and at worst a budding megalomaniac.

9th January 2008

All too conscious today of the pain of ostracism, of being invisible, emotionally castrated, undesired.

Why is it that whenever I look at a watch, or clock, the time is always thirteen minutes past the hour?

Why is it that everything I touch turns to shit before my eyes?

Too much medication and not enough fornication.

I've seldom felt so sick.

2nd December 2007

Yesterday was one of those days when, no matter how hard I tried, all I could think of was the pain, the failure, the disappointment and the loss. Indeed, like a Chinese finger trap, the harder I tried to wriggle free of these thoughts, the tighter I became enmeshed in them.

I must be very, very evil to be punished so horrendously, and with such adamantine persistence.

15th October 2007

Tonight. Perhaps tonight I'll do it. After all, in a finite universe you can either keep on ducking and diving until you're finally, inevitably grabbed from behind, and dragged down against your will, or you can stand still, and welcome it with open arms, as the friend it hates to be.

Either way, it gets you; it's just a matter of when, and how.

And afterwards, past and future coalesce, and nothing ever was or will be.

23rd September 2007

I finally finished my book, leaving myself safely imprisoned in the bowels of the Castel Felice, consigned to decades of regret, denial and intermittent torment. Despite the fact that I have physically returned to Australia on several occasions since 1970, the world of possibilities, energy and self-fulfilment from which I was untimely ripped back then can never be re-entered, other than through the flawed filter of my recollection.

17th April 2006

I dreamed I was in love and it felt real. Warm, fervent, palpable, moist.

Unrequited.

Then I fell asleep, and everything was all right.

30th March 2006

Forced myself to leave the house, but only managed to get a few yards down the street before the waves of panic emerged, and I felt compelled to return home. Once there, cocooned in reminiscences that have probably become increasingly bogus as their power over me has grown, I studiously endeavoured to refrain from wanting.

Lack of exercise has made me flatulent, and the house begins to reek of half-digested vegetable matter.

7th March 2006

Managed to attend my weekly group therapy session – first time in a month. As usual, I was the only man there (men, as a general rule, are inherently self-sufficient, and so do not need therapy).

We discussed the things we fear most, and all but one of the women cited death. When I told them death was one of the few things I didn't fear I don't think they believed me. I tried to explain. "Death is the absence of everything, including fear," I said. "Everything I fear is bound up with living, because living generates desire, and desire is never satisfied." Aware that I was sounding a little fatuous, like some coffee-table, West

Coast Buddhist, I added. "I don't mean that in any pseudo-spiritual or esoteric sense. I mean it in hard, practical terms. Whatever you want, the opposite happens – in experiential terms, that's as close to an observable physical law, such as the law of gravity, that I've come across."

At that point, Sally accused me – quite gently, it must be said – of wanting to seem macho and tough, at which I had to laugh. "If I was really macho and tough," I countered, "I wouldn't be so terrified of life."

13th February 2006

The bad news I had been expecting and dreading since November finally arrived today. It made me laugh. I felt released, invigorated, vindicated, free. I rolled on the floor, ablaze with mirth. I rocked with laughter till the tears flowed.

The first century Jewish itinerant philosopher Joshua is alleged to have said "You shall know the truth, and the truth shall make you free".

Death is the truth. Death, decay, despair and disappointment. Everything winds down. It is belief in anything else that wounds.

30th November 2005

Had my last psychology session with Louise today. Took great care to generate the most acceptable apparent demeanour and attitude: guarded optimism mixed with recognition that "I've still got a long way to go."

In reality, felt denuded, distraught, bereft of hope or solace. Almost like a bereavement, with my aspirations as the corpse. Was just beginning to derive real benefit from the sessions, and now they're ending. Like having your crutch whipped away and being forced to try to walk with a broken leg.

Will have to try to continue the exploration alone. Not sure it will, or can, be as effective that way, but must try. After all, the alternative is…….

Unthinkable……

19th June 2005

Life is pain, frustration, disappointment, irritation, anti-climax, thwarted ambition, failure.

It is a shrivelled old man without any teeth attempting to eat an ice cream.

An open wound teeming with maggots.

A beautiful girl inside a desiccated hag. A desiccated hag inside a beautiful girl.

15th June 2005

The doorbell rang. Ignored it. Lay on the bed, staring at the ceiling, my mind a maelstrom of thoughts, impressions, recollections.

Nothing tangible can be trusted. Nothing tangible, least of all other people, will save you. Only memories are real. Only memories matter. Refuse the rest.

3rd March 2005

Is there any escape from noise? Since Negativland first posed the question more than a third of a lifetime ago, the answer has not changed.

Take this morning, for example. To the rear of the house, a banshee wails, in attempted time with some obscure eternal rhythm, oblivious that her desires are unattainable. Meanwhile, out front a congregation of men is frantically, and deafeningly, endeavouring to postpone the inevitable.

I suppose, on reflection, that that's the most that any of us can ever manage, or even aspire to – but does it always have to be so loud?

15th February 2005

Spent the afternoon on line - websites about suicide, mainly, of which there are, not surprisingly perhaps, a profusion. Certain methods appeal; most do not. Death from exposure is an early favourite, not least for its metaphorical resonance. Weather's getting warmer though, so may have to reconsider. Don't mind a modicum of pain, but on no account must there be any mess.

Latest episode of 'Scrubs' the best yet. Laughed myself hoarse.

17th February 2004

Was thinking today about the time we crossed the Atlantic in 1970 and struck the edge of a cyclone. Mountainous waves surging over the bows and crashing against the windows of the ballroom, which was on the top deck, and which was where most of the passengers had gathered to watch. Remember feeling awed and terrified. Apparently, there were genuine fears for the ship's safety, or so I later learned. Given everything that's happened, and not happened, since, I really wish she'd sunk.

1st February 2004

Today I wrote and slept.

I hated what I wrote, but enjoyed the process of writing it. I tend to feel the same way about my writing as I feel about myself. Sometimes I find it almost tolerable; usually, however, I loathe it.

Sleeping is better than writing as it brings you closer to the truth. I do not sleep nearly enough.

29th December 2003

Occasionally my faith is challenged by events which appear to imply the existence of an escape route. For hours, sometimes even days, I am lulled into a pathetic, unseemly optimism which holds me hypnotised, like a moth drawn to a flame.

Never underestimate the power of delusions.

15th January 2002

I bought this journal, and the fountain pen with which I have been making entries in it, several days ago on one of those arbitrary whims to which I all too frequently defer.

There is something therapeutic about the physical act of writing, as distinct from manically tapping away at a computer keyboard, and I also reasoned that, by using a fountain pen, a writing tool with which I am unfamiliar, I would need to think more about, and hence, one hopes, be more therapeutically enhanced by, the whole process.

I am not altogether sure it is working.

So what has been occurring in my life?

My days are split between research and writing for my website, spells of torpor, attending to various bodily needs and functions, occasionally watching TV, and reading - all against an omnipresent backdrop of anxiety, angst and anger.

Last Wednesday I saw my 'loony doctor', as P.G. Wodehouse would put it, who recommended that I begin taking lithium alongside the two anti-depressants that I'm already on. I have yet to fathom what, if anything, I feel about this.

19th February 2000

I still feel rudderless and stinted. My faculties are blurred and viscid. I can't imagine ever 'recovering', whatever that means. I almost wish I could die, but I reckon death only ever occurs when you don't want it to.

2nd October 1999

She left me, of course, as I always knew she would. I'm only surprised it lasted this long.

How do I feel? Perplexed. Uncertain. Superfluous. But mostly relieved, even though this time 'round the train ended up actually getting derailed.

31st August 1999

Jennifer's girl has died, and far from feeling bereft or bereaved I feel blessed, rejuvenated. It's the best thing to have happened since That Night in Hong Kong. Doubtless this is entirely hypocritical of me, but who's to know?

3rd March 1998

Still moribund and listless. Is there no end? The arrow may have been plucked, but the wound is still a gaping one.

25th January 1998

It didn't really happen. Except that it did. And I myself am not writing this entry; it is some obscure and enigmatic stranger, with no foothold whatsoever in my life. This mythological personage received a 'phone call at 6.45am, approximately three hours on from The Incident That Never Really Happened.

I feel I must reiterate at this stage that I do not in actual fact have anything at all to do with the writing of this entry. Oh, admittedly my hand holds the pen, and there is a sense in which I am <u>mechanically</u> involved, but the actual process of authorship is the responsibility of someone else.

I forget exactly who.

And so I watched from some enormous distance - through a telescope to a large extent - as this unreal and presumably imaginary stranger departed to a distant place, no longer his own, where nothing happened.

Except that it did.

I think I've got this wrong ......

In the end, I decided to pretend that Someone Had Died. An interesting, original, but ultimately futile version of solitaire. The odd thing was, if I tried really hard, I was able to suspend my disbelief to the extent of actually experiencing genuine grief, a bit like watching a movie or reading a book that so sucks you into its pseudo-reality that what you understand as actual hard core 'real reality' is forgotten about and wholly replaced by the counterfeit version.

The word 'reality' should always come with inverted commas 'round it. I've had faith in so many things that have ultimately turned out to be either lies or illusions that one more surely won't make much difference. Surely ......

14th June 1997

Yesterday, for the first time since getting married eighteen years ago, I made love with a woman other than my wife. It was a transcendental, almost wholly dream-like experience. It put me very much in mind of the scene towards the end of 'For Love Alone' in which the protagonist spends the night entwined in the arms of a friend of her husband's, sharing a deep, impassioned love devoid of any responsibility, demands or expectations, but replete with an exquisitely innocent joy that knew no boundaries.

She was even younger looking than I expected, and immeasurably more beautiful. She had a lilting, playful voice that occasionally grew throaty, though whether from a sudden upsurge of passion, or simple phlegm, I found it impossible to tell. She sounded a good twenty years younger than she was, and looked at least ten. Her English was excellent - much better than that of any of my students.

She collected me from my flat at twenty to one, and we exchanged pleasantries, mainly about our mutual interest in writing, as we drove the two miles or so to her studio. (The term 'studio' was totally appropriate, for this would prove to be a place of high art.) The small hallway as you enter is full of paintings, all Oriental (although whether Chinese, Japanese, Korean or whatever, I know not), of various styles, mainly featuring women. After taking off my shoes we chatted about the paintings for a while and then passed through into the main part of the studio which is, quite literally, like another world.

I took a shower and donned a kimono, as did she, and then we sat and talked of love for half an hour or so. In the end, though, talk is relatively meaningless, and it seemed clear that we were both doing little more than scraping the surface of the fundamental, ineffable truth that underlies all else.

She rose to her feet eventually and said, "All you have to do is relax and let me love you".

"I'm sure I can manage that," I joked, endeavouring to hide my nervousness, as she led me into what, in hindsight, I can only

describe as the Inner Sanctum. Here, for the first time in my life, I would experience all the pure, uninhibited, innocent joy that love, and only love – devoid of strings, obligations and consequences – can bring.

She started by standing behind me and gently touching my head, ears, neck, shoulders and back. Her hands were like gossamer, her movements slow and sensuous. After a time I began to feel as though I was in the presence of an angel, or at any rate not a creature of flesh and blood, so tender, chaste and innocent was her touch.

That was a word that kept resurfacing in my brain – 'innocent'. Everything was a million miles away from the carnal, guilt-sodden, brazenly acquisitive images of sex that constantly bombard us today in western culture. This was love without either restraint or lust. It was also love without commitment or responsibility, other than in the here and now of shared bliss. Ai and I were not in a relationship. We were not even, in any meaningful or enduring sense, friends. Yet that which was inherently female in her spoke to that which was inherently male in me with a gentle depth that rendered all such social conventions temporarily meaningless.

As the intensity increased – although it was an entirely controlled, serene intensity, completely devoid of frenzy, haste or desperation – I began to lose awareness of myself as a distinct and separate human being, to feel all barriers seemingly dissolve. I am not a remotely mystical person by nature, but that is the best way I can think of to describe it.

We ended up on the bed, although I cannot recall how. The physical contact between us felt almost seamless; I could barely tell where one person stopped and the other began. Even talking like that of 'persons' seems somehow to miss the point. Crazy as it sounds, it was as though we had become a single being, half male and half female, created through, suffused in, indeed defined by, love. I could just as readily have moved abruptly or quickly as I could have sprouted wings and flown. If this implies an element of restraint it was tantamount to the nurturing, consoling restraint that a mother bestows on her baby, a restraint which focuses only on the baby's best interests.

I do not think a single square centimetre of flesh, on either of us, was missed. I have a vague recollection of her mouth around my manhood, doing things with her tongue of unimaginable, exquisite gentleness, evoking pleasure of such intensity I was provoked to laugh aloud. When we fucked, it was like sailing on a gently swelling sea, beneath a sky of unrelenting, hopeful blue.

Just as I was on the verge of coming, I chose to stop, and we lay back forever in one another's arms, all futures merely theoretical.

6th December 1996

Organisation breeds confusion .....

A paradox. The anti-Midas touch.

A sealed letter plonked anonymously in my palm - the student disappears amongst a crowd of her fellows. I decide it can wait until break time. Then, over Singapore noodles and stewed mushrooms, the grand opening ceremony:

Dear Teacher Albert:

How are you, I am writing this letter to your At 12 o'clock tonight. I am very thank teacher Albert helped me learnt English in five months. I can read, can wrote, can spoke and can learn little English. When, I went to another classroom to learn English, I am very remember your classroom. Now my far your classroom I very sad, because this classroom is myself souvenir in five months to learn English. I see you very tired. When you teaching for ours. because new and old student in classroom.

Can you will help me to come back your classroom to learn English. If I can't to come back your classroom, I never go to school, and I stay at home self-educated English.

I hope you will help me to return your classroom and you understand me letter. Because midnight I would like sleep. I stopping here and I hope you will answer for me.

good luck for you

student

Huan Cheng

After school, I drove with Guiren, Cheng's brother, to the apartment that they both shared. I suppose I had to. I tried my best to reassure Cheng, but all it brought was tears. Guiren was also crying, though behind a guise of attempted jocularity. It seems these things take time to iron out.

Next day, Guiren arrived, all smiles.

"Where's Cheng?" I asked.

As Guiren's face trembled like a jelly. "Him n-no come to school. B-becow t-teacher come. Him h-h-hap emotion."

The blight of the human race. It perhaps explains the opening line of this entry.

18th August 1992

As a boy I used to pick fights simply for the thrill of inflicting and experiencing pain. My adrenalin would surge and I would lose myself in the flurry and ferocity of the moment.

How then did I come to be the pathetic physical coward I am today? Did I somehow get out of the habit of being brave, or was my courage stripped from me - by events, circumstances, disappointments, failure? More to the point, is it possible to recapture bravery once it's been lost?

Somehow I doubt it.

20th June 1991

If there exists a universe for every possibility then there must be an infinite number of universes, and more Albert Langleys than could be counted in a million life times.

2nd July 1990

It has been claimed that we are all the products of our choices. I agree that choices are to blame, but those choices are not principally ours.

23rd November 1989

All people are intrinsically beautiful, but some elect to disguise that beauty behind make-up, anger, self-consciousness or fear. Others kill the beauty in themselves by becoming wholly self-absorbed. Underlying and informing all of this is the readily observable fact that most people do not even know what beauty is, and so in chasing what they imagine to be beauty they actually end up becoming uglier than ever.

11th January 1988

Not a lot to put. Life continues to be predominantly miserable and monotonous. No, I don't mean that. The basic problem is that I can't be bothered. About almost anything you care to name. Laziness? Perhaps. Despair? More likely. Sickness? Doubtful.

4th April 1986

Each of us invents, inhabits and to some extent maintains his own reality, which is something as uniquely and unrepeatedly ours as a finger print. It is something incommunicable, like colour to the blind, yet real and undeniable as stone.

26th October 1984

Today, for the most part, I lived elsewhere. Not that that is strange. In fact, it's fairly commonplace.

Perhaps it would be more strictly accurate to put 'elsewhen'. For there is nothing now. The past is all I have. My yesterdays are all that's real.

29th September 1984

There was a man who, overnight, developed an aptitude for hypochondria. Nothing else was different .....

19th June 1984

Life is enigmatic; so persistent and formidable, yet, ultimately so meaningless. It terrifies and transfixes me. These words that I am writing will one day be the partial legacy of a former human being. Sad, that. Or else inconsequential. (Both perhaps?) I'm off to bed, no doubt to cry, or else laugh, myself to sleep.

26th April 1984

Today I am old. My sagging body goads me. Although the sun is shining, I am grey inside. Despondent. Hemmed in, demoralised, tormented.

18th February 1984

Jennifer is sitting downstairs talking to her mother. At least, I think it's Jennifer. The face is still the same, but hearts change. Everything changes.

"We are all the victims of each other's carelessness."

People clutch at anything that doesn't move.

Walter and Eileen split up the other day, as did Mark and Amy. Josie and Pete also seem on the verge .. ...

Everything is pointing at a climax; nothing genuinely survives, except .....

Except the one thing that exists.

13th January 1984

For just about as long as I can remember, life, for me, has consisted of an almost unrelenting mental hell. There are occasional periods when the flames momentarily recede, but before you can so much as catch your breath, they're back, with added force, and it's all you can do to stifle the moans.

21st November 1983

I feel thoroughly demoralised and disenchanted. Almost stunned.

But what exactly do I mean? Who is this 'I' I write about?

I do not know. I do not think it can be known.

The last few years of my life have seen, I suppose, an intensification, albeit an unstructured one, of my attempts to find myself, to understand, to shatter all the symbols and the concepts which obscure the underlying truth. To re-awaken, as it were, what is really there.

I've failed.

My mind is more constrained and fouled by concepts than it ever was. I cannot see the wood for the trees.

In all my years of chopping and changing, searching and wondering, pondering and agonising, I myself have hardly shifted. Oh, the ways I give accounts of my experience have altered - seemingly. But what are words? What are thoughts? Most certainly, they're not the thing; they're not 'reality'. They're not -

When all is said and done, <u>they're not</u>!

15th May 1983

Is there any hope for me, I wonder? Twice now I've almost caught the tossed ball of faith, only to fumble it on both occasions. I, and I alone, am the author of my own decay.

Decay, in fact, is just the word to summarise my present state. Nothing pure or wholesome now remains. "I am the very worst of sinners", pushed around and tainted by interminable flights of fancy – moulded by the vacillating 'spirit of the age'.

Capricious as the wind.

I die each day, a thousand deaths, as helpless as a seed released onto the breeze, to land eventually who knows where?

20th February 1983

I've just recalled the world I made those hallowed summer's nights so long ago, while waiting for the world I had not made, which never really was, to end. Although I never sensed its lilting breezes, or perceived its earthy smells, I knew it with a certainty that I've never since been able to reclaim. The lacerating seconds quailed. I dreamed, and sighed, as though possessed. "Tomorrow and tomorrow....... "

Comforting: a lullaby of truth. The words were unimportant, but the music -

Ah!

I swayed and sagged upon the branch of hope - the only thing that plausibly sustains.

I dangled there, protected by the freedom that divides. The gap. The space. The measureless uncertainty of nothingness.

I think I reached the boundary of faith: a gleaming, nugatory paradox. How curious it felt to warm oneself on embers that ostensibly had died! Impossible. Absurd. I laugh about it now.

A friend I had has metamorphosed in reverse. I can't conceive of anything more horrible. To <u>un</u>believe yourself insane.......

Oh, well.

Within - across - below the damning darkness that surrounds us there are many voices calling, many hands outstretched. A meagre touch is all it takes to murder one's awareness; regression is accessible to all.

The virus of presumed attainability.......

I've risen now. I've seen the light.

Excuse me if I squint a bit.

27th March 1982

Today I went to play football. So the sun shines, the wind rages, and my heart is low inside.

I remember hefty punts and droppies cancelled out against the same inevitable wind so many years ago, outside my current universe. The child's voice still insists, with ludicrous conviction, "It isn't fair!"

29th January 1981

Once a state penal institution, Formby Hall only periodically reverts to its former character and temperament. As the brief winter afternoon darkens swiftly into night, I find myself oppressed, intimidated, brutalised. The stark tyranny of loneliness enfolds me in its clamp-like, unremitting hand. The room is swathed almost impenetrably in blackness. I contemplate a memory of freedom.

In the corridor, a noise of footsteps. Gaunt, metallic, harsh, drawing swiftly closer. A clatter of keys. "You'll lock up then, will you Al'? I'm just off."

It is of course a tantalising, tortuous dream. There is and can be no escape.

"Righto Harry. Thanks."

My pen continues to assault the vacant page, eradicating time. Occasionally, an unexplained fluidity of words would rise to penetrate eternity. But that was rare.

Awakened to the startling passage of the hours I prepare myself purportedly to leave. I seem to fumble for the correct key, occasionally beset by surging desperation. But ultimately at liberty to go.

A soundless inner voice proposes mirth. I stagger on in bold, ebullient strides. A semi-suicidal form of self-deception. As tapping key on glass he seems to take away my final tangible bond. There is now the omnipresent sea of blackness all around.

I find I must control the urge to run, to scurry madly, blindly through the terrifying, terrorising gloom. To walk with measured certainty across the most perplexing skein of darkness pulls with painful gravity against my feet's preposterous, importunate urging. I am panting in the cold, antagonistic wind.

The station's murky, tepid light allures, if only tenuously. There has to be a gradual progression – such darkness cancelled out by sudden bursting forth of inexhaustible effulgence would disorientate if not destroy. But as from now, futility decides to wane. The future seems assured.

The tingling of a bell – invariably anti-climactic – followed by the calm, conclusive Closing of the Gates. The signalman with slow, complacent steps does not appear in tune with or aware of the encroaching imminence of eternity. But then again, he has his blazing fire and stack of magazines.

The train a vivid jewel on the black, interminable backdrop. A sumptuous oasis almost lost in the midst of ceaseless sands. A vestigial fragment of civilisation in an almost omnipresent wilderness. My escape is now assured – at least until I pause to analyse my situation. We hedonists are never truly free, "for however high crypto-eagles aspire to soar, in thoughtscape or dream, their human natures cannot but cling to any circumstantial straw which may indicate an ordered universe."

17th April 1980

Sitting in a crowded bedroom drinking cold coke and waiting in vain for conversation. Face flushed and body tired and hot from too much embarrassment, too much yearning. Half past eight the door slammed behind, a muffled sound of laughter. "We don't want you here." The old persecution complex re-emerging.

24th September 1979

I was married last week. The people sang and stomped and all but danced. Even my dad, whom I'd thought frozen into immobility by a stern religion, even he rejoiced, and lifted up a heavy heart.

I pondered as I held my bride's hand how soon the vivid certainty of it all would dwindle into fond but hazy memories. And yet, it seemed the whole experience was itself situated somewhere just a yard or so from what we call reality. An almost dream. The calm, recumbent air molested by camera clicks, the smudged red lips of not-quite-knowns, aghast against my face, the trembling warmth of Jock's soliloquy. All forever never there.

We paused at Jennifer's mum's to re-design the wedding car. A brown austin allegro, we said, would be nice. And off we drove against the clear, impossible sky, that God had presumably made especially to celebrate our union.

While at table, disembowelling mushroom omelette, I fiddled with my ring and thought 'this woman is my heart mate from now, until our blood has ceased to circulate in our bodies'.

The loose ring would soon grow firm around my finger.

Through the night we tried in vain to make our bodies coalesce. It didn't matter. All that really signified had been transferred and united already. Had been made plain. So what of dying flesh?

"To love, to cherish, to have, to hold, from this day forward, for better, for worse, for richer, for poorer, in sickness and in health, as long as life still binds us to this earth."

The words have somehow jumbled in my jumbled mind; but meanings take on many different forms. Our every gasping future breath redoubled by a sharing that must embrace entirety. Nothing kept in hidden pockets.

Now I sit in somewhat mucky surroundings pondering the culmination of a segment of my life. This room, devoid of what the western world would term 'home comforts' (though in reality, containing luxuries in almost every corner), this room now constitutes my home.

(I listen to the sun-diluted wind whistling about the bushes; here inside a cosy kernel of my womb there is calm.)

In years to come, the memories which this day, these days, make will circulate in my brain and become inseparable from the pseudo-Americanisms of Linus Campbell, the tears of unwanted leave taking (another significant time of omelettes), the red-faced roaring at a vital winning goal, the long nights of talk and beer and smoking in the college bar with Alan and Ruth. For only now has more than one dimension to it. Only now, in truth, has anything at all to do with time. All my pasts and all my futures constitute (it might sound a bit banal, but think) a kind of eternal omelette, with an occasional mushroom here or there, and maybe a tomato or two, to represent variety in taste. It's all one, however; and ultimately my wedding day and all its sound and colour is just the same as depositing unwanted ants on bare and innocent skin.

24th September 1978

Dreams are much less real than imagination (?) but much <u>more</u> real than love.

7th May 1977

There are times – like now, for example – when I all but cease to function. I am, to quote the jargon, "functionally transfixed". I don't know where to turn. Assistance seems entirely unattainable. I've almost reached the point, on more than one occasion, of wishing myself dead.

God, if God exists, is not only imperceptible, but wholly beyond the scope of our comprehension. There are many gods created by the hands and minds of men but none, so far as I can see, that transcend in any way the merely human. Perhaps that's to be expected. Illiterate savages can have no conception of the written word; the understanding which a dog has of most of its owner's behaviour will be negligible and, presumably, wholly confined to a canine sphere of relevance. So the empirical absence of a transcendent deity is not, in itself, tantamount to a refutation of the <u>*idea*</u> *of deity. But I must admit it doesn't help.*

As I've been sitting writing this the sun, after a prolonged period of slumber, has reappeared, if somewhat insipidly. My spirits have accordingly revived, or at any rate begun to. Whimsical and frail, my mind is on the verge of cracking open. "I am dying, Egypt, dying!"

In the intermission Jennifer came and we attached ourselves to one another, limpet-like. The flow of pain was briefly staunched. All delusion of course, but so is so much else.

27th November 1976

They go away. They usually return. This time, her hair is dangling down like creepers. She is wet. She smiles. "I brought the food." Her eyes are big with happiness. She smiles - I think about the taste of food. She looks at me with happy eyes, her face grown bright with expectation. "Shall we eat?" The question is a lure. I think about the dangling, twirling line, the helpless fish unwieldy on the end. I think about the going and the coming, how they usually but not invariably unite. I think about the taste of food. My wet mouth says, "Sure, let's." I think of how the mouth becomes enlivened with the oozing moisture of intent.

Begin. The acceptable procedure. Having gone, and now returned, she has the happiness to smile. She looks at me and I at her. As we both consume the food our throats are gradually restored. We find the nameless joy of hidden, unexpected morsels; the wetness is astounding. "More," I say, and grasp at that which cannot be denied, although its nature will, inevitably, and maybe more than once, be changed. She kills the wetness of her gleaming fingers on her downward-dangling hair. I do the same, but mine is stretching heavenward. I move across the difference - the fatness of our bellies lulls. I lie upon her. Directions, always moving, alternate completely. I hang above her briefly - strongly; something loosens. The food inside us gurgles. "More," she insists, but I cannot move. I fall beside her like a landed fish. She makes a tiny noise which irritates. "It's over." I am certain that the future is ordained. She says again: "More - more." I say that it is over. "No!" Her eyes are even bigger now but loathsome; it is often thus. The coming and the going - they are one, but not the same. The difference which divides us reappears.

22nd February 1976

It seems that Ruth has resolved not to acknowledge what happened between us after last year's Stoneyside Christmas party. That's her privilege, I suppose, but it doesn't mean that nothing actually occurred - or does it? Is her denial tantamount to an excision?

It can't be, for after all there were three of us involved in the events of that night, and Alan and I will never, ever forget, that's for sure. In denying what she voluntarily engaged in that night Ruth is effectively refusing to accept part of her own experience, which is no different really from a refusal to accept oneself. Mistakes, if that's what it was, are as much a part of life as successes, and arguably more instructive.

10th December 1975

Head like granite. Stomach? Yes, but upside down and swirling. Unbalanced, speech slurred. "Morning, Jim." Lips move, but ears need oiling. "Jock's a sod." Looks like a laugh. Agreement. Wobble to door and out; into bog. Slosh is too loud and hurts my ears. "Christ, what have I done?" I say, and feel the words vibrating, Daren't pull the flush. A dream. HW telling dirty jokes in the Welly with eyes of cold steel. Or hot. Can't tell. Walking eases it. Sober. A girl I know says "Hi". She divides in two. "Hello Anthea, Juliette." A response of sorts. Eyes staring into beer which bubbles in triumph. Should I disrupt it, transform it? No, not here, not now. Forster's 'Passage To India' is recalled. Dinner. Must fight it - "A happy Christmas to you" - swallow, force it down - "All the best" (his hand grips mine). "Don't get drunk," I say, and wonder at my courage. Really should be happy but it serves me right. Company is excellent, but unappreciated. Feelings not switched on. "Goodbye, see you next year, have a happy Christmas," Smiles that might be joyful. And me?

I feel I'm on a barren rock at the edge of a barren island miles from anywhere. My mind is blitzed by wind and water, sunshine and seagull droppings. My body feels detached and fragile, somehow damned.

29th September 1975

I was standing in a hallway. A huge, seemingly endless hallway. I was quivering, half in fear, half in anticipation. An ancient man with a beard of quicksilver leered down at me, and spoke: "Your name". I told him. "Age?" I was silent. "Age?" he repeated coolly, "I -" It just fizzled out. "What is your age?" retorted the man, and the hallway rumbled. "I'm not sure I understand the question," I pleaded. "Just exactly what do you mean by age?" I woke with a start.

2nd June 1973

Surprise, surprise - Jane Irons came avec sa famille pour nous visiter. I didn't recognise her at first but on closer scrutiny it became apparent that it really was her. Her sister, Susan, was more easily recognisable, as was her mother. It was a tremendous thrill to come into contact with someone from Australia after all these years although I did not actually talk to Jane herself.

19th February 1973

Today had an exceedingly high Australiansed air about it. Nearly every day is flavoured in that way to some degree, but today much more so than most.

3rd October 1971

I want to go home. PLEEEEEEAAAAAAASE!!!!!!!!!

25th June 1970

I hate St Edmund's. I hate the snivelling headmaster, I hate the brothers, I hate the boys with their ridiculous accents and their cold toast lunches, I hate our fat lump of a form teacher. I HATE THEM ALL AND I HATE THIS COUNTRY!

13th February 1970

Arrived in England. TERRIBLE!!!!!

PART TWO:

THE MIGRANT'S TALE

Denouement

There would be times, I somehow intuitively realised, when I would lust after death with a fervour that was almost irresistible, and yet death would continue to elude me, preferring to hold back until my circumstances were such as to make its intervention all the more unpleasant.

Death is no-one's friend; it hates to be welcomed with open arms, and does not respond to even the most cordial of invitations.

Only when life had lulled me into acquiescence, optimism and equanimity would death arrive, and, without knocking, force its way into the supposed sanctuary of my innermost thoughts, where it would stand, twice as large as life, grinning avariciously, barring my only escape route.

This I knew, with irrevocable certainty.

But there would also be times when I would forget, or pretend it was not so, or convince myself that death was just a myth, like God, or the equality of the sexes, or Father Christmas.

Consequently, when the Last Day in which I had endeavoured so ardently not to believe for so long finally arrived, I failed at first to perceive it for what it truly was. There was no angelic trumpet blast, and God did not descend in majesty from on high on his throne of judgement, but the unleashing of divine wrath was in the offing nonetheless.

From the moment I awoke, I was conscious of a subtle difference in the atmosphere: the air was somehow taut, as though being stretched to its limit like an enormous piece of elastic, and as the day went on my physical surroundings seemingly began to wobble, and flicker in and out of focus, under the strain. At some point, I knew - although not precisely when – it would snap asunder, releasing hell fire, or purgatorial flame – it mattered little which – to engulf, eviscerate, and purify.

During the morning I mucked around, or at any rate went through the motions of mucking around, because when all was said and done I was still a young teenager, and hence still not wholly committed to acceptance. When the removal lorry lumbered around the corner into our street, however, and disgorged a quantity of nameless, faceless men who proceeded to take away our belongings, denial became almost impossible, and although the air temperature was in the high nineties, I felt chilled to the very marrow.

That afternoon, there were two of me, one palpable and active, the other disembodied and disowned, watching from afar in a state of mingled bemusement and regret. It was the ghostly me who climbed into the car when the time came for the drive to Outer Harbour, while the tangible me regarded the process with detachment and, perhaps, a small amount of derision, before, finally, turning away and re-entering the building that would always, at least to most intents and purposes, remain home.

1963

The Leaving Of Liverpool

It was the winter of the Great Freeze, and our train from Liverpool to London kept having to stop for long periods so that snow could be removed from the line. I seem to recall that we had a whole compartment to ourselves, but other than that, and the repeated delays, I have no distinct memories of the journey. However, I can imagine my mum – to my dad's thinly concealed disgruntlement – smoking incessantly in order to camouflage the intense feelings of uncertainty, anxiety and malaise with which she must have been battling as she allowed herself to be peremptorily extricated from the only home she had known in twenty-eight years.

My dad, who had religion for his solace, and whose behaviour and conversation were invariably rooted in a very stark but narrow framework of moral certainty, would have suffered no such feelings of uneasiness. In all likelihood, he would have devoted considerable time to enlightening me about various aspects of our journey, as well as about the train on which we were travelling. Since his word was never to be doubted or questioned, I would have listened with genuine curiosity and interest, consigning to my short term memory arcane details of steam engine design, the names of the home grounds occupied by football teams in the towns and cities through which we passed, and other matters, probably of dubious validity, long since forgotten.

The fourth member of our party was my sister, Theresa. Despite still having a couple of months to go before her third birthday (making her almost four years younger than me) she had already begun to exhibit considerable independence of mind by steadfastly refusing to don the warped moral strait-jacket proffered with such disingenuous conviction by my dad. Despite his best attempts to get her to contort herself into the right shape to wriggle into it, she had made it clear that she preferred clothing of a less confining nature. At the time, I regarded her attitude as exemplifying the same kind of wanton self-regard that my dad had tacitly helped me to discern in my mum. Before too long, however, I would be envious of what I would begin to see as her superior sense of selfhood.

We spent the night in a warm, garishly colourful London hotel. In the morning, we sat all sat together at a table and ate breakfast, which was brought to us by waiters who called my dad 'sir' and my mum 'madam', almost as though we were rich. Once breakfast was finished, we packed our things and caught the boat train to Tilbury.

Australia was much further away in those days. It was half way around the endless, slowly turning world.

My chief recollection of the three week voyage to Australia aboard the SS Stratheden is of almost continual, vibrantly iridescent sunlight. Even the Bay of Biscay, built up in my imagination from my dad's words of foreboding as a place of gargantuan, ship-smashing waves, was traversed with ease, beneath a sky of ardently omnipresent blue.

Whilst aboard the Stratheden I tasted cucumber and spinach for the first time, played quoits with my dad and Theresa, and splashed about in the shallow end of the ship's swimming pool.

We stopped briefly at Port Said, Aden and Colombo. At Colombo I got off the ship for the first time since Tilbury, and we spent an entire afternoon meandering around the multi-coloured city streets, being virtually deafened by a cacophony of human voices – hawkers, traders, the almost incessant exchange of greetings and farewells – and traffic noise. We returned to the ship in a rickshaw pulled by a nearly naked man whose muscles coursed and rippled conspicuously and constantly beneath his ebony skin.

A young Ceylonese girl and her parents boarded the ship at Colombo. She was about my age, with long dark hair hanging down to below waist level, and skin the colour and (I imagined) texture of dairy milk chocolate. Within moments of seeing her for the first time I had decided that she was far and away the most beautiful human being, or indeed thing, I had ever seen. The regal way in which she moved, combined with her irreproachable loveliness, convinced me that she was of royal birth, and I mentally dubbed her 'The Indian Princess'. A few days into our voyage across the Indian Ocean, she appeared at the pool-side in a bottle green one piece swimming costume, and I experienced an unfamiliar but not unpleasant tautness in the pit of my abdomen, together with a brief surge of indeterminable yearning, and my assessment was reinforced.

At Home In A Palindrome

My Indian Princess disembarked at Fremantle, a place of sizzling pavements, and broad, bright thoroughfares that almost seemed bejewelled, where everything was seemingly swathed in effervescent white light. A fitting home for a princess, I imagined, and a place I would quite like to have stayed, but we were bound for Adelaide, a fact with which I was not entirely pleased. Of all the possible destinations available to us – Melbourne, Sydney and Brisbane were the others – Adelaide had, to my youthful ears, the harshest, least inviting sound.

And sounds mattered. As a toddler, I had pledged my allegiance to Everton rather than Liverpool not, as I think my dad imagined, merely to spite him, but because I preferred the sound of the word. 'Liverpool', to me, sounded – and sounds – both coarse and unprepossessing, whereas 'Everton' appeared to have a kind of rich, mellow warmth that intrinsically appealed.

Words are not the things they denote, however, as I was soon to discover, although my first impressions of Adelaide were far from positive. It was late morning when we disembarked at Outer Harbour, and it appeared to me that every fly in South Australia had congregated on the wharf-side to welcome us. Within seconds of leaving the ship it seemed that every inch of exposed flesh on my body boasted its resident member of the clan muscidae. Doubtless this is something of an exaggeration, but that is how it seemed.

They were canny, too, those flies. They knew the difference between a casual, aimless swish of the hand, and a determined swat intended to inflict harm. In response to the former they remained rooted where they were, blithely oblivious. If they felt themselves genuinely threatened, however, they would swiftly take flight, only to land again moments later, often on more or less the same patch they had just vacated.

It soon became apparent that mine was not the only body to which the flies gravitated. Everyone else was under siege as well, especially – or so it seemed to me – the males. My dad in particular was proving irresistible.

Once we got inside the customs building, the onslaught abated. The thing I noticed most then was the heat. During the preceding fortnight or so I had experienced the highest temperatures of my young life, but for some reason the heat here in Adelaide seemed unprecedentedly oppressive. Perhaps it was because the ship journey had been in the nature of a holiday, whereas I had now come to the place which was to be my home. How do people manage to live, work and play in such heat, I wondered?

From Outer Harbour we travelled in a truck to Glenelg Migrant Hostel. I sat in the back amidst our possessions, exposed to the elements, enjoying the cooling breeze which had the happy side-effect of warding off most of the flies, and marvelling at the broad thoroughfares, the seemingly omnipresent greenery, and the vibrant technicolour garb which seemed to be favoured by most of the pedestrians.

I loved Glenelg, which in addition to being a delightful place – a bit like a Southport in the sun – was also, I was soon reliably informed, a palindrome. To my ceaselessly questing six and a half year old mind this was an immediate cause of fascination and intrigue. Across a page in my exercise book I wrote the word repeatedly: forwards, backwards, left to right, right to left, up and down, down and up, and each time it was the same:

GLENELG   GLENELG   GLENELG   GLENELG
G   G   G   G
L   L   L   L
E   E   E   E
N   N   N   N
E   E   E   E
L   L   L   L
G   G   G   G

I secretly hoped that we would remain in Glenelg, somehow imagining that to live in a palindrome would entail exposure only to forces that were positive, life-affirming and constant.

A couple of days after our arrival at the hostel, my sister succumbed to chicken-pox. When I had had chicken-pox a year or so earlier my mum had counted precisely half a dozen spots, a fact to which, given that I was soon to be six years of age, I had attributed very definite, if not particularly legible, significance. Theresa, though, was covered in spots. I recall thinking that she seemed to have as many pock marks as there were stars in the night sky, and Mum needed constant vigilance to prevent her from scratching herself raw.

So the doctor came, and we had to pay him, which my dad said was wrong. He prescribed a strong smelling pink ointment which had to be applied several times a day, and said that Theresa must be kept indoors, and out of direct sunlight. A tall, wiry, bespectacled man, with curly black hair, and a sallow complexion, he attracted my unwavering attention throughout his visit. I found his manner of speech particularly intriguing. He spoke in a peculiar, whining voice, which grossly mispronounced all the vowels. After he left I mimicked it. "Sarnloit", "chickun-pox", "guhrl."

While Dad went hunting for work and housing, and Mum looked after my sister, I was free to explore. I soon began to relish the open spaces, the heat, the almost constant sunlight. Even the flies seemed less troublesome. The larger ones were sometimes quite dozy, and if you were quick you could catch one. Then you could have some fun extracting revenge. Flies without legs could still fly, I discovered, while flies without wings could walk, as could flies with only four, or even three, legs. Flies with just one wing remained earthbound, however. Best of all, a friend I made at the camp showed me how to use a magnifying glass to create fried fly.

One morning, Mum gave me an enormous green piece of fruit, almost as large as a grapefruit, to eat. She said it was a pear, but it was like no pear I had ever seen before. It was also the juiciest, most delectable thing I had ever eaten. Dad scornfully remarked that size wasn't everything, and that English pears, although much smaller, were far nicer tasting.

However, I was beginning to realise that many of my dad's dogmatic pronouncements were not the incontrovertible truths I had hitherto taken them to be, but merely his opinions – and with regard to the relative merits of English as against Australian pears, his was an opinion which I most emphatically did not share.

Opinions And Comparisons

Smithfield Hostel was outwardly more austere and primitive than Glenelg, but despite – or perhaps partly because – of that, I loved it even more. We had moved to Smithfield after a couple of weeks in Glenelg because we had been promised a house in nearby Elizabeth West. It was also much more convenient for Dad, who had begun working at the Holden's car factory in Elizabeth.

If the set-up at Glenelg had resembled a holiday camp, Smithfield, with its green-painted hut complexes perched six feet above the ground on stilts, was more like an army encampment deep in some faraway tropical rain-forest – except that the surrounding terrain could scarcely have been less jungle-like. For one thing, there were hardly any trees, and, apart from the lime green of the camp huts themselves, the predominant colours were various shades of yellow and brown. It was – as I would later recite with captivated glee

– 'a sunburnt country', a land still almost wholly in tune with, and in submission to, the elements.

Which, I somehow felt (if not quite thought), was how things ought to be.

When my dad complained, as he was wont to do, that everything was depressingly barren and parched compared to the lush green foliage of the English countryside, I somehow felt my feelings vindicated. Perhaps, at some level, I was beginning to rebel, but I like to imagine that I was beginning to see that most things in life were open to interpretation, were matters of belief not assurance.

My dad believed that green was an inherently more attractive colour than yellow and brown, whereas I could see beauty in both. However, there was a freshness and a novelty about the scorched Australian landscape that somehow rendered it, for the time being at least, more appealing.

The Wilson Brothers

It was while we were at Smithfield that I first met the Wilson brothers, Martin and Robert, who hailed originally from Nottingham. Martin – tall, and solidly constructed, with a grimly sardonic smile almost permanently contorting his features - was eight, but seemed much older.

He had already resolved, to his own satisfaction, most of the major philosophical and practical quandaries of life, and tended to be openly impatient, and at times scornful, of anyone with differing views. He found belief in God particularly preposterous, and spent much time vociferously and ardently denouncing it to all who would listen.

The younger brother, Robert, was not quite six, and he and I hit it off immediately. We shared the same vigorously questing imagination and exploratory zeal, and many a happy hour was spent pursuing and inflicting temporary captivity – or worse – on small, comparatively defenceless invertebrates, racing one another across the nearby scrubland or sheep paddocks, or acting out scenes from our favourite cartoons. Much smaller and wirier than his brother, Robert evinced a lithe fluidity of movement that put one in mind of a cat, but in almost every other respect – playful ebullience, sociability, desire to be liked – he was more akin to a puppy dog. Carrying both comparisons further, he was adept at anything requiring guile or subterfuge, but was also prone, at times, to over-estimating his own ability, and to thereby pushing himself beyond his limits. This particular weakness was something Martin was all too often able to exploit in ways which reinforced the brothers' already glaringly lop-sided pecking order.

The Wilsons, it emerged, were going to be our near neighbours in Elizabeth West, and Robert would go on to be my longest and, although it was not a term I would have used at the time, closest Australian friend. As the years passed, our interests and passions evolved and developed in almost perfect sync, sometimes in ways that made almost everybody else seem like aliens. In seven years, I cannot recall a single harsh world being exchanged between us. It was in all respects a friendship made – and ultimately obliterated – in heaven.

As for Martin, however, he would go on to become something quite other than a friend.

The Milk Of Human Kindness

When I was seven years old, I attended Broadmeadows Primary School for a few months. My class teacher there, Miss Jackson, was a singularly wonderful human being. In contrast to the overwhelming majority of teachers I was to come across in life, she actually seemed fond of children. Moreover, she appeared to understand us, to be interested in and empathise with our fears, desires, uncertainties and needs.

One day, as I scampered across the school playing fields in response to the morning bell, I tripped over and careered headlong into a large and extremely deep, muddy puddle. Coated in mud from the neck down, I could see no alternative but to slink back to Smithfield Migrant Hostel, where we were staying at the time, for some maternal reassurance and compassion. What I got instead was a severe scolding, followed by a hurried wash and change of clothes, and an injunction to "be more careful this time" as I was all but flung physically out of the door and back to school.

I reached my classroom more than an hour late, in a condition not far short of apoplectic terror, convinced that Miss Jackson was going to kill me. She was sitting at her desk, and everyone in the class had their heads down, writing. She turned her head to look at me as I entered the room, but said nothing. I shuffled across to her, and stutteringly tried to explain why I was late. "Come here, Albert" she said, and with immense reluctance I moved closer, whereupon she swept me up in her arms, pressed her fragrant cheek against my still somewhat grimy one, and said, "That must have been awful." Literally choked by a compound of unfamiliar emotions, it was all I could do to nod my head and splutter "Yes."

"I bet you could do with some milk now, couldn't you?" she asked and, not waiting for an answer, got to her feet, took me by the hand, and led me out of the room, along a succession of corridors, then out across the playground to the staffroom, where our morning recess cartons of milk were stored when they first arrived. She sat me in an armchair, brought me milk, and said, "You stay here and rest until recess, OK? Then, if you're feeling better, you can go outside and play."

After receiving a second carton of milk during recess I ventured out into the playground on limbs grown light with exhilaration and relief.

Miss Jackson's attitude and reaction should not really have surprised me. Looking back, I cannot recall her ever admonishing one of her pupils. If we did something inappropriate, wrong or inadequately she never told us we were 'bad', but she had a subtle way of conveying her disappointment, and this was usually sufficient to get us to amend or improve our behaviour. Her love of learning (and of us) was such that we felt energised and inspired, and most of us genuinely wanted to learn, both for the obvious senses of joy and fulfilment it yielded, and out of a wish to please Miss Jackson. Most of the teachers I was to encounter in life appeared anxious to suppress the natural vitality and exuberance found in the overwhelming majority of children. Such teachers were motivated, in the main, by fear, distrust, and the desire for a peaceful life. Miss Jackson, on the other hand, regarded our inherent *joie de vivre* as genuinely precious, as something to be cherished, cultivated and harnessed. It was obvious that she had retained her own inner sparkle to a much greater extent than most other adults, and perhaps this was partly why we tended to respond to her so positively.

On the afternoon of my final day at the school she called me up to the front of the class and, with her arm around me, spent about half an hour talking about various things: my family, where I was going to live, what I wanted to be when I grew up. She asked me whether I had enjoyed being in her class, to which I of course said "Yes". Then she gave me a final squeeze and said, "I won't forget you. I hope you won't forget me."

I doubt very much that Miss Jackson, or whatever she is known as today – if, indeed, she is still alive – can remember more than a small percentage of the children to whom she proffered those presumably standard words of farewell. (They were definitely standard while I was there, at any rate, because I had witnessed the same ritual enacted on several occasions with other children before it became my turn.) I, however, still think of her occasionally, and her memory is a welcome antidote to the peremptory bouts of cynicism by which I find myself so frequently assailed.

A Coat Of Flies

One Saturday afternoon Dad told me he was going to walk to Elizabeth West to take a look at our new house, which was nearing completion, and did I want to go with him? What he failed to tell me was that, taking into account all the detours and wrong turns we would make, it would end up being a journey of more than ten kilometres. I would arrive back at the hostel that evening badly sunburned, dehydrated and fit to drop, for my dad, in his wisdom, had not seen fit to take any water with us, while the very notion of using some kind of sun protection would not have entered his head. Indeed, no sooner had we started walking across the paddock that lay just outside the perimeter fence of the hostel than he removed his shirt in order to expose himself to the allegedly health-inducing properties of the sun's rays.

He was almost immediately thwarted in this intention, however, thanks to Mother Nature, who saw fit to apply a sun-screen of her own devising, and of a most unique and unexpected kind. Since that first morning at Outer Harbour I had grown so used to the omnipresent flies that I had barely noticed them – until today, that is. A sudden meteoric rise in temperature after a cool week had brought them out in their hordes, and it soon became apparent that, for a fly, the best place to be on such a dry, sweltering afternoon was somewhere on the broad expanse of my father's perspiration-saturated back. Within a couple of minutes of his removing his shirt, the skin on his back had disappeared beneath a seething, oscillating morass of black.

I was both disgusted and amused. "You're wearing a fly coat!" I taunted, and swished half-heartedly at his back. My dad, who was in one of the lugubriously pensive moods to which he intermittently succumbed – his 'worries', he called them – merely grunted.

So on we went, me, my father and the flies, and by the time we reached the main road it was obvious that only the flies were enjoying the trip. Dad was still in an inexplicably surly temper, having declined my invitations to play both 'Twenty Questions' and 'Truth or Dare?', and I was beginning to flag. We had already walked considerably further than the distance between the hostel and my school, and by this time I realised that I would much sooner have remained behind and gone hunting for lizards, caterpillars and grasshoppers with Robert.

When we finally reached civilisation, my dad replaced his fly coat with his shirt. He seemed to perk up a little, too, although when I asked him for a drink he told me that I would have to wait until we got back to the hostel.

After walking along the main thoroughfare, Peachey Road, for what seemed to me like an eternity we took a right turn and I was presented with two wonderful sights, one of which could scarcely have been more welcome, and the other of which almost heralded an epiphany. It was a shopping centre, complete, I had no doubt, with innumerable bottles and cans of tantalisingly cold and fizzy fluids; and right alongside it – amazingly, incongruously – was something no six and a half year old boy could conceivably resist – a tank engine. Not some quarter-sized, unrealistic-looking model of a tank engine such as I had sometimes come across in playgrounds back in England, but the real thing. For a short while, my tiredness and thirst were almost academic, and I resolved that, with or without my dad's approval, I was going to examine it in detail. Fortunately, a contretemps was avoided as Dad seemed as intrigued as I was. He had a keenly avaricious interest in vehicles of all kinds, and my passion for trains was almost certainly something which, in large measure, I had inherited from him.

The tank engine was situated just outside the main entrance to the shopping centre, on a single segment of track. Apart from us, there was nobody else around, and so we were free to undertake an unencumbered inspection tour. We began by clambering inside the driver's cabin where everything was almost exactly as it would have been when the engine was in service. For a while, we played together happily, with Dad as the engine driver, and me as the fireman. After a while, I left the cabin to explore the rest of the engine, a process which had been facilitated by the strategic placement, all around it, of climbing frames and ladders.

Eventually, however, I became conscious of my thirst once more, and returned to the cabin to ask Dad to buy me a drink. He would not hear of it, however, telling me that he was not going to waste good money on rubbish like coca-cola when there was as much free water as we wanted back at the hostel. "Why didn't we bring some water, then?" But he told me that going thirsty for a while was good for me, and that I ought to offer my discomfort up to Our Lady as a kind of prayer. I was spuriously, if only briefly, appeased by this suggestion, whereupon my dad, seizing the moment, said, "Not far to go now. Let's press on."

Getting In Tune With The World

Our walk to Elizabeth West had taken place in late March, but the house was not ready for occupation until more than two months later. This was because, far from 'nearing completion', all that had existed when we arrived had been a set of foundations in the middle of a large patch of barren brown earth, a sight that had set the seal on an afternoon that, for me, had been memorable for almost all the wrong reasons.

When the day finally came for us to take possession of 42 Charmouth Road there was considerable excitement, mingled with relief. Robert and Martin moved with their parents the same day, to a house just two doors away around the corner, which you could more easily reach by clambering over an intervening iron fence.

My parents, it later emerged, celebrated our arrival in a time-honoured manner, but I was in a somewhat less celebratory frame of mind, as I had the impending prospect of starting at a new school to look forward to. It was a Saturday when we moved into our new home, and on the following Monday I was scheduled to commence at St Thomas More Primary School in Elizabeth North. My father had arranged for a near neighbour, Mr. Rensenbrink, a Dutch gentleman whom he had met at Sunday Mass, to drive me to school on my first day, along with his son Hans and daughter Gabrielle, who were already pupils there themselves. Mr. Rensenbrink was a short, thin, scrupulously clean man with slightly thinning brown hair, an amiable smile, and who wore an unusual, to my eyes, square-framed pair of spectacles. By strange coincidence, he worked at Glenelg Migrant Hostel, which was where he would be travelling after he dropped us off a kilometre or son from the school. He spoke fluent English, albeit with a pronounced Dutch accent, but Gabrielle and Hans sounded like dinkum Australians.

Despite being more than a year older than me, Hans was at least four or five centimetres shorter. He was the sort of boy who, without trying or even wanting to, could uncover latent maternal feelings even in hearts grown cold through years of cynicism, dissatisfaction and disappointment, as I would soon discover. He had what is sometimes called a natural charm, and his striking good looks – blond hair, blue eyes, perfectly balanced facial features – were reinforced by impeccable grooming. Not even Jeeves could have found fault with the way he was turned out.

Some idea of the alarmingly alien nature of his mindset can be gauged from the fact that the first thing he did on arriving home from school each afternoon was to clean his shoes until they shone, in preparation for the next day. Indeed, although he was wearing a vibrant red duffle coat when we first met, it was his iridescent black shoes that really caught the eye. He was superficially friendly enough to me, but I sensed that he was acutely conscious of our age difference, and was anxious to ensure that so was I. Over time, however, and for a variety of reasons, this would change.

Gabrielle, who was twelve, was in her final year of primary school. She too wore a duffle coat, but the fact that it was dark grey gave a stark indication of a key difference between her and her brother. Although it would be misleading in the extreme to call her plain, she was nevertheless as unostentatious in both demeanour and appearance as Hans was foppish. She also struck me as an authentically kind-hearted person who seemed genuinely aware that attending a new school for the first time was likely to be, for me, a highly nerve-wracking experience.

When we arrived at the school, Hans went off immediately to join his friends, but Gabrielle took the time to take me on a quick tour of the various classrooms and outbuildings before introducing me to Mrs. Deliquin, my class teacher.

Mrs. Deliquin proved to be a strict, but not unkind, teacher. At any rate, she manifested none of the random cruelty I was soon to encounter in certain of her colleagues. Her approach was simple but effective, and she seemed genuinely to want us to learn. Consequently, unlike the majority of teachers I was to come across, she tended to explain things in detail, and repeatedly, in a variety of different ways, until she felt confident that we all understood. In some subjects, such as English, this often ended up becoming rather boring, but in Maths it was a godsend. In the end of year exams I finished among the top ten in the class in Maths for the first and only time in my school career, and this was certainly no coincidence. Rather, it was a vindication of Mrs. Delinquin's measured, and almost uniquely patient, approach.

My first half a year or so at St Thomas More's was a predominantly happy time. I made friends, gradually learned to speak 'Australian', and became increasingly immersed in, and in tune with, a world that had quickly shed any initial sense of strangeness to become entirely familiar and congenial.

The Sick That Comes Out Of Your Mouth

Last Thursday I was sick. It was the sick that comes out of your mouth. My mum gave me cordial to drink and she took my tempriture. In the afternoon I was allowed to watch TV but I was to sick so I went to bed. When I went back to school my sister got sick as well.

Meeting Linus Campbell

The sound of heavy rain falling on a tin roof remains one of my fondest memories. On this particular Saturday, it had started raining in the early hours of the morning, and did not finally abate until midway through the afternoon. At that point Mum said that I could go out to play if I wanted, but not to get all muddy, and to return home straight away if it started to rain again.

About a hundred metres up the road from us, and on the opposite side, was a large expanse of waste ground I had informally christened 'The Dump'. It was an ideal playing area, rendered all the more attractive to me on this particular occasion by the existence of a large number of rain puddles, one of which must have measured a good five metres by three. Ignoring my mother's injunction 'not to get all muddy' I had soon miraculously transformed myself into a prehistoric duck-billed dinosaur, and was happily splashing about from one primeval lagoon to another.

At first, I had the entire Dump to myself, but it was not long before another boy arrived, looking uncannily like Paddington Bear, in a blue sou'wester, bright red Wellington boots, and yellow rain hat. He seemed about my age, or perhaps slightly younger, and he was stooping down beside a rain puddle, apparently examining something.

I went over to investigate. "What are you doing?"

He looked around, and up at me. He had a thin face, with a pronounced hooked nose, large brown eyes topped by immense, bushy dark brown eyebrows, and a pointed chin surmounted by a small mouth that seemed to be slightly off-kilter. "I'm making a boat," he said, and showed me a long, thin, vaguely boat-shaped piece of wood that he had been whittling away at with his pen-knife. His accent sounded American, but he seemed friendly enough. "Let's see you sail it then," I said, and, after contriving a few final refinements with his pen-knife, he obliged. Soon he had fashioned a boat for me as well and we were racing them across the rain puddles.

"What's your favourite dinosaur?" I asked.

His mouth became even more uneven, and he screwed up his face slightly. "I'm not particularly interested in dinosaurs," he informed me.

It was my turn to screw my face up as I attempted to come to terms with this astonishing admission. Finally, in an attempt to reassure myself that I had not heard correctly, I blurted out, "How do you know when a brachiosaurus is asleep?"

The look he gave me suggested that he neither knew, nor cared.

"By the dinosnores!" I announced triumphantly, and erupted into laughter.

Once I had calmed down, the boy, who had steadfastly refrained from reacting in any way to my joke, got slowly to his feet and said, "Let's race our boats across that big puddle, shall we?" He began to wander off.

"Er…okay," I said, running after him. As we squatted down next to the large puddle ready to start our race I endeavoured to re-establish my credibility by asking him his name.

"Linus Campbell," he said, " and don't laugh."

"Why would I laugh?"

He looked discomfited. "You know – 'cos of Peanuts."

He had lost me completely by this point, but reluctant to diminish myself still further in his eyes, I laughed and said, "Oh….. yeah – of course……"

But he could tell I was still confused. "Haven't you ever read Peanuts? Linus is a major character."

I thought how clever and grown-up he seemed, using big words like 'character', which I was not entirely sure I understood. In the circumstances therefore, I felt it best to admit that no, I had never read, or even heard of, Peanuts.

Linus, it emerged, was actually almost a full year older than me. He was not from America, although his accent was still suggesting as much on the day I last saw him, almost seven years later, but rather from

Glasgow, in Scotland, where his parents and multifarious siblings still lived. He had come to Australia with his grandparents, and lived directly opposite The Dump, in a house just three doors along the road from ours.

"Why don't you live with your mum and dad?" I asked.

"I like living with Gran and Pops," he replied, in a tone of voice that made it clear he was not willing to explore the subject any further. Linus remained an important part of my life throughout my stay in Australia, but I scarcely learned any more about his past than I did on that occasion. However, as already alluded to, he was not exactly a physically prepossessing specimen, and over the years he intermittently suffered from some quite debilitating bouts of ill-health, occasionally requiring hospitalisation; I therefore strongly suspect that the reason his parents were willing to consign him to the care of his grandparents was that a warmer climate had been recommended for him, for health-related reasons.

That first day, we played together happily for several hours, until it was beginning to grow dark. When an ancient-looking, child-sized woman with white hair appeared at the gate of one of the houses opposite, Linus suddenly got to his feet, and announced, "I have to go – see ya!"

After walking about ten metres, however, he slowed down, then stopped completely, and turned back to look at me. "Triceratops," he said.

He certainly was a strange one, this Linus Campbell, I thought, not for the last time, unable to hide the puzzlement from my features.

"My favourite dinosaur," he explained. "It's a triceratops."

"Oh!" I exclaimed, feeling both relieved and reassured. I grinned widely. "Mine's the allosaurus," I announced proudly.

I went home myself soon afterwards, content in the knowledge that I appeared to have made a good friend. As I was soon to discover, however, friendship could sometimes combine with perplexity and antagonism to produce a *ménage-a-troi* calculated to unnerve, annoy and - paradoxically - stimulate and enliven.

The Great Divide

Purely by chance, the majority of the houses on our side of the road seemed to be occupied by British families, while those on the opposite side were mainly home to Australians. In the house opposite but one to ours on the right lived an Australian woman called Margaret, who had been the first person to welcome us when we arrived. She and my mum soon became good friends, and I would often arrive home from school to find them both sitting at the kitchen table, drinking tea, chattering incessantly, and shrieking from time to time with high-pitched, almost manic laughter.

Margaret had two children, Paul, aged five, and three year old Melanie. I sometimes played with Paul, while Melanie became one of my sister's best friends. I never saw Margaret's husband, and so I naturally assumed that he worked nights, just as my dad on occasions had to. Consequently, whenever I visited Margaret's house to play with Paul, I made sure I was as quiet as possible, for fear of disturbing his sleeping dad.

I later learned that my solicitude had been entirely unnecessary, as Margaret was, in fact, rearing her children alone. I assumed this made her a widow, but my mum explained that sometimes things were not that straightforward. Such was the cocoon of pseudo-respectability in which I existed in those days that it was several years before I came to appreciate that Paul and Melanie in fact had different fathers, to neither of whom their mother had ever actually been married.

The principal attraction of Margaret's house was its preponderance of animal guests (although I sometimes got the impression that it was really Margaret and the kids who were the guests). In the back garden there were rabbits, guinea pigs and a stumpy tailed lizard called Simon, while the kitchen sink was home to an enormous fish known as Sam that Melanie and Paul used to lift out onto the draining board to stroke. While in the sink, the poor animal had no room to move, let alone swim, and used simply to lie there, curled up with its perpetually gaping mouth almost touching its tail. I kept expecting to hear that it had died, and been ceremonially served up with roast potatoes and vegetables or a crisp green salad, but I never did. For all I know, it's there to this day.

Next door to Margaret, and directly opposite us, lived an Australian boy called Colin, whom I soon befriended. He was a couple of years older than me, with unkempt, jet black hair, and enough freckles to have made a profitable business out of selling them. The freckles were so compacted that at a distance Colin seemed to have a perfect sun tan. His nickname for me was 'Shrimp', which I never really understood, as I was nearly as tall as he was, if rather less well-developed.

I think it was Colin who introduced me to footy. He had a plastic football that we used to kick to one another, initially in one or other of our front gardens, and later, as I grew more proficient, across the road from garden to garden. My kicking was pretty haphazard at this stage, and often I would fail to make the distance, or the ball would skew off the side of my foot and land either in Margaret's garden or, more rarely, the garden at the other side. If Margaret happened to be in her garden when the ball landed there she would swoop on it with all the panache of a Lindsay Head or Johnny Cahill, and kick it back to me, usually with unerring accuracy. As she did so she would often playfully taunt me with "Ratbags to the backlines!" or some other such castigation, whereupon I would set my teeth in concentration, determined to prove her wrong – and invariably either stub my toe while attempting to kick, or propel a grubber straight into our garden fence.

From time to time, Colin also used to like to play one-on-one, which usually resulted in me being covered in dirt and grass stains, barely able to move from soreness, and grinning almost maniacally from ear to ear. In later life, only orgasms would come close to producing the level of pleasure I felt after those early inductions into a game I would soon come to regard with a devotional fervour that evoked a genuinely religious sense of transcendence.

On the morning of the 1965 grand final, Colin told me that he would be going to the match in order to watch his dad, who would be playing for Port. I just laughed at what was clearly a somewhat pathetic attempt to tease me. After all, I saw Colin's dad – a frail, balding, bespectacled man who looked older than my own dad – arriving home from work some nights, and if he was a league footballer then I was a boiled potato.

Once again, as with Margaret's non-existent husband, the truth took a long time to register, and even then I was unable really to get to the bottom of the matter because Colin and the two adults with whom he lived had long since moved away.

The Death Of Santa Claus Part One

The Wilson brothers may only have been separated by a couple of years chronologically, but in terms of outlook, behaviour and character they could scarcely have been more different. Martin was determinedly self-reliant, at times seemingly almost to the point of xenophobia. There was an intrinsic aggressiveness verging on brutality about him that suggested a deep-set disappointment with the world, or at least with his own experience of it. Over time, this intensified, and became, for me, an intermittent source of real uneasiness and even, on one occasion, outright terror.

Robert, by contrast, exuded a kind of puppy dog gregariousness to which it was hard not to be drawn. Like me, he had an insatiable curiosity about the world, and his place in it, which was never sullied by the kind of cynicism exhibited, and at times luxuriated in, by his brother. Occasionally, indeed, it felt like Robert was actually *my* brother, not Martin's – the brother I had never, or only very briefly, had.

Martin's and Robert's parents, who preferred to be known as Syd and Cathy rather than the more usual 'Mr. and Mrs. Wilson', seemed to me to be partners in a much fuller sense than my own parents had ever been. They not only appeared to enjoy one another's company, but they actually did things together, such as going out to a restaurant, a club, or to the cinema, drive-in or theatre. They even went away on annual family holidays. On Sunday afternoons during winter, Syd would play soccer for his works team, and Cathy would invariably accompany him. Often, Robert and I would tag along as well, although watching a game of soccer was the very last thing on our agenda. In the early days, we would spend our afternoons climbing trees, or searching for insects and lizards if the weather was warm enough, or staging mock ninja fights. Before very long, however, such childish pursuits were cast aside as we both became consumed with an insatiable passion for footy, and thereafter we devoted our time to honing our kicking and ball-handling skills, engaging in one-on-one contests, or re-enacting incidents from the matches we had watched on television the previous night.

Sometimes, of an evening, Syd and Cathy would go out together, just like my mum had told me she and my dad used to do before they were married. On such occasions, Martin and Robert would be left in the ostensible care of my parents, which in practical terms meant that I would be presented with a marathon evening of play, discussion and, if Theresa was allowed to stay up late as well, sister-baiting.

Despite being an avowed atheist, and always being anxious to present an image of himself as an unequivocally rational being, Martin was, in actual fact, a creature of considerable inner contradiction, tension and confusion. He appeared to derive a substantial amount of pleasure from scaring, confusing and upsetting those younger or weaker than himself, and my sister was one of his favoured victims. However, although some of the methods he used might loosely have been described as having a basis in logic, most manifestly did not. For example, he was extremely keen on ghost stories, many of which were told in the first person, and presented not as fiction, but as events that he, and sometimes his brother Robert also, had actually experienced. Typically, Martin would insist that most if not all the lights in the room were turned off in order to produce the desired ambience, and the tales tended to feature much in the way of moaning and wailing, coupled with sudden bangs and other loud noises, all of which were guaranteed, before long, to reduce my sister to a quivering, near hysterical mess. One particular story, which featured the Wilsons being forced to spend the night alone in a deserted castle haunted by the headless ghost of Ann Boleyn, caused Theresa to have nightmares for months afterwards, but despite – or perhaps, perversely, because of – this, she always seemed eager to hear more such tales.

One of Martin's biggest coups came when he systematically dismantled Theresa's faith in Father Christmas. Theresa would have been aged just over three and a half at the time. We were at the Wilsons' house on this occasion, and Martin was in an overtly confrontational mood. Robert, Theresa and I were discussing what presents we would like for Christmas, and Theresa said something about writing a letter to Santa Claus (or, more likely, getting me to write such a letter for her). Martin snorted with contempt. "There's no such person as Santa," he said. "Your mum and dad buy your presents from the shops."

Robert, obviously a little taken aback by this unprovoked assault, hissed warningly, "No, Martin…….."

But Martin said, "Shut up – she deserves to know." And then, to Theresa. "Your parents lie to you about Father Christmas. He's just make believe, like Cinderella or Snow White or the three little pigs. Ask Albert."

Theresa looked at me with a mixture of silent entreaty and defiance.

Gee, thanks Martin, I thought, as, somewhat feebly, I endeavoured to balance frankness with a brotherly solicitude for my sister's emotional well-being. "Why would Mum and Dad lie to you?" I asked.

"To keep you as their baby," Martin interjected. "To keep control over you. Is that what you want, to go on being Mummy's little baby, sucking a dummy and wetting your nappy all your life?"

Theresa, who still secretly sucked a dummy, and who on occasion still wet the bed, judiciously elected to say nothing.

Martin, however, sensing that he was on the verge of a kill, was relentless, and he proceeded, with scrupulous logic and clarity, to dismantle, piece by piece, the now tottering edifice of my sister's faith in what he scornfully termed 'The Santa Claus Myth', destroying in the process an integral aspect of her nascent, hitherto undiluted perception of the numinous. Much of what he said was, in all probability, beyond my sister's understanding, but even at this early age she boasted a questing and analytical mind, and could see that some of Martin's arguments were incontrovertible. When he had finished, Theresa sat quietly sucking her thumb, obviously somewhat cowed and shaken, but determined not to show it.

Martin, however, was not satisfied with simply undermining my sister's trust in her parents, and her sense of childish wonder. Wanting to strike while the iron was still hot, he moved on to what he saw as another cornerstone of human dependence, ignorance and immaturity. "It's just the same with God," he told her. "He's just a fairy story, too."

"He is not so a fairy story!" retorted Theresa, sure this time that she was being teased. "God lives in heaven," she added, authoritatively.

"Oh, yeah? And where's heaven?"

Theresa pointed solemnly upwards.

"On the roof?"

"No, silly! Up above the sky."

"*Above* the sky?"

She nodded.

"But there's nothing above the sky. The sky's above everything, and goes on forever. Scientists have proved it with their telescopes."

But Theresa was roundly scathing of such barefaced fatuousness. "He's up above the sky, like magic – and you're just a stupid boy!"

Nevertheless, her unquestioning assurance had been shaken, and it would not be very long before her embryonic faith in God would suffer the same fate as her belief in the existence of Santa Claus.

Snowy The Rabbit

Robert and Martin had pets. There were the dogs, Susie and Sammy, and up to three cats at any one time. Then of course there were Margaret's kids, Paul and Melanie, with their unique exotic menagerie, while our next door neighbours, Tony and Jean, had Kim, the pure white samoyed.

All of which constituted, to Theresa and me, a real bone of contention. "Why can't we have a pet?" we'd demand repeatedly, usually of Mum who, we intuitively realised, was the parent with the ultimate veto on such matters. Besides, we knew she was quite besotted with Kim. ("What about a samoyed, Mum?")

"Pets are hard work," she'd say. "They don't simply look after themselves."

This, I knew, was true. As a three year old I had had two pet goldfish, Laurel and Hardy, but in all the confusion, excitement and upheaval surrounding the birth of my sister, they had been completely forgotten about, and had died.

However, I was older now, I reasoned, and sufficiently responsible to be able to take care of a pet, even one a good deal more responsive, communicative and intelligent than a fish.

In the end, in a gesture which, in hindsight, I can interpret as plainly palliative, my mum, astonishingly, relented. I arrived home from school one afternoon to find a large wooden hutch in the back garden. Inside was a pure white rabbit which, while not the dog or cat I had really wanted, was unquestionably a pet.

"We'll call him Snowy," I decided at once.

"Snowy-Snowball!" countered my sister, in a plaintive whine. For some reason, she regarded the rabbit as hers, and hers alone, and would continue doing so regardless of being told otherwise.

Although Snowy/Snowy-Snowball would doubtless have been happier with a harem of pliant does at his disposal (not to mention a single, unequivocal name), he appeared to be reasonably contented (at any rate, as far as it is possible to judge such things with rabbits). He had plenty to eat, enjoyed the run of the back garden for much of the day, and was relaxed when handled (other than by my dad, who for some reason seemed to imagine that rabbits enjoyed being picked up by the ears).

One morning, however, we awoke to find that Snowy had seen fit to abscond, and was nowhere to be found. Dad consoled my sister by assuring her that Snowy was probably fine; he had no doubt gone to join his wild bunny friends out in the bush. By this stage, however, Theresa had become more or less immune to parental platitudes, and tended to turn to me whenever she wanted an unvarnished version of things. “Where’s my bunny gone?” she asked me.

“He wasn’t your bunny!” I retorted, and, with considerable relish, went on to tell her that I imagined Snowy (“Snowy-Snowball!”) had either been run over by a car or else killed by a dog or cat.

Theresa received this intelligence with surprising equanimity, nodded thoughtfully, then declared, “It’s his own silly fault for running away.”

Nevertheless, I suspect she nurtured a vague hope that she might awake one morning to find him nestling cosily in the corner of his hutch. After a couple of weeks or so, however, it was clear even to Theresa that Snowy-Snowball would not be returning. It was then that we decided to put in a joint bid for a replacement – “one that can live in the house,” we suggested, “so it won’t run away.”

Unfortunately, Mum was not so easily cajoled this time. In fact, the task proved impossible. She merely sat back (she seemed to be doing an awful lot of sitting these days), hugged her enormous belly, and said, “I’m afraid there’s going to be a much more important new addition soon.”

Theresa looked mystified, but I knew exactly what Mum was on about. I looked resentfully down at Theresa, recalling the time when she had been an “important new addition”. Considering the way that things had turned out since, I would much have preferred a puppy, and as I reflected on the likely contents of my mum’s gargantuan stomach I found it difficult to suppress a flicker of resentment and unease.

The People Next Door

During our family’s first year or so in Australia only my mum showed any signs of missing England. Admittedly, my dad was often wont to compare Australia unfavourably with the Old Dart in various ways – it was “parched and dry and barren”, or “full of ballyhoo” – but his behaviour tended to belie this apparent disapproval, and it seemed obvious to me that he was happier than he had ever been in Liverpool, at any rate during my lifetime.

Two main things happened to attune my mother to life in Australia. First of all, she made friends. On the very morning of our arrival, Margaret from across the road called to welcome us to the neighbourhood, and thereafter she and my mum became frequent visitors to one another’s homes. Our immediate neighbours on one side were a Glaswegian couple, Maggie (thus named in order to distinguish her from Margaret) and Archie, together with their two young kids, Davey (five) and Shona (two). Maggie and my mum also became good friends, although it seemed to me that Maggie (and Archie and the kids) spoke some weird and unintelligible foreign language. Why couldn't they speak American like Linus?

Far and away my mother's closest friend, however, and perhaps her biggest antidote for homesickness, was Jean Pengelly who, along with her husband Tony, and gorgeous white samoyed Kim, became our other next door neighbours a month or so after we first moved in.

To me, as a seven year old, both Tony and Jean seemed physically enormous, indeed bigger than any other human beings I had previously encountered. It would not have at all surprised me if it had been announced that traces of giants' blood had been found in their veins. I was often left literally open-mouthed in my awe of both of them, but particularly Tony, who genuinely used to terrify me (though not, I am reasonably sure, deliberately). Things stayed that way until an incident on Christmas Day 1966 which instantaneously transformed him into a veritable hero. With my dad away in Tasmania at the time Tony was the person my mum turned to when we couldn't get my motorific torture track, the 'must have' Christmas present for every young boy in 1966, working. Tony managed to spot the problem almost right away and, having fixed it, spent the next hour or so playing with it with me - something my dad would almost certainly not have dreamed of doing.

Both Jean and Tony were from the south-west of England – Jean from Devon, Tony from Cornwall – and both had the deeply sallow skin and deceptively lugubrious demeanours sometimes said to characterise the inhabitants of that region. In actual fact, once I got to know them better, it was clear that both possessed sophisticated, lively and occasionally quite impish senses of humour.

Mum's friendship with Jean was slow to develop, perhaps in part because Jean was not the sort of person predisposed to open up or confer trust all that readily. However, it was to be an enduring and extremely profound friendship, which would last until my mum's death in 1987. In the short term, it helped my mum adapt to, and embrace, the new life in Australia for which I doubt she was in any way emotionally prepared when we first arrived.

While Jean had been en route to Australia aboard the SS Oriana she had befriended Maureen, a young, single Scotswoman who also ended up living in Elizabeth West. For a time, Jean, Maureen and Mum formed a solid, if ostensibly unlikely, trio. Maureen was far and away the youngest of the three, both in years and outlook, and she was frequently described by Mum, with obvious admiration, as 'trendy'. When she returned home to Scotland after a couple of years, having failed to find the man of her dreams that she had been seeking, she left a highly significant legacy to my mum – and, indirectly, if perhaps even more significantly, to me – in the shape of her substantial and varied record collection. Comprised almost entirely of seven inch singles, this collection, to which I listened avidly and incessantly, effectively ignited what was to become a lifelong obsession with popular music in almost all its forms.

The second thing which ultimately helped attune my mum to life in Australia was the birth of my sister, Anna, who, almost from the start, gave the conspicuous impression that she was very much a child of the soil. Whenever she was outdoors, Anna was in her element, and her insatiable, unquestioning love of the world around her inevitably rubbed off on Mum.

By the time we left Australia, at the unilateral behest of my dad, my mum was every bit as much in love with it as were Theresa, Anna and I. Her friendship with Jean had acquired such importance to her that she implicitly regarded their enforced separation as tantamount to a divorce. However, there could be no question of our staying: my mum had promised to love, honour and obey, which meant that my father's dictates, however idiosyncratic, whimsical or arbitrary, had to be adhered to. Within the kingdom of his own household, my dad was no constitutional monarch; he was an absolute ruler, appointed, approved and sustained by divine whim and sufferance.

Strangers In A Strange Land

When Mike and Jimmy suddenly showed up unannounced at the start of the summer school holidays it felt as if we had been invaded by aliens. Jimmy had been a near neighbour of ours in Liverpool, while his friend Mike was from the infamous Scotland Road, and spoke with machine gun rapidity in an almost impenetrable accent. Both in their early twenties, they had decided to take a working holiday in Australia before resigning themselves to lives of grim predictability and routine, interspersed with brief occasional moments of forgetfulness.

My mum, who was only a little older than them herself, and who alone of the four of us was seriously missing England, was unequivocally delighted by their arrival, and insisted that they remain with us for several days.

Neither Mike nor Jimmy had much time for kids, although Mike did occasionally make an effort.

"Betyerdedpleezdtheblueswuntheleegaywack?" he would say, punching me playfully on the arm, aware that I was, like him, at least ostensibly, an Evertonian.

In truth, however, although Dad had informed me of Everton's championship success, it was not something that had made all that much of an impression on me. Nevertheless, I agreed politely that, yeah, it was great.

Jimmy, by contrast, seldom if ever addressed me directly, making me feel as if I was either invisible, or else some kind of common, but not particularly useful, household item, such as an egg separator. Instead, he spent most of his waking time in the kitchen with Mum, both of them smoking incessantly, drinking endless cups of tea, and laughing uproariously at shared reminiscences. Sometimes Jean, Margaret or Maureen would show up, and my mum would revel in the role of interpreter. I especially enjoyed it when Maureen came; she would often bring a stack of 45s, which Mum would play on her recently purchased pride and joy, a new, deluxe, state of the art, Radio-Rentals radiogramme. To this day, I cannot listen to Elvis Presley, Frank Ifield, Johnny Cash, Chubby Ckecker, Helen Shapiro, Chuck Berry, Buddy Holly or Eddie Cochran without recalling that intimate, somehow almost surreal kitchen scene: Theresa and I on the floor, playing with Lego or toy farm animals or model cars, and the adults at the table, swathed in cigarette smoke, and laughter, and the all too brief shared illusion that life was, after all, worthwhile.

After Mike and Jimmy had departed, I asked my mum, "Why'd they have such long hair? It looks sissy."

"Because of the beetles," she replied, but it would be a while before this apparent non-sequitur resolved itself into the seeds of a lifelong salve.

Foghorn Leghorn

The only person at St Thomas More's who seemed to take exception to me - or, more specifically, to my being English - was Martin Barrett, a self-obsessed, somewhat effeminate boy who was in the grade above me. I found his hostility quite ironic given that, with his garishly ruddy complexion, he looked much more like the archetypal pommie than I did. Nevertheless, if his always scrupulously enunciated word was to be believed, he was actually from a town in New South Wales called Woomargama – a fact which I would later turn to my advantage, and his immense discomfort, on the football field, when, during an intra-school practice match, I hit him with the most vehemently vigorous hip and shoulder bump I ever managed to concoct, leaving him spread-eagled and semi-conscious.

Although he was older than me by more than a year, and bigger as well, Martin never resorted to physical forms of harassment, preferring to focus on subtler, essentially psychological methods of intimidation. I found him more of an irritant than an object of real fear, although I was always careful not to overstep the mark when responding to his barbs, particularly before I had had my self-confidence bolstered to some extent by Colin's programme of self-defence training (by which time, perhaps sensing that I was no longer the easy, unresisting target he had initially taken me for, Martin appeared to have lost his appetite for bullying).

Aside from his ugly red face, the most conspicuous thing about Martin Barrett's appearance was his enormous nose, which in my view had a somewhat beak-like appearance. Predictably, this led to my referring to him as 'Martin Parrot', initially only under my breath or when talking about him behind his back, but later, after I had learned that he had nothing substantive with which to back up his tawdry jibes and cheap insults, to his face. By grades five and six I was openly referring to him by a wide range of ornithological appellations – 'bird brain', 'chook face', 'Foghorn Leghorn' – and was delighted to find each of them not only hitting home with a surprising degree of effectiveness, but being increasingly adopted by large numbers of both my, and his, classmates.

'Foghorn Leghorn' was perhaps the name that suited him best as he had a voice which, particularly in grade seven when it was breaking, closely resembled that of the cartoon rooster. The last time I heard him using it he was whimpering pathetically, but more of that in its proper place.

1964

“What do you call three Catholics waiting at a bus-stop?”

There were three of us at the bus-stop, waiting to catch the bus home from school. Martin Barrett’s younger sister Debbie, and Alexandra Templeton, both of whom were in my class, were standing next to the bus-stop sign, talking to one another, while I was sitting on the pavement with my back to a telegraph pole.

A trio of boys in the uniform of nearby Elizabeth North Primary crossed the road just in front of us and started to head our way. As they approached, one of them gave a sudden snort of laughter, and said, “Hey fellas, what do you call three Catholics waiting at a bus-stop?”

“Dunno, Stevo’, what do you call three Catholics waiting at a bus-stop?”

“Unlucky!”

Seconds later, having been wrenched unceremoniously to my feet, I found myself doubled over as one of the boys pinned my arms painfully behind my back, while another had me in a headlock. The third boy, the one who answered to Stevo’, then delivered a ferocious punch to my solar plexus.

Debbie and Alexandra looked over at us with scant interest.

Turning toward them, Stevo’ said, “Is it true that all Catholic girls wear black knickers?” They studiously ignored him. “Give us a look then,” wheedled Stevo’, “’cos if you don’t” – he sidled back in my direction – “I’ll thump him again.”

Moments later, having predictably still received no response from the girls, he did so, with added venom, and I felt as if I was going to throw up. After this had happened two or three more times, the boy who was pinning my arms behind me helpfully suggested, "Give him a blood nose, Stevo'."

Stevo' looked only too ready to oblige, but I was saved by the arrival of our bus. "Let him go, fellas." I was promptly released, although one of my captors kneed me fiercely in the back as he did so. "Same time tomorrow, kid?" ventured Stevo', flicking my ear, as the three of them sauntered off.

Alexandra and Debbie, who throughout the encounter had not muttered a single word, went straight to the back of the bus after paying, while I sat near the front, clutching my stomach in pain, and forcing myself not to cry. The next afternoon I walked home from school, as I would continue to do until I moved to St Mary's in Elizabeth Park three years later. I also conceived the unspoken resolution that the next time there was bullying to be done, it would not be me on the receiving end.

What I Watched On TV Last Night

Last night I watched Popeye. Popeye went to see Olive Oil at her house. Pluto came and bashed Popeye up. He ran away with Olive. Popeye came to fight Pluto again but he bashed him up again and tied him to a lampost. Pluto tried to make Olive kiss him but she wouldnt so he tied her to the train lines. Then the train was coming. Popeye sqeezed his can of spinich out of his jersey and eat it to make him strong. He burst his ropes and ran to fight Pluto again. This time he bashed him up. The train had nearly got Olive but Popeye punched it and smashed it in bits. He kissed Olive and that was that.

How Not To Derail A Train

After my encounter with Stevo' and his cronies I decided that it was not worth risking a repetition by catching the bus home each afternoon, and that I would walk instead. By doing this, I was not only able to avoid being bullied, I was also able to save 6d a day in bus fares to supplement my 8d a week pocket money (a penny for each year of my life). This gave me the comparatively respectable weekly income of more than 3 shillings, which was enough to enable me to bolster my 'How and Why Wonder Book' collection every fortnight or so.

Occasionally, I would walk home from school alone, but usually it would be with a group of other boys. My most frequent companions were the Fowler brothers, Graham, who was my age, and Gary, a year younger. Gary in particular had a pronounced mischievous streak that I found appealing. We came up with plenty of ways to amuse ourselves during our journey home. In spring, for example, we often played Squash the Caterpillar. On some days, the footpath between Womma railway station and Elizabeth West was littered with woolly bear caterpillars, which presumably felt reassuringly safe and secure in the realisation that there were few predators that found them palatable. They had reckoned without me and the Fowler brothers, however.

The object of Squash the Caterpillar was self-explanatory. With each step you took, you were required to convey at least one woolly bear caterpillar into oblivion. As soon as you failed to do this, you were 'out'. Gary Fowler was impressively proficient at this game, often making it almost as far as his front gate without a single ill-directed step, leaving a two kilometre long trail of mutilated corpses of the arctiidae family in his wake.

The game appealed to me on many levels. I found the 'splat' as you brought your foot down hard on each unsuspecting victim immensely satisfying. I was also intrigued by the thought of the split second transformation of something living into something dead. Many transformations were reversible – when you doused the candles on the altar after Mass on Sunday you knew that, come the next Sunday, they would be lit again – but when you squashed a caterpillar you were creating its ultimate, incontrovertible fate.

After a while, however, the appeal of stamping repeatedly on helpless invertebrates began to pall, and I started to hanker after something more audacious and challenging. One afternoon, as we were waiting at the Womma station level crossing for a train to pass, it came to me. "Why don't we see if we can derail a train?" I suggested.

Graham looked a bit perplexed at that, but then turned scornful. "That's mad," he said. "You'd end up in Borstal."

Gary, though, appeared intrigued. "How'd we do it?"

I said I knew a place, not far from the line, where some old railway sleepers had been discarded. "There must be about twenty of them," I said. "We could pile them up across the rails and see what happens."

"OK," said Gary, "when?"

"Why not now?" I said, and so it was agreed – almost.

"I don't want anything to so with this," said Graham, but he followed us just the same, and I could see that he was having a little trouble quelling his fascination, if not his outright admiration.

"Let's just try a couple at first," I suggested, when we reached the ditch in which the sleepers were lying. "We can always try more if that doesn't work."

Graham's sense of horror suddenly resurfaced. "Work!" he almost shrieked. "What do you mean, work?" His normally flushed face had paled. He looked from Gary to me as if trying to discern a flicker of common sense in either of us. Then, exasperatedly, "You're really planning to do this, aren't you?"

Gary and I ignored him.

"You're both nuts!" wailed Graham, but still he tagged along.

Gary said, "Go home and suck your dummy if you're scared," and we both laughed.

Getting the sleepers up onto the track was hard work, and we ended up with mud all over our hands and the fronts of our school uniforms. However, we finally managed it, and, after dusting ourselves off as best we could, crouched down behind some nearby shrubbery to await developments.

The first train to pass was travelling the wrong way, but a short while later we heard the distant wail of a horn emanating from down the line in the Adelaide direction, heralding the imminent arrival of our prey.

It proved to be even better than we could have wished. The approaching train was a Bluebird, an express on route to Port Augusta. This meant that it would not stop at Womma, but would hurtle through at somewhere in the region of seventy miles per hour.

Seconds before impact, the potential seriousness of what we had done finally hit me, and I was suddenly beset with qualms. What if the train actually was derailed, and people got injured, or even died? Gary and I would be murderers, condemned to a lifetime diet of bread and water, forced to do hard labour for the rest of our lives, or maybe even hanged. For some unknowable reason, I imagined confessing my sin to Father Ballantine, who said, disinterestedly, "And are you truly sorry, my son?"

"Yes, Father."

"Very well. Now say a good act of contrition, and for your penance say two Our Fathers – one for each of the deceased – and a Hail Mary for every broken bone. How many did you say it was?"

"Ninety-seven, father."

"Ninety-seven Hail Marys, then."

There was a sudden, almost deafening bang and the sleeper on the far side went scudding along the rails for about ten yards before bouncing into the ditch which ran immediately adjacent to the tracks. Meanwhile, the sleeper nearer to us shot up into the air in our direction and, after contriving a lazy but quite spectacular somersault, came to rest, almost vertically, against one of the track-side fence posts.

The Bluebird hurtled on without a pause, completely unscathed.

As Gary's eyes met mine, there was a brief glimmer of mutual alarm, and then, with exaggerated fervour, we both burst out laughing. Graham briefly glared at us with heightened disdain before striding purposefully off, as if frightened of being contaminated by proximity. "You're both nuts!" he yelled back and, on reflection, perhaps he was right. We were also very relieved.

Colin To The Rescue

One day, I was walking back from Elizabeth West Shopping Centre with Colin, when we were approached by two boys, one of whom deliberately collided with me as we tried to skirt past them.

"Hey, watch it!" I protested, whereupon he slowly twisted his face into a sardonic grin, sidled up to me, and with his nose almost touching mine said, "Gunner make me, pommie?"

He was about the same height as me, or perhaps slightly shorter, but with acres of puppy-fat. Both he and his mate, a gangly, angular-looking boy, who was staring in what he presumably thought was a menacing way at Colin, had crew-cuts. The short, thick-set one pushed me hard in the chest and said, "Why doncha go home, pommie?"

"That's just where I was going," I replied, manifesting a brazenness I certainly did not feel, "at least till you got in the way."

Clearly my response was not to his liking, for he grabbed the neck of my T-shirt and forced me up against a nearby garden fence. Meanwhile, just out of my line of sight, I heard a scuffle break out between Colin and the other boy.

"Why doncha stay in yer own fuckin' country where they don't mind the smell?" hissed my assailant, at which point, to my surprise as much as his, I kneed him in the vitals as hard as I could. Even as I was doing it, I was questioning my own wisdom, but I was determined not to suffer the same indignity as I had at the hands of Stevo' and his chums. As it happened, fortune was smiling on me that day, for as I wriggled clear in what I fully expected would be a futile attempt to avoid the horrendous beating that lay in store for me, I saw to my surprise that the second of our assailants was already out of commission. He was crouching on the grass verge between the pavement and the road with his hands covering his face. He may have been moaning slightly. A couple of trickles of blood were beginning to ooze out between his fingers. The next thing I knew, Fatso was hurtling past me, and had collided, stomach first, with the garden fence. He barely had time to let out a gasp before Colin had seized him by the neck, somehow forced him down onto all fours, and rammed his face down hard against one of his, Colin's, own knees, which he had been simultaneously thrusting sharply upwards. Fatso gurgled and whimpered, covering his badly wrecked nose with his hands. Colin flung him disdainfully aside and, turning to me, said, "OK, Shrimp?"

I nodded, feeling out of breath, but exhilarated.

"Let's scoot then," he proposed. "I feel a sudden need to wash me mits."

Needless to say, I was more in awe of Colin than ever after that. I begged him to show me how to defend myself properly, and he agreed. Although I realised that I would not have lasted ten seconds in a serious fight with someone as brutally effective as Colin, I nevertheless managed to master at least the rudiments of 'fighting dirty', and this not only bolstered my confidence, it also came in practically useful on more than one future occasion. To my shame, however, I only rarely utilised my new-found skills purely for self-protection, for as the years went by I acquired an arrogance that tended to be fuelled and reinforced by imposing my will on others, either by means of direct acts of violence, or the threat of such. There was something addictively alluring about having direct control over the experiences and destiny of another human being, however briefly. It was much better to be a schoolboy than a caterpillar.

Meet The Flintstones

The senior priest in our parish was Father Ballantine, who in terms both of physical appearance and character reminded me of Fred Flintstone. He was a heavily-built, thick-jowled man in his mid- to late forties, with jet black hair, and a deep, booming voice. Superficially amiable and garrulous, he had a fickle and at times quite ferocious temper which, particularly during my time as an altar boy, I learned to be wary of. The standards he required of his altar boys were extremely high, and he always let you know in no uncertain terms if he felt you had failed to perform up to his expectations, however slightly. If you made a really glaring mistake, however, such as forgetting to ring the bells at precisely the right instant during the consecration of the Eucharist, you could expect an ear-bashing so loud and vitriolic that, according to my dad, it could clearly be heard outside in the church car park.

Whenever Father Ballantine was required to drink from the chalice during Mass, he pulled a face. When I asked my dad why, he told me that Father Ballantine hated the taste of wine. “But it’s not wine,” I protested, eager to show off the knowledge that had won me first prize (a framed picture of the pope) in my class for religious instruction that year, "it's the transubstantiated blood of Christ!"

Dad looked a trifle uncomfortable. "It still looks and tastes like wine," he said, "but in essence, yes, it's the very blood of Christ."

"Oh," I said, outwardly compliant, but inwardly reflecting that, if he had flapped his arms, thrown back his head, and crowed like a rooster it would have made as much, if not more, sense.

Father Ballantine's assistant was Father Chekovich, a young priest of Polish extraction, fresh from the seminary. He was tall and lean with prematurely thinning hair, an effervescent smile, and a ruddy complexion – nothing like Barney Rubble to look at, but he shared the Flintstones character's easy-going nature. At any rate, to most of the altar boys, Fathers Ballantine and Chekovich were invariably known as Fred and Barney.

("Who did you get on Sunday?"

"Fred."

"Oh, bad luck – I had Barney again. Third time in a row.")

Given their respective personalities, you might reasonably expect that Barney would be the preferred choice as a confessor, but this was where the leopards changed their spots. Fred seemingly found the sacrament of penance ineffably boring, and always tried to get confessions over and done with quickly. He was perfectly happy for you to supply him with the tersest, most rudimentary description of your sins – "four fibs, two lies, disobedient to my parents twice" – so that he could proceed straight to the token penance and hastily muttered absolution. You got the impression that he was bursting for a fag the whole time, which he probably was.

With Barney though it was always:

"And what exactly would you say was the difference between a fib and a lie?"

"Why do you think you appear to have such a problem being honest?"

"In what precise ways did you disobey your parents? Did you receive a punishment for your disobedience?"

And you could expect a seriously hefty penance too, not just a handful of 'Our Fathers', 'Hail Marys' and 'Glory Be To Gods'.

"It's important that you demonstrate the sincerity of your contrition, my son," he would venture, by way of explanation. "Now go, and sin no more."

You sometimes got the impression that Barney genuinely believed that God's grace was sufficiently powerful to enable you to live a perfect life, if only you had sufficient faith, whereas chain-smoking, impetuous, occasionally foul-mouthed Fred Flintstone had had far too much of the sordid side of life flung at him down the years to succumb to such ingenuousness. Moreover, with Barney you always somehow felt that he might be sufficiently astute to find out about your real sins, rather than the unsophisticated, arbitrary concoctions with which you habitually presented him.

Failing To Hit The Target

Hans's mother was terrified of death, of which I suspect she had seen more than her fair share, and was energetically scrupulous in her efforts to extenuate its impact. She was Hungarian, and spoke hardly any English. As far as I know she never left the house, other than to work in the garden, and once a year, at Christmas, to attend a midnight Mass celebrated in Dutch (which she spoke fluently) at a church in Elizabeth South. She must have felt extremely isolated and vulnerable, with most of her life spent immersed in her housework or gardening, or lived vicariously through her family. Although she was kind-hearted enough in the main, the terror that was lurking just beneath the surface, and that you could sometimes see reflected in her eyes, would on occasion bubble up and issue forth with an uncontrollable potency that was quite alarming to behold.

She must have spent hours each day cleaning her home, which was always spotless, while her back garden was a veritable wonderland of burgeoning fecundity and colour. Once, on a visit there to play with Hans, I went to the lavatory, and, without realising it, accidentally overshot my target slightly. When Mrs. Rensenbrink found out she reacted with such virulent fury that I genuinely feared for my life. For the only time in my experience she actually left her home as she herded me unceremoniously along the street and around the corner to my house, all the while berating me (I assume) in a mixture of Hungarian and Dutch, with the odd English phrase ("dirty dog-boy!") thrown in. It was only actually during her faltering attempts to convey the nature of my crime to my mother that it dawned on me what I was alleged to have done.

Mum frowned, shook her head ruefully, and tut-tutted with sufficient incredulity to get Mrs. Rensenbrink, finally, to calm down, but I still somehow felt that she would only be properly appeased if granted a front row seat at my public hanging, drawing and quartering.

"It was only a little drop of pee, Mum," I said, after my accuser had left.

Trying unsuccessfully to suppress a smile, my mum replied, "Yes, I know, but I think it might be sensible to sit down next time to you have to go to the toilet at Hans's. Either that, or hang on if you can until you get home."

Wise words, which in recent years have assumed a new and hitherto unimagined significance for me, so much so that, almost every time I am forced to answer the call of nature in someone else's home, I find myself thinking of Hans's mother, and dutifully sitting down.

A Malign Injunction

In grade three I sat next to David Starcevich, whose mother was the class teacher. I have no idea how experienced a teacher she was, but she gave the impression of being somewhat naïve, and you got the feeling that, had you wanted to, you could have got away with near murder in her class. Some in fact did, but for whatever reason or reasons – perhaps, at least in part, because I sat beside her son – I was never inclined to wage war on her.

David Starcevich was an immense, lumbering boy with all the grace and facility of movement of a giant sloth, and a personality to match. Hardly surprisingly, we did not exactly hit it off. As far as David was concerned, I was a goody-goody, while he to me was just about the dullest human being I had ever come across. He was exceptionally intelligent, however, at least in the narrow sense acknowledged by the school authorities, and frequently vied with Mary Winterbottom and Katie Bowyer for the dubious honour of being named dux of the class. (It was a dubious honour in that most of the boys, and quite a few of the girls, were chary about being labelled a swot.)

David's older brother, Martin, who was in grade seven, was, physically, the biggest boy at the school. He boasted the same levels of personal charm and grace as his younger sibling, but they were combined in his case with a demeanour that exuded real menace and malevolence, making him a source of genuine fear to boys of my age and younger. By all accounts, he was not averse to throwing his weight around, and the acknowledged best policy when dealing with him was to remain as invisible as you could.

Consequently, when both of the Starcevich brothers sauntered out of an alleyway just in front of me as I was on my way from the bus-stop to school one morning, the first thing I sought was a place to hide. I was too late, however, for instead of walking on, the brothers had come to a halt, and turned to face me, almost as though they had actually been awaiting my arrival.

Caught between the urges to brazen it out and flee, I merely stood there, watching.

"This him?" said Martin to his brother.

David nodded.

Martin then addressed me. "Davey reckons you're a goody-goody," he said. "Are yer?"

Too scared to think of a cheeky riposte, I merely muttered "No".

Martin harrumphed. "Dead naughty then, are yer?"

I looked away.

"Tell us what yerv done that's naughty," Martin persisted.

(Attempted train derailment, perhaps?)

"Well?"

I shrugged my shoulders.

Suddenly grabbing hold of me, Martin twisted me 'round to face him, and then stooped down so that he was at my level, eyeballing me. "Bein' good's sissy," he said, "and I don't like sissies." He shook me briefly, but hard. "Understand?"

When I said nothing, he shook me again, more vigorously. "I said understand?"

"Yeah," I mumbled.

"Good. I'll be gett'n regular reports off Davey, and if I don't find out yerv been naughty soon, we'll be having another talk, OK?"

"How will David know I've been naughty?" The words were out of my mouth almost before I was aware of it.

"What?"

"How will he know? He'll only know if I get caught, and why would I want to do that?"

Martin looked momentarily flummoxed, a reaction I fully expected him to attempt to camouflage by giving me another shake. Instead, however, he said, "Do someth'n sneaky, yer mean?"

I nodded.

He thought about this for a moment, but then said, "Nah, yerv gotter get caught, and punished. Bein' sneaky's no different than bein' good really. It only goes ter show yer a coward."

"So I've got to be stupid, then, and get caught?" I replied (and nearly added, "like David"). "What's the use of that? Half the fun's in getting away with stuff."

David, who so far had not said a word, chipped in then with, "This ain't a discussion, Langley – yer'll do as yer told."

Martin added, "Just be naughty, OK, and things'll be fine."

They ambled off.

I pondered this superficially glib parting shot, and as time went on it began to seem more and more beguiling. By 'being naughty' I would be imposing my will on the world, rather than being brow-beaten and shaped by it. However, I was still convinced that it was only worth doing if you took measures to prevent yourself from being caught.

"I know it hurts - it's meant to!"

St Thomas More Roman Catholic Primary School was run by an order of nuns known, I can only assume either tongue in cheek or with somewhat perverse humour, as the Sisters of Mercy. The headmistress, Sister Mary Christopher, typified their attitude and outlook.

I have no idea how old Sister Mary Christopher was. To me, as a seven or eight year old, she seemed beyond age. The skin on her face was ghost white, with the apparent texture of sandpaper, and she had tiny, pockmark eyes that seemed perpetually focused on her own inner turmoil. If Hans's mother was afraid of death, Sister Mary Christopher was terrified of – and hated – life. The only time she aspired to any kind of observable energy or impetus was when she was inflicting pain. During morning assembly, for instance, she delighted in administering public canings. Her victims – almost always boys – would have been pre selected for her by their respective class teachers, and would often be unaware of what was in store for them. As far as Sister Mary Christopher was concerned, this only served to reinforce her feelings of relish and stimulation, because an unwary victim was somehow more vulnerable and helpless, and correspondingly that much more likely to disintegrate into tears, than one who was mentally prepared,.

Once her array of victims had lined up before her, Sister Mary Christopher's slit-like reptilian eyes would actually open wide, and for a brief few seconds her desiccated body would be infused with animation and the re-ignition of long suppressed and unacknowledged sexual yearnings. I used to imagine her lying in her bathtub, crying with despair and rage at her drooping, crease-laden mammaries, and futilely feeling herself in a bid to rekindle some long obliterated vestige of warmth.

Sister Mary Christopher's cane was white with a red tip, like an enormous match. She put so much effort into caning that you thought – indeed hoped – that she might do herself an injury, but if she did she never let on.

"I know it hurts – it's meant to!" were the trademark words with which she would cajole each of her hapless victims – a wholly redundant assertion that nevertheless somehow had the effect of exacerbating the humiliation being experienced.

One morning during assembly, Sister Mary Christopher read out a letter that she had received from the mother of a classmate of mine, Anthony Lindner. In it, Anthony's mother remarked that she was disappointed with her son's performance in the recent mid-year exams, and would therefore be grateful if he could be encouraged to "buck up his ideas" by being given "a good hard smack or two". Consequently, despite having done nothing specifically wrong, Anthony was required to submit himself, in front of the entire school, to the vituperative chastisement of the ostensible hand-maiden of the God of love and mercy, whose weathered face temporarily reflected His glory by contorting into a grin, or leer, implying near orgasmic gratification.

I myself would not have any first hand encounters with God's ostensible hand-maiden until I was in grade six, and then only briefly

However, in grade seven – which was the class that she herself taught – I would have enough encounters to leave me scarred for life.

Mesozoic Era Musings

"The Mesozoic Era lasted a hundred and twenty million years," I recited. "It was split into three periods – the Triassic period, the Jurassic period, and the Cretaceous period."

Wilbur ventured a brief nod. "When did the first birds come about?" he asked.

"Some time between the last years of the Triassic period, and the first years of the Jurassic."

"What was the first bird called, and what does its name mean?"

"Archaeopteryx, and its name means ancient wing."

"OK, now it's my turn – ask me about dinosaurs."

Wilbur and I were reclining on the grass in a secluded corner of the school playing field. If Robert Wilson was the nearest thing I had to a brother when I was at home, Wilbur De Groot was his equivalent at St Thomas More's. Thinly built, with prominent nose and chin, and ice-white, spiky hair, Wilbur, like Hans, came originally from Holland. He lived in Elizabeth Downs with his parents and baby brother Johann, and for the first two and a half years of my time at St Thomas More's we were inseparable. Our principal shared passion was 'How and Why Wonder Books', which we collected and read avidly, often memorising entire sections and then testing one another on them.

Every few weeks we would be allowed to spend the weekend together, either at Wilbur's home or mine. At night, lying head to toe in the same bed, we would endeavour to ward off sleep for as long as we could by insectivorously picking away at choice aspects of the knowledge in which we both delighted.

"Which would have been harder to kill, ankylosaurus or stegosaurus?"

"Which planet would you most like to go to?"

"What book d'you reckon you'll get next? I can't decide between 'The Polar Regions' and 'Lost Cities'."

"I've already got 'The Polar Regions'. You can borrow it if you like. Did you know that the Aurora Borealis is yellow and pink, but the Aurora Australis is green? I think I'm gunna get 'Explorations and Discoveries' next, or maybe 'North American Indians'."

And so on and so on, deep into the night, until one of us – usually Wilbur – finally fell asleep.

My recollections of those weekend sojourns are closely tied up with memories of important and dramatic historic events. I was staying at Wilbur's when news came through of President Kennedy's having been shot in Dallas. Likewise, I can recall sitting in Wilbur's living room watching grainy black and white TV coverage of Winston Churchill's state funeral. In his thickly accented but fluent English, Wilbur's dad enjoined us 'never to forget this moment'; the world, he said, was bidding good-bye to one of the greatest heroes of the twentieth century, if not of all time. Whether or not I agreed with this assessment, I have forgotten neither Mr. De Groot's words, nor the setting in which they were proffered.

Childhood friendships can seem almost intractably intense and all-consuming, and yet ultimately they are as precarious as a house of cards. When Wilbur and I were in grade five, Wilbur's parents decided to remove him from St Thomas More's and send him instead to the local state primary school in Elizabeth Downs. After spending more time with Wilbur during the preceding two and a half years than I had with almost anyone else, and having got to know him on as deep a level as I was probably capable of doing at the time, I was only ever to see him once more (although he would feature regularly and prominently in my dreams for decades). That was on a Sunday afternoon more than two years later, when his parents paid an impromptu visit to mine. The intervening years had wrought considerable changes in both Wilbur and me, and we were awkward and uncertain with one another, scarcely knowing what to say, or even what physical posture to adopt. In the end, I was relieved when he left, conscious perhaps at some level that, as is almost invariably the case in the end, the woolly bear caterpillar of our friendship had been peremptorily squashed beneath the jackboot of arbitrary circumstance.

The Day Of Judgement

One of the best things about my dad was that he gave Theresa and me plenty of what would nowadays be called 'quality time'. He would take us for walks, read or make up stories, and play games, several of which could loosely be described as educational.

One of Dad's favourite such games was called Day of Judgement, and involved his taking on the role of God, with Theresa and I as ourselves. We had to imagine that it was the Last Day, an impression my dad would seek to reinforce by blowing briefly on an imaginary trumpet ('the last trump') in order to summon the souls of everyone who had ever lived to gather before his throne (actually, a kitchen chair) and be judged. (Strictly speaking, it should have been an angel sounding the trumpet, and not God, but I pretended not to notice this obvious *faux pas*.) You also had to imagine that Theresa and I were in the midst of an enormous multitude of dead souls, all awaiting their own individual hearings. I wondered to myself what mechanism God would use to determine who went first. Even if he decided to summon everyone in straight alphabetical order Theresa and I were destined for a wait of, oh, a couple of hundred years at least.

In the game of course, the two hundred year wait was ignored, and Theresa's name was the first one called.

"Ah," said God, kindly, as Theresa stepped forward, "I see that you are one of my precious little ones, and have yet to reach the age of reason. I see no sin in you, and so you can come and live forever with me in paradise."

At this, Theresa climbed up onto God's lap, and smiled beatifically down at me, her vagrant older brother, as I fought to contain a sudden surge of nervousness. The cause of my unease had been God's mention of the age of reason, which was the age at which a person was deemed to be morally responsible for his or her actions. Moreover, once you had reached the age of reason, you were supposed to be capable of more or less any manner of wickedness. Given that the Catholic church had decreed that a child reached the age of reason at the age of seven, this meant that I now had a whole year of potential murder, highway robbery, grand larceny, adultery and attempted train derailment under my belt. There were other mortal sins, as well, some of which I might have committed without even knowing it (not that that would have been any excuse, of course).

Come to think of it, I was not entirely clear on what grand larceny and adultery, both of which Mrs. Starcevich had mentioned during RE, were. For all I knew, I might already have committed both.

So there I stood, an eight year old grand larcenist and adulterer, not to mention attempted train derailer, awaiting the judgement of a God whom I was relieved to realise was actually only my father, and who could not really see into the innermost recesses of my depraved, sin-saturated soul.

"Albert Fraser Langley," intoned the divine judge of all in a thick Liverpool accent, while my newly redeemed sister playfully tugged at the hairs issuing from one of his ears.

Half cautious, half amused, I shuffled forward to Face the Music.

"Hmm," said God. "You, I see, unlike your sister, have already reached the age of reason, and although you have been a good boy on the whole you have nevertheless committed some sins – disobedience, lies, even one case of swearing."

This last was in reference to the occasion a couple of weeks earlier on which I had inadvertently let slip the word 'bloody', normally reserved for use when I was with my friends, in the delightfully astonished presence of my dad.

"I am afraid," continued God, "that you are not quite ready yet to come and live with me in heaven, so I shall have to send you to purgatory for a while, so that you can be cleansed of your sin."

"Oh, fuck!" I said spontaneously, then promptly clapped my hand to my mouth in horror.

If I was horrified, this was as nothing compared to the reaction of God, who appeared on the verge of an apoplectic fit. My sister meanwhile giggled appreciatively.

When God had finally managed to calm down, he asked, "Do you know what that word means?"

"Er," I said, thinking quickly. "It's a bit like flippin' or bloomin', isn't it?" – citing a couple of the rather tame slang expletives favoured by my dad who, unlike my mum, never swore.

"No," said God, sternly. "No – it's not a bit like those words. It's a very, very, very bad swear word, and you must never use it."

"Is it?" I innocently asked, consciously assuming my most cherubic, choir-boy like facial expression. "But people use it all the time."

"What people?"

"Mike and Jimmy used it," I replied, which was certainly true. "And Mum, and you, and Mar-"

"When have you heard me use it? I never use it!"

"Don't you? Oh, I thought you did." (Actually, I knew very well that my dad never swore, but I could see no harm in endeavouring to cloud the waters a little.)

"No – I don't – and neither must you. I'll accept that you didn't know how wrong it was, and I'll let you off this once, but you must never, ever use it again. Do you understand?"

"Yes," I said meekly, secretly delighted at the impact that the word, the meaning of which had only been taught to me a few weeks earlier by Hans, had had, and resolving to embellish my conversation – out of Dad's hearing, of course – with it on a regular basis henceforth.

"Now, where were we?" mused the omnipotent one.

"You were just sending me to purgatory."

"Oh, yes. I'm afraid your sins mean that you're not yet ready to join me in paradise, and so I am going to have to send you to be purified in the flames of purgatory for a few thousand years."

Once, on a mutual dare, Robert and I had poked our fingers into the flame of a lit match, which was an experience neither of us much cared for, and would be extremely unlikely to repeat. I tried to imagine the intense pain I had briefly experienced on a small part of my finger expanding to cover my whole body, and then going on, without abatement, for year after year after year.

And all for a few measly lies and a slightly less than optimal obedience record.

"Flames?" I said, disbelievingly. "A few thousand years?" God's face was sympathetic; Saint Theresa was picking her nose. Ah well, in for a penny, in for a pound. "FUCK!" I yelled.

The Death Of Santa Claus Part Two

Some mornings I would awake to find that the atmosphere in my bedroom had congealed overnight, leaving me in a kind of cocoon or bubble of inertia. Inside my skull, my thoughts would seemingly resound, echo and reverberate. External sounds would become exaggerated and blurred, and I would be beset by a churning sense of nausea.

Everything, it seemed, was slowing down – which, nevertheless, still represented an acceleration of the actual state of things, in which the inevitable decline towards decay and dissolution was barely perceptible.

"What do you reckon happens when you die?" Martin asked my sister, intent upon her further enlightenment.

She considered for a moment, wary by now of his tricks. "They bury you in a graveyard," she finally decided.

"And that's it, is it? No more Theresa?"

"I go to live with God in heaven," she suggested, almost reluctantly, smelling a trap.

"But you're dead – how can you go and *live* anywhere?"

She struggled briefly to comprehend what Martin was getting at, before tentatively venturing, almost as a question, "My soul goes on living………."

"Your what?"

"Soul, silly! That keeps on living even after I die. It goes on forever."

Martin produced an evil looking smirk. "OK, so where is it now, then – your soul?" He spat the final word out like a rotten piece of fruit.

She searched his face for some indication that he was making fun of her, but still being of an age when all smiles appear agreeable, acquired sufficient confidence to point meaningfully at her stomach. "In here," she said.

"Inside your tummy?"

She nodded.

"All mixed up with your breakfast?"

Theresa briefly looked as though she was going to engender a retort, but she obviously thought better of it, because she nodded, albeit with scant conviction.

"So if I cut you open I'd be able to see your soul for myself, would I?"

"You're not going to cut me open!" she exclaimed.

"No, of course I'm not – but just suppose."

However, Theresa, who was growing tired of being forced to swim out of her depth, chose to erect an implicit barrier of sorts around herself by beginning, with single-minded determination, to suck her thumb.

"People have died and then come back to life, you know," said Martin, coaxingly.

This was more familiar ground. "I know," acknowledged Theresa. "Like Jesus."

Martin, resisting the urge to spar with such an obvious non sequitur, remained focused on his underlying point. "Much more recently than Jesus. They've died on operating tables – their hearts have stopped – and then the doctors have managed to resuscitate them."

"Resu – what?"

"Bring them back to life. Start their hearts up again."

Theresa looked both intrigued and a little confused at this point, and Martin, sensing he risked losing the initiative, moved swiftly to consolidate his position. "So these people know what it's like to be dead," he said, simply.

The room went quiet. Theresa was clearly on the verge of being overwhelmed by this entirely unexpected piece of intelligence. Eventually, in a hushed tone of voice, she asked, "What did they say it's like?"

Martin paused dramatically, presumably for effect, but succeeded only in completely sabotaging his whole offensive, going as it were from within a hair's breadth of conquest, to the frustrating anti-climax of an unforeseen, but nevertheless unequivocal, stalemate. “They’ve all said the same thing,” he informed her, and paused again to magnify the tension. “It’s like a deep, deep sleep with no end.”

The taut atmosphere suddenly slackened. Robert and I, who knew better than to interrupt when Martin was waxing homiletic, looked across the room at one another with raised eyebrows – the self-proclaimed supreme logician had, it seemed, been unceremoniously hoist on his own petard.

Theresa may only have been four and a half, but she saw almost straight away that there was something seriously flawed about Martin’s pronouncement. “But there was an end,” she said. “They came back to life again.”

Suddenly aware of what he had done, Martin made a desperate last ditch attempt to change the thrust of his attack. “But none of them mentioned heaven,” he informed her, “or God. It was just – nothing.”

Theresa eyed him coolly, with diminished respect. You don’t know any more about death than anyone, her eyes said, while her voice announced, “I don’t want to talk about this any more.”

Later, when she and I were on our own, Theresa asked me what I thought would happen after she died. “We’ll all have a big party,” I told her, thereby simultaneously taking her mind off the matter as she mounted a furious assault on my person, and exempting myself from tendering the painful admission that I did not have the faintest idea.

It still seemed, however, that on those mornings when I awoke enmeshed in inertia, I was as close as I would ever come to some plausibly coherent insight. Five and a half years later, as I sensed my inner vitality slowly bleeding out of me into the surrounding darkness at Outer Harbour, my intimation became unquestionable.

A Friend Of Mine

My friend Hans lives near us at 21 Kilmington Road. He lives with his dad and his mum his brother and two sisters. He is the youngest. His dad is from Holland and his mum is from Hungry. Sometimes I go to school with Hans in his dads car. It is a green volkswagon. When Hans gets out the car to go to school his dad kisses him goodby. This is because they are Dutch.

Monkey Business

When I first saw my new baby sister Anna she seemed too small to be human. My mum has been hoodwinked, I decided; the hospital staff had swapped the baby for a bald ukari, one of the red-faced South American monkeys I had recently seen at the Adelaide Zoo.

My theory broke down, however, when Mum pulled back the blanket that was wrapped around Anna's head to reveal a dense thatch of jet black hair. Clearly, this was no monkey; it was, alas, another sister.

When Mum had first announced that she was 'expecting', my initial reaction had been one of disappointment. There goes my chance of having a puppy, I thought. After a while, however, I became reconciled to the idea, reasoning that to have a younger brother to boss around might actually be quite enjoyable – and, in its way, not unlike having a puppy.

The possibility of the baby turning out to be a girl did not enter my thoughts. It had been a girl last time; therefore it would be a boy this time. Anything else would be blatantly unfair.

Yet here I was, standing in the maternity ward at Gawler Hospital, while my mum proudly showed off her grotesque, red-faced, black-haired, purportedly female monkey-baby.

Purportedly female........ that was it! Perhaps the doctors and nurses had made a mistake. After all, the baby was so diminutive that it's willy must be virtually invisible.

I resolved to bide my time, and await an opportunity to inspect the evidence for myself – with a magnifying glass, if necessary.

A Birthday Without Presents

My eighth birthday was on a Friday, and, as a treat, my dad had promised to take me to Salisbury, where the shops were open until nine o'clock at night, in order that I could choose a birthday present for myself. The colossal sum of two whole pounds had been set aside for this purpose – enough to purchase ten 'How and Why Wonder Books' had I been so inclined, although I was sure I would be able to find something even more tantalising if I looked long enough.

To be made a fuss of like this was especially agreeable given that my baby sister Anna, born less than two months previously, had occupied the unequivocal central position in both of my parents' – and indeed Theresa's – affections for what I considered to be a grotesquely excessive period of time. After all, she did nothing all day except eat, sleep, cry, pee and poo – I could do all of that, and more.

During the train journey from Womma to Salisbury I did, I thought, a commendable job of keeping my churning sense of anticipation more or less in check. As things turned out, this was quite fortunate, for no sooner had we disembarked from the train at Salisbury station than my dad informed me that he did not have sufficient money to give me the two pounds he had promised. He then endeavoured to console me by adding that he hoped to have it in a week's time, but if I could not wait that long, he could afford to let me have ten shillings today instead.

If a week is a long time in politics, it is an eternity in the mind of an eight year old. Besides, the whole point of our trip to Salisbury was, I had been led to believe, to enable me to choose a birthday present for myself. Gravely disappointed therefore though I was, I nevertheless had little hesitation in selecting immediate gratification, however partial, over the unimaginably distant prospect of boundless wealth. Having spent most of the preceding week in a state of ever-increasing anticipation – the equivalent, if you like, of sexual foreplay – and the journey from Womma to Salisbury in a condition of intense arousal, I had effectively passed the point of no return, and to deny myself satisfaction now might well be damaging to my health.

Or so, at any rate, I reasoned.

My dad was predictably scathing. "Patience is a virtue," he advised me, and went on to lecture me, at length, on the enormous range of inimical consequences likely to stem from weakness of character. I barely listened. Wasn't honesty a virtue too? Why then did you lie to me, Dad? And why did you wait until we'd got to Salisbury to tell me that you weren't going to give me the two pounds you'd promised?

I thought of asking all these questions, but I knew better. My dad would only do what he always did, which was to transfer the burden of blame and guilt onto me, for in the special, idiosyncratic universe that he inhabited, he was never wrong.

It developed into a somewhat tortuous, guilt-ridden night, with my dad continually expressing his disappointment at my 'weakness of will' and lack of patience. He even accused me of being greedy, and "Greed is one of the seven deadly sins", he somewhat sanctimoniously informed me. It seemed clear to me, even then, that the entire situation had been deliberately engineered by my dad as a kind of test, and that by failing it I was effectively declaring myself to be morally redundant. How many more thousands of years of purgatorial agony could I expect to endure now, I wondered?

So much for a happy birthday.........

In the end, despite trembling physically with reluctance, uncertainty and guilt, I spent my ten shillings on a small model train set with a basic track layout, but one that could be continually expanded. It may not have been precisely what I had imagined buying earlier, but it was much better than going home with nothing, I decided.

Over the next few weeks I managed to extract a surprising amount of amusement from my ostensibly unremarkable purchase. Included in the box with the train and its basic oval of track was a leaflet detailing all the other trains, track types and accessories that you could buy to expand your layout, and I began planning to do just that.

Before I could implement my plans, however, we received a fateful visit from the De Groot family who, having learned of our new arrival, were anxious to engage in the protracted sequence of billings and cooings stipulated by society as an appropriate means of acknowledging such an event. Thus, while Wilbur and I retired to my bedroom to conduct a prolonged discussion on dinosaurs, or astronomy, or the development of powered flight, the adults sat around drinking tea and deluding themselves that the cacophony of scarcely human sounds they saw fit to make for Anna's benefit were actually anything other than palliatives for their own intense unease.

Anna, in any case, carried on sleeping, oblivious.

Meanwhile Theresa, temporarily deprived of her current favourite toy, consoled herself by playing 'Mum' to Johann, Wilbur's eighteen month old brother. In a credible effort to amuse him, she gave him some of my toy cars to play with, which he ignored, and then the small train set that I had purchased for my birthday, with which he was immediately, and obsessively, besotted.

Later, as the De Groot family was preparing to depart, my mum pulled me discreetly to one side. "Johann really seems to like that little train set of yours," she remarked. "Why don't you give it to him?"

I blinked up at her, unsure I had heard correctly. Mum, it seemed, was suggesting that I give Johann my recently acquired train set, which I liked, simply on the grounds that he, Johann, also appeared to like it. Was that really how things worked? If I manifested a liking for Wilbur's latest 'How and Why Wonder Book', or Linus's bike, would they be obliged to give them to me? Or was it perhaps a peculiarly Dutch custom, like fathers kissing their grown sons as they bade good-bye to them of a morning?

Presumably suspecting that I found her logic somewhat less than wholly persuasive, Mum changed tack slightly, and said. "Oh, come on, you wouldn't want to disappoint him, would you? He's only little."

Then he's got a whole lifetime of big disappointments ahead of him, I thought, and it would do him no harm to start getting used to it.

At that moment, Mrs. De Groot came over, carrying Johann. "Ve vaunt to tenk Albert for de luffly trenset, don't ve Johann?"

Mouth open, thoroughly bemused, I stood there gaping like a landed fish. Try as I might, I could not recall the point at which I had agreed to a transaction of such dubious equitability.

Sensing that my beneficence was perhaps a touch less unequivocal than she had been led to believe, Mrs. De Groot judiciously unfurled an olive branch: "Unt Elbert shell heff a How unt Why book!"

Which, I could not prevent myself from thinking, was worth at least six bob less than the train set. Did she expect me to dance with glee?

However, it all became academic when Mum interjected, "Oh, we wouldn't hear of it. Albert's getting much too big for such babyish toys anyway, aren't you, Albert?"

Yes, I thought, since buying the thing a couple of weeks ago I've virtually doubled in size……. However, conscious that the slight pressure which my mum had just begun applying to my upper arm was tantamount to an injunction to obeisance, I merely muttered "Yes,"

After the Dutch raiding party had departed, Mum helpfully explained to me that, by giving my train set to Johann, I had demonstrated possibly the most important of all virtues, generosity. "Generosity," she told me, in all apparent seriousness, "is its own reward."

For once not daring to venture a retort (although a certain 'F' word was balanced tentatively on my tongue), I simply sighed, thinking that this was, in all probability, the single most ridiculous thing I had ever heard my mum say. With the benefit of more than forty years of experience and hindsight, however, I can now see that it was probably among the wisest, for generosity spawns the most enriching and ennobling gift of all: appreciation.

"*I* know who *I* like."

In most respects, Mrs. Starcevich was a resolutely traditional sort of teacher, combining a predominantly chalk-and-talk centered approach with a pronounced lack of flexibility and imagination. However, just occasionally, perhaps in the mellow afterglow of a rare night of voracious sexual experimentation with a compliant partner, she allowed us to do things which, by the normal standards of the school, were almost recklessly unconventional. On particularly clement days, for example, she sometimes despatched us to the playground with our chairs and reading books, where we would sit in groups, and take it in turns to read aloud. The groups were based on ability, and I was in the top group, a fact which pleased me enormously, not because I was in any way proud of my reading ability, but because this meant that I was in the same group as Katie Bowyer.

Quite tall for a girl, with lightly tanned, youthfully flawless skin, and short, straight blonde hair, Katie Bowyer was the first girl to have generated real appreciation, and no small degree of passion, in me since The Indian Princess. Admittedly, I was only eight at the time, and so the word 'passion' needs to be qualified, or at least contextualised, to some extent. Given that puberty was still an unimagined horror lying in wait for me in years to come, my passion was manifestly not tied up with notions of sexual conquest, or even, in any clearly definable sense, of sexual gratification. Nevertheless, there was an unmistakable, if somewhat incoherent, sense of yearning there, rooted, I think, in a fundamental appreciation of beauty, and a desire to be esteemed.

That said, I would have been as keen to give tangible, physical expression to my passion as I would to kiss my sister, or make an impromptu gift of my favourite toy to my best friend's baby brother.

With the groups spread out all over the playground, and Mrs. Starcevich only able to be within earshot of one, or at most two, groups at a time, we obviously did not engage in much reading. Instead, we talked. Given that eight year old boys and girls of my generation tended to inhabit totally separate universes for the most part – indeed, one of Mrs. Starcevich's favourite, and least popular, punishments, was to force you to sit next to a member of the opposite sex for the day – this often ended up being more enlightening, as well as arguably of greater educational value, than reading about the improbably tepid adventures of Lok and Shan, the cave boy and cave girl, or the latest easily spelt activities mastered by Dick and Dora, or their annoyingly anodyne pets, Nip the dog and Fluff the cat. ("Jump, Fluff, jump!" "Run, Nip, run!" "Scratch Nip, Fluff!" "Bite the postie, Nip!")

I believe it was Mary Winterbottom, the cleverest girl in the class, and Katie Bowyer's best friend, who ignited the touch paper. "Let's all talk about who we like," she said.

Most of the girls blushed and giggled, while the boys simply looked disgusted. There were more girls in the group than boys, however, and in the end, simple weight of numbers carried the day.

Susan Atherton went first. "I like Barry Ryan," she admitted. Fortunately for Barry, he was a lousy reader, and so was about a hundred yards away on the other side of the playground.

"Doesn't he kind of smell?" asked Mary.

"Ooooh, no!"

Shrieks of girlish laughter.

Just as it was dying down, I heard a familiar voice announce, "*I* know who *I* like."

I looked across to the opposite side of the group to find Katie Bowyer, the speaker, staring straight at me, with a playful, almost coquettish, grin on her face.

Cascades of conflicting emotions enveloped me. I was gratified, bemused, sceptical and – most of all – embarrassed. Acutely, overwhelmingly, inescapably embarrassed. Worst of all, I could not hide it, to the infinite amusement of most of the girls. Feeling like a cornered animal, I impulsively struck out at what I perceived to be the cause of my pain. Shaking my fist at Katie, I contorted my face into what I hoped was an expression of suitably implacable derision and hostility. At the same time, I desperately struggled to give appropriate verbal expression to my feelings, but all I managed to come up with was, "Ooooh…….. you!"

Katie simply sat there, calmly, maintaining a prima donna's right to silence. Then she gave a coy smile, winked at me, and blew me a somewhat over-exuberant kiss – which last action reduced the entire group, including the boys, to hysterical howls of laughter.

During my time in grade three, variations on this incident were played out several times, presumably because my classmates found my reactions, which I was never satisfactorily able to control, so hilarious. Nevertheless, despite the intense discomfiture to which I was all too readily reduced on these occasions, my indeterminable yearning persisted. Was it, I wondered, a sin? Should I confess it to Father Ballantine? (No way!) How many years in purgatory was it worth? Surely, the overpowering embarrassment to which I was being intermittently subjected was punishment enough.

Katie, no doubt, thoroughly enjoyed seeing the agitation she could so effortlessly elicit. Whatever her initial motives for implying some kind of fondness for me had been, any warmth of feeling was all too rapidly subjugated to a perfectly understandable desire to see me squirm.

I resolved never again to allow my affections to be dangled before my nose like dirty laundry. With one notable exception, I succeeded.

Deception As An Art Form

The Starcevich brothers continued to berate me for my alleged irreproachability from time to time, but their strange reluctance to reinforce their message by pugilistic means transformed them, in my eyes, from a real threat to a mere nuisance. This is not to suggest that I became entirely comfortable during my encounters with them, and I still endeavoured to avoid them whenever I could. But no amount of verbal aggression, however vitriolic or insistent, was ever going to get me to change my behaviour.

I was perfectly aware of the potential benefits to be gleaned from overt acts of misconduct, of course. For one thing, your status in the eyes of your peers could be enhanced no end, as could, albeit to a somewhat lesser extent, your sense of self-esteem. However, I considered such rewards to be of negligible appeal compared with the feelings of achievement and superiority to be derived from 'pulling a fast one'.

With that in mind, an important development during my time in grade three came with our introduction to the delights of cursive hand-writing. Right from the start, I was fascinated, both with the mechanical (but seemingly almost magical) process of conferring meaning on a blank page, and with the immense variation in potential ways to achieve this. Hand-writing, it seemed, was as uniquely distinctive an expression of personhood as physical appearance, finger prints, or the sound of the voice. This begged a question – how much of a person's intrinsic self was embedded in such things? If I could somehow be made to look exactly like another person, would I thereby become that person? What if I learned to speak like them?

What if I learned to write like them?

Shortly after progressing to grade four, I began to spend hours with my collection of Mobil football photos, endeavouring to reproduce the footballers' autographs. At first, I would trace them. Then, when I believed I had got the hang of the idiosyncrasies inherent in the letter shapes, as well as the flow and orientation of the words, I would start to do them freehand, slowly at first, then gradually faster and faster as the process became more natural and automatic. Initially, the standard of my attempts varied greatly – my 'Lindsay Head' was excellent, almost impossible to tell from the original; 'Robert Martin' and 'Bob Edmonds' were passable; but I found 'Peter Anderson' and 'Terry Short' almost impossible to master. In the end though, after hours and hours of painstaking effort, I could produce credible versions of all forty autographs in the series.

This was all very well in itself, but it was hard to imagine any practical use for my new-found ability, at any rate while it was restricted to reproducing the signatures of footballers. The hand-writing of my mum and dad, however, to which I next turned my attention, was another matter entirely.

The Kalawara Ninjas

The climax of each school year was the Christmas concert, for which rehearsals sometimes began as early as April. In grade two we had done a traditional Nativity play, in which I played the role of a shepherd. The only thing I can remember about it is how itchy and hot I felt in the hessian sack I was required to wear, for reasons just as impossible to fathom now as they were back then.

From grade three onwards, the boys and girls, having passed the threshold of reason and thereby shed their youthful incorruptibility, performed separately, presumably to prevent the kind of prurient, inter-sex fraternisation so beloved of children of that age. In grade three, this meant the boys dressing up as frogs, and serenading the audience, comprised mostly of parents and other relatives, on the multifarious delights attendant on living in a pond, the obvious advantages of hopping over walking as a method of locomotion, reminiscences of life as a tadpole, and our overriding, but repeatedly thwarted, ambition to go-a-wooing (which I understood to mean producing a wooing noise, somewhat like an owl). I imagine the whole thing was utterly, transcendently dire. My dad, at least, appeared to think so.

"Did you like our singing?" I asked him proudly afterwards.

"It was terrible," he informed me. "Out of tune, out of time, and flat." (If honesty to the point of candour is a virtue, my dad's sanctity was, and is, unquestioned.) Then, perhaps realising that by being so brazenly frank he ran the risk of upsetting me somewhat – or, more likely, out of a desire to be perceived as complimenting my mum's needlework (she being within earshot) - he added, "I liked the costumes, though."

Ah yes, the costumes. In my view too, they were far and away the best thing about the 1964 St Thomas More Primary School Christmas Concert. A muted pea green in colour, they were single piece garments that covered the entire body except for the face and hands (which, during the performance, were suitably coated in matching green grease paint). To me, their use as frog costumes was of distinctly secondary importance to the purpose for which they had obviously been principally created, which was to provide me, to the measureless envy of most of my friends, with a custom-made, entirely authentic-looking ninja outfit.

For several years during the 1960s, imported Japanese TV programmes littered the airwaves. Of these, far and away the most appealing to the average eight or nine year old boy was *Shintaro*, which featured the adventures of the eponymous hero, a medieval Samurai, as he travelled around the country righting wrongs, the majority of which seemed to be perpetrated by evil ninjas. Helpfully, these ninjas always alerted you to their iniquitous intentions by wearing black. Supporting Shintaro in his quest were a band of honourable, white-robed ninjas, whose primary purpose seemed to be to highlight their master's near illimitable combative prowess by means of their own, equally supreme, ineptitude. Even as an eight year old I was fully aware that virtue, or its lack, did not really conform to a straightforward colour code, and this was one reason that I was delighted to be breaking new ground by becoming, as far as I was aware, the first ever green ninja – or, to put it another way, the first ever ninja not to wear his morals on his sleeve.

Every ninja worth his or her salt (yes, there were even female ninjas) needs a secret society to which to belong, and it was here that the nascent organisational and creative talents of Martin Wilson came to the fore. I have no idea what happened to Martin in later life, but at the age of nine or ten, before the onset of the overtly distasteful misogyny and inflated opinion of self which characterised his early adolescence, he gave every indication of having all the makings of a first rate impresario, stage manager, or even director. The most obvious evidence of this came via the regular concerts which we – he, Robert and I, plus Theresa on occasion – performed for his and Robert's parents. These concerts, which tended to be loosely constructed hash-megandis of songs, short plays or sketches, and comedy routines, were all arranged and, where necessary, written or composed – with considerable adeptness and imagination – by Martin. He was also the only one of us to display more than a modicum of aptitude for performing, which makes the genial forbearance shown by Eddie and Janet, our regular (and indeed only) audience, all the more commendable.

Martin's talents were also given full rein in the genesis and development of an organisation which, for a brief time, was the focus of considerable amounts of our energy and attention, the Kalawara Ninjas. Deriving its name from the local playground and sports fields, membership of this body was open to all the kids in our neighbourhood, providing they successfully completed a series of carefully devised 'trials by ordeal'. The trials, which included things like drinking at one go a special 'cocktail' made to Martin's own secret (and supremely foul-tasting) recipe, and squeezing the stem of a rose bush until blood oozed out between your fingers (my idea), seemed to have the surprising effect of putting off a number of potential initiates, including Linus Campbell and my sister. Hans, on the other hand, who had a conspicuously bloodthirsty imagination, would certainly not have been repelled by the initiation tests *per se* – indeed, he would probably have come up with a few tests of his own that the rest of us might well have balked at – but the prospect of going home with dirty shoes or hands was simply not to be countenanced. Similarly Colin, as easily the toughest boy of our age in the neighbourhood, would undoubtedly have sailed through the initiation sequence without blinking, but make believe games of this sort were never his cup of tea. Moreover, as his family did not possess a TV set, he probably had no idea what ninjas were.

In the end, our much vaunted secret society comprised just three members: Martin (the Samurai), me (Chief Ninja), and Robert (Honourable Dogsbody). One Saturday morning, laden with supplies, weapons (wooden swords, and throwing stars fashioned out of tin lids), plus the sort of boundless, questing, insatiable curiosity and imagination that only childhood can elicit, we embarked on our maiden adventure. In our minds' eyes at least, this would take us far beyond the boundaries of civilisation, and deep into the uncharted chaos, thinly veiled menace, and unprepossessing uncertainty of the region that Martin, in one of his less inspired moments, had christened The Badlands.

1965

The Monkey Learns To Talk

According to Mum, Anna was more precocious as a baby than either Theresa or me. She was certainly not wanting for stimulation. Theresa in particular seemed to regard her as a prized new addition to her collection of dolls and cuddly toys. She already had a doll which cried, as well as one that wet the bed, but now she had one that could do both, sometimes simultaneously, as well as producing spectacular quantities of poo.

Babies typically exhibit a keen interest in their surroundings, and in Anna's case this was most pronounced, and especially so when she was outdoors. From a very early age, she would gaze around in apparent wonder and exhilaration at the enormity and ever varying splendour of the world, sometimes even eliciting an impromptu gurgle of pleasure.

At the age of eleven months she uttered her first word. Quickly learning that, whenever she did so, she was guaranteed an animated and appreciative reaction on the part of anyone within earshot, she began to utilise it almost unceasingly.

The word in question admirably summarised her view of the world; it was 'Out'.

"Out!" she would declare as she was lifted from her cot in the morning.

"Out!" as she sat in her high chair, ignoring her breakfast.

"Out!" as she was required to perch on the pink plastic bowl, the purpose of which still eluded her.

"Out!" she would chant, with excited approval, as she was removed from her pyjamas, and dressed in clothing appropriate for the day ahead.

Anna's desire to be outside in the open air was, it seemed, insatiable, all-consuming and ever present.

Almost equally insistent was her refusal to wear shoes, which she habitually, and with ever growing expertise, removed as soon as they were on her feet. If left entirely to her own devices, she would probably still be walking around barefoot to this day.

Anna's first friend was Daniel, the son of Jean and Tony from next door. Actually, to call Daniel a friend is somewhat misleading, as it implies equality of status, whereas for the most part he was accorded treatment more appropriate to a lackey – or, on those rare days when Anna was feeling particularly kindly disposed, perhaps a pet. Meagre of stature, and wholly amenable and guileless of temperament, Daniel was admirably suited to his role, and no matter how many times he was verbally or physically maltreated, he seldom allowed either his psychological or palpable bruises to keep him away from Anna's prepossessing company for long.

Several months younger than Anna, Daniel was also a somewhat slower developer, particularly linguistically. He had immense trouble articulating Anna's name, for instance, which, for several months, was inexplicably pronounced 'Faffy'. Equally inexplicably, Anna for a time seemed actually to prefer this rendering of her name, and would often use it when referring to herself.

As a youngster, Anna manifestly eschewed both the intellectual and the subliminal, adhering implacably to the straight forward maxim 'might is right'. This attitude was particularly observable in her dealings with Daniel. For the most part, the pair of them would play together quietly and peaceably. However, the moment you heard a conversation starting up you could rest assured that, within a matter of minutes, Anna's Nietzschean propensities would be being given full, unmitigated rein. Eventually, the dialogue would generate a difference of opinion with which Anna would find herself unable to cope dialectically. There would then be a brief silence, presumably while she made a last effort to come up with a sufficiently telling verbal riposte, and then Daniel would erupt into tears. Moments later you would hear the frenzied patter of his bare feet as he scurried homewards in pursuit of maternal consolation, all the while wailing pathetically "Faffy hit me!" Meanwhile Anna, looking relaxed and a trifle smug at having made her point so eloquently, would bide her time, confident that Daniel would all too soon be back to resume their discussion, having sensibly adjusted his opinions to conform with hers.

One of Anna's and Daniel's favourite topics of conversation was size.

"My mummy says I'm bigger than I was last week," Daniel would declare. "She measured me on the wall."

With an amused, slightly indifferent smile, Anna would reply, "Yes, Daniel, I can see you're much bigger than you were."

"Soon I'll be bigger than you! Soon I'll be the biggest!" Daniel would flex his non-existent biceps to emphasise his point.

"No," Anna would respond. "You are big, Daniel, but you'll never be bigger than me."

"Soon I'll be as big as my daddy!" Daniel would proclaim, eyes agape at what he clearly felt was an imminent prospect.

Anna would laugh, in a self-contained, somewhat patronising kind of way. Daniel's dad was six foot three inches of sheer muscle.

Blinded and intoxicated by the sheer magnificence of the future vista he had concocted, Daniel would effectively beg Anna to bring him back down to earth with a thud. "Soon I'll be bigger than you! Soon I'll be able to bash you up!" And he would cavort around, adopting a succession of pugilistic and virile poses, until inevitably reminded of the utter absurdity of both his words and aspirations by Anna's irrefutable fists.

Then "Mum!" he would howl. "Faffy hit me!"

None of this is to imply that Faffy did not know how or when to be deferential herself. If Theresa doted on her to the extent of treating her much like a favourite doll, the feelings were certainly, to some extent, reciprocated. Indeed, Anna seemed as keen to please and impress Theresa as she was to lord it over Daniel. She also seemed to look up to me, perhaps sensing that, with my love of sports and other outdoor activities, I was something of a kindred spirit.

As for me, however, although I was pleased with the fact that Anna was a veritable tomboy, and certainly nothing like the temperamental cry-baby Theresa had tended to be at the same age, I nevertheless could not refrain from continuing to wish that she had possessed the extra appendage that would have made her, from my point of view, so much more amenable as a companion.

The Girl With The Variegated Eyes

Grades four and five shared a single classroom. This meant that the class teacher, Sister Mary Vincent, had more than eighty kids to look after – or, as she more probably regarded it, to keep under control. For, on the evidence of her treatment of us, Sister Mary Vincent's educational philosophy was based entirely on a single principle, which was to obliterate in her pupils all traces of imagination, creativity, curiosity, and, most especially, of individuality and personal uniqueness. Adherence to this principle meant that we, her pupils, were required to render complete and unhesitating obedience to her every instruction – "or woe betide you". It also meant that subjects such as maths and spelling, in which one's achievements were objectively measurable, were deemed, in principle, to be of much greater importance than subjects which only allowed for subjective methods of assessment, like composition or art.

All of this is not meant to imply that Sister Mary Vincent herself was devoid of imagination or inventiveness. When it came to the matter of devising appropriately demeaning and unsavoury forms of punishment, for instance, she could be positively inspired – of which, more later.

Despite Sister Mary Vincent's best efforts to trammel, cow and intimidate, I found being in grade four, for the most part, an enjoyable, and at times genuinely enriching, experience. For one thing, I got to sit next to my best friend Wilbur, for the only time in my school career. I also got to share a classroom with Hans, who was in grade five, for the first time. And, perhaps most significantly of all, the frequent punishments to which I was subjected engendered a certain kudos, and saw me attain significantly greater popularity among my classmates than I had ever previously enjoyed.

Oh, and there was Andrea Godfrey. Although I retained a certain residual fondness for Katie Bowyer, I realised by this stage that, far from reciprocating my affections, as I had initially thought, she actually took pleasure in humiliating me. Consequently, albeit with a measure of reluctance, I decided it was time to move on to pastures new, making absolutely sure in the process that this time I would reveal nothing of the urgent, giddying, nameless passions seething away beneath my studiously concocted façade of choir-boy-like innocuousness.

My conviction that it was time for a transferral of affections became fully confirmed the day I was made aware that, in one respect at least, Andrea Godfrey was not like other girls.

A year or so older than me, she was in grade five, which meant that while I had hitherto had a kind of peripheral awareness of her, I had never really had occasion to look closely. Following a revelation made early in my first term in grade four, however, looking closely was something I conspired to do at every available opportunity, if only surreptitiously.

It would probably be fair to suggest that Andrea Godfrey was no conventional beauty. Of medium height and build, she had short, straight black hair, and her face was predominantly pale, with a light sprinkling of freckles. It was, I thought, a pretty face, but others might conceivably have regarded it as plain. She came across as an eminently sensible girl, combining considerable intelligence with common sense, good humour, and a kindly disposition.

All of these traits were, in my view, appealing, and might on their own have been sufficient to attract me to her. However, the rubber stamp on my affections was applied during a maths lesson on percentages.

Usually, grades four and five worked separately, but occasionally, if Sister Mary Vincent felt that the subject was appropriate, she would give us a joint lesson. The lesson on percentages was one such instance:

Percentages In Our Class

There are 81 children in our class today.

42 children are in grade 4 = 52%

39 children are in grade 5 = 48%

There are 44 girls = 54%

There are 37 boys = 46%

31 children have black hair = 38%

25 children have brown hair = 31%

23 children have fair hair = 28%

2 children have red hair = 3%

44 children have blue eyes = 54%

34 children have brown eyes = 42%

2 children have green eyes = 3%

1 child has 1 blue eye and 1 green eye = 1%

Andrea Godfrey's eyes were two different colours! This astonishing revelation transformed her, in my estimation, into a beauty of incalculable distinctiveness and splendour. There was, literally, no other like her – within the confines of our classroom, at any rate. Admittedly, there was also no one like Victoria Cameleri, the only Maltese child in the classroom, or the one Welsh boy, Dafydd Gynne. But this was somehow different; this had to do with something intrinsic and inviolable, rather than being a simple matter of geography.

From that day on I worshipped silently from afar – quite literally from afar, in that our desks were on opposite sides of the classroom. Whenever Andrea Godfrey answered one of Sister Mary Vincent's questions I would analyse her words for hidden dewdrops of wisdom to which, once uncovered, I would commit myself with almost religious zeal.

"If you chance upon a broken-bodied child lying in the road having been struck by a car, you should attempt to comfort the child, make it

warm, and keep it awake if possible, but under no circumstances should it be moved until an ambulance arrives."

These clear and simple guidelines have remained with me ever since, although I have never, alas, found myself in a situation requiring their deployment.

My rapidly developing skill at subterfuge enabled me, I am relatively sure, to keep my percolating passion for Andrea Godfrey a secret, and this in itself was a kind of aphrodisiac. However, whereas my lust for Katie Bowyer had been almost wholly visceral, my feelings for Andrea were, by comparison, rather esoteric. In a way she became almost an object of devotion, and hence, in any truly carnal sense, both unobtainable and undesired.

At the end of the year, Andrea moved up to grade six, which had been relocated to a new school complex, called St Mary's, at Elizabeth Park. No sooner was she out of sight than she withdrew herself from my contemplation. I was ten years old by this time, and hitherto unimagined urges were beginning to envelop me. By happy coincidence, the perfect reinforcement of those urges showed up in my grade five classroom on the opening day of the 1966 school year.

The Wheel Of Fortune

My dad had been chosen to appear on *Adelaide Tonight*, as a contestant on 'The Wheel Of Fortune'. Even my five year old sister was allowed to stay up late to watch.

When Ernie Sigley introduced him, my dad looked surprisingly relaxed – much more so than I would have been. Was this a good sign, I wondered?

He sent the wheel of fortune spinning, and when it finally came to rest, Sigley announced, "Well, Bill, just listen to this. Answer this one question correctly, and you will receive" – cue musical fanfare, lasting several seconds longer than it ought to have – "luxury wall to wall carpets throughout your home!"

The audience dutifully "oohed" and "aahed", while, in our living room, a look of unadulterated avarice briefly contorted my mum's normally placid features.

Sigley hid behind a ludicrously exaggerated grin as he waited for the clamour from the audience to die down, then said. "And your question, Bill, is this." He paused, his face grown suddenly solemn, and stared portentously into the camera. "In which year" – another melodramatic pause – "Bill, are you ready for this?"

"Sure thing, Ernie."

"OK, Bill. Here it comes. In which year" – Sigley paused again, and may even have winked at camera – "was the Great Train Robbery?"

Close-up on my dad, who had immediately screwed up his face, either in concentration or from despair. Seconds passed.

"I'm going to have to press you, Bill……."

Eyes tightly closed to emphasise his uncertainty (was he praying? was anybody listening?), Dad lurched at the answer like a drunk stabbing blindly at a wine bottle with an upside down corkscrew. "Nineteen…..sixty…two?"

There was a massive collective groan from the audience, while Sigley contrived an expression of smugness masquerading as compassion. "Oh, Bill, Bill, Bill!" he chortled-wailed. "So very close! It was actually nineteen sixty……..three."

Dad nodded ruefully, as though he had actually known all along.

Then, as upbeat music started playing, Sigley went on. "But no contestant ever leaves *Adelaide Tonight* empty-handed – and so, Bill, as your consolation prize, we hope you'll accept" – the camera cut to a pouting, glamorous-looking blonde woman, and then started panning out slowly – "this beautiful, fake angora hearth rug!" The blonde woman helpfully indicated the microscopic, snow-white rectangle of carpet that had appeared in camera shot beside her, and ventured a winsome smile that she had no doubt spent hours perfecting in front of a mirror, or a lover.

And that, suddenly, was that.

"Bed time," said Mum, looking resigned, if a trifle diminished. She, no doubt, was inured to disappointment and anti-climax, whereas to me they were comparatively unfamiliar. I went to bed feeling that something small and indefinable, but nevertheless important, had died within me, and despite what Martin Wilson had claimed, once something had died there was never any possibility, ever ever *ever*, of resuscitation.

Going To The Footy

On Saturday I went to the footy. It was Port and Centrals. I went with Robert and Martin and their mum and dad. We had a picnic. Every time Port kicked a goal all the Centrals barrackers bood but I barrack for Port so I cheered. Port won by 9 points. Five Port players were in Melbourne or we would of won better.

The Death Of Santa Claus Part Three

I became an altar boy entirely because of the perks associated with the role. Only a few of these perks, such as the tips you invariably received for serving at a wedding or a funeral, were of a pecuniary nature. Most were more esoteric. I derived particular pleasure from occupying a central role in what, for many Catholics, was a highly intimate devotional experience, the partaking of the actual body of Christ in the Eucharist. When I held the communion plate up to the chin of Katie Bowyer or Andrea Godfrey I felt as if I was somehow being granted brief, privileged access to the stark reality of their innermost emotions, thoughts and yearnings. Peering surreptitiously into their eyes, I believe I captured them in a moment of rare vulnerability and exposure; they were bare before me, and I had the potential either to molest or to assist. The fact that I invariably elected to assist did not in any way diminish the sense of power I felt. It was, in all respects, a compulsively visceral, unabashedly sexual thrill, and as such was infinitely preferable to mere money.

There were other, less intense fillips too. I enjoyed the fact that, unlike among my teachers at school, to whom I remained more or less invisible (although this was soon to change), I was clearly Father Ballantine's favourite. This led to my being treated as a *de facto* 'head altar boy', which meant that any of the more interesting or responsible jobs – assisting at communion, ringing the bells, lighting and extinguishing the altar candles – were mine for the asking. (It also meant that I was often given the task of training newcomers - a duty which ultimately, and irrevocably, succeeded in sabotaging my love affair with the cassock. Asked by Hans to "show him the ropes" I happily obliged, only to discover that my friend's ability to charm extended beyond members of the opposite sex. Father Ballantine rapidly became besotted, to the extent that Hans replaced me in the unofficial altar boys' pecking order. Feeling snubbed, I put up with the situation for a brief time before resigning.)

In Father Ballantine's eyes, ringing the bells at appropriate times during Mass was an altar boy's most important function. There were only about half a dozen such instances to remember, and yet it was amazing how often a boy would need a nudge from one of his fellows, or a glare from Father Ballantine, to remind him. I had a reputation for never forgetting, which is why Father Ballantine usually insisted that I had charge of the bells whenever I was assisting him. Father Chekovich, however, adopted a much more egalitarian approach, with sometimes comical results. On one occasion, a certain unnamed boy who features elsewhere in this story somehow contrived to ring the bells, loudly and pronouncedly, at a completely inappropriate time, eliciting a ripple of laughter from the congregation, and a bemused stare from Father Chekovich; afterwards, the priest saw fit to have a quiet word with him. Had Father Ballantine rather than Father Chekovich been officiating, the boy would probably have been excommunicated.

Perhaps my greatest achievement as an altar boy was to obliterate my sister Theresa's religious faith. When she attended Mass with my dad the pair of them invariably used to sit near the rear of the church, which meant that my sister's view of what was happening at the altar was restricted. When, during key moments in the service, she heard the faint tinkling of bells, she quite naturally assumed that this was God's way of signalling his approbation. As soon as she discovered, courtesy of me, that there was nothing remotely divine going on after all, her perception of the nature of the universe was dramatically and irrevocably changed. The fact that my ostensible service of God had perversely succeeded in bolstering the ranks of the world's agnostics appealed to me no end, as did the scarcely credible fact that my five year old sister had believed in a God who elected to employ campanological means when communicating directly with humankind.

Martin Wilson might have managed to disabuse Theresa of her comparatively harmless belief in the red-suited, white-bearded old man who conferred presents on the world's children at Christmas time, but by extricating her – albeit inadvertently - from the much more invidious mire of religious mumbo jumbo I had, I liked to think, rendered her a much more telling and enduring service.

Vincent The Viper

Only Sister Mary Christopher was allowed to use the cane. The other teachers had to make do with a ruler, or the back of the hand. As far as Sister Mary Vincent was concerned, this was highly unsatisfactory, and a source of considerable, very obvious irritation. But she was not to be defeated.

Looking back, I am not sure exactly why she earmarked me to be the regular butt of her most fiendishly distinctive brand of chastisement. Most teachers – including Sister Vincent initially - tended to ignore me, which was how I liked it. By half way through my time in grade four, however, Sister Mary Vincent seemed to have decided that I was sorely in need of corrective intervention, and that in order for it to be effective it needed to be applied at least once, and sometimes twice or more, daily.

At first, this simply meant a hefty smack or two with a ruler, either on the hand or – much worse – the back of the leg. However, it soon emerged that the only noticeable effect this had was to magnify the esteem in which I was held by my classmates. Even David Starcevich, whom Sister Mary Vincent ironically appeared to like (perhaps discerning in him a similarly malicious turn of mind), seemingly found it hard to quell his admiration.

Sister Mary Vincent was never so calculatingly, invidiously inventive as when presented with a dilemma. On this occasion, it seemed clear that what was needed was a punishment that would demean and distress me, whilst simultaneously depriving me of the mitigating solace afforded by my fellow pupils. In the end, the solution she concocted fit the bill superbly; it was, in all respects, a concept redolent of unadulterated, diabolic genius.

If Sister Mary Vincent shared Sister Mary Christopher's intrinsic vindictiveness and hatred of all that was spirited, individual or Quixotic, she was nevertheless, in purely physical terms, her antithesis – red and shiny where the headmistress was pallid and sand-papery, angular and imposing rather than flat and moribund. She was also considerably more animated and intense, if rather less prone to sudden, frequently alarming mood swings. Although in terms of general iniquity and malice there was probably little to choose between them, there was no doubt in my mind that Sister Mary Vincent was, by some measure, the more potent adversary, as her compulsive malevolence was much more imaginatively deployed, and hence was infinitely harder to evade. Moreover, unlike her boss, she actually appeared to realise that I existed, which inevitably had the effect of augmenting my potential validity as a target.

Such was the extent of Sister Mary Vincent's wickedness, she was even known to punish girls. Indeed, on one epochal occasion, which had a particular significance for me, she actually smacked a girl. But more of that at the relevant time.

Not all of my feelings regarding Sister Mary Vincent were negative, however. She inspired a considerable amount of loathing and dread, to be sure, but intermingled with such feelings was more than a modicum of admiration. Like her, I was occasionally subject to sadistic impulses, and fully appreciated the frisson to be gleaned from according them imaginative rein.

If you want to understand the essence of the psychology of effective torture, you need only watch a cat playing with a mouse, one moment molesting and humiliating, the next tantalising with spurious offers of liberty. For it is in the context of apparent security and self-confidence that pain is most acutely felt.

Before leaving England, I used from time to time to play with Billy, a toddler who lived a couple of doors away from me on the same street.

At the time of the incident I am about to describe, I would have been about four and a half, while he would have been at least a couple of years younger. He regarded me with a combination of trust and low key adulation, while I, in return, was affectionate, playful and protective. Together, it seemed, we inhabited a mutually constructed bubble of safety and contentment, a veritable haven from a sometimes waywardly vindictive world.

One especially warm summer's day as we were playing happily together on the pavement just outside our homes, I was suddenly, for no apparent reason, presented with a starkly vivid and powerful mental image of Billy drowning in Coronation Park lake, splashing frantically and wailing plaintively as he tried without success to attract the attention of passers-by.

As I came back to myself, and was confronted by the immediacy of Billy's supple, vulnerable flesh, his myopic, idiot eyes, the paltry flicker of his upstart imprint on a world in every sense too big, too real, too unforgiving to sustain him, I recognised him, probably for the first time, as a fellow victim, as someone who was born to suffer. The hands he sometimes stretched towards me, whether in supplication, or beseeching support or reassurance, were meant to be impaled; they might, indeed, have been inviting nails.

"Look here, Billy," I said, "I've got something for you."

Without even seeing what it was, he cooed his appreciation, as do nearly all the condemned.

With almost devotional precision and solicitude, I placed a squirming ant upon the unprotesting whiteness of his neck.

"Ooooh – tickle!" said Billy, laughing, for this, of course, was just a game.

I promptly added another ant. Then another. And another. Soon ants were crawling over virtually every centimetre of exposed flesh on Billy's body, while others had begun exploring beneath his clothes.

I laughed, perhaps not quite unkindly. "Now Billy's the ant boy!"

But Billy's acquiescence was on stilts. He tried to emulate my laughter, but his skin was harbouring rebellion. His bottom lip became unwieldy. He collapsed.

"Ants!" he whimpered. "Ants – no like!"

But I was forced, or chose, to misconstrue. "Yes, Billy – lovely ants!" Depositing a mercilessly writhing handful on his scalp.

"No, no, no!" wailed Billy, as the weight of sudden insight began to pull. It tugged at him in unfamiliar ways, as everything became inverted.

I laughed aloud, delighted to have given such release, although I was simultaneously aware of having cauterised.

"Delighted as I always am to see my pupils deriving pleasure from their education, I fail to see exactly what you're finding so hilarious, Mr. Langley. Perhaps you'd condescend to enlighten us?" Sister Mary Vincent's deceptively playful, lilting words were skewers to my reverie.

Knowing better than to attempt to answer my accuser's actual question, I said, as meekly as I could, "I'm sorry, sister."

She made the same face my baby sister Anna made when breaking wind, and sighed. "I fear we may be taxing you, young man," she said, removing a piece of paper and a pen from her desk drawer. "Happily," she added, and she looked it, "it's not an insoluble dilemma."

As Sister Mary Vincent began writing something on the piece of paper, an almost imperceptible hum arose, which gradually magnified. Contributing to this hum was Wilbur, who whispered, helpfully, "You're for it now….."

"Quiet!" shrieked the banshee of Christ, as she removed an envelope from her desk drawer, and placed the piece of paper on which she had just written inside it. "You!" she hissed, pointing in my direction. "Out here – now!"

I lurched into the unknown on palsied limbs.

"Take this to Sister Mary Damien," she told me, handing me the envelope.

I blinked up at her, trying to discern a hint or two as to my destiny from the expression on her face, which was, however, neutral.

"Now!" she caterwauled, propelling me toward the door with a brutal shove.

Without really taking the time to think the matter through, I saw no option but to comply.

Damien The Demented

Sister Mary Damien taught the babies' class. She was extremely tall and thin, with a swarthy complexion that had the apparent texture of worn leather. Both her face and hands were covered in dark brown moles of various sizes and shapes. The largest were the dimension of a sixpence, and sprouted an assortment of thick, greyish hairs. I had never previously enjoyed a first hand meeting with Sister Mary Damien, but I already knew that I found her penchant for smiling incessantly, with what I imagine she thought was winsome charm, rather irritating, not least because she happened to be, physically, just about the most hideous-looking human being I had ever seen.

Having knocked on the door, and been invited to enter, I walked over to Sister Damien, who was sitting at her desk, and handed her the envelope. "Thank-you, dear," she said, in a breathy, cherry-sweet voice more appropriate to a child of five than a full-grown woman.

I waited as she tore open the envelope, and, smiling iridescently, cast her eyes over the contents of Sister Mary Vincent's missive. I wonder if they like one other, I mused, Sisters Damien and Vincent. Do they perhaps go shopping together? Or sit curled up alongside one another on the sofa, drinking cocoa, and chortling at *Bewitched*, *The Dick Van Dyke Show*, or *The Flying Nun*?

Or did they endeavour to avoid one another at all costs, addressing one another with studiously manufactured politeness, through serried teeth, whenever communication was unavoidable?

Having read the note, Sister Damien screwed it up into a tight ball and dropped it into the metal waste paper bin at the side of her desk. She sighed, presumably with pleasure, for she was smiling even more pronouncedly, like a Cheshire Cat, or a four and a half year old boy collecting ants on a sunlit Liverpool side street.

When she struck me across the head, it was with such force that, for a split second or two, I actually lost consciousness, coming 'round just in time to prevent myself from falling over. By then, Sister Damien had grabbed me roughly by the collar, and was herding me towards the corner of the classroom nearest the door. "You can stand there quietly and face the wall," she breathily informed me, "until I decide that you're ready to join us."

Then, addressing the forty or so confused looking five and six year olds in her class, she announced, "We have a new boy with us today, children. I hope you'll help him feel at home. Sister Mary Vincent sent him to join us because he's been finding the work in grade four too hard. Please be kind to him – it isn't his fault he's so stupid."

The children dutifully giggled, albeit with some apparent uncertainty, while I stood gazing at the wall, battling intensely with a torrent of debilitating feelings, of which humiliation, stupefaction and anger were foremost. I was forced to remain in the corner until after recess, when I received my formal induction into the multifarious delights of Sister Mary Damien's quaintly surreal approach to education.

"A is for apple – yum yum!" I reluctantly recited, all the while attempting to ignore the intrigued stares of my temporary classmates. "B is for bird – tweet tweet!. C is for cat – meow! D is for dog – woof woof!"

All the time, sharpening and polishing her knife with palpably transparent glee, Sister Damien appeared to be focusing all her attention on me, her God-given talisman of hope. She smiled, of course, and continually, luxuriating in the glitteringly idiosyncratic mirage of redemption she had concocted. From time to time she sought to reassure herself, as well as to remind me of my status, by stabbing at me, half playfully, half in earnest, and grinning with gratification as I flinched.

"If I have ten grapes, and eat three, how many grapes will I have left?"

"Seven, sister," I replied, sullenly.

"Good boy!" Her merry, lilting voice a cat-o-nine-tails.

During both recess and lunch time none of my friends, other than Wilbur, would have anything to do with me, and even Wilbur seemed subdued as he gazed with thinly concealed longing at the rest of the grade four boys playing ringy-up, or brandy on the wall, or kick to kick. I stared at them too, vicariously enjoying the sudden, sharp pain as the fiercely flung tennis ball rebounded off a leg, or back, or arm, or buttock.

Mental pain was worst I began, if tentatively, to understand.

According to my school diary, the ensuing three week period saw me demoted for the day, mostly to grade one, but once or twice to grade two, no fewer than half a dozen times. Sister Mary Vincent, it appeared, was fully aware of the crushingly demeaning nature of the punishment she had conceived, and derived explicit solace from administering it. It might indeed have been an act of worship, with the seraphic host visibly endorsing it by igniting the majestic candle into which Sister Mary Vincent's luminescent face had seemingly, one might have believed miraculously, transformed.

At night, in bed, I lay curled up in a ball, like a threatened caterpillar, wide awake, denuded and confused. Escape seemed quite unlikely, but I somehow realised that, unless I made at least a gesture of defiance, I ran the risk of consigning myself to a lifetime spent squirming on the end of a hook.

The Day I Forgot My Kicking Boots

At the age of nine, football rapidly began to supplant astronomy, natural history and (attempted derailment of) trains in my affections. Thanks to Colin, I had already learned the rudiments of the game, and during grade four I began to play it at school during recess and at lunch times. Virtually all the boys at the school, from grade four upwards, used to take part in these impromptu games, which conformed only very loosely to the official version of the code as defined by the Australian National Football Council.

For most of the younger boys, such as me, participation in the games tended to be tangential and circumspect. We were more like on-field spectators, neither expected nor required to take an active role. When, therefore, I somehow managed to kick the winning point in one game, I almost succeeded in convincing myself that I now knew what it felt like to play in a premiership team. (Sadly, in reality this was not to be an experience I would ever enjoy.)

My first official game of football was for a combined grade four and five team against our counterparts from Elizabeth North Primary. Until 1968, all St Thomas More's matches were played away from home, or at neutral venues, as we did not possess a suitable oval of our own. This particular match saw us donning the school's recently purchased set of sleeveless, lace-up football guernseys. Predominantly red in colour, with white yokes and edgings, they were several sizes too big for most of us as they had chiefly been bought for the use of the school first XVIII, which comprised boys from grades six and seven. Nevertheless, it was the first time I had ever worn a proper footy jumper, and in my mind's eye I might have been fronting up for Port Adelaide at Alberton.

I seem to recall that there were a total of about twenty-four guernseys, all numbered sequentially. However, we only took the bare eighteen players, and hence the first eighteen jumpers, with us on this occasion, and the level of confidence which my team mates had in my ability was amply shown by my being presented with the number eighteen jumper. However, far from feeling insulted or demeaned by this, I was actually quite pleased, as this happened to be the number worn by probably my favourite footballer at the time, Eric Freeman.

Elizabeth North Primary was the closest school to ours geographically, but, as I had discovered to my cost at the hands of Stevo' and his cronies a couple of years earlier, the relationship between the two sets of pupils was anything but neighbourly. Hardly surprisingly therefore, when teams from the two schools clashed at sport, particularly football, affairs could sometimes become a little wayward. The fact that the games were invariably umpired by teachers from Elizabeth North did little, if anything, to assuage matters, especially given that the extreme financial hardship under which state schools were forced to operate at the time precluded the purchase of whistles for sports umpires. Or so it seemed.

Presumably as I was quite tall for my age, I was selected to start the match at centre half back. Because I had no preconception of what a full-blown football match was like I hurled myself into the fray with an abandon and a ferocity that I would later find it hard, if not impossible, to reproduce. Most of the play occurred in Elizabeth North's forward lines, and so I seemed to see a lot of the ball. In fact, I must have ended up having well in excess of twenty kicks, on which basis you would be forgiven for expecting to see my name listed high among my team's best players. However, simple statistics can be deceiving. Of those twenty or so kicks, I imagine the most penetrating would have travelled all of three metres. Quite a few were grubbers, and at least a couple were so ineffectual that they failed even to clear the player on the mark.

The reason for my execrable kicking was simple. The only footballs I had previously kicked were Colin's plastic one, and the moth-eaten undersized balloon used during our impromptu recess and lunch-time games at school. For the match against Elizabeth North we used a nearly new, senior-sized Ross Faulkner football that had been inflated to its maximum pressure. When my sandshoed right foot connected with this redoubtable sphere it was the equivalent of trying to hit a cricket ball with a badminton racket. And did it hurt! In later years, I would go through entire matches kickless and feel less embarrassed. Nevertheless, each failure did at least have the positive effect of making me desperate to get hold of the ball again as soon as possible in order to put things right.

The more desperate I got though, the worse my kicking became – and my indignity did not even end with the final siren for, as chance would have it, when it sounded I had just marked the ball, and so was allowed one final kick. (Strictly speaking, as I was well over a hundred metres from goal, the teacher/umpire should simply have asked me for the ball, but he presumably nursed an expectation that I would provide him with some further amusement – a hope I was all too ready to indulge him in.)

Biting my tongue to reinforce my concentration, I steadily, carefully dropped the ball and flung my foot at it with enough energy to wind a rhinoceros. Meanwhile, perhaps out of a sense of self-protection, the ball somehow conspired to elude my flailing foot entirely, and bounce harmlessly away. For once, the arch foes of Elizabeth North and St Thomas More's were united in a common spirit of mirth as, to a boy, they laughed uproariously at my expense. Meanwhile, the umpire, having scooped up the ball, ruffled my hair in a not altogether unfriendly way, and said, "Try 'n remember your kicking boots next time, ay Blue?"

A Flawed Alliance

"What do you mean you weren't sick?" asked Wilbur. "Why didn't you come to school then?"

I produced a somewhat smug smile, and tapped my nose.

Wilbur initially looked disgruntled, then suddenly excited as enlightenment dawned. "I'll bet you only pretended to be sick," he declared. "Faked a temperature, forced yourself to puke – fooled your mum that way." He seemed impressed, though whether with himself or me was hard to tell.

"Not even warm," I said, lying back on the lawn in our favourite corner of the school playground, and chewing serenely on a desiccated stalk of grass.

"What then?" demanded Wilbur. "You know you can tell me, whatever it is – I won't squeal." He looked at me almost imploringly. "We're mates, aren't we?" he felt it might assist his cause by adding.

I casually removed the grass stalk from my mouth and tossed it aside before manoeuvring myself into a sitting position. "I just felt like a coupla days holiday," I told him. "That's all – no big deal."

Wilbur balanced my disclosure on his own tongue and started to evaluate it by tentatively chewing. "But what about your sick notes?" he demanded. "I saw you giving 'em to Vincent – so don't deny it!"

"What about 'em?" I replied.

"Your parents must've at least thought you weren't well to give you a sick note," he suggested. Then, suddenly animated again, "Or did they have special permission to take you somewhere?" His born again face was riding on the breeze, alert with all the possibilities of freedom.

"Cold, cold, cold," I taunted, as I stretched myself out once more across the saving lawn.

"Ahah – of course!" exclaimed Wilbur, giving himself a theatrical smack on the side of his head with the palm of his hand. "You had to go the dentist, didn't you? That's not quite the same as being sick." By proffering a qualifying remark like this, Wilbur presumably believed he was bolstering his chances of being right, and his normally pallid face was flushed with certitude as he warmed to the imminent prospect of his achievement.

I rose again to a sitting position and helpfully commenced a summary of the key facts that Wilbur had so far uncovered, counting them off sequentially on my fingers as I spoke. "OK, point one – I wasn't sick. Point two – I never pretended to be sick. Three – my parents didn't have permission to take me anywhere. Four – no, I didn't go the dentist's. Five – yes, I did give notes to Sister Vincent when I came back to school after being off. Six – the notes said I'd been sick. Seven" – and here I looked mischievously into Wilbur's eyes; I may even have winked – "Seven," I repeated, " – neither of my parents wrote, or knew anything about, those notes." I grinned, with what was in truth only a vague approximation of triumph, as I had started feeling bored. "Add all that up, and what do you get?"

A shadow of alarm momentarily darkened Wilbur's features, but was quickly replaced by a combination of incredulity and awe. "Have you been playing hooky?" His words were precious jewels, wrapped up in a deceptively nondescript cloth bag, and then carefully removed.

Blithely, to fuel the vestiges of my enthusiasm, I nodded.

For a few moments, Wilbur seemed to have forgotten how to breathe. "Why'd you do it?" he eventually asked, determinedly suppressing his astonishment, but forced to gulp in any case from trepidation, or alarm.

"I'm sick of spending the day with the babies," I informed him. "It's driving me nuts."

Wilbur knew to at least appear consoling. "It doesn't seem fair," he agreed, "the way she only seems to pick on you."

"Anyway, I'd had enough," I went on, flicking exasperatedly at the ground with my index finger. "I've no desire to be a martyr," it somehow seemed appropriate to add.

Wilbur was regarding me with seemingly unabashed admiration. He might indeed have swooned, had not conviction suddenly burst like an over-inflated balloon. "Hang on a minute," he said, "what about the sick notes? You said they were sick notes, but your parents didn't write them........"

"That's right," I conceded, suddenly enjoying myself once more.

"That means," said Wilbur, visibly daring himself to draw the obvious conclusion. "That means – if – if you – you didn't?"

I grinned, and nodded. "Yep," I said, unnecessarily.

"But – but – but – ." Wilbur's mouth was farting in bewilderment and disarray. For a couple of seconds, he looked as though he would have liked to have refused to believe, but a sudden wave of admiration swept aside all doubts. Wilbur was rolling on the grass then, contorted by mirth into a helpless abandonment of unremembered limbs. "That's fuckin' amazing, Langley!" he chortled repeatedly, only partly for reassurance. "Absolutely fuckin' amazing!"

All at once, he came to a stop, and sat, staring at me, in the thrall of a sudden, overwhelming impulse. "We should do it together," he said simply.

I stared back at him, uncertainly. If the Starcevich brothers had contrived the simplistic (and erroneous) theory that I was a goody-goody, there could be little or no doubt that Wilbur was the genuine article. "Are you sure?" I prodded, suspecting that his reaction had been distorted, or perhaps even created, by the senses of relief and liberation he was feeling at having finally uncovered my secret.

"Of course I'm sure!" he insisted, a little too swiftly and determinedly to convince.

"All right then," I said, "let's do it tomorrow. I'll be waiting for you in the scrubland near your house at half eight in the morning. We can go up into the hills, or spend the day at the Centre together."

"No worries!" agreed Wilbur, with a keenness that was almost tangible. His traitorous eyes, however, told a different, more predictable tale.

The Joys Of Friendship

Linus's grandparents reminded me of my mum and dad, or rather of how I imagined my mum and dad would end up. I never observed any demonstrable affection in their relationship, and to all intents and purposes they inhabited separate worlds. They did not even sleep in the same bedroom as one another. In a sense, the only important thing in life they had in common was a shared solicitude for the welfare of their grandson.

I found Linus's gran to be a cheerful, uncomplicated, essentially kind-hearted person, who almost uniquely among the adults of my acquaintance, seemed actually to like me. I have reason to suspect that she disapproved of the fact that my parents frequently resorted to corporal punishment with me, but only very rarely with Theresa. Consequently, she would often give me treats, such as lollies, chocolate, or home-grown grapes from the garden, or engage me in conversation of a sort that implied a real respect and interest. (Most adults never conversed with you: they either told you what to do, or simply ignored you.)

Linus's grand-dad – always known as 'Pop' or 'Pops' – was equally good-humoured, but rather less enamoured of me. On occasion, he would take both Linus and I out, most often to the footy, but sometimes to other places. These were seldom happy trips, as putting Linus and I together for a prolonged period of time was more or less tantamount to lighting the touch paper leading to a large quantity of gun-powder in an enclosed space. The length of the touch paper might vary, but the end result was always the same. Although Linus's grand-dad was scrupulously careful to deal – or at least be seen to deal – evenhandedly with the inevitable contretemps that emerged between his grandson and me, I got the impression that, deep down, he actually blamed me for them. At any rate, after one particularly acrimonious afternoon spent watching West Torrens play Sturt at Adelaide Oval, he decided that enough was enough, and there were no further trips. Even back then, I could see his point of view. After a week spent working hard on the railways, the last thing he needed was to have his Saturday ruined by a pair of fractious, bickering, ill-tempered boys.

If Robert and Wilbur jointly fulfilled the role of 'brother as soul mate', Linus was their exact converse, the quintessential brother as rival. In effect, if not reality, he was an only child, occupying centre stage in his grandparents' affections, and used to getting his own way almost without question. As a result, he did not cope at all well with the give and take which are so essential to a healthy friendship, and which tend to be second nature to kids with siblings. Linus was also a year older than me, which I suspect he felt meant that I ought to subordinate my will to his in cases of disagreement. Given that I was used to endeavouring to impose my will on that of my younger siblings in the context of a parental regime which palpably favoured them, this was never going to happen.

One of the first trips that Linus and I took with his grand-dad was to an air show at nearby Edinburgh airfield. Linus's grand-dad did not have a car, and so we walked. The air show itself was much less my particular cup of tea than Linus's, which automatically confirmed him in the dominant position he imagined was his by right. For most of the afternoon, therefore, he was happily able to impress me with his knowledge of the various aircraft on display, although in truth my interest was negligible.

If that seems a little sarcastic, let me stress that Linus's knowledge on matters such as these was genuinely impressive. If I sometimes found his attitude of assumed superiority difficult to tolerate, I nevertheless admired, indeed looked up to, him greatly. Of all my friends, he appeared to possess the liveliest and most wide-ranging intelligence, and it seems to me highly probable that another reason for the antagonism which so frequently erupted between us was that I was jealous. Privately, I aspired to many of the attributes that Linus seemed so admirably to manifest, but my inherent state of confusion about the world, coupled with the battle I was engaging in to free myself from the collective delusional psychosis in which I had been enmeshed almost since birth, conspired to render these aspirations unattainable. This inevitably produced a high level of frustration, not to mention a certain feeling of inferiority, both of which might well have been alleviated to a degree had Linus ever displayed any genuine warmth of feeling, or even a touch of humility, towards me, but for reasons outside his own control this was never possible.

It was on the return journey from Edinburgh airfield that things got out of hand. We were still walking along the road adjacent to the airfield when Linus and I came across a toy scooter which had been abandoned, although it was hard to see why as it was still in almost pristine condition. Thinking that Christmas had come early, I promptly claimed it for my own, feeling both confident and justified in so doing on the grounds that Linus already had a scooter of his own, not to mention a bicycle, while I had neither. I should have known better. Linus immediately claimed that he had seen the scooter first, and it was a clear case of 'finders keepers'. A vigorous tug-of-war then ensued during which the scooter risked being broken in two. Finally, Linus's grand-dad intervened, and wrenched the scooter out of our hands. Confident that the justice of my case was undeniable, I was reasonably relaxed at this development, but it quickly became clear that justice was the last thing on Linus's grand-dad's mind. All he wanted was a peaceful walk home. "Neither of you can have it," he declared, and for a few minutes we walked on in silence, Linus and I on either side of him, alternately eying the scooter he was carrying and one another with mingled avarice and acrimony. Linus's grand-dad was obviously uncertain what to do next, but when we reached a large, muddy ditch at the side of the road he finally decided. Walking to the edge of the ditch, he held the scooter high above his head, almost in triumph, and hurled it as hard and far as he could down into the mud.

Linus seemed perfectly equanimous about the way matters had been resolved, and I could not help imagining that he had not really cared about having the scooter for himself, but had merely wanted to ensure that I did not get it.

I do not know whether Linus's gran was told about our little difference of opinion, but somehow I suspect she was. At any rate, I do not believe it was a coincidence that, when I had a day off school a few weeks later for some Catholic holy day of obligation or other, she called at our house during the morning and asked if I would like to borrow Linus's bike for the day. Linus had never even allowed me to touch his bike before, let alone ride it, and so, whatever Linus's gran's motives were in allowing me this dispensation, I was hard pressed not to interpret it as a belated conferral of justice.

Hiding From The World

When the rain started, I headed for my favourite bolt-hole, an old abandoned water pipe that lay on some wasteland just outside Elizabeth North shopping centre. Curled up in the middle of the water pipe I still felt fairly cold, even in my duffel coat, but at least I was afforded a measure of protection, not only from the rain, but also, to some extent, from the lacerating impact of my own thoughts.

It was five to ten in the morning, which meant that I still had almost six hours to endure before home time. Had Wilbur been with me they would have been six hours of fun rather than endurance, but Wilbur, exhibiting the characteristic common sense that made him in so many ways my superior, had let me down, as in all honesty I had known he would, and so my third day of truancy, like the previous two, would be a prolonged, intermittently excruciating battle with the feelings of inadequacy engendered by my afflictions at the hands of Sisters Damien and Vincent.

At least I would have the illusion of being in control, however, of having at least retaliated, if not quite triumphed.

Earlier that morning, I had remained aboard my bus for two stops longer than usual, eventually alighting at the end of Tolmer Road, a couple of hundred metres or so from Wilbur's home. At almost exactly half past eight, and somewhat to my surprise, Wilbur had emerged from his house and ventured across the road to the patch of scrubland in which, perched behind a tiny bush in a gesture of concealment, I was waiting, as per our agreement.

Things were not as they seemed, however. "I can't come," said Wilbur, without preamble, his studied frown not quite masking the underlying sense of relief I was hardly surprised to discern. "Dad said he'd drive me to school this morning because it looks like it's going to rain."

"Oh," I said, which in the circumstances seemed the safest.

Wilbur muttered something about being sorry, said he'd see me at school, and left me to confront both my demons and my destiny alone. His departing footsteps were the hurried, ungainly ones of the not quite penitential.

Because of the impending rain, I decided to head for one of the local shopping centres rather than venture into the hills, where finding shelter might prove a problem. Curled up in the water pipe I experienced an illusory sense of inviolability. Being enclosed was tantamount to being set apart, to being held in loving arms.

The rain became torrential. To pass the time, I recited lists of trivial facts that I had committed to memory: the average distances of each of the planets from the sun; the names of all the footballers in the 1965 Mobil Footy Photos card series; premiership teams since 1907; obscure statistical information about various dinosaurs – height, length, weight, number and size of brains; the names of the fifty American states; the world's capital cities and their populations; the names, nicknames and colours of footy clubs from Victoria, Western Australia and Tasmania; and so on.

Eventually, the rain abated, and so I walked across the intervening strip of wasteland into the shopping centre in order to check the time. To my horrified disbelief, I discovered that it was only twenty-five to eleven. Nevertheless, I returned to the sanctuary of my water pipe, and spent a few minutes eating a couple of my lunch time sandwiches. Then I visited the toilet, and on my return to the water pipe decided to eat the rest of my lunch.

Returning to the shopping centre, I peered into the window of the library to scrutinise the clock on the wall behind the counter. It read eleven fifteen. I would have liked to have gone into the library and spent some time reading, but I knew it would be too risky. However, the thought of reading gave me an idea: I returned to the water pipe, took my Wide Range reader out of my satchel, and spent what I convinced myself was a good three hours or so immersed – as far as that was possible - in the irreducibly tame, straight-laced, passionless tales contained therein.

When I next visited the library to find out the time it was twenty past twelve – still nearly four hours before I could realistically head home. I might have elected to move on and find myself another hiding place, but the rain had begun again in earnest, and so I had no alternative but to return to the water pipe.

Although my school uniform was hidden from view beneath my duffel coat, I carried a satchel, and was clearly a boy of school age. It might seem strange therefore that no-one confronted me, and asked me what I was doing at the shopping centre. However, although I was only nine years old I had already acquired mastery of the art of remaining invisible, an achievement that most people do not manage until it is effectively thrust upon them during old age. While playing truant I visited shopping centres in Elizabeth North, Elizabeth Park, Elizabeth Downs, Elizabeth Vale, Elizabeth Fields and the city centre. I paced the streets of all these suburbs and more. I lay in water pipes, sat at train stations, and played on swings, slides and climbing frames at various playgrounds. Not once during all this time was I so much as spoken to by an adult.

Perhaps I actually am invisible, I thought. Perhaps I don't exist.

At two thirty or so the rain relented once again and I decided to head for home. I would tell my mum that we had had football training, but the coach had cancelled it because of the weather, and sent us home early. She would believe me. She almost always did.

Rumbled

The penny finally dropped for my mum when, for the third time in little over a week, I alleged that my early arrival home from school was attributable to a cancelled football training session.

"I thought you only had football training on Fridays," she said. This was a Wednesday.

"Oh, this was a special extra session," I explained.

"But it was cancelled?"

"Yes."

"Just like last Friday?"

"Yes."

"And last Wednesday as well?"

"Er, yes."

"I see. So what else did you do at school today?"

"Oh, the usual stuff."

"Like?"

"Sums. Reading. A spelling test."

"And did you get any homework?"

"No – I mean yes."

"You don't seem sure."

"I nearly forgot."

"What homework have you got then?"

"Writing and sums."

"Good thing I reminded you, isn't it? You'd better do it then."

"OK."

A little unnerved, I retired to my bedroom to do my imaginary homework. A couple of minutes later my mum came in and closed the door behind her. Uh oh. Perching herself on the edge of my bed she said, "Why don't you tell me what's really been going on?"

Carefully manufacturing a look of innocent bemusement, I blinked up at her. "Huh?"

"I know you haven't been going to school," she told me. "I found out from Mrs. Rensenbrink."

A surge of panic rose, which I struggled to keep from inflicting itself on my features. Best say nothing, I thought, and did.

"Well?"

Keep calm, don't say anything, avoid her eyes – perhaps she'll give up and go away........

"Well?" she said again, much too soon, and I was forced to acknowledge that my chances of escape did not look promising. So, somewhat hesitantly, with what I hoped was just the right air of indignation, I told her about my victimisation at the hands of Sister Vincent, and my persistent, almost daily, demotions to the babies' class. When I had finished, Mum looked, and was, furious – but not, I was surprised and extremely relieved to discover, at me. "How long has this been going on?" she asked me.

"Coupla months." I saw no harm in exaggerating matters.

"A couple of months! Why didn't you say something?"

I just looked at her. Tell your mother your most shameful secrets? Who was she kidding?

“We pay a lot of money for you to attend that school,” she informed me, with obvious bitterness. “In return, we expect you to receive a proper education, not waste your time doing grade one work!”

It was, I had to admit, a pretty valid point, albeit one that had not occurred to me. I wondered briefly how much money my parents had effectively thrown away subsidising my dozen or so days in Sister Damien’s class, not to mention the days I had refrained from attending school at all.

“Right,” said my mum, using the business-like tone of voice that was frequently the precursor to a thrashing, but on this occasion her ire was directed elsewhere, “if you promise me never to play hooky again, you won’t be punished.”

It seemed a wholly reasonable deal to me, so I nodded.

“In the meantime,” she went on, “your dad and I are going to have a quiet word or two with Sister Mary Christopher.”

With that, she got to her feet and headed for the door, only to pause just before she reached it, as though she had suddenly remembered something. Turning to me with a wry smile on her face, she said, “How’s your homework coming on?”

Somewhat reluctantly, I uncovered the exercise book that I had been covering with my elbows throughout our discussion, exposing to my mum’s inquisitorial gaze my somewhat extravagant, half-finished drawing of a triceratops engaged in a frantic and bloody life or death tussle with a tyrannosaurus rex.

"Mmm. Delightful," said Mum, although she clearly meant the precise opposite.

Not that I cared. Energised and inspired by my unexpected acquittal, I set to work embellishing, and subtly amending, my drawing. Against all the apparent odds, the beleaguered triceratops was destined to survive, in the process consigning its seemingly invincible adversary to an abrupt, appropriately turbulent demise.

I never again played truant, and although I remained one of Sister Mary Vincent's favourite penological targets, my regular exposure to the deranged wrath of her colleague, Sister Damien, was over. Whether the pair of them are still alive, or enduring perpetual torment in the deepest recesses of the non-existent hell in which I still irrationally believe, I cannot find it in my heart to wish them well.

1966

Mont Plonk And The Chosen Three

When he finally reached the summit of the divine mountain, the renowned and venerable samurai Mikalo stood with his back to the slowly setting sun, spread his arms out wide in a gesture of benediction and thanksgiving, and addressed his faithful followers thus:

"In the ever illustrious name of the Kalawara ninjas I hereby claim this great mountain, along with all the land visible as far as the horizon in every direction."

The acolytes cheered.

"Let this mountain henceforth be a place of celebration, thanksgiving, remembrance and sanctuary."

Despite not understanding some of their leader's words, the acolytes cheered once more.

Then, crouching to his knees, Mikalo stretched forth his hand to indicate a six inch long semi-circle of dog faeces that had been rendered black and brittle by prolonged exposure to the sun. So desiccated had it become, that even the flies eschewed it. "Nothing happens by chance or outside the controlling harness of divine will," Mikalo declared. "Therefore, in the full and certain confidence that to do so is to align ourselves more completely with the purposes, resources and actions of the divine intelligence, I hereby have pleasure in naming this mountain………… Mont Plonk!"

The acolytes became suffused with excitement, and began waving their swords exultantly above their heads. "Mont Plonk!" they chanted, almost drunkenly. "Mont Plonk! Mont Plonk! Mont Plonk!"

Mikalo, who in terms of the self which he habitually proffered to the world for scrutiny was actually highly sceptical about the existence of a divine intelligence, nevertheless evinced apparent conviction by virtue of his aptitude for role play. Aware, at some level, that we are all comprised of many, often mutually contradictory, personae, he was briefly relishing the specious consolation to be derived from wearing a bridle.

The acolytes were similarly enhanced, if not quite liberated, whilst simultaneously abandoned to an image of consummation.

It had been a long, challenging, at times unglamorously irksome day. Even during the initial part of the journey, while they were still travelling through civilised parts, there had been problems. On one occasion, a group of ragamuffin children had taunted and insulted them. A short while later, they had been pelted with stones by another gang of urchins.

"A ninja does not respond to intimidation from those beneath him in status," Mikalo reminded them, and they walked steadfastly on, neither changing pace nor displaying any outward signs of emotion.

They encountered their first significant challenge when they arrived at the River of Relinquishment, which must be traversed in order to enter the Badlands. Although the dry season had already started, the river still flowed deep, and, as everyone knows, a ninja, being a creature of air and fire, does not get his or her feet wet if it can be helped. "We shall build a bridge," announced Mikalo, and he promptly set to work gathering stones for that purpose from along the river bank. The acolytes fell to assisting, and soon they were able to commence the process of laying down a pathway of stones across the mighty waterway. Their crossing proceeded smoothly until, half way over, one of the acolytes, Dogsbody, could not resist the urge to stoop down and examine the bed of the river for signs of frogs or yabbies or fish. Suddenly, he overbalanced, and catapulted head-first into the water. "Oh, shit!" he exclaimed.

The great samurai Mikalo, who was already on the Badlands side of the river, was livid. "Have you no self-control?" he scolded.

Meanwhile the second acolyte, the one who gloried in the title of Chief Ninja, had paused in his progress across the bridge, and had turned around with the intention of helping his comrade, only to lose his footing, and plummet backwards into the water with a mighty splash. "Cripes, my new sandshoes," he wailed. "Mum'll kill me!"

Together, the two chastened acolytes clambered back onto the bridge and scurried across to join their leader, whose florid face, sardonic smile and gleaming eyes suggested a degree of amused satisfaction that, as one entirely wedded to The Cause, he could not possibly have been feeling.

The River of Relinquishment flows from north to south, and the Chosen Three were now standing on its western bank, confronted by a vast expanse of grassland. Spectacularly green and lush for the time of year, it stretched for an unknown distance away to the west, but had nevertheless to be negotiated before the Badlands proper could be reached.

"Many tales are told of those who have entered the Fields of Doom never to return," Mikalo the samurai informed his followers, in a hushed voice not entirely devoid of excitement. "Extreme caution, therefore, is needed."

Turning to the Chief Ninja, who was busy pouring water out of one of his sodden sandshoes, Mikalo said, "You, in your perfect camouflage of green, will lead the way. I will follow, and you, Dogsbody, will bring up the rear."

And so they ventured across the legendary Fields of Doom, slowly, warily, slithering like snakes, the green carpet giving way before them like a parting sea.

The grassland came to an end as abruptly as it had begun. Ahead lay an enormous expanse of open countryside, completely barren, brown, and hostile apart from an improbably large slab of slate grey rock in the middle distance, a handful of uninspired, underdeveloped shrubs, and, almost on the horizon, a couple of green-tinged clumps of what perhaps were gum trees.

The Chief Ninja waited until his leader and Dogsbody had crawled alongside him and then said – because, as second in command, it was his right – "What now?"

Mikalo pointed in the direction of the isolated rocky outcrop. "The Altar of Enlightenment," he said, almost reverentially. "I have heard tell of it, but never thought to see it with my own eyes."

"What's the Altar of Enlightenment?" asked Dogsbody, impertinently.

The samurai graciously chose to ignore the indiscretion, and said, "First we must reach it, and then I shall tell." With that, he heaved himself to his feet, and sprinted off across the intervening wasteland, followed soon after, albeit at a less frenetic pace, by the acolytes.

The Altar of Enlightenment was almost perfectly rectangular in shape, proving, or at least strongly suggesting, that it was man-made. Some six metres long by four metres wide, it rose almost a metre from the ground on its eastern edge, descending to just over half a metre high on the opposite side. Dogsbody immediately started to clamber up but Mikalo placed a restraining hand on his shoulder. "Wait," he commanded.

Sniffing querulously, Dogsbody nevertheless obeyed.

Mikalo then extracted his still nearly full water bottle from his sack and commenced a slow, anti-clockwise circuit of the altar, pausing every few paces to sprinkle several drops of water onto it. As he did so, he muttered indecipherably, and made seemingly random arcane gestures, vaguely comparable to a priest bestowing a blessing, with his right hand.

The acolytes sniggered, but by the time Mikalo had completed his circumnavigation and rejoined them they had recomposed their features, and were standing dutifully to attention. "Since I have temporarily annulled the negative energies associated with this place," the samurai announced, "it will now make an ideal staging post."

The two acolytes looked at one another with thinly concealed amusement, each silently challenging the other not to snigger again. In this, they might not have been successful if Mikalo, having already climbed onto the altar, had not immediately instructed them to follow him.

"What negative energies?" asked the Chief Ninja, as the three of them sat down together near the centre of the altar.

Mikalo looked grim. "In ancient times, this was a place of ritualised torture, execution and sacrificial offerings – both animal and human," he explained. "Such activities leave marks."

"Marks?" asked Dogsbody.

"Scars upon the cosmos," Mikalo said, whose face, impressively, was almost preternaturally emotionless.

There was a brief pause, and then, "What sort of methods of execution were used?" the Chief Ninja could not prevent himself from asking.

"Oh, the usual," Mikalo answered, somewhat blithely. "Disembowelling, beheading – both partial and complete, crucifixion, slicing in two, throttling, burning or boiling alive, tearing limb from limb, hanging, variations on the death of a thousand cuts……."

The acolytes contrived to seem appalled. "Beheading wouldn't be too bad," mused the Chief Ninja. "Or slicing in two, or hanging. But I wouldn't want to be burned to death or crucified."

"Me neither," agreed Dogsbody. "I'd like to be beheaded by a guillotine, but not an axe or sword," he decided.

"Enough!" said Mikalo. "We have scarcely begun our journey, and must complete it by nightfall. Let us quickly refresh and fortify ourselves, and then continue."

The next stage of the trip was easily the most onerous, if also in some respects the most unmemorable, as, under the heightened ravages of the searing sun, they made their way across the Desert of Confusion.

After travelling for at least an hour, Dogsbody said, "Those trees on the horizon are just a mirage, aren't they? They don't seem to be getting any closer."

But Mikalo simply said, "Everything is as it should be," and proceeded to increase the pace a little.

Shortly afterwards, both of the acolytes ran out of water. Mikalo, on the other hand, despite having expended some back at the sacrificial altar, still had almost half a bottle to spare.

"Such wanton intemperance is unforgivable," he said, and might indeed have been felt to taunt, had not his status as a samurai precluded such censoriousness.

And no, he later told them, I shall not share my remaining water with you – although not out of selfishness, he hastened to reassure himself, but merely to teach you a lesson.

But neither of the acolytes was thirsty.

Suddenly, almost miraculously, they found themselves in the proximity of a small clump of gum trees, known, according to Mikalo, as the Forest of Forgetfulness. "This is a place of spiritual refreshment and retreat," he informed his followers, stressing the word 'spiritual' in a way that, in truth, only he was sufficiently sophisticated to find meaningful.

Indeed Dogsbody, who liked to think of gravity as an irritation rather than a law, was already half way up the nearest tree.

"That ruddy kid brother of mine," hissed Mikalo, *sotto voce*, to the Chief Ninja, who wondered briefly whether 'ruddy' was a bona fide swear word, of a sort to elicit purgatorial flame and torment, or just a harmless slang expression.

"You'll only make yourself thirsty," Mikalo said to Dogsbody, who had neatly perched himself between a fork of branches two thirds of the way up the tree, and was looking down on his associates with what might have seemed, but almost certainly was not, an element of smugness. Blessed with a roseate disposition that derived from his natural disinclination to reflect on things, Dogsbody, for the most part, simply was.

In retaliation, or perhaps to quench his thirst, Mikalo indulged in a swig or two of water, but this only had the effect of encouraging the Chief Ninja to emulate the arboreal exploits of his younger comrade, albeit with noticeably less verve and skill.

"We'll rest then," suggested, or conceded, Mikalo, and, propping his weary form against the weathered trunk of an almost entirely negligible gum tree, he did so.

God Runs Out Of Fags

"Some of you," said Father Ballantine from his pulpit, in an ominously relaxed and quiet voice, "put as little as fifty cents into the offertory plate each week."

He paused, giving the silence time to cajole, then suddenly bellowed, "Fifty cents! Fifty – measly – cents! That's not even enough to buy a packet of cigarettes!"

He paused again, as if daring somebody to answer back. "Is that the price you put on your faith?" he asked, almost sorrowfully. "Is that the value you place on God sending his only begotten son to suffer and die in your stead?"

Red-faced with the effort that indignation demands, his eyes danced across the serried ranks of the congregation, hoping either to engage or, it might have been, impale.

I, however, had been left far behind, having become transfixed by the mental image of God going into the local deli to ask for twenty Viscount, only to be told that he did not have sufficient money.

"I'm sorry, God, mate," said the shopkeeper, "but fifty cents ain't nearly enough to buy a packet of smokes these days, yer know."

"Damn and blast!" exclaimed God. "It's those bloody faithless cheapskates at St Thomas More's – they're less committed than a bunch of eunuchs at an orgy!" He sighed morosely. "More than half of 'em are pommies, yer know," he added in a low, meaningful voice, tapping his nose, while the shopkeeper looked, but was not in the least, consoling. "Ah well," chuntered God, foraging on the counter for a pack of juicy fruit and a Milky Bar. "I was thinking of trying to give up anyway, so I reckon I'll take these instead."

At that point I tuned back in to Father Ballantine, who now, it seemed, was talking about television. "And then there's *Star Trek*," he veritably spluttered, rolling his eyes as though in disbelief, or else in the sudden thrall of ecstasy. "Has Satan ever had a more compelling piece of propaganda? Yet some of you will sit for hours immersed in such rubbish and never even set aside a quarter of an hour to pray together as a family."

Enmeshed in the ineffable truth of what he himself was declaring, or more likely simply short of breath by virtue of his habit of smoking forty a day, Father Ballantine was breathing hard, and glowering with what I imagined must be righteous indignation.

"Dad," I said, a short while later, as we were walking home from Mass, "do priests ever sin?"

"Yes, of course they do," my dad replied.

"Well, who hears their confessions then – bishops?"

"No, just other priests."

I found this disclosure barely credible.

"What about nuns, then?"

"Do you mean, who hears nuns' confessions?"

"Yes – I mean, no. I mean, do nuns commit sins?"

"Of course they do!"

"Even mortal sins?"

"Yes, sometimes. Even mortal sins."

"Hmmpphh….."

I imagined Sister Mary Christopher in a bandit mask, threatening a moist-skinned, vacant-eyed bank manager with her red-tipped weapon of choice. “Just put all the money in this bag,” she commanded, smirking at his discomfiture. Then, when he had finished obliging, she began to smite him repeatedly with her cane, all the while pronouncing gleefully, “Oh, I know it hurts – it’s meant to!”

To me, at the age of ten, the world somehow seemed a vastly more complicated place than it had even a year earlier. Sin was omnipresent and inescapable. You could even sin while watching your favourite programme on television. Once, during confession, Father Chekovich had said to me, “God sees right into the depths of your soul, my son. He knows not only your thoughts, but your very motivations. It is not sufficient simply to do what is right – to obey your teachers for fear of getting punished, for example – you must do what is right out of a genuine, heartfelt love of God.”

At the time, I had not really understood what Father Chekovich was driving at, but after mulling it over for a while, it finally made sense.

God demanded nothing more nor less than perfection, and the more I thought about it, the more it seemed to me that perfection was unattainable. My dad was always haranguing my mum for her “vile, despicable habit” of smoking – and yet Father Ballantine, God’s anointed priest, smoked, by his own admission, forty a day. Nuns wore wedding rings to show that they were married to God and yet my dad had told me they were capable of mortal sins – of murder, grand larceny, even deliberately missing Sunday Mass.

If perfection was truly unattainable, where did that leave God?

When, on the Sunday of Father Ballantine's wide-ranging if bombastic sermon, the offertory was collected, I watched out of the corner of my eye as my dad, for the first time ever in my recollection, placed some paper money on the plate.

The Great Farting Epidemic

Darryl Callaghan was an acknowledged master of the surreptitious fart, a fact which alone was sufficient to earn him virtual celebrity status among most of the rest of the boys in the class. However, his talents did not end there. A decade before the emergence of punk rock Darryl was impressing his classmates with his idiosyncratic penchant for adorning various parts of his body with safety pins, which he somehow managed to insert into his flesh without either flinching or drawing blood. Perhaps, I pondered, recalling an episode of *Lost In Space* (or was it *Star Trek*?), Darryl was not actually a boy at all, but an android……..

On those days when the wind was low, Darryl would compensate to some degree by generating loud, authentic-sounding fart noises via the time-honoured technique of placing a cupped hand under his naked armpit and swiftly and energetically bringing his arm down to his side. This was guaranteed to infuriate Sister Mary Vincent, although she seldom if ever managed to identify the miscreant.

Not that Darryl was always so fortunate. In academic terms, he was what might most charitably be termed an under-achiever, a state of affairs which nowadays would almost certainly lead to his being provided with remedial help of some sort. As far as the Sisters of Mercy were concerned, however, there was only one cure for stupidity, which was to harass, brutalise and flay it into oblivion. As an incentive to our intellectual growth, Sister Mary Vincent would declare, "Now, children, it's time for a spelling test. I expect you all to achieve a mark of at least six out of ten. Boys who get five out of ten or less will be smacked – one smack for five out of ten, two smacks for four out of ten, three smacks for three out of ten, and so forth. Any boy who gets nought out of ten" – and she would almost invariably stare meaningfully in Darryl's direction at this point – "will have the pleasure of half a dozen first hand encounters with Sister Mary Christopher's cane during tomorrow morning's assembly." And she would lick her in truth almost invisible lips in anticipatory relish. "Girls," she would then say, "will not, of course, be smacked, but will do an equivalent number of recess detentions instead."

Darryl, who seldom managed more than one or two out of ten in any test, whether spelling, dictation or mental arithmetic, received his repeated thrashings with the same equanimity and easy-going grin as he bore his self-inflicted safety pin wounds.

Darryl's trend-setting proclivities also extended to the realms of style and fashion. Presumably bored with using his legs as surrogate pin cushions, he was the first boy in the class to progress from wearing shorts to long trousers. Perhaps even more significantly, he was also the first boy in our class to take up smoking. I am not sure exactly when this was, but by the time he was in grade five he was a hardened chain smoker – when out of the classroom, of course. By this time, several other boys in the class had also started smoking, but Darryl's head-start was such that, in terms of noticeable side-effects, he was already well into the home straight.

As a ten year old, Darryl had a voice reminiscent of Hollywood actor Lee Marvin, albeit with an Australian accent. Indeed, his pronouncements were typically so deep and gravely in tone that their content, which seemed to consist almost exclusively of words like 'smokes', 'root', 'woofters' and 'frenchies', usually uttered with a feeble, almost self-effacing guffaw, seemed irrelevant.

The mere mention of 'frenchies' was enough to make any self-respecting male in grade five degenerate into fits of helpless giggles, irrespective of whether they had any clear notion of the nature of the object in question. Most, I suspect, did not. In my own case, as someone who had no idea what an erection was, let alone how penetrative sex occurred, the word 'frenchy' was just inherently funny, without any reference to its alleged meaning. Similarly, words like 'stiffy', 'poofter', 'wanker', 'cunt' and 'prozzie' had the undeniable effect of tickling you onomatopoeically in a way that disclosure of meaning would perhaps have undermined.

Almost uniquely, Darryl's popularity among his peers did not depend, even in part, on any kind of athletic prowess. Indeed, he openly eschewed all forms of physical activity with the exceptions of lighting up, belching, creating farting noises in the way described above, and, of course, and most especially, farting itself. I can not recall ever seeing him so much as breaking into a trot, let alone running. When forced to participate in football matches his sole apparent intention appeared to be to get, and stay, as far away from the ball as possible (which if he could manage it meant the nearest toilet for a sly smoke).

Despite this wilful indolence, however, Darryl Callaghan was arguably, with the possible exception of football and cricket captain Barry Ryan, the single most respected boy in the class.

That popularity and esteem reached its peak in grade five during what, in hindsight, came to be known as the Great Farting Epidemic. Inspired by Darryl's example, virtually all the boys in the class endeavoured to develop prowess in the skill of letting one rip both odorifously and unobtrusively. When, as sometimes happened, particularly in the first half an hour or so after lunch, fifteen or twenty boys more or less simultaneously felt constrained to alleviate their colic in the tried and trusted fashion, the result was sublimely, indescribably asphyxiating.

Sister Mary Vincent, who beneath her carefully concocted veneer of assurance was actually quite a confused and disappointed soul, would wrinkle up her nose, and her facial expression would oscillate back and forth between bemusement and irritation, as she instinctively looked for someone to blame, and hurt. "Open some windows please children," she would say, sniffing repeatedly as though endeavouring to convince herself that she was not imagining things. "We seem to have acquired a quite unpleasant odour from somewhere."

If for nothing else, Darryl Callaghan deserves to be remembered with esteem bordering on veneration for his feat in forging a workable ongoing alliance between boys of very disparate personalities and ideals, not to mention digestive systems. This achievement was actually almost wholly incidental in that it derived, not from any overt act of will, or from strength of character – for, if Darryl had any character at all, it was virtually indiscernible – but from the inherent urge which all human beings possess, at least initially, to ride the crest of the prevailing wave, rather than be overwhelmed by it.

Darryl presumably died many years ago, most likely from lung cancer. However, imperturbable epicurean that he was, he will no doubt have done so in a happy frame of mind, with the flavour of his last consoling drag still both massaging his taste-buds and camouflaging the underlying sense of angst that being human generates.

The Girl Of My Dreams

My brief, intense passion for Jessica Silverton was fuelled largely by her physical resemblance to Angela Cartwright, the young actress who played the character of Penny Robinson in the popular US TV series *Lost In Space*. She had the same immense, almost bulbous eyes, willowy frame, and lush dark hair, typically worn tied back in a pony tail. There were some significant differences too, however. Whereas the character of Penny came across as being something of a tomboy, or at any rate as someone not averse to action and the sometimes rumbustious rough and tumble which was an inevitable component of life aboard the intergalactic space vessel the Jupiter Two, Jessica Silverton was quintessentially female, to such a degree that she might almost have been a caricature of femininity. When she walked it was as though the very air around her rippled, even intermittently cavorted, in appreciation. She almost seemed a creature of liquid, rather than flesh and blood. Her smile, which, sadly, was all too rarely unfurled, became, to me, an implicit source of inspiration, like a blessing. When she laughed, which was even less frequently, I felt myself all but obliterated by the bliss I imagined, or knew, was cascading from her features.

The possibility of my actually, personally eliciting that laugh would sometimes wash over me in the night, causing me to tremble with desire. A kind of consummation, fervid, frail and indecipherable, loomed.

To the best of my recollection, however, I never so much as exchanged 'hellos' with Jessica Silverton, which, after the debacle involving Katie Bowyer, was perfectly fine with me. Besides, there were always my dreams, which even back then I was beginning to prefer to my actual waking life.

Ah, those dreams! In them, Jessica Silverton became accessible to me in ways I scarcely understood, involving both my body and that nebulous extension of it that I still, through force of habit, or delusion, called my soul. In some entirely primal, incoherent, emblematic sense the pair of us became, not Albert and Jessica, but the ultimate personification of Male and Female, united, by a process that resembled osmosis, into one, indivisible entity.

This, I came to imagine myself believing, usually a matter of seconds before awaking, incontrovertibly alone, to the confines of my sweat – or sin – soaked bed, is real. Is life. Is all that can or should be sought.

I knew. Till stymied by my own redundant perspiration.

One afternoon, on a whim, I followed Jessica as she left school, anxious, indeed almost desperate, for reasons I could not properly articulate, to discover where she lived. Perhaps I felt that by so doing I would somehow be acquiring a measure of control over her, achieving a kind of ownership. Perhaps I was simply nosy.

I followed at a distance of roughly a hundred metres. My stealth training as a ninja made concealment easy. I would hide in alleyways, or crouch down behind parked cars, peering surreptitiously out to monitor my target's progress, then scurrying rapidly after her whenever she turned a corner.

Perhaps to my astonishment, perhaps to my relief, I discovered that my imagined soul-mate inhabited a semi-detached house not dissimilar to my own, albeit with the luxury of a tiled, rather than a tin, roof. If this rendered her a little more human, even mundane, in my eyes, which arguably was bad, it also made her more accessible. At least in theory. My dreams accordingly became less esoteric. There was flesh involved, and ways of interaction that were almost carnal.

But Sister Mary Vincent, perhaps not quite unknowingly, extinguished our connection with a single, palpably half-hearted gesture.

Every weekend we were required to have our diaries, which contained a record of all the work completed during the previous week, signed by one or other of our parents (or, in the case of Dafydd Gynne, his grandma). On Monday morning, doubtless as an ostensible fillip to her spite, Sister Mary Vincent would check all our diaries to make sure this requirement had been attended to. Needless to say, anyone whose diary did not contain a parental signature was punished, the boys corporally, and the girls with detention – except for one seminal occasion involving the Girl Of My Dreams.

One of my favourite mental exercises concerning objects of desire like Katie, Andrea and Jessica was to identify, and then luxuriate in, the things we had in common. Sometimes, when such things appeared scarce, I would endeavour to create them. In the case of Katie Bowyer, for example, I spent several months endeavouring to imitate her pronounced Staffordshire accent, convinced that by so doing I would somehow, at some indeterminable level, establish a connection with her. All I actually managed to do, however, was attract confusion, amusement or scorn at my preposterous way of talking.

As far as Jessica Silverton was concerned, though, there was no need for me to resort to mimicry as we already shared something quite conspicuous and, in my eyes at least, special. When it came to the weekly matter of ensuring that our diaries got parentally endorsed, we were equally remiss. Quite why Jessica, who was normally a model of compliance and respectability, should have had such a persistent problem with this one particular requirement is a mystery. Perhaps she had a poor memory. Perhaps she hated both her parents. Perhaps, beneath her veneer of scrupulous conformity and rectitude, she harboured revolutionary ideals. I do not know. All I do know is that, after four or five consecutive weeks of non-compliance on Jessica's part, Sister Mary Vincent finally lost patience.

"It appears you don't find detention much of an inconvenience, Miss Silverton," she observed, in a deceptively gentle tone of voice to which I had learned, from dire experience, to attribute terror and foreboding. "Let me see" – her pursed lips disguised the fact that she had already, incontrovertibly decided – "Yes, I think the answer is clear. Since you display the same wilful ignorance as a boy, it only seems right that you should be treated as one." And her oily flesh was incandescent with arousal. "Kindly proceed to the front of the classroom, Miss Silverton."

A dull murmur arose, and gradually grew louder. Not only was this unprecedented, it was also, surely, in defiance of the Geneva Convention. Or something. In any case, to smack a girl was unthinkable.

But Sister Mary Vincent, as I knew to my cost, was never one to let the boundaries of common sense or accepted behaviour stand between her and fulfilment. Like a stunned beast in an abattoir, Jessica Silverton staggered toward her inevitable, if unimagined, denouement.

So caught up was I in the drama unfolding before me that I neglected something quite important. Like Jessica, I habitually forgot, or omitted, to get one of my parents to sign my diary of a weekend. Unlike Jessica, however, I avoided retribution by the simple expedient of forging my mother's signature (my dad's was so unbelievably idiosyncratic that it actually looked like a forgery, so I thought it best to use my mum's). Except that this weekend I had forgotten, and it was not until Sister Vincent was a couple of desks away that I realised. I hastened to endeavour to remedy the matter, but I was too late.

"What's this?" exclaimed Sister Vincent gleefully, her almost invisible lips glistening with anticipation. She loomed before me, swaying slightly, as though about to swoon. Her eyes grew fervent. "The very nerve!" she gasped. "A forger!" And, with obvious delight, she clipped me hard across the head, then wrenched me to my feet by the neck of my jumper. "To the front, Mr. Langley," she veritably chortled. "A double dose for you, I fancy – and an hour's detention tonight to boot."

I slouched as insolently as I could to the front of the class, joining half a dozen boys, and Jessica. By the time Sister Vincent had completed her rounds another couple of boys had joined us. One of them, Darryl Callaghan, the only boy in the class to wear long trousers, was painstakingly rolling them up in anticipation of his imminent chastisement, a cheesy grin, as always, embellishing his features. As he stood there, he muttered something indecipherable, but presumably amusing, at least to him, and chuckled almost self-effacingly.

"Perhaps this will teach you," was hardly Sister Vincent at her most inspired, but I was too excited to be critical. The prospect of physical pain seemed entirely inconsequential in the context of the seminal event I was about to witness: a girl – a girl! – was about to receive a belting. And not just any girl either, but the one that I had chosen to presume to call my own.

Whack! That was Darryl Callaghan.

Whack! Then Anthony Lindner, who presumably refrained on principle from allowing his mother access to a pen.

Whack! Whack! I endeavoured not to wince as both of my calves were unceremoniously flayed.

Possibly because of her own fear, or maybe as a result of an uncharacteristic attempt at chivalry on the parts of the remaining boys, Jessica Silverton found herself at the very end of the line. When Sister Mary Vincent reached her, she paused in a way that might have been intended to seem dramatic, and said, "And as for you, Miss Silverton," before solicitously applying her ruler to her victim's bare calf with rather less force than would be needed to momentarily stun a fly. If Jessica felt anything at all, let alone pain, she must have skin like gossamer, I mused.

Her reaction, therefore, was little short of startling. Her pert, slightly upturned nose curled up still further as though she were about to cry, her lower lip and chin began to wobble, her eyes grew scarlet and puffy, and her cheeks became inflamed. By the time she headed back to her seat she was sobbing uncontrollably.

As I returned to my own seat, I experienced a strange feeling of abandonment, indeed betrayal. Not even my cry-baby sister Theresa would be reduced to tears by what amounted to a tentative exploratory caress from a wholly innocuous piece of wood. Feminine charms and grace were all very well in theory, I reflected, but not in invertebrates.

I turned around and, with cool deliberation and detachment, took one last disdainful look at Jessica Silverton's bloated, anguished features. Angela Tewksbury was attempting to console her by patting her sympathetically on the arm, but even she, I could see, was feeling somewhat bemused, and even a touch embarrassed.

For an all too brief time, Jessica Silverton had introduced me to the wayward, bitter-sweet complexities of unrequited lust. With her, I had become more fully aware than ever before of the real nature of the activities she made me want to engage in. There were still a number of conspicuous blanks to be filled in, most notably in connection with that area of my body that my dad had taught me to treat with fear, suspicion and circumvention. Nevertheless, although the specifics were ill-defined and somewhat confusing, I was now entirely aware, for the first time in my life, that what my father called my 'private parts' – and hers too, presumably – were pretty centrally involved.

Or would have been. As I watched the hitherto resplendent focus of my lust transform herself into something wholly lacking in either self-respect or moral fortitude it occurred to me – alas, not for the last time – that a mirage can evoke desire as readily as an oasis.

The Wisdom Of Mother Christopher

One morning at school assembly Sister Mary Christopher informed us that she was henceforth to be referred to as 'Mother Christopher'. This, we were given to understand, was tantamount to a kind of proto-canonisation.

But what for, I wondered? What exactly had she done to warrant such an accolade? Perhaps even more to the point, what particular attributes and skills had Sister Mary Christopher exhibited that were deemed worthy of reward by the Sisters of Mercy?

This was something I found perpetually bemusing, not least in terms of semantics. The fact that the same word could sometimes be used to describe two or more completely different things was well known to me. Someone who was healthy could be said to 'well', for example, but a 'well' was also a repository of water. The world 'blind' meanwhile, had, according to my dictionary, over thirty distinct meanings.

Clearly, here was another such word – 'mother'. According to my previous understanding, this word referred to the relationship between a female who had given birth to a child, and that child. The act of giving birth, in effect, created a mother.

But Mother Christopher, as far as I could tell, had never given birth. Nuns seemingly never did.

Mothers also took care of the children they had borne. They fed them, clothed them, taught them things, bathed them, tucked them up in bed, read them stories, sang them to sleep, played with them, soothed their pains and their ills, and consoled them when they were upset. Occasionally, they also upbraided and chastised them, even smacked them, but seldom in a way that overrode or undermined the essentially nurturing nature of their role.

I tried to imagine Mother Christopher bathing my young sister Anna, tucking her up in bed, and then reading her a bed time story. The image, however, refused to coalesce in my mind's eye. Indeed, the thought was almost nauseating. Quite simply, Mother Christopher's hands were not made to undertake activities requiring gentleness, solicitude and care. Her whole *raison d'être* was to circumscribe and debilitate, to reinforce rather than quell suffering. Like the salt monster in *Star Trek*, she seemed to extract not only fulfilment and a revitalised sense of purpose from the act of inflicting pain, it actually appeared as if she was being physically nourished by it. Her normally pallid, starchy flesh would briefly glow, as though suddenly infused with moisture. Her eyes, which usually seemed to be focused inwards, would sparkle almost manically, affirming, albeit a touch perversely, the indissoluble nature of her connection with all that was squalid, rudimentary and mundane.

Mothers also existed and acted independently of their offspring, of course. They did the housework, shopped, drank tea incessantly, visited, and were in turn visited by, the neighbours, went to Tupperware parties, watched boringly sentimental old movies on the television, argued interminably with their husbands…….

All things which Mother Christopher would, surely, never even think of doing.

Or would she? Did her newly bestowed status elicit certain new responsibilities, and perhaps even awaken some long dormant subliminal urges? Did she now go shopping for groceries at 'Coles' every Friday night, or sit dabbing her eyes in front of the television as Humphrey Bogart reassured Ingrid Bergman "We'll always have Paris."

Is she perhaps continually reminded of all that she has lost, of all the possibilities and potential she has sacrificed upon the altar of her own bemused acquiescence?

I wonder this because it seemed to me, even as a ten year old, that Mother Christopher was someone who had been constrained, indeed configured, by disappointment. It was there in her tone of voice, her physical stance, the way her dark, diminutive, essentially unseeing eyes impaled her.

By the time I arrived in grade seven, the class that Mother Christopher herself presided over, I had begun to realise that disappointment was, in fact, only the most conspicuous expression of a deeper, more insidious ill. For when you poked and prodded at the callous of her disappointment, she would wince and squirm, obviously discomfited. Had you then been capable of surgically removing the callous you would have exposed the source of that pain, which Mother Christopher herself occasionally could not resist revealing.

"Stop your work," she would say, her tone of voice suggestive of mild panic, or disorientation. There would sometimes be a clearly visible sheen of perspiration on her upper lip, or forehead.

She would stand or sit there, staring intently at something either far behind us, or else imprisoned in her skull.

"Life," she would announce, trembling perceptibly in deference to the word, "is like a thread of cotton." And the sigh this realisation led her to unfurl was almost stentorian.

We sat, either listening or pretending to, feeling not so much bewildered as embarrassed.

As Mother Christopher purported to inspire us.

"We dangle over the abyss," she explained, "supported only by this flimsy thread of cotton, which could snap at any time. And then.........." Her eyes would roll inanely in their sockets. Her chin was that of a trembling, scolded child.

In a confidential, almost conspiratorial, tone of voice, she contrived the closest thing to an explanation she could muster.

"Nothing."

Neither consoled nor intimidated by this somewhat far-fetched revelation, we nevertheless knew enough to seem diminished. Once, Victoria Cameleri had even whimpered.

These impromptu existentialist interludes were as close as Mother Christopher ever came to fulfilling her statutory duty of providing us with appropriate religious instruction.

Occasionally, the sermon would be varied. Instead of representing life, the thread of cotton would become our sanity, with the underlying abyss becoming madness. On these occasions, Mother Christopher's distress became more visible, and its effect on us was greater. To die, after all, was inevitable, if scarcely credible, whereas to go insane was somehow to lose everything that made us human, to become controlled rather than controlling, to be imprisoned in a motiveless, perfunctory existence.

"Pray," enjoined Mother Christopher, with a rare approximation of religious fervour, "that God protects you from the nightmare of insanity."

And I knew then, as clearly as I know today, that the engine of her disappointment was fuelled by terror of the odd, the different, the absurd, and that she genuinely believed that by surrendering her independence to the wimple, the habit and the veil she would be effectively immunising herself against the arbitrary havoc wrought by madness. For madness, in Mother Christopher's eyes, was non-conformity run rampant. It was the almost inevitable by-product of desire pursued outside the protective umbrella of obedience.

Perhaps, in the end, that was the reason for her proto-canonisation. In her desperation to preserve what she had come to regard as her sanity she had painstakingly extinguished every last vestige of independence, initiative, inspiration and independence, becoming in the process, albeit as a side effect, almost the perfect nun – a person devoid of personality, a woman bereft of any kind of feminine sensibilities, a human being for whom humanity was a virtual dagger in the heart.

She had also – because, when all is said and done, she was still a creature of flesh and blood, of appetites, sensations and experiences – grown very, very disappointed.

The Politician

In grade five I shared a front row desk with The Politician. That was not his real name, of course. Indeed, had you told me back then that this superficially unremarkable, wafer thin, shy albeit quite amiable boy would go on to fashion a successful career for himself in South Australian politics I would have assumed you were either lying, or had mistaken him for someone else.

If there was a clue to The Politician's future direction in life during our time at school together it probably lay in his gregariousness and general popularity. Never one to take the lead, or suggest himself capable of ingenuity or inventiveness, he consoled by virtue of his acquiescence and amenability.

The Politician's easy going personality was undoubtedly a product of nature not nurture. His father, a large, moustachioed, rather terrifying sergeant major type with a voice that was at once cacophonous and piercing, ruled over The Politician and his younger siblings with a combination of militaristic fervour and, it seemed to me, a complete lack of either affection or kindness. His word was law, and instantaneous, unmitigated obedience was not so much demanded as taken for granted.

His wife, a small, shrew-faced woman with a propensity for wearing far too much make-up, was scarcely less intimidating. On one occasion she arrived at our house wishing to see my mother, whereupon I ran indoors to announce her arrival with the first words to enter my ten year old head, "Mum, The Politician's mother's here to see you!"

Getting punished for misbehaving was an integral part of growing up. Usually it consisted of a brief rebuke, or a sharp slap administered almost as a reflex gesture, and quickly forgotten about. In my experience, however, punishments were not exclusively reserved for misdemeanours. The Politician's mother, on hearing me referring to her as such, upbraided me with a vehemence that would not have been out of place had I been guilty of describing her as a prominent member of the personal harem of Satan himself. My mother seemed as taken aback by this show of vitriol as I was, but of course in those days adults maintained a kind of tacit solidarity when in the presence of children however extenuating the circumstances.

The repercussions did not end there. Over the next three years, whenever I encountered The Politician's mother, I was invariably and routinely reminded of my *faux pas* by being castigated for it yet again. No doubt in the view of The Politician's mother I had sullied her identity by, in effect, subordinating it to that of her son, but if so she selected the perfect form of retaliation by ever afterwards defining me exclusively in terms of what, by any reasonable standards, was a wholly negligible offence.

The Politician himself was much too prepossessing a character ever to have harboured a grudge. If he had a weakness, it was that he was so wholly devoid of artifice and cunning as to lay himself open to all kinds of oppression and abuse. That was in theory. In practice, it never happened because The Politician was almost universally perceived as an all round top bloke, more than compensating for his deficiencies in intelligence and ingenuity with liberal measures of affability and charm.

My relationship with The Politician was a strange one. It was magnified to some extent by the fact that his father and my father, despite boasting wholly disparate characters, enjoyed a seemingly close and harmonious friendship. The harmony was on open display each Sunday morning at Mass, for while The Politician's father played the church organ my dad would sit directly alongside him to provide what he quaintly described as "the leading voice". When Anna was christened it seemed only natural that it was The Politician's parents to whom my dad turned when seeking a godfather and godmother. On a more everyday level, our fathers spent quite a lot of their spare time socialising, with the inevitable consequence that The Politician and I frequently found ourselves thrown together, making ours an almost wholly incidental friendship rather than a friendship of choice. I suppose the fact that we ended up sharing a desk in grade five must have had the effect of bolstering that friendship to some extent, but the bottom line was that we saw the world in very different ways, meaning that underlying all our dealings with one another there existed an inviolable reserve which kept us, figuratively speaking, at arm's length.

The Politician and I seldom encountered one another after we commenced secondary school, for he was in the purportedly happy position of attending a prestigious Catholic high school in the city, whereas I was consigned to the ignominy of the local state secondary. My father would very much have liked to see me emulate The Politician, but the fees were prohibitively steep. On one occasion he endeavoured to persuade Mother Christopher that I was blessed with hidden scholarship potential, but given that Mother Christopher possessed only the flimsiest notion of who I was, it was hardly surprising that he failed entirely. Had he succeeded I would almost certainly have had a less stressful, considerably happier, but arguably less challenging subsequent life.

1967

The Hub Of The Wheel

It may have been coincidence, it may have been divine or else demonic will, it may have been a catalyst, it may have been my imagination. I do not know. Whatever the reason, the arrival at school of the three Hirsch children coincided with a marked change in my outlook on life. No longer were my perceptive faculties exclusively located above my neck. My awareness of the things around me was now transmitted, at least as often, and sometimes indeed with exaggerated vividness and intensity, through my groin.

The proximity of Marlene Hirsch, for instance, had such a pronounced, indeed seismic, effect upon my equilibrium that I was sometimes hard-pressed to remain standing.

The Hirschs arrived in Elizabeth from Millicent, a small town in the south-eastern corner of South Australia, via Germany. They all had scrupulously sculpted, exquisitely balanced features, alabaster skin, fair hair, and merry, lithesome eyes that seemed to promise either romance or adventure – or, in Marlene's case, perhaps both.

Carl, the oldest of the Hirschs, was as tall as an adult, and extremely strongly built – a bit like Martin Starcevich, without the personality disorder. I only ever saw Carl each morning and afternoon on the school bus because he was based, along with the other grade sevens, at the newly built extension to the school in Elizabeth Park, known as St Mary's.

A year younger than Carl, Soren also commenced his time at the school at St Mary's, and so my initial contact with him was limited. However, when I too transferred to St Mary's the following year, Soren and I became the firmest, if in some respects least likely, of friends.

Shorter than his brother, but still quite tall for his age, Soren was exceptionally lean and wiry and, while in grade seven, was the focus of considerable adulation for being, by some measure, the fastest sprinter in the school. He was also an extremely lively and amusing, if occasionally exasperating, companion.

Marlene Hirsch, alas, was never my companion, amusing, exasperating, or otherwise. What she was, though, was the closest thing to feminine perfection I had ever seen. Not that others would necessarily have agreed with me, but then perception of genuine beauty was, I somehow suspected, akin to divinely imbued, prophetic insight, and as such was accessible only to a rare few.

The closest thing to a direct personal encounter I ever experienced with Marlene came one Friday evening after football training when I was in grade six. A group of about a dozen of us decided, for a reason or reasons I shall probably never now recall, to walk home together, dropping people off as we went, and essentially circumnavigating the entire north, north-west and west of the city in the process. That, at any rate, was our declared intention.

Most members of the group were in grades five and six, but there were also a couple of grade sevens, Soren Hirsch and Francesco Viera, to whose incontrovertibly superior wisdom the rest of us, quite naturally, deferred.

In some respects, Soren and Francesco might almost have been a single entity, with Soren very much the controlling influence (though scarcely what could be called the brains of the operation). Where Soren went, Francesco followed. Whatever Soren said, Francesco agreed with, and would often repeat, like a faulty echo, merely changing one or two of the words, or their order, in a somewhat feeble gesture of autonomy. On the rare occasions that Francesco felt sufficiently audacious or inspired to venture an original utterance of his own he would be careful to construct it in such a way as to permit effortlessly speedy modification should Soren's reaction – which Francesco would continually, solicitously monitor – suggest in any way that this might be advisable.

One upshot of this was that Soren had comparatively little experience of, and equally little tolerance for, dissension. Indeed, so used was he to getting his own way that, on the rare occasions that others elected not to defer to him, his reaction could be waywardly, even violently irrational. You sometimes got the impression that Soren was much less interested in truth than he was in eliciting approbation. If you disagreed with him, he took it as a personal affront, and his sense of personal betrayal was such that not even undeniable, categorical proof that he was wrong would sway him.

This, at least, is just about the only feasible explanation I can proffer for the bizarre sequence of events that Soren proceeded to orchestrate that Friday night. "I know a quick way home," he told us, as we exited St Thomas More's by the main gate. With that, he turned left, and headed due east, towards the Adelaide Hills – precisely the opposite direction from that in which most of our homes lay.

"Yes," said Francesco, eager, as ever, to convey the impression that this was a plan to which he had contributed, "this is a really good short cut."

Whether intrigued, amused, or simply acquiescent, we all dutifully followed. Perhaps, we may have thought, among the unimaginable complexities to which life under Mother Christopher's grade seven tutelage exposed you, was a technique for contravening certain supposedly inviolable physical laws.

Superficially alluring though this thought was, I was sufficiently mature at eleven to realise that truth, however multi-layered, did not include compartments labelled 'paranormal' or 'sublime'. More likely, I imagined, Soren simply had some kind of ruse, or practical joke, in mind.

And so we trundled on, ignoring the fact that the hitherto distant hills, which lay in the opposite direction from home, were gradually getting closer. However, when the road along which we were walking began to slope upwards, Barry Ryan's trust for one was ruptured. "This ain't the way home," he announced, his tone of voice perhaps a touch less conciliatory than he intended.

Soren said, "It's just a different way, Bazza," which Francesco reinforced with "Yeah, Bazza, it's a short cut."

But Barry Ryan had come to a stop, his normally quite defiant chin having now become positively rebellious. "Home's back that way," he insisted, pointing behind him, and endeavouring to elicit, with a plaintive stare, the support of others in the group. "Well, ain't it?"

No one answered, although Gary Fowler looked across a little uncertainly at his older brother, Graham.

Technically, of course, Bazza undoubtedly had a point, and I am sure that each and every one of us knew it. However, at some other level we were aware that if we were to allow ourselves to be guided and constrained by technicalities we would end up living pretty charmless, denuded lives. And so, as though inextricably enmeshed in a collective cobweb of anticipation, we avoided Bazza's eyes, and guilelessly succumbed to the only kind of life experience that can, when all is said and done, redeem.

"See, Bazza, nothing to worry about," said Soren, with slightly excessive fervour.

"No worries, Bazza," added Francesco, with a grim smirk that may have been his version of a reassuring smile.

When we finally reached the boundaries of civilisation Soren cheerily informed us, without missing a beat, that now it was time to turn left.

So we did.

"Who's gunner win tomorrow, Bazza?" I asked, referring to the big interstate football match in Adelaide that several of us were planning to attend. In truth, I was not remotely interested in Bazza's answer, but I imagined that by diverting his attention from the objective reality of our plight I might, in some way, reinforce the solidarity of the group.

"The Vics, of course," he replied. "Without Big Bill we'll get crucified in the rucks. Their rovers are better too. And Royce Hart'll probably kick seven or eight on Elleway." He stuck his chin out, as he almost always did, to reinforce, or else to challenge.

This last was too much, however. "No way!" I demurred, caught up in the topic despite myself. "Ron'll be 'way too tough for that weedy Tasmanian poofter!" I was consciously eschewing eloquence in order to forge a more elemental connection, sensing perhaps that Bazza needed to find an alternative outlet for his simmering rage.

"Nah," he retorted. "Elleway only looks good for Port cos all the full forwards in the league are useless."

"Eric Freeman's a good full forward."

"Yeah, but he plays for Port, and 'sides, you're just biased."

"What about Sashy then?"

Bazza nearly choked on phlegm. "That great lump of lard!"

But we had reached another pivotal point in our pilgrimage, as Soren breezily announced, "Left here, fellas."

"Now you'll see," said Francesco, who may even have believed it. However, if he had hoped that his words might provoke an inquisitive craning of necks, he was to be disappointed.

At long last, however, we appeared to be walking downhill.

Bazza and I continued to talk about the footy, with the Fowler brothers, who were also intending to go to the match, occasionally joining in as well.

The sun had set by the time we reached Elizabeth North Shopping Centre, which lies a mere half a kilometre or so from St Thomas More's.

However, by resorting to Soren's short-cut it had taken us somewhere in excess of an hour and a half to get there.

"This is me," said Bazza, who lived just a couple of streets away from the shopping complex. He was terse-lipped and pale, and studiously avoided eye contact with everyone as he hurriedly effected what no doubt felt like an escape.

Stephen Owen, John Conolly and a couple of others were quick to follow, although their homes lay at least a couple of kilometres away to the south. I engaged in what I hoped was a surreptitious but meaningful exchange of glances with The Politician and the Fowler brothers, my nearest neighbours in Elizabeth West, but any precipitate action on our part was speedily circumvented by Soren, who said, "Not far to go now, fellas. This way."

"Nearly home," embellished Francesco, whose complete and unequivocal faith in Soren was clearly such as to be independent of experience or circumstance.

And so our pilgrimage resumed, adhering, so far as I could tell, to no predetermined plan or structure, but nevertheless being embraced by Soren – and, to some extent by Francesco – as a kind of evocation of divine will.

With me, the Fowler brothers, and The Politician as the soon-to-be-incinerated sacrificial offerings.

We reached the railway crossing at Broadmeadows, which was about a kilometre away from where Soren and Francesco lived in Elizabeth Field. The rest of us, though, still had four or five kilometres to go.

With uncharacteristic boldness Francesco, who perhaps gleaned a certain inspiration from having at last reached familiar territory, informed us that we were almost home.

"You might be," returned The Politician testily. "We're still as far away from home as ever."

But Soren, who presumably considered words superfluous in the face of such indefatigable logic, merely laughed, and Francesco, after evincing a momentary suggestion of discomfiture, joined in.

I, by this time, had immersed myself completely in what I had increasingly begun to perceive, if still somewhat imprecisely, as a kind of rite of passage. I may even have been grinning.

Soren's house proved to be almost identical to mine, at least superficially: west facing, red bricked, the trademark tin roof, and a front porch and veranda tacked on to the south wall like a wholly incongruous last minute afterthought.

As befitted tradition, we trooped around to the back of the house, whereupon Soren clambered onto the porch and rapped sharply on the fly door to attract attention. Moments later his mother appeared, looking a trifle quizzical, but boasting a kindly, winsome smile that put me in mind, paradoxically, of Sister Damien.

My eyes did not linger long on Mrs. Hirsch, however, for peering around from behind her, still dressed in her school uniform, was Marlene, who was gazing unmistakably, or so I felt, in my direction.

As Soren, somewhat ramblingly, and with minimal attention to the facts, attempted to provide his mother with an explanation of his lateness,

I allowed myself to stand transfixed, slowly becoming enmeshed in a connection that I was scarcely able to believe was being forged. A second or two spent staring into Marlene's eyes was tantamount to a sliver of eternity, and seemed to yield a wordless explanation of all that was necessary. Perhaps I realised even then that this is as close as we would ever come to being lovers in any conventional, fleshly sense, but the moment contained enough of an intimation of transcendence to sustain me for a life time.

To touch was not to love, I saw. To touch was an act of desperation, a refusal to accept, and she and I would never, ever touch.

Mrs. Hirsch was addressing me now, her tone of voice at once implying solicitude, and complete obliviousness as to what, in every sense, had just transpired. Feeling everything with almost too great an intensity to bear, I reassured her blithely, drawing flashes of approval from my beloved, so that ever after, without the sullying need for any kind of intercourse, our destinies, indeed our very cores, would be wholly, haplessly, inexorably intertwined.

For I was Johann Ulrich Voss, and she was Laura Trevelyan. I was John Evelyn, confused, duplicitous, misled, alongside the vestal incorruptibility of his Margaret Godolphin. We would die apart, unmourned and possibly unremembered by one another, but somehow still entrenched in that moment.

The rain had started by then, of course ("heavy ground – suit the Vics"), but I even succeeded in turning that to my advantage, with a parting shot that was the equivalent of a vow of eternal fidelity. And so, embedded more deeply than ever in the reality that fate had seemingly proffered, I wandered home, reluctant even to speak, aware that henceforth only through silence and solitude would the true shape and contours of our marriage be affirmed.

By happy chance, I went to the following day's football match alone, as all of my friends had been 'grounded' (The Politician for a full month!) for their collusion in Soren's and Francesco's Grand Tour. Freed from distractions, I was able to concentrate exclusively on the on-field action, and as it went on the match developed, for me, into a kind of religious rite. The fact that I escaped the same censure as my fellow miscreants is almost impossible to credit unless you believe that our destinies are shaped either by fate, or by some divine or demonic will.

Which only goes to prove that the truth is not always as obvious or logically inferable as we would like to imagine.

The Chamber Of Horrors

The highlight of the school trip to Murray Bridge was a cruise aboard a paddle steamer. During this journey, half a dozen or so of us, drawn together by coincidence rather than design, congregated in the stern.

“This is idyllic,” said Angela Tewksbury, who liked to use words she imagined the rest of us had never heard of. “If I half close my eyes, I could imagine I was on the ship going back to Ingerland.”

Angela also had a tendency to be profligate with her syllables, something which had become even more noticeable since Mother Christopher had confessed herself enraptured by the sound of the Queen’s English being regally enunciated.

Before I really knew what I was doing, and without knowing why, I said, “If we were, I’d drill a hole in the deck so that we sank!”

Everybody turned to look at me, Angela along the bridge of a nose that seemed to be reacting with distress to something malodorous. The other girls in our group manifested similar disdain as they elected, *en masse*, to withdraw to somewhere more congenial.

Because I was a boy, and boys were tough, I snorted derisively at their retreating backs, but inwardly I was perplexed and more than a trifle embarrassed. Why had I made such a ludicrous assertion? The two boys who had stayed behind with me, Hans and The Politician, both displayed solidarity by laughing.

“Girls just don’t have a sense of humour,” observed Hans, whose opinion on the subject had to be respected because he was the acknowledged class expert on members of the fairer sex. Once, it was rumoured, he had even kissed one, and not just on the cheek either.

Hans’s own sense of humour, indeed his view of life as a whole, was notoriously macabre. When his sister Gabrielle had been killed in a car accident he had, almost with relish it seemed, described how her body had been "turned to mush" by the impact of the crash. During our walks home from school together he took delight in concocting a series of increasingly gruesome tales for my edification. The central figure in most of these stories was the outwardly respectable, even amiable, Mr. Butcher, a tailor whose basement was filled with implements of torture, which he utilised with great zest and imagination on hapless visitors to his shop. His means of ensnaring his victims was cunningly simple: each of his changing cubicles had a trap door which Mr. Butcher, stationed in the basement, could open with a lever. The victim would then plummet down to be confronted by a smiling Mr. Butcher, armed with a loaded revolver. Hans's descriptions of each of the implements, and the uses to which they were put, were at once meticulous and almost loving. You got the impression that he would genuinely have enjoyed watching them being used.

During the summer holidays Hans and I constructed what we described as a 'Chamber of Horrors' in the ramshackle tin shed my dad had constructed, if that is quite the word, in our back garden. Once we had finished our modifications and refinements, we made it available, at two cents a head, to all the young girls of the neighbourhood, whose collective response was surprisingly wholehearted and keen - or perhaps not so surprisingly, given that their two cents bought them a few choice seconds of close proximity to Hans, the undisputed local resident dandy.

Once a girl entered the chamber the door would be closed behind her, leaving her in total darkness. Hans and I would then proceed to make truly laughable assortment of eerie noises, which nonetheless often proved quite successful in eliciting a yelp or even a small scream, of fear. There then followed thirty seconds or so of complete silence, which Hans guilelessly referred to as "the softening up session". All this time I had been standing slightly behind and to the right of the victim, whom I would then imprison in my arms, placing my right hand over her mouth to stifle any histrionics. This was Hans's cue for his *piece de resistance*, which involved his shining a torch on his own face, which had been smeared with jam to make it look bloody, and which was contorted into an expression of extreme agony coupled with terror. I would then relinquish my hold on the girl, whose 'ordeal' would be concluded with a prolonged sequence of groaning and wailing from both Hans and me, together with a relentless banging and hammering on the tin walls of the shed. Astonishingly enough, a fair proportion of our victims emerged from the experience agreeably shaken, although I have little doubt that virtually all of them would have preferred to have had Hans, not me, groping them from behind.

Not Waving But Hanging

I was swathed in sunlight, arms outstretched as though attached to an invisible cross, legs rotating haplessly, or perhaps determinedly. It was as though I could feel myself disappearing.

The swimming instructor, whose separate identity I had never properly allowed myself to imagine, was counting towards infinity: “Twenty-one, twenty-two, twenty-three, twenty-four.......”

As though such things were meaningful.

But as for me, swathed as I was in sunlight, simultaneously protected and imprisoned by a membrane wrought from my very essence, floating aimlessly and haplessly and hopefully.......

As for me.

Denouement loomed, cascading from the unbelievable swimming instructor’s lips, a vibrant trout evading frantic bears’ paws.

As “Thirty-seven, thirty-eight, thirty-nine” - an echo from another world, amazing and unseemly, my somehow not quite plausible limbs refusing to conform.

Until it came to me: the countdown was a prelude to a kind of birth, or rescue. Veneers, I saw, can almost always be destroyed.

But the spurious allure of treading water, swathed in sunlight, arms invisibly affixed, vision stymied - all of this was preferable, somehow, to the stark indignity of exposure.

Perhaps believing that our inability to swim derived from fear of water, she had got us to submerge ourselves, and then, aloof, uncaring, her reassuring stopwatch tightly squeezed, had presumed to calculate the actual extent of that fear.

"Forty-seven, forty-eight, forty-nine......."

But I was not afraid, for I had undergone all of this before, innumerable times, and I knew that the ultimate upshot would be that I would break the surface of the water gasping loudly, ostensibly triumphant, but still incapable of swimming a single stroke.

Toad Comes To Tea

Recently I invited my then friend Toad to tea. We had just moved to the neighbourhood and Toad was the only friend I had, so mum had persuaded me to ask him to tea and maybe later to spend the night. As we had only just moved into the neighbourhood we did not know about Toad's boastful personality.

At about six o'clock a huge Rolls Royce came screaming round the corner and came to a halt outside our house. Moments later a splendid Toad dressed in a glorious dinner suit stepped out of the car and began striding up the garden path. We ran to the door to welcome Toad who came in snorting about us not having a doorbell because such a dignified person as he should not have to humble himself by knocking.

Much later (at two forty in the morning to be exact) Toad still boasting about his brave deeds in world war two was eventually forced to leave by my angry father. My family was very dissappointed in Toad's behaviour and I was very sad to lose such a seemingly fine friend but I was soon consoled as I found many new friends.

The Black And White Of It

For the 1967 school concert, the grade six boys, of whom I was one, played the part of Al' Jolson style minstrels, complete with regulation black and red grease-painted faces. The fact that this was well before anyone had dreamed of such concepts as political correctness was amply demonstrated in my hearing by Mother Christopher who, when asked by a parent what the grade six boys were going to be in the forthcoming Christmas concert, proffered the admirably succinct, and readily acknowledged and accepted, reply, "Nig-nogs."

Priests And Nuns

Nuns and priests differed greatly from each other, and not merely in ways that were obvious, such as gender. Probably the most important distinction between them was in terms of their religious views, with nuns worshipping an Old Testament God whose central dictum was "an eye for an eye and a tooth for a tooth", whereas priests advocated a version of Pauline Christianity in which they, the priests, occupied the central role as living manifestations of the diminutive, self important, jumped up little egotist himself. Priests were much easier than nuns to deal with because all you had to do was pander to their foibles, which were easily identifiable. Nuns, however, tended to have so many different foibles jostling for precedence that you could as soon pander successfully to them as hit the jackpot at roulette. (Actually, it was more like Russian roulette, albeit that your shots were aimed at your foot rather than your head.)

The only nun I ever knew who broke the mould was my grade six teacher, Sister Mary Pia (known to us boys, with crass inevitability, by a name I shall not insult your intelligence by repeating). There were times when you could almost believe she cared about you. What other nun would squat down beside you as you were sitting on the ground lacing up your football boots and actually talk to you intelligently about footy?

"Who do you go for then, Albert?"

"In the footy? Port, sister."

"Oh, yuk! Sturt's much better."

"Nah, Port'll win this year."

"What's your favourite position?"

"I dunno, sister. Centre probably."

"Reckon Johnny Cahill's a good centreman?"

"The best!"

"What about Bob Shearman?"

"Mmm, yeah," I allowed graciously. "He's pretty good too."

Compared to the sufferings I had to endure under Sister Mary Vincent's regime, life under Sister Mary Pia was almost idyllic. You had to be exceptionally naughty indeed to induce her to use the ruler on you, and even then it was usually just a half-hearted slap rather than Mother Christopher's full on tennis serve or one of Sister Mary Vincent's sharp, vitriolic stingers.

The fact that my dad was working away in Tasmania for much of 1967 combined with the pronouncedly more relaxed atmosphere at school to make it one of the two most memorably enjoyable years of my life.

Ensnared

Three of us - Soren Hirsch, Francesco Viera and me – were standing downstairs on the crowded, homeward-bound school bus when, out of the blue, Soren asked me, "Which girl in your class do you fancy then, Al'?"

I spluttered my distaste. "Girls!" I exclaimed. "Yuk!"

"I bet there's one you secretly like, and I betcher I can guess who it is," ventured Soren.

"Nah!" I said, a bit nervously.

"Now let's see. Is it Katie Bowyer?"

"Oh, don't be ridiculous."

"Is that a yes or a no?"

I gave vent to a prolonged sigh of surrender. "No," I said.

"Mary Winterbottom?"

"What?"

"Do you like Mary Winterbottom?"

"No!"

"Jessica Silverton?"

"Na-ah." (Not this year anyway.)

"Jane Irons?"

I snorted loudly. "Oh yeah, sure!" I proclaimed sarcastically.

Soren looked thoughtful for a moment, then went on. "Victoria Cameleri?"

"Jesus, no!"

"Judy Watson?"

"No already!"

"What about my sister?"

My heart gave a sudden, tumultuous lurch. "No way!" I exclaimed, much too quickly and stridently. I was sure I could feel my face flushing.

"Ahah! So it *is* Marlene, then? I knew it!" He was grinning evilly.

"I said no way!" But the note of panic in my voice told a different story.

"Hey, Francesco! Do you want to tell her, or shall I?"

Being put on the spot like this was not something Francesco enjoyed.

He gave a short laugh, and looked at Soren, then at me, then back at Soren. "Er ….." he said, helpfully.

"Hey, I know," taunted Soren, "I'll go upstairs and tell her now." And he made as if to push his way past me towards the stairwell at the rear of the bus.

"No!" I almost shrieked, causing several heads to turn in my direction. I was really panicking now for it seemed I was hopelessly trapped.

Soren paused, looking equivocal. "Tell yer what," he said, finally, "admit to me that you like her, and you have my word that I'll never, *ever* tell her."

O Christ, what to do? Seconds ticked by and then Soren made as if to move past me once more. "Okay, okay," I said desperately, "I admit it."

Soren stopped, and smiled with apparent compassion. "There now, that wasn't too hard, was it?"

Then he turned to Francesco and said, "I won't need to tell her anyway, will I?"

Once again, Francesco looked uneasy. "Uh?" he muttered, trailing, as usual, about half a million miles behind the conversation.

Soren saw that he would have to spell it out. "I won't need to tell her," he explained, "because when we get off the bus, you'll do it for me, woncha?"

And I felt the floor of the bus ripple and shudder beneath my feet. I had been well and truly ensnared, and all I could do was hope and pray that Soren was teasing me, and would not make good his threat. Knowing

Soren's nature, however, and in particular his penchant for tricks and japes, it was, I realised, at best a rather tenuous hope.

1968

An Afternoon Of Fun And Games

After living next door but one to us for close to five years Robert and Martin and their parents moved a couple of miles away, to a newly built house in Elizabeth Field. Despite the handicaps of distance, however, Robert's and my friendship continued to flourish. We saw each other on most weekends, while during school holidays we spent as much time together as we possibly could.

My relationship with Martin, however, effectively disintegrated the day the Wilson family moved house. Despite being only a year older than me, Martin was, or liked to think he was, immensely mature for his age. He proved this by reading, or affecting to read, substantial tomes dealing with subjects like political theory, sociology and the lives of influential statesmen and thinkers. He called himself a Marxist, forswore all animal foodstuffs, and developed a somewhat idiosyncratic passion for rugby. For his thirteenth birthday this egalitarian, peace loving vegetarian asked his parents for, and was duly given, an air rifle.

One of the best things about Robert's and Martin's new abode was that it was situated directly opposite a large, sumptuously grassed football oval, and this was where Robert and I spent much of our time together. Sometimes we were joined by other boys, and we would stage impromptu matches, four or five a side, using the entire oval. Hans, who had moved to the nearby Smithfield Migrant Hostel where his father had been appointed warden, sometimes umpired these affairs. He would undoubtedly have preferred to have joined in as a player, but was strictly prohibited from getting his shoes dirty.

When it was just Robert and me we would often play out imaginary games, commentating loudly as we did so. On other occasions we would engage in goal kicking competitions, which Robert, despite being smaller, lighter, and a year younger than me, nearly always seemed to win. It was while we were engaged in one such competition that Martin, presumably bored of taking pot shots at old tin cans, decided it would be more enjoyable and challenging to put himself and his new possession to the test by firing it at living, moving targets. Us.

At first, I could not quite believe what was happening. There was a sudden sharp whizzing noise as something bounced or skidded on the grass a few yards from where I was standing. Then, a little further off, there was a loud ringing noise as something struck one of the goal posts with considerable force. "Come on," said Robert, "he's shooting at us," and he snatched up the ball and started running across the oval in the direction of the changing shed.

I was still feeling bemused, but then I caught sight of a familiar figure standing about thirty or forty yards away behind the goals, partly obscured by a bush. It was Martin, and he was taking aim with his air rifle. I hared after Robert just as a pellet landed almost exactly where I had just been standing. I quickly overtook my friend and reached the changing shed a few seconds before him. I then looked back to see Martin languidly sauntering across the oval in our direction, presumably believing that we were effectively trapped. The changing shed provided a modicum of cover for the moment, but once Martin arrived the game would be up. "Is he serious?" I asked Robert breathlessly. In answer, he rolled down his football sock, in the process providing ample visible evidence of just how serious Martin was. "He's not trying to kill us," Robert said, which I suppose was mildly reassuring. "He just aims low, trying to get you in the leg."

"But that's crazy!" I exclaimed. "Why don't you just tell your dad?"

Before Robert could answer, we heard the crack of Martin's rifle and dust flew on the ground a couple of metres away. In desperation we ran around to the changing shed door. It was locked. "We'll just have to make a run for it," I suggested. Robert nodded, then did something wholly inexplicable, and kicked his football high over the shed in Martin's direction. Perhaps he intended to distract his brother, or felt that carrying the ball was slowing him down. A sharp crack followed by a light thud told us that Martin had found this unexpected new target irresistible.

We sprinted away across the soccer field that was situated alongside the football oval, heading in the direction of the small children's playground that lay on the far side of the playing field complex. We heard a couple of shots ring out as we ran but neither of us was hit. When we reached the playground we stopped to catch our breath and consider our options. Martin was still ambling in our wake, about three hundred yards away. "It's a good thing he's such a lazy cunt," said Robert. "We stand a chance if we manage to keep our distance."

"What if he starts running?"

"Martin? Run? He hasn't run in years - other than when his dinner's being served anyway."

"But how can you let him get away with it? Your dad'd kill him, surely?"

Robert sighed, and shook his head. "I have to live with the bastard," he observed, obviously believing that this constituted an adequate explanation. "Anyway, he's getting a bit too close for comfort now. Let's scarper."

All of this was but a prelude to one of the longest afternoons in my young life. For more than two hours the cat and mouse chase continued, with, I was convinced, only Martin's indolence enabling us to escape unscathed. The ordeal finally ended when Robert's and Martin's parents returned home from wherever they had been. "Have a nice time together boys?" asked Mrs. Wilson, clearly assuming we were all still the best of pals. "Great!" said Martin, smiling almost beatifically. "Eventful," muttered Robert, avoiding everybody's eyes except mine.

Girls And Boys

Of the twenty or so boys in her grade seven class Mother Christopher was only aware of the names of a handful. Anthony Lindner and Darryl Callaghan were known to her because of the regularity with which she felt compelled to mortify their flesh in public, but in sharp contrast there existed a couple of boys who actually elicited something akin to admiration. The pair in question were Hans Rensenbrink and Barry Ryan, but the sources of their appeal to Mother Christopher were very different.

In Hans's case it was all to do with sex. Combining blond hair, startlingly good looks, an impeccable dress sense and an almost regal demeanour it was a very rare female indeed who was immune to his allure. And Mother Christopher, however grotesquely atypical of her sex she might had become, was nevertheless undeniably female.

Barry Ryan was a vastly different proposition to Hans. Captain of the school football and cricket teams, laconic, rough around the edges and as affable as a labrador, as far as Mother Christopher was concerned he ticked all the right boxes on the proforma headed 'Ocker Aussie'. For although she was sufficiently old fashioned in outlook to retain more than a vestige of respect for the Royal family, and to harbour an oft-enunciated affection for the old dart and its customs, she was at bottom fiercely Australian, and liked her boys in particular to embody those characteristics which, somewhat romantically, she elected to believe had shaped the nation.

On the whole, however, boys were of only negligible interest to Mother Christopher, who spent most of her time immersed in hushed conversation with a small coterie of girls who collectively inhabited a square of four first and second row desks. These were Mother Christopher's pride and joy, her scholarship girls, on whom she saw nothing wrong in concentrating almost all of her pedagogic endeavours. All eight of the girls were eminently qualified to sit the Catholic high school's scholarship examination, for all boasted skin as fair as freshly fallen snow, and eyes like lapis lazuli. It was not that Mother Christopher entertained racist notions, it was simply that her eyesight was poor. Thus when Hans's sister Gabrielle died, Mother Christopher stood before the class, body shaking with barely suppressed tears, and announced that both recesses were cancelled for that day as it would be inappropriate for us to enjoy ourselves in the wake of such a tragedy. It was the same when Marlene Hirsch, she of the milk white skin and golden hair, suddenly lost her father. However, when pretty, petite Victoria Cameleri was similarly bereaved nobody in Mother Christopher's class would even have known about it had they not been present at Sunday Mass when it was announced from the pulpit. Poor Victoria, you see, was Maltese, and her jet black hair and flawless but sallow complexion rendered her effectively invisible as far as Mother Christopher was concerned.

Life for the invisible majority of Mother Christopher's pupils was, in the main, rather carefree and relaxed, if a trifle mundane. Lessons tended to consist of long periods of idleness interspersed with occasional exclamations from Mother Christopher to the effect that she had "found a simply marvellous sum" and we must all "down tools and have a go at it right away". The injunctions to down tools and attempt the sum were, for most of us, equally redundant in that we had not in fact been doing anything, while in order to solve the sum we would have needed to be familiar with concepts which Mother Christopher had only ever seen fit to divulge to her 'chosen few'.

School fees at St Mary's were in the region of $300 per term. That, at any rate, is what my dad paid. Presumably, if parents wished their child not merely to attend, but actually to receive an education, those fees would have been substantially higher.

Television Commercials

A Commercial I Like

A television commercial which I enjoy viewing is one which advertises Jet's dog food. This commercial appears frequently on channels 10, 7 and 9. I like the commercial because it shows unnatural skill in a dog. As the commercial begins, two children are playing near the garden path on which is lying a skateboard. Suddenly a dog appears on the scene, jumps onto the skateboard and skilfully ~~man manueveres~~ rides it into the kitchen. Here its mistress has fixed some 'Jets dog food' he moves over to it and the commercial ends.

A Commercial I Dislike

The commercial I dislike most is an advirtisement for Canberra television sets. This advertisement appears only on channel 9 on a Sunday. Noel Teasdale captain coach of Woodville Football Club appears in this commercial looking as if the world was coming to an end and proceeds to tell why Canberra Television sets are the greatest. With advertisements like this I don't think Canberra television will sell many television sets.

An Old Adversary

As I stepped off the school bus I nearly collided with a boy wearing the predominantly green uniform of Elizabeth Technical High School. Then I noticed who it was – Martin Barrett, who I had not seen for almost a year.

My reaction was quick, and I do not know who was more surprised by it, my old adversary or me, because a split second after recognition had dawned I had grabbed him by the neck of his jumper and thrust him hard against a nearby telegraph pole. "What a lovely surprise – I don't think!" I said. It was Billy Sutton all over again, only this time my victim was older and bigger than I was (albeit also rather flabbier). With my right hand firmly holding onto his jumper I wrapped the fingers of my other hand around his throat and squeezed. Martin's face turned even redder than normal, and he whimpered pathetically, sounding more like a newly-hatched chick than a full grown rooster.

Then we both had our second surprise, for I suddenly saw that the person who was behaving truly pathetically was me not Martin, and I relinquished my grip. “See you ‘round, Marty,” I said, patting him almost fondly on the left cheek - the one I had almost broken once during a football match - and watched, feeling simultaneously angry and deflated, as he scurried off. All of the times that he had taunted, tantalised and teased me went with him.

A Family At War

In my recollection, it almost seemed to be happening in slow motion. Calmly, deliberately, my mum would pick up a cup, saucer or plate, and then hurl it hard at the wall behind my dad, who was sitting, arms folded, unflinching, wearing the almost benign smile he tended to adopt whenever he believed that he was suffering for Jesus. In later years my mum would inform me that, during the first three years or so of her and my dad’s marriage, she smashed at least four complete sets of crockery in this way. Why? Not because she hated my dad - that would be a much later development - but rather because of a fundamental philosophical difference between them, which throughout their three decades of marriage never came close to being resolved. In essence, whereas my mum was a self-declared hedonist, my dad viewed all pleasure with suspicion, as having the potential to engender, even encourage, sin. The upshot of this was that they disagreed about virtually everything. Indeed, just about the only matter on which they saw eye to eye was the (in their case not so holy) state of marriage, which sadly for both of them they regarded as a life sentence, irrespective of the hardships faced or level of discord between them. As far as they were both concerned "Til death us do part" meant precisely that, whereas if ever a couple afforded a stark example of the desirability of divorce, it was my parents.

The dichotomy between them was most sharply realised in their attitudes to money, and in particular the Langley family finances. As far as my mum was concerned, these were simply a resource to be utilised, while my dad's attitude to them was both very different from my mum's and, not to put too fine a point on things, rather weird. Essentially. if not quite consciously, he believed that the family's economic resources were extensions of himself, and as such should be subject to the same levels of maintenance and care as his own physical body. Whenever he was required to pay for something - anything at all, regardless of the cost - he made it manifestly clear that he was only doing so with the utmost reluctance, almost as it were under protest. It was exactly as though he were paying not with money, but with freshly gouged out chunks of his own flesh.

It was the same with our pocket money, which he would deliver to us with an expression of such torment on his face that, on occasion, it was all I could do not to hand it straight back.

When, on 14th February 1966, Australia 'went decimal' my dad's immediate - and doubtless gleeful - response was to halve both

Theresa's and my allowances. Up until that point we had, each week, received amounts in pence equivalent to our ages - I, for example, got nine pence. Henceforth, however, I would have to be satisfied with a weekly allowance of just nine *cents* - one cent being, as every Australian schoolboy and schoolgirl of the time knew well, worth precisely half of one penny. Theresa and I were, to say the least, indignant at what we regarded as a palpable injustice, but there was nothing we could do. Both of us were well aware by this time that our dad's notion of justice had little if anything to do with fair play, reasonableness or equitability. Rather, it was a matter of what he felt he could get away with. As a boy growing up in Liverpool his mum had given him a penny's pocket money every week for each year of his age, and if that had been good enough for him then, irrespective of inflation, food rationing, war, tempest, fire, flood and decimal currency, it ought to be good enough for us, too.

In 1967 Dad was made redundant by Holden's and was unable to find another job offering a similar rate of pay locally. He therefore decided to look interstate, and ended up working at a mining camp near Queenstown in Tasmania. I can still vividly recall how genuinely upset we all seemed whilst seeing him off at Womma Station, but it was not long before we began to appreciate just how much better all our lives were going to be without him.

To live in the same house as both my parents was to be exposed to an almost constant stream of bickering. Although my mum no longer resorted to crockery smashing in order to make her points she and my dad seemed capable of finding reasons to disagree about even the most innocuous of subjects. However, once they got started on one of their genuine 'pet themes' - money, my mum's smoking, my dad's slovenliness - you knew they were set fair for the rest of the day and the only way you would get any peace was by leaving the house. (Anna's predilection for the Great Outside was almost certainly derived, at least in part, from her feelings of distress at my parents' continual squabbling, and her perfectly understandable desire to place herself out of earshot.)

With my dad gone, the general atmosphere at home improved immeasurably. Arguments and disagreements still occurred, but they were much less frequent, and tended to be conducted at a vastly lower decibel level.

The improved social picture - in itself reason enough to relish my dad's absence - coincided with a dramatic economic upturn. Both Theresa and I had our weekly allowances increased from eight and ten cents respectively to two whole dollars, which was more money than either of us had hitherto ever owned. Shortly after my dad left it was my birthday, and for the first and only time in my life I was allowed to have a party. Among my presents were not just the proper leather football I had been craving for more than two years, but a complete football kit as well.

I can still clearly remember the day, early in 1968, when my dad returned home from Tasmania. Within perhaps five minutes of his arrival he and Mum were arguing at the top of their voices. I cannot recall the precise cause of their disagreement, but I am fairly sure it had to do with money. Theresa and I glanced at one another as if to say "here we go again." This was how it always ended up, and always would. There is and can be no escape.

Palmer's Tree Explained

"It's called Palmer's Tree," explained Hans, who typically had trouble with unfamiliar words of more than two syllables.

Linus and I looked suitably perplexed.

"Here, I'll show you," said Hans, and he held his hands out in front of him, palms down with fingers outstretched. "See how thick and muscular the fingers are? That's because these are what are called working man's hands. Now let's look at yours."

As there seemed to be no good reason not to humour him, we complied.

"Ah, now, this is interesting," said Hans excitedly. "You two's hands are actually very similar. See how skinny they are and how you've both got long, thin, weedy fingers? They're what's known as girls' hands."

"Girls' hands!" exclaimed Linus, whose fuse was shorter than most. "Wadderyer mean I've got girl's hands? In my experience, girls' hands tend to belong to girls."

"Not according to Palmer's Tree," explained Hans. "According to Palmer's Tree girls can have have all different kinds of hands and so can boys. Jane Irons has got working man's hands like me," he affirmed, as if that proved his point.

"What cereal packet did you learn this from?" I enquired sardonically.

"It wasn't a cereal packet - it was a book. A real book. From the library."

"Christ, Hans," I remarked, "I didn't know you could read."

"He means a picture book, don't you, Hans?" asked Linus.

"Ha bloody ha," said Hans. "You're just upset 'cos I said you've got girls' hands."

"Hans, in order to get upset, we'd need to take you seriously," countered Linus, " and in order for us to take you seriously, you'd need to grow several million new brain cells."

"If it's any consolation," said Hans, ignoring or perhaps not quite understanding Linus's jibe, "some of the most famous men in history have had girls' hands. Isaac Einstein, Adolf Hitler, President Kennedy - even Jesus."

There was nothing either Linus or I felt able to say to that. However, we did not wish to let Hans believe he had conquered us with his idiocy, and so we simultaneously undertook to use our girls' hands in a way that brooked no argument.

The Boy Who Saw

Far and away the most conspicuously unusual boy in my class was Dafydd Gynne, who was partially deaf in one ear, and walked with something of a limp on account of one of his legs being four centimetres shorter than the other. Dafydd bore these afflictions stoically, even cheerfully, maintaining that "We are all deformed in some way." His most visible deformity, if such it could be called, was his head, which appeared much too big and bulky for his slender, almost sinuous, body, and which harboured an intelligence that, while a trifle ponderous, was amazingly acute. Not that you would know this from his school reports, for it was not an intelligence that could properly be measured in any conventional sense. Rather, Dafydd boasted what was effectively a kind of x-ray vision, enabling him to view the world in a uniquely penetrative way. When Wilbur De Groot departed St Thomas More's in 1966 it was Dafydd who replaced him in my esteem, if not quite my affections. On a purely intellectual level, he intrigued and captivated me, but there was too much coolness and introspection in his character to elicit anything more than the most platonic kind of admiration.

Originally from Swansea in Wales, Dafydd was an orphan who lived with his grandmother in Elizabeth Field. The fact that he had suffered much in life was relatively easy to infer, but Dafydd was not prone to embellishing this impression with details. During his time at St Thomas More's and St Mary's the Sisters of Mercy missed few opportunities to augment Dafydd's misery. This was particularly so in grade seven, under

Mother Christopher, who on more than one occasion inflicted a ferocious caning on Dafydd simply because she didn't like the way in which he was looking at her.

By grade seven, Dafydd and I were ostensibly inseparable, although never really what you would call close. Nevertheless, familiarity gave rise to a certain degree of solidarity, even loyalty. On a couple of occasions I intervened to prevent Dafydd from being bullied, and he repaid me with a silent, ardent faithfulness that at times seemed almost aggressively credulous. It was as though the act of maintaining his subservient relationship with me represented a central core in his belief system, informing both his level of motivation and his self-image. I am fairly sure that Dafydd was never happier than when sitting or lying alongside me in our favourite corner of the school playground. Given the way in which our relationship would ultimately end, this was perhaps both understandable and appropriate.

Surprisingly, given Dafydd's intelligence and my scepticism, much of our time together was spent discussing what can only be described as matters of the soul - the soul in which neither of us, in actual fact, believed. (Dafydd took his agnosticism much farther than I did in that he never, to the best of my knowledge, attended Sunday Mass.) "Life without pain is meaningless," Dafydd was wont to quote, and he might well have derived real solace from the thought. "Death is really nothing but the absence of pain," he would add, daring me to heresy with his stark, cold eyes.

Depending on my mood, I would either contemptuously dismiss the challenge, or rise to it like a fish confounded by an angler's lure. "Death is more than just the absence of pain," I might say. "It's the absence of *all* sensory experience."

"What of the person who is blind, deaf and dumb?" countered Dafydd.

"They still have touch," I replied. "They can still feel through their skin."

"Yes - pain."

"No, not just pain. There are loads of other sensations."

"It's only pain that really counts. All the rest is meaningless."

"You're pain-obsessed!" I'd shout, inducing Dafydd into a rare display of the emotion that usually simmered just beneath his exposed outer shell. "Can you blame me, Al'?" he'd say, making no effort whatsoever to staunch the sudden explosion of wetness. "Can you honestly blame me?"

I would struggle to construct a meaningful response to this, finally opting for an equivocal "Er, mmm", which Dafydd received with the dignity of a crowned Head of State.

Perhaps, on reflection, I am wrong to think of Dafydd as having been intelligent. Perhaps he simply boasted greater awareness than the rest of us. Wilbur, too, exuded the nonchalance of knowing to a remarkable degree, but you could hardly call him clever. He was, if anything, the quintessential idiot savant.

Dafydd's insight was seldom exhibited in spectacular fashion, at any rate as far as mere mortals like me could tell. This was because he effectively saw everything in full colour, leaving those of us who only saw in black and white with no real framework for judging what he said.

“Mother Christopher is suffering,” he would remark. “She only hits out because she’s desperate.”

“She’s just an evil old cunt, Dafydd.”

“No - not evil. Just in pain.”

“There’s plenty of pain all right, but it ain’t hers.”

“Pain isn’t so terrible,” laughed Dafydd. “It helps make things clearer.”

Which was so plainly ridiculous I was unable to think of anything to say.

“Like when you’re sick,” Dafydd went on, “everything is deeper, sharper and more intense. Things move slower, too - even the air moves slower.”

“Dafydd, you’re an idiot!” I retorted, somewhat more vehemently than I had intended because, in truth, there was a part of me, just a part, that understood. Then, more quietly, I added “Isn’t there anything in life that makes you spit, Dafydd? Something or somebody that you hate.”

Dafydd sighed. “Hating is hard,” he said, “but - yes, sometimes I hate myself.”

This was almost too preposterous, but despite an overwhelming urge to run away and leave him, I never did. For cruelty was, I knew, occasionally the child of desperation or despair, so it was arguably just possible that Mother Christopher ....

Or even Albert Langley ....

The Vagaries Of Reality

Even at the age of twelve I was aware that reality was fundamentally, indeed uniquely, different for every individual human being. We all inhabited different universes, and this was true at the elemental, core level. It was not merely a case of seeing things differently; they genuinely were different.

The universe inhabited by Mother Christopher was as alien and bewildering to me as a universe where time ran in reverse, or one in which people talked out of their anuses rather than their mouths. I liked to speculate as to what was hidden under Mother Christopher's voluminous robes, not in a manner that was lewd or prurient, but simply because it seemed to me wholly improbable that an actual human body could be attached to that haggard, disappointed, slightly bewildered face.

A story she related on more than one occasion was how, as a very young child growing up on a dairy farm in the south-east of the state, she had one day been startled into stupefaction by the sudden emergence from out of the shimmering haze that fringed the distant horizon of a group of fifteen or twenty people wearing hardly any clothes, and with skin like burnished ebony. "Darkies" or "blackfellas" she called them, and she instantly, instinctively knew that where they went, death followed. Shortly afterwards she lost her mother to tuberculosis, which needless to say proved her point. "They're not like us," she declaimed, as her eyes took on the same haunted, far away look they wore when she talked of madness. "Don't let anybody tell you that they're human, because they're not. Oh, they're slightly smarter than a dog or cat, I'll grant you. But they can't think and communicate like we do."

When she used the word "we" she was only really referring to those members of the human race who, for whatever reason, good or bad, were visible to her. I was perhaps fortunate in this respect in that I spent more or less the whole of 1968 outside the venerable Mother's ken. This meant that I could get away with such things as forgetting to do my homework or talking in class - crimes that, if perpetrated by the likes of Dafydd Gynne, Anthony Lindner or Darryl Callaghan, even Barry Ryan, would almost certainly have elicited six of Mother Christopher's spiteful best.

In November the whole class had to undertake a series of examinations in a range of subjects, some of which we had not actually studied all year. In order to be allowed to progress to high school a pupil was required to attain an overall pass grade in these examinations. I, however, was absent from school with suspected hepatitis throughout the examination period and so, technically, ought to have been required to repeat the year. Two years earlier, when he was in grade five, this had actually happened to Hans Rensenbrink, who although a year older than me was now a classmate of mine. Lance Campbell had suffered a similar fate at Elizabeth West Primary School while in grade six. In my case, however, the question of my having to repeat the year was never even raised, presumably because Mother Christopher had entirely failed to notice my absence. Had I been compelled to spend another year under Mother Christopher's tutelage

I suspect that the frail thread of cotton from which my sanity was allegedly hanging would very soon, and very emphatically, have snapped.

Denial

By the end of 1967 more or less everyone in grades six and seven seemed to know that I was fond of Marlene Hirsch. Fortunately, and perhaps a little surprisingly, there were relatively few occasions when I felt myself compromised by this state of affairs. One person, however, seemed to take particular delight in teasing me about it.

Jane Irons was a near neighbour of mine who had arrived in Australia from Somerset a couple of years earlier. She was, in some respects, a female counterpart of Barry Ryan as she was tall and strongly built, excelled at sports, and seemed to be a natural leader, captaining both the school basketball team and her house, St Mary's. Unlike Barry, however, she was also extremely good at school work, so much so that in 1968 she became one of Mother Christopher's elite coterie of scholarship girls.

During 1967 and 1968 the nearest the school bus stopped to home was Elizabeth West Shopping Centre. This left me with a walk of over a kilometre, and my regular companions on these walks were Hans Rensenbrink and Jane. Close associations of this kind between members of the opposite sex were comparatively rare, but Hans, who after all was a year older than me, and Jane had fairly mature outlocks, and seemed to get on well together. As for me, I suppose I was tolerated because I was Hans' friend, but relations between Jane and me were less than cordial. She clearly looked down on me, and whenever she spoke to me there was an unmistakable trace of a sneer in her voice.

Jane's discovery that I harboured a high regard for her friend Marlene was grist to the mill as far as Jane was concerned, and she never wasted an opportunity to taunt me about it. "I bet you'd like to give her a snog, wouldn't you, Albert?" (Alone among my school acquaintances she called me Albert rather than Al'; the only other person who did this was my mother when she was annoyed with me.)

"No way!" I exclaimed, hoping that my vehemence would simultaneously deflect the attack and camouflage my true feelings.

It was Hans, however, who dug the knife in deeper, albeit unintentionally. "I don't know what you see in her, mate," he interjected. "I can't stand fat girls."

"She isn't fat!" I almost shouted, thereby aggravating my situation still more.

Jane, who was on the stout side herself, looked askance at Hans, and may even have blushed, although with her naturally florid complexion it was hard to tell. Then, to me, she remarked, "No, she isn't, is she Albert? She's just right, isn't she?"

"Look, I don't even know why we're talking about her. I don't like her, okay?"

Jane looked smug. "She knows you like her, you know."

Like a securely hooked fish I wriggled and squirmed in desperation. "I don't, I don't, I don't!" was the best response I could come up with, and both Jane and Hans laughed, the former with triumph, the latter almost as a reflex.

On one memorable occasion the bitter pill of Jane's taunting contained a hidden core of unexpectedly delectable sweetness.

Our 1968 school trip took us south by coach to Victor Harbor, where we spent an unusually frolicsome day away from Mother Christopher's asphyxiating stare, she having elected to remain at school. On the journey home I sat alongside Stewart Clark, who promptly fell asleep. With no one to talk to my mind turned to Marlene, whom I knew was sitting on the long seat at the back of the coach with four or five of her friends. From time to time their shrieks of laughter could clearly be heard, a noise I found peculiarly alluring. Although not normally given to outlandish flights of fancy, I resolved to see if I could establish a connection with Marlene by force of will alone. No doubt had I been fully awake and alert I would have regarded such an undertaking with the disdain it deserved, but I was extremely relaxed, on the verge of dozing off in fact, and somehow, at that moment, it seemed a convincingly plausible idea.

I let my arm droop over the side of my seat so that it would be clearly visible to those sitting behind me including, I hoped, Marlene. Then I gently flexed my fingers back and forth, creating as it were a lure, or so I chose to believe. I continued this for some time, with my eyes closed, whilst cultivating, in my mind's eye, a detailed representation of Marlene's face. Come to me, I was almost not quite saying. Let us be as one.

Just as the school bus was wont to do, the coach deposited us at Elizabeth West Shopping Centre, and Jane, Hans and I commenced our walk home. Jane seemed in an unusually ebullient mood which I took to be a wholly natural response to an enjoyable day out. However, after we had been walking in silence for a couple of minutes she suddenly presented Hans and me with a question. "Guess what us girls were talking about on the coach?"

I reacted scornfully. "Who cares?" But Hans, ever the diplomat, invited Jane to enlighten us.

"We were talking about which boys in our class we like the best," she announced with a smirk of unmistakable, if slightly malicious, triumph.

"We all know you fancy Darryl Callaghan," I retorted, hoping thereby to deflect what I suspected was going to be some unwanted, probably acutely disquieting, attention.

"Oh ha ha," responded Jane, with relaxed contempt. "And guess what, Albert, you got your wish."

"You mean you're going to suddenly disappear in a puff of smoke?" I jibed, still trying desperately to avoid the fate I somehow simultaneously longed for.

"Marlene Hirsch likes you, Albert."

My pulse was racing, and I was breathing far too quickly. "So what!" I squeaked.

"So when's the wedding going to be?"

Hans, who seldom exhibited much interest in anyone's affairs other than his own, inadvertently came to my rescue. "What about me?" he demanded. "Who likes me?"

"Oh, almost everyone," said Jane nonchalantly, before adding, with what might have been a modicum of distaste, "You're very popular."

"Who though? Who?" persisted my saviour, with the result that by the time Jane had finished trotting out, and Hans commenting on, all the names of his multifarious admirers, we had reached my front gate. Jane, obviously a little irritated at having had her attack so comprehensively derailed, still took the opportunity to fire off a final salvo, "Night night, lover boy," but its effect on me was minimal.

Hans, in any case, was still thoroughly absorbed in his favourite subject - himself. "Leonora Wilkinson – yuk! Did she really say she liked me, or are you pulling my leg?"

But I did not hear the remainder of the exchange because I had quickly put myself beyond earshot, and back into a realm of my own creation, where everything had suddenly been rendered surprisingly amenable. I therefore basked in the feeling, knowing it would not last.

1969

A Journey Of Discovery

Although Linus Campbell was far from the most robust of boys, in 1969 it surprisingly emerged that he boasted quite exceptional qualities of endurance. The revelation came after he decided to join Central District Harriers under the coaching of a wily, patient and good-humoured Geordie, Frank Abbott. Frank was quick to discern that Linus was no sprinter, but that what he lacked in outright pace he compensated for in reserves of stamina. Even without having undertaken any training he was faster over 800 metres than any other boy at the club. A month or so into Mr. Abbot's training regime he was finishing the distance so quickly that he was leaving his nearest rivals trailing nearly 100 metres behind him.

It so happened that the commencement of Linus's athletics career coincided with one of the more cordial phases in our relationship, and it did not take much for him to persuaded me to accompany him to Harriers training sessions. Although I regarded myself as reasonably fit and quite a fast runner I was soon to be disabused on both counts. For one thing, my sprinting style was all wrong as I tended to waste energy flapping my arms about like a wayward bird whilst simultaneously taking short, staccato steps which left me feeling breathless after forty or fifty metres. By the end of my first training session I had, thanks to Mr. Abbot's attentive, targeted coaching, lopped more than a second off my time for the 100 metres. Further improvement followed in subsequent weeks, but in truth I never became a better than average athlete. The principal benefit which I gleaned from my athletics training was improved fitness, which had the happy side effect of greatly improving my performances in the sport I loved above all others, football. Over the course of the 1969 football season I went from being a somewhat flat-footed, kick-a-quarter centre half forward, to the team's star centreman. For the first and only time in my life I was acknowledged by my peers as a genuinely proficient exponent of a specific sporting activity, and this inevitably generated marked improvements in both my self-esteem and confidence.

These two attributes were very much to the fore the evening I enjoyed the undoubted highlight of my time as a Central District Harrier. One of the many friends I had made since joining the club was the coach's daughter, Josephine. A year or so younger than me, Josephine was quite diminutive for her age, but surprisingly strong, as I discovered during the impromptu rough and tumble wrestling sessions in which we were wont to engage whenever a convenient opportunity presented itself. That these sessions were harmless and innocent I have little doubt in that they invariably took place in full view of Josephine's father.

Our twice weekly training sessions were always rounded off with a timed run around the entire training ground, a distance of roughly 800 metres. I normally covered the distance in about three minutes, but on one noteworthy April night it took me close to half an hour. During that evening's training session Josephine and I had, as usual, spent some of the designated rest time between activities embroiled in playful bouts of wrestling. One pleasurable side effect of such gambols was that we gradually acquired a fairly intimate knowledge of one another's bodies. By the end of training on the night in question that knowledge could fairly be described as all embracing in that the tactile limitations imposed by our clothing had been almost wholly circumvented.

By the end of training the sun had set and so final run took place in near darkness. On the far side of the field from where our coach was stationed was some fairly dense shrubbery, and it was there, almost as if by pre-arrangement, that Josephine and I interrupted our circumnavigation of the oval to undertake a circumnavigation of a much more agreeable kind. It was, I suppose, a semi-logical culmination of the frolics we had been enjoying over the preceding months. In Josephine's case, it may in part have been motivated by curiosity about the contours and crevices of the male form, for she was one of two girls, whereas I had sisters, and the distinguishing elements of female anatomy were therefore familiar to me.

Eventually, we finished our exploratory fumblings, all of which had taken place without a single word being exchanged between us, rearranged our hair and clothing, and, somewhat breathlessly, resumed our circuit of the oval.

If Mr. Abbot suspected anything he gave no evidence of it. He did not even chastise us for taking so long completing our run. Nor did he seemingly notice that, for almost the entire duration of our journey home in his car, Josephine, who was sitting on the back seat between me and Linus, had her hand securely deposited inside my tracksuit bottoms, where, with perhaps surprising expertise, it was managing to elicit in me a degree and form of pleasure that I had never hitherto experienced, nor would again more than half a decade.

Coming Of Age

My first day at Elizabeth West High School was taken up with IQ tests, on the basis of which we would be streamed. I ended up in one of the two top streams, F1, with the 'F' standing for French, my language of choice. The alternative to French was German, which Linus chose, as did Marlene Hirsch. They were placed, respectively, in G1 and G2.

Our class teacher was Mr. Hickinbotham, a Geography specialist, who was replaced midway through the year by Mrs. Slade, who also taught Geography. Both seemed to me entirely negligible characters, at any rate in terms of any measurable impact or influence they had on me.

However insipid in character many of them might have been, at least all the EWHS teachers were human beings and not nuns, although the headmaster, Mr. Hannington - always referred to by us as 'Batman' because of the large, swishing black cape he wore - approached his vocation with a lack of compassion and inflated sense of self-importance that any Sister of Mercy would be pleased to emulate. Afflicted to the brim with religion, he seemed to spend most of his time patrolling the school corridors, grim-faced and earnest, intent upon perpetrating the will of Jehovah on the frail, defenceless flesh of those less worthy than himself. Potentially at least, this could be anyone in the school, but in practice it tended more often than not to be the poor and the meek - or, to put it another way, those who would feel the pain most acutely.

My desk-mate was a Scottish boy called Marcus Fray, with whom it would be fair to observe I did not always enjoy the most cordial of relations. Meanwhile, the desk immediately in front of me was home to Penny and Leanne, who were completely unlike any girls I had ever previously encountered. It was all in the way they tended to look at you, which was as though they had X-Ray vision and could see right through your clothes. Or perhaps it was rather that they gave the impression that they wished they could. Many of my most potent wet dreams of the period, as well as for several years afterwards, involved this pair whom I came, with crass unfairness, to dub 'The Sisters Of Sin'.

My best friend during my time in F1 was Simon Anderson, another Scot, and far and away the smallest boy, in every respect, in the class. His conspicuously retarded physical development was a source of considerable amusement to several of the better developed F1 boys, and was frequently not just alluded to but, in the changing room showers after PE lessons, forcibly exposed.

Simon was so small and light that he could perch on the cross bar of my bike and I would barely notice the extra weight. We travelled far and wide like that, but we also walked a good deal. Simon had found a cave in the Adelaide foothills which we both, on occasion, visited. It would play an important part in my life later in the year, as well as resonating in a quite discomfiting way for decades afterwards.

Despite his diminutive stature Simon was both older and wiser than I was, and his influence on me was both profound and, in the main, beneficial. At the beginning of the year, mentally invigorated by my achievement in making the top stream, I was determined to study hard and obtain the best marks I could. My school report at the end of the first term was replete with praise; only in Maths did I fail to finish in the top ten in the class, a state of affairs which would never again come anywhere close to being repeated.

As the year wore on, Simon helped me to see how shallow and irrelevant much of the school curriculum was. Even French, in which I had achieved top marks in the first term, was scarcely going to benefit me in later life unless I went to live in France, or decided to become a linguist. I had thought that history might prove enlightening, but the dilapidated old creature who taught it clearly had no genuine passion for the subject and as a result made it seem as desiccated and irrelevant as she was.

On Saturday evenings Simon and I sometimes hung around with another boy from F1, Steve Peterson, who was eager to get us to join him in dipping our toes into what, for Simon and Steve, though not for me, became the inescapable quicksand of addiction to nicotine. Steve would steal a single cigarette from his mother's purse, and we would pass this around between us, each taking a couple of long drags before conveying it to his neighbour. For Steve, this almost ritual act of smoking a single cigarette between the three of us became, I suspect, the highlight of his week. For me, however, smoking was somewhat *passé*, having been the 'next big thing' 'way back in grade five (and no, I had not myself partaken, although the pressure to do so had been intense). So I went through the motions of jumping on Steve's bandwagon but, as a somewhat more illustrious personage than me would later, famously declare, "I never inhaled."

Steve and I differed on other matters besides smoking. He was a fanatical devotee of soccer, whereas I preferred football. In the summer, he played tennis, while I favoured cricket. A proud Londoner, Steve was staunchly English, and poured scorn on my infatuation with Australia because of the, to me, entirely irrelevant fact of my having been born in England.

Over and above all this, we both had very different personalities, which led on more than one occasion to jousting of a more than merely verbal kind. For my part, there were times in 1969 when I was consumed by an intense, inexplicable anger, coupled with an overwhelming urge to hit out. On one notorious occasion the butt of my anger was Marcus Fray, whom I savagely bludgeoned into semi-consciousness in a prearranged post school fight, but the most regular victim of my wrath was the hapless Steve. In at least one respect he was his own worst enemy, for he boasted an ugly, monkeyish face with large, protruding ears that just begged to be boxed, and box them I did, repeatedly, and with obvious relish, sometimes in direct response to something he had done or said, on other occasions purely for the hell of it.

Physical appearances notwithstanding I was not, it has to be admitted, the most captivating of thirteen year olds.

I did have an authentically tender side, though, which was perhaps manifested most pronouncedly in my relationship with Simon. Perhaps because of his smallness, perhaps also because of the way he tended to shuffle about in his oversized clothes like a young puppy just beginning to find its feet, I treated him with exaggerated solicitude, almost as though he were a pet rather than a friend. That this was as patronising of me as it might have been deemed considerate is unquestionable but I do not believe that anything could have induced me to inflict on Simon treatment of a similarly brutal, domineering kind to that which I visited on Marcus and Steve.

Why was I so angry? Undoubtedly one major reason was that I did not want to return to England, but felt powerless to do anything to prevent it. My anger may also have been, in part, a reaction to the increasingly stifling yoke of Catholicism. However, many of the causes probably lay so deeply embedded in my subconscious that only an expert psychoanalyst would stand any reasonable chance of being able to expose and label them.

The Apollo 11 Mission

I received most of my information about Apollo 11's flight through newspaper and television. However I found a small amount by listening to the radio.

Probably I would have felt happy when the first man stood on the moon or when the men had landed safely on the moon. But I wouldn't have known what was happening if I didn't read the newspaper or listen to the radio. So mass media played an important part in the moon mission.

On television I received probably the most information about the journey to the moon, however newspaper gave me cuttings that I can keep forever. Then there is radio, what does radio do? Well the fact is that radio was the main link between us here on earth and the spacemen when they were 240,000 miles away.

Most of the people I know were very interested in the Apollo 11 mission only one person that I know didn't express his opinion. If he was in a good mood he was all for the mission and if he was cross or in a bad mood he thought the mission was a waste of time. I won't mention his name in order to not discriminate him. My sister is for the mission and is keeping a scrap book of the mission. Nigel the boy who sits next to me thinks it is a fantastic scientific achievement and thinks that all the money that has gone towards the mission was used for a good cause.

The Big Match

Anticipation had been growing for more than a month, ever since the school committee meeting at which Dave Cloke of G1 had approached the F1 representative, Tom Sergeant, with the idea of staging a football match between our two classes. A date was quickly settled on, and 'Paddock Man', the G1 class teacher, who also coached the school's first year football team, was roped in to umpire. The idea struck a chord with most of the boys in F1, even those who did not normally like sports, because there had always been something of a rivalry between the year's top two classes.

The match is one of very few from the period about which I can recall specific incidents and details, presumably because, from a personal standpoint, it was without doubt one of the best games that I ever played. Not that it was perfect mind you, as the opening seconds confirmed. The G1 ruckman won the tap, and directed it perfectly to his rover, who happened to be Linus Campbell. Linus and I were engaged in one of our periodic feuds at the time, and were not on speaking terms, and so it was a trifle unfortunate for him that he was standing right next to me. I tackled him front on, with considerable ferocity, albeit fairly, and as he hit the ground I found to my surprise that I had somehow ended up holding the ball. I was off at once, hurtling goalwards with one thing only on my mind – glory.

One bounce, two bounces, three, four – within seconds I was in goal kicking range, having in the process ignored several good leads, including one from Steve Peterson at full forward. Just as I was steadying myself to take a shot at goal I felt something cannon into me from behind and my arms were simultaneously pinned to my sides by firm hands. The ball popped from my grasp, and I clattered to the ground on top of a squirming body whose owner roughly pushed me off him. Paddock Man, having already blown his whistle, cried out "Holding the ball!" and I looked across in order to determine the identity of my captor. It was Linus, and he was wearing a distinctly fulsome grin of triumph.

"You utter bloody selfish fuckin' cunt, Langley!" was Steve Peterson's loudly voiced assessment of my crime, but although I knew that he had every right to be annoyed, I reacted with equal anger. "Piss off, monkey face!"

Tom Sergeant, who was team captain, offered me some rather more measured criticism. "Remember it's a team game, Al'."

And, for the remainder of the match, that is precisely what I did. After my initial *faux pas*, it soon developed into one of those all too rare games in which, seemingly, I could do no wrong. My athletics training had helped make me fitter and faster than almost any other boy on the field, and for the next hour or so I ran, ran, ran, and where I ran the ball followed. There were no more long, weaving solo excursions, though. Every time I gained possession my first action was to look for a team mate in the clear to whom I could pass the ball. If no such person presented himself, I kicked the ball as hard as I could in the direction of our goal, in true, tried and tested Port Adelaide fashion.

Football, though, as Tom had pointed out, is a team game, and man for man our team was simply not as good as G1's. Basically, the difference lay in the number of good players the respective teams boasted. G1 had at least half a dozen members of the school team, whereas we had only two – Tom and me. Given this, we could take at least a modicum of pride from our achievement in keeping the final margin down to just a couple of goals.

Afterwards, the two team captains got together in order to nominate the best player afield. There was no trophy, but the winner would have his name read out before the whole school during the following morning's assembly. I happened to be standing not far from Dave and Tom as they were discussing the matter, and so distinctly heard the G1 skipper opining, "I reckon the BoG was one of your guys. That red-haired kid – what did ya call him? Al'?" I failed to catch Tom's reply, but he must have concurred because on the morrow it was my name that emerged, with obvious distaste, from the mouth of our hallowed leader during assembly.

My reaction was a mixture of pleasure and embarrassment, tinged with melancholy, as if I realised that days like this would be unlikely to be repeated all that often, if indeed ever, in the future.

The Séance

One day one or other of The Sisters Of Sin brought a Ouija board to school. Over the course of the ensuing week or so they conducted a series of séances in the cloakroom adjacent to the F1 classroom. Had

Batman got wind of what they were doing it is distinctly possible that he would have rescinded his self-imposed stricture of never inflicting corporal punishment on girls, but by some miracle of diabolic intervention all of the séances were conducted free of sanctimonious interference.

In those days, I was almost as dubious about activities that purported to involve contact with 'the other side' as I am today, but that did not prevent me saying "yes" when the Sisters Of Sin invited me to take part. There were four of us involved: Leanne, Penny, me and, as chance would have it, Steve Peterson, and the question with which we confronted the spirits was "What is my destiny?" Penny went first, and the rest of us placed our index fingers on the upturned bottom of the glass, and waited. The response was not long in coming as the glass, impelled by who knows what arcane power, slid smoothly across the board and stopped at the letter 'R'. "Who's moving it?" I demanded, but Penny and Leanne just hissed at me to be quiet. "You have to concentrate," said Penny, and within moments the glass was on the move again, on this occasion stopping at the letter 'A'. A third time the glass moved, sliding towards the centre of the board before returning whence it came – 'A' again. The next movement was the most chaotic, but also the last for now. It ended with the glass touching the letter 'F' – 'RAAF'. "No way!" shrieked Penny, and we all laughed, for the notion certainly stretched one's credulity. Penny was no 'yes' girl.

Steve went next, and this time the glass spelt out 'T-R-A-V-L'. "What's that supposed to mean?" he complained.

"It means you're going far," I quipped.

"But there's no 'e'."

"Ghosts are notoriously bad at spelling," I countered.

But Leanne was telling us to hush. "My turn now," she declared.

Leanne's turned out to be the longest go yet, but its meaning was unambiguous. 'M-O-R-E-S-E-X' – whereupon the séance nearly broke up in a collective fit of giggles. Finally, though, Penny managed to restore something approaching decorum. "We gotta do Al's," she insisted.

Certain by now that it was The Sisters Of Sin who were propelling the glass around the board I nevertheless had no hesitation in going along with the charade. Mine proved to be another two-worder: 'I-N-S-I-D-E-D-I-E'. Steve stifled a chortle. Despite myself, I felt as though a small block of ice was slivering slowly down my spine. "What's that supposed to mean?" I asked, with somewhat more emotion evident in my voice than I might have wanted.

"It probly means yer gunner die at home, in bed," suggested Penny.

"Or else in a hospital," was Leanne's equally mundane suggestion.

I, of course, was fully aware that the whole escapade had been a somewhat artless contrivance on the part of two inherently mischievous girls, and so to look for meaning was preposterous. Wholly, ineradicably, incontrovertibly preposterous, and just to prove it I harrumphed loudly as I got to my feet, and overheard myself assert as much, albeit in rather fewer syllables.

Hellfire And Damnation - And All Within Arm's Reach

My dad spent most of 1969 working in Alice Springs. Just as during his Tasmanian sojourn his absence rendered life at home considerably less stressful. It is therefore quite ironic that the single worst act of cruelty he ever visited upon me was concocted and administered while he was physically separated from me by hundreds of miles of desert and scrubland.

Life with my mother rather than my father in charge was, in the main, a relaxed, happy-go-lucky affair. My dad's absence also meant that I tended to be accorded discernibly greater respect as nominal 'head of the house'. Personally, I would have been delighted had this state of affairs continued indefinitely, but the declared aim of my dad's working away was to enable him to accumulate sufficient funds to pay for our return to England in a year's time. For while the rest of us loved Australia, he had decided that only by returning to England would we be able to enjoy the sort of family lifestyle he deemed appropriate. For one thing, he would be able to get a job close to home, rather than being forced to live away for long periods. Another key advantage of living in England would be that I and my sisters would all be able to access Catholic schools without the need to pay exorbitantly high fees, or indeed any fees at all. As 1969 wore on, this second reason irked me more and more, as during my year of state-funded education at Elizabeth West high school I learned more and was considerably happier than I had ever been at either St Thomas More's or St Mary's. As for the first reason, as I have already intimated, life at home with no father present was, in almost every way conceivable, immeasurably preferable to life when he resided among us. Absence, in this particular case, certainly did not make the heart grow any fonder.

For my thirteenth birthday my dad sent me a package containing two small booklets: an aboriginal lexicon, and *What Every Catholic Boy Needs To Know About Puberty*. The former booklet intrigued me, and I was soon amusing myself by writing diary entries using aboriginal words. I still have the diary to this day, but the lexicon was lost years ago, rendering the entries wholly indecipherable.

Notwithstanding my first impressions, *What Every Catholic Boy Needs To Know About Puberty* would go on to have a much more far reaching effect on me than the lexicon. Written by a celibate Catholic priest, it contained a wealth of information about a condition previously unknown to me, but which I was fascinated to discover I had been experiencing for more than a year. Among the helpful guidance imparted to me through this book was the revelation that the urges and impulses I had been having in relation to members of the opposite sex were inherently sinful. So was touching my own penis for any purpose other than to facilitate urination. Most disturbing of all I discovered that the activities in which Josephine and I had engaged on that memorable night in April were not merely sinful, but mortally so. Consequently, if I died before confessing this into a priest I would be consigned to the searing flames of hell for all eternity.

The section of the book which I found most illuminating was headed 'Masturbation' which, I discovered, was the act of touching oneself in order to experience sexual gratification. Such an act was, it goes without saying, inherently sinful, but if you touched yourself in such a way as to induce what was known as an 'orgasm', you were irrevocably damned (unless, of course, you made a full and earnest confession to a priest). At first, I was not entirely sure what the word 'orgasm' meant, but when the venerable father went on to write about 'wet dreams' I began to get an inkling, for these were events which fell within the realm of my experience. Apparently, a wet dream was a sinful human response to a lewd temptation of Satan. The good Catholic, when confronted by such temptations, would do everything in his power to deflect or ignore them, for the act of sin lay not in the temptation itself but in succumbing to it. Succumbing to it meant, in effect, spilling one's semen - known as 'ejaculation' - and for a male human being there was one situation, and one situation only, in which it was not a sin to ejaculate. That was when a married man had sexual intercourse with his wife with the express hope that in so doing conception would occur. Because for the wife to conceive and bear offspring was, it seemed, the sole purpose of sex, and the pleasure which the husband derived from the process was effectively a divine reward for his fidelity and obedience.

Clearly my next visit to confession was going to be somewhat complicated. In the meantime, I would have to find a way to thwart the sinful advances of Josephine, as well as endeavour to avoid looking at

Marlene Hirsch, an act that on occasion attended to elicit a carnal response of dubious legitimacy. So ready was I to immerse myself in the cauldron of guilt which the book generated that, to all intents and purposes, my life as a sexual being ended there and then, and it would be more than half a decade before it even began to be reawakened.

A Garden I Know

My friend Hans used to have a wonderful garden. However due to his father's business they had to move. In the front garden there was a huge willow tree, which shaded the windows at the front of the house from the sun. The lawn was short and well kept by Hans' mother who was very interested in gardening. All around the fences at the front of the house were roses and other flowers.

If the front garden is appealing then the back garden is even more so. At the back were six tall fruit trees of various types while one corner of the garden was reserved for some small flowers of all different colours, while another corner was planted with strawberries. A narrow stone path led all the way around the garden.

Unfortunately when Hans' family left the people who moved in were not the gardening type and now the garden is covered with weeds and tall grass and some of the fruit trees are dead or dying.

Shooting Myself In The Foot

My mum was crying, something that, in my experience, was quite unprecedented. What was the matter? Had she burned herself while cooking? Had she perhaps been peeling onions? But there were no onions visible, and indeed no food of any kind. Besides, it was not dinner time, or anywhere near it.

What was one supposed to do in such a situation?

My first impulse was to, in effect, declare that this was not a matter that concerned me by leaving the room. However, in my father's absence I was, as my mum was wont to remind me continually, 'the man of the house', and therefore I ought at least to see if there was anything I could do to help. "Er, what's wrong, Mum?" I ventured rather meekly.

She immediately endeavoured to disguise the fact that she had been crying. "Oh, it's nothing," she said, which might have been reassuring had she not thought fit to add, "Why on earth does your dad want us to go back to England?"

It was not a question I felt pleased to be asked, but I knew the answer. "He wants me, Theresa and Anna to go to Catholic schools, and he wants to be able to work closer to home," I dutifully recited.

Ignoring the latter point, my mum launched an unexpectedly vigorous attack on the former. "Bloody Catholic schools!" she exclaimed. "What's so good about them? You're much happier at Elizabeth West than you were with those horrible nuns."

This was certainly true. Indeed, I had probably never been happier. However, I had found the unfamiliar sight of my mum crying extremely unsettling, and if worrying about whether or not it was a good idea to go back to England had induced such a startling reaction, I felt duty bound to attempt to reassure her. “Oh, it’ll be fine,” I lied, before rubbing salt into my own wound by adding “and it’ll be great to have Dad at home all the time, won’t it?”

Rather than answering my question she chose to concoct one of her own. “Are you sure you don’t mind going back to England?”

“Of course not!” I insisted, and the Catholic part of me even managed to generate a small but discernible wave of pleasure at the self-mortification my deceit was masking. Besides, it was still six months before we were due to leave for England, and six months to a boy of thirteen is a long, long time.

A Climb Of Faith

It ought not to have been a hazardous journey, but between us we conspired to make it so. We set out early in fine weather, with adequate provisions. Our conversation was desultory. Houses and gardens grew brighter and more ornate as we went. The sun continued to be kind to us.

If anyone had asked us where we were going we would both have answered identically, but the meaning which lay behind the simple words “The Cave” was, for each of us, entirely different. So much is true for every linguistic interchange involving humans but some of us manage nonetheless to remain convinced that we are heading, essentially, in the same direction.

In our case, that direction eventually began to involve an upward incline, at first only slight, but before long quite sharp. Small boys confronted by such circumstances sometimes turn and head for home, but we persisted. It was only ever onwards, only ever upwards then, as the ground beneath our feet became a purely incidental factor in our progress.

As we passed the final houses we conspired with one another to produce a silence that was actually a good deal more intelligible a form of communication than words. Our bodies clawed and scrambled helter skelter up the final slopes but mentally we had already completed the ascent. Ahead lay escape, if only for an instant, and I would sit cross-legged on the floor convinced beyond all question, for perhaps the only time in my entire life, that hope was not a meaningless conceit.

If that was, in a tangible as well as both a metaphorical and metaphysical sense, the zenith of our experience, the onset of what would develop into the nadir was swift and inescapable. Our rations exhausted, we tried in vain to slake our thirst at various seemingly likely locations on the journey home, but it seems that exposure to even the most tangential fringes of enlightenment exacts a heavy price. And so we staggered, not quite vanquished, home.

The Worst Christmas Ever

When we broke up from school at the beginning of December the summer holidays stretched out ahead of me like a vast, sumptuous, as yet untasted feast. As for what was looming at the start of the new year, that was so unimaginably distant as to feel not even mildly threatening.

That December was the most carefree, enjoyable time of my life, especially the three weeks or so before my father returned home from Alice Springs. The vast majority of my days were taken up with playing cricket at the Kalawara Reserve, from eight or nine in the morning until sunset, with an hour's break for lunch. Sometimes there were enough of us for two full teams, but usually games were five or six aside, with everyone fielding except the two batsmen who were 'in' at the time. I was a capable medium pace bowler, a competent enough fielder, and a thoroughly lousy batsman. I loved bowling, and to this day regard the feeling associated with uprooting a batsman's middle stump with a perfectly delivered yorker as transcending even the ecstasy of orgasm.

On the hottest days, a group of us sometimes went to one of the local swimming pools, either Elizabeth or Salisbury, instead of playing cricket. Such days were almost as enjoyable because of the sense of timelessness they evinced. I had never cared much for swimming when forced to go at school, but during the summer holidays with friends it was somehow different.

A few days before Christmas my dad returned home and, as if in response, the atmosphere turned sultry. With our departure to England now only a fortnight away it was starting to assume a reality and an inevitability that I did not like.

It did not help when Simon said to me, as he was wont to do increasingly, "You're making a big mistake. You're going to regret it."

I was making a mistake? What choice did I have?

Well, perhaps there was a choice. "I could run away to The Cave," I suggested to Simon, who rather surprisingly did not react with scorn.

"I could bring you supplies," he said, almost eagerly, " and let you know when the coast was clear."

That was all well and good, but "What then, though?"

We were both silent. Simon was clearly taking this surprisingly seriously, but the difficulties seemed insurmountable, even to an outlandishly imaginative pair of thirteen year olds.

After a while Simon, rather tentatively, almost as if he were thinking out loud, unfurled his *coup de grace*. "What about Linus's folks, eh Al'? His gran really likes you. What if they adopted you?"

Of course! It was the obvious solution. Despite the fact that Linus and I did not always see eye to eye, I felt certain he would welcome me with open arms. He could be the brother I had never, other than for a few brief hours back in 1959, had.

I felt a fleeting tingle of anticipation, almost of optimism, but deep down I knew I was kidding myself. However horrifying the prospect of returning to England seemed, there was no way I would be able to bring myself to desert my family. It was not just a question of loyalty, but also of fear – fear of what would happen to me, fear of what my dad might do, fear of what it might do to my mum.

On Christmas Eve my dad, Theresa and I went to midnight Mass, which of course took place during the first hour or so of Christmas Day. In previous years this had been, for me, a time of almost unbridled joy, but this year could scarcely have been more different. On those past occasions Mass had been a time of excitement and anticipation, a prelude to the wonder and magic of Christmas. This year, however, there were no feelings of excitement, and the anticipation had been replaced by a sickening sense of foreboding.

I looked around the packed Church hall at the faces of people who had grown familiar to me, some of whom I could actually say I loved (if only to myself). It suddenly struck me with the force of a fierce punch to the solar plexus that, in all probability, I would never be seeing any of these people ever again. Throughout Mass, I did not join in any of the responses, or sing any of the hymns. I hated Catholicism with its selfish, small-minded God who was made in the image of the man standing directly alongside me, my dad.

Later, in bed, I thought about Marlene Hirsch, for whom I had nursed a secret longing for more than three years, and whom I had managed to convince myself I was destined to marry. Suddenly, from somewhere deep within myself, a surging wave of emotion rose to engulf me, and I spent the entire remainder of the night enmeshed in a cloying web of uncontrollable, unrelenting tears.

1970

All Aboard!

I navigated the gang-plank almost breezily, as though my body was operating independently of my mind (which, in a sense, it was).

As I entered the ship I began squinting in an attempt to come to terms with the sudden onset of gloom. A photo taken at the time shows me open-mouthed with astonishment as though unable to acknowledge what was happening. I am holding a small canvas bag out in front of me as though in supplication, or attempted appeasement of the gods in whom, even now, I sometimes cannot stop myself believing. “Here, take this,” I might be saying. “In here is everything I own.”

But gods, even non-existent ones, are not so easily deceived, and the canvas bag remained in my possession as I descended, still squinting perplexedly, ever further into darkness.

The cabin which my mother, sisters and me would call home for the next six weeks might easily have masqueraded as the ship’s bowel. Males and females sleeping together in the same room was, I knew, inherently sinful, unless one of two conditions applied: either they had to be married to each other, or doing so was a means of saving money. Anything that saved you money was fine, which is why my dad would spend the six weeks of our voyage sharing a cabin on a different deck with three other men, all strangers to each other, all prisoners, separated only by a mutual force of will, never touching.

My mother and I had the top bunks, Anna and Theresa the lower. At night I would lie on my side, watching mesmerised as, within the confines of her night dress, my mother's wayward, undulating breast sagged first one way, then another, in time with the rhythmic waves, which of course could not be conveniently ignored. One night my mother's actual breast escaped the confines of her nightie and was sinlessly conspicuous for hours, becoming ever more absurd and flaccid, like a punctured sack of air.

I am still squinting as I write this. Still perplexed. Still not quite believing.

My younger sister spent almost the entire voyage in the bunk below my mother's, alternately writhing and retching, abandoned to her misery like some frail piece of flotsam propelled beyond reach of the waves by a mighty, vagrant act of nature. Turning slowly paler in the sunless centre that we all, but she with most conviction, had been trapped inside, she would emerge at journey's end a pallid, frightened grub, tottering insanely on limbs fresh grown and hence, as yet, barely usable.

Back then, Anna was The Baby, and hence accorded almost universal obeisance and solicitude, while the rest of us were left to fester unobserved.

Being unobserved became for me, in time, much less a goal than an intrinsic attribute of personality. I would spend most of the ensuing decade honing and perfecting the art of remaining invisible, with or without recourse to the bolt holes I habitually, if somewhat artlessly, contrived to construct for myself.

Whether I did this in order to punish or reward myself was something I was never wholly able to decide. Perhaps I was, and am, a masochist. Few people who have passed through the proving fires of Catholicism are not.

So I would sprawl across my sin-soaked bed, my bed of nails, and glory in each inward spasm of suffering, each flesh superating stab of flawed belief, and would continue doing so, I knew, until the precise, actual moment of my death.

The Worst Sin Of My Life

Shortly after we had boarded the ship a loud gong had sounded. "That'll be for dinner," announced my dad.

I took no notice, as I was talking to Linus, who had come to see me off. Sharon McCarthy, Theresa's best friend, was also there, as was the entire Pengelly family of parents Tony and Jean, and sons Daniel and Lawrence.

My dad, however, was seemingly oblivious of their presence, and was intent on only one thing. "Are you coming, Al'?" he enquired.

"Eh?" I responded, only half paying attention.

"If you want a meal, you'd better come along."

"A meal? Why would I want a meal?"

"It'll be your last chance. Come on."

"But I'm talking to Linus."

"If you don't come now you won't get a meal until tomorrow morning. I'm not going to buy you anything to eat later. Not when there's a perfectly good meal already paid for."

"I don't want anything to eat. I want to explore the ship with Linus."

"Well, don't blame me when you're hungry later."

This went on for about five minutes. In the end, as was invariably the case in such wars of attrition with my father, my resistance crumbled.

"Oh all right," I conceded. "Let's go – but I want to be back in time to see Linus again."

"Don't worry, we'll only be about half an hour."

So I said, "See you later" to Linus, little realising that I never would. Because far from being a quick thirty minute affair, dinner aboard the Castel Felice comprised three formal courses languorously served over a period of almost two hours. By the time we had finished, the ship had already set sail. Knowing I had let my friend down badly I raced out onto deck to see if I could at least spot him on the quayside, and wave goodbye. However, we were too far out, and the tiny figures on the shore were unidentifiable. I would later write to Linus on several occasions, trying as best I could to explain my unforgivably selfish behaviour, and to apologise. He never replied.

How *was* I to explain my behaviour? It was a question that would haunt me for decades; indeed, it still does, for even today I cannot speak or hear spoken the word "meal" without being transported back in time into the body of that lonely, crestfallen youngster who felt as though the world he loved had gone forever.

My suffering on that night did not did not end with the ship's departure. A couple of hours later my dad invited me to go for a walk with him and, still feeling irretrievably diminished by what had transpired earlier, I consented without a murmur. Eventually we ended up in the ship's lounge. "We'll have a drink," my dad decided.

Eventually, the waiter, a tall, suave Italian with a crisp, pencil thin moustache, arrived, looking a trifle disconcerted. "Er, ze boy, sir," he said to my dad, pointing at me, "ee aza no tie. Ee a *muss* have a tie."

"Oh," said my dad meekly, and he got up as though to leave. "I'm sorry – I didn't know."

"Ah, no, sir," said the waiter, "is okay zissa one time. Please to av a menu."

My dad thanked him, and sat back down. He put his glasses on and ran his eyes over the menu. "It looks as though they do food here, Al'," he informed me. "Would you like a sandwich or something?"

Consigned To Oblivion

A fortnight or so into the voyage, I made my way out onto deck, carrying the large orange I had selected from the fruit bowl at the end of dinner. The night air was cool but seemingly still, and I decided to go to the stern of the ship where the disco was located so that I could listen to the music whilst eating my orange.

Right at the ship's stern was an elevated observation deck, where I now climbed. Unlike on the sheltered main deck, here it was windy. From directly below Glen Campbell could be heard singing the singularly appropriate line "I can feel your sea winds blowing" from the song 'Galveston'. It was a song I had come to know well during our voyage. It always, for some reason, made me feel wistful, sometimes almost to the point of tears.

It was a bright, clear, moonlit night, with the Pacific Ocean, which tonight was worthy of its name, stretching out, clearly visible, as far as the horizon in every direction. I went to stand with my elbows resting on the port rail, and began peeling my orange.

"She was twenty-one," lamented Campbell, "name of Galveston."

I looked to my left, to where Australia lay, and felt a slight tickle of remorse, which was gradually exacerbated by the mournful tone in the singer's voice as he bewailed his own loss. Eating my orange would be a distraction, so I resumed peeling. However, I was not to be allowed so convenient an escape route, for as the song reached its climax the orange slipped from my grasp, and tumbled, almost it seemed in slow motion, down, down, down into the vast forbidding emptiness below. I was left holding only peel. All that remained of the orange was its odour and taste, the latter actually just a faint mirage of anticipation. It was then that I finally comprehended, in full, what had happened, and without my orange to console me turned away from the omnipresent ocean, and went down below to where I could, perhaps, reclaim my delusion for a little longer.

PART THREE:

DAYS OF SUNLIGHT AND SORROW

1960 and thereafter

1.

Despite all the disappointments that the decades have wrought, Albert Langley's regular visits to Coronation Park occasion, if not quite hope, at least a fleeting illusion of solace. It is as though his conviction is a ghost limb, subject to all the apparent pangs and irritations of the real thing, and just as persuasively palpable, but ultimately unable to withstand the weight of his disillusion. Brief recourse to distraction is preferable to none at all, however, and this, presumably, is why he chooses to persist.

Shrunken, both in flesh and soul, and prosaically, if not quite shoddily, dressed, he is careful to avoid all visible reminders of these deficiencies as he moves, or is pulled, towards his goal, which in a physical sense at least has always been the same. Indeed, he has undertaken these same trips almost every Wednesday for the past half century, and if they seldom leave him feeling fulfilled, or even enlivened, they are nevertheless essential to his *raison d'être*. They represent, it might be said, a kind of parody of his life, and as such can neither be avoided nor, entirely, embraced. The person who through force of circumstance has emerged as Albert Langley is enslaved to these walks, embedded in them like a fossil. There is and can be no escape, except perhaps within the pages of a book.

The sky is green with weight, a dark, unwieldy green, which brooks no argument, and seems to imply asphyxiation, in spite of which the air, though motionless, is palpable. It is precisely the sort of day that Albert relishes most. It feels as though the entire world is being safely shielded from the wrathful eye of God by a vast, impenetrable canopy.

The deepest pools are stagnant ones, thinks Albert, and is almost overwhelmed - though fleetingly - by lust.

Coronation Park, opened early in the twentieth century, has, over time, supplanted elegance with dilapidation, fostering a formless, haphazard, wild sort of air, to which Albert feels himself inexorably drawn. The park represents, in part through symbol, but chiefly by giving rise to actual, tangible reminiscences, an exposition of the feminine - or, more properly, of that which Albert has discovered, and believes he understands, of his own intrinsic femininity.

Such things are as much an affliction as belief, and just as impossible to ignore.

Rain, thin, invidious and web-like, adding to the oppressive nature of the day, has already begun by the time Albert reaches the park gates. The atmosphere is cloying, and Albert, frail and semi-porous, wobbling on barely competent feet, is forced to pause for breath. He has circumnavigated this park so many times that he is aware, at some level, of the position of every morsel of rock, each sliver of vegetation. Every step he takes is capable of eliciting a whole cascade of memories, of spawning comfort, fear, desire or disappointment, of caressing him gently like a lover, or stabbing him suddenly and ferociously in the solar plexus.

Much less the victim than this state of affairs might lead one to suppose, Albert Langley permits himself to be shunted along without discernible unease. If not quite mollified, he is nonetheless as physically relaxed as he ever manages to get these days, and might, if anyone were watching, be imagined a man of reasonable, even robust, health.

But Albert is to all meaningful intents and purposes invisible, camouflaged by decades of relentless disappointment. His own eyes have long been blinded to all save interior visions, and even these are only indistinctly glimpsed, like gossamer wraiths across a backdrop of infinity.

More than half a century has now passed since Albert first visited Coronation Park, accompanied by his father, a sallow-faced man whose standard facial expression wavered somewhere between perplexity and wry, almost fatalistic, amusement. William Langley had made it through the war years virtually unscathed, but could be counted as a victim nonetheless as a consequence of wounds inflicted by an even more invidious enemy than the Nazis. These wounds still gaped, and would sometimes be unveiled for his son's scrutiny and admiration.

"Can't we go the park ay, Dad?"

His voice resounding through the ages, like a gong.

The man, his father, invariably laughed at that, wobbling uncontrollably like a marionette. "Always the flippin' park," he moaned, but good humouredly, content that all other possible destinations should remain, at least for now, merely hypothetical.

Albert's pulse began to quicken as soon as they passed through the park gates. Fresh blood was welling up as his brain became a welter of wayward desire and motivation, spewing forth a torrent of excited prattle.

"Are we goner go in a boat, ay Dad? An' go 'n see the fish? In the hot-house! An' make a wish in the wishin' well, ay Dad?"

But the principal focus of Albert's interest had never been horticultural. Indeed, the physical environment itself was not something with which he was ever more than perfunctorily concerned; he much preferred to submerge himself in the ostensibly less intrusive realms which he, and he alone, could access.

At the park, perhaps more than anywhere else, he found it easy to abandon himself – which, he later learned, was the ultimate goal of all genuinely great minds – for at the park he was hemmed in, contained, constricted by illimitable greenness. Redemption, he decided at a very early age, was quintessentially and flamboyantly green in hue, and invariably involved containment and concealment. After all, did not Christ himself command us to forsake the world?

"We're off now, Sunshine."

"Arr-ay Dad!"

"Don't 'arr-ay' me. Your mum'll have our tea ready."

And so they had to go, exposing themselves once more to the hostile light.

The trees, he saw, as they reached the park's ornamental gates, were somehow more distinctively individual than people. This amused, and nearly frightened him.

"Ay Dad," he said. "'Ow cum all the trees is green?"

His father's eyes became appalled, not blinking. His mouth was making furtive movements towards the shape of a half remembered word.

“Are green,” he finally elected to reply, preferring to deflect the attack.

But Albert was relentless. “And the blue sky, Dad! Why’s it blue, ay? Why int it red or somethin’?”

“Flippin’ wrap-up, Albert – don’t be daft. It just is. It’s just the way things are.”

“What things, Dad?”

“All of ‘em. Everything.”

“But who made ‘em, Dad?”

“Why, God, of course.”

Of course of course ....

“How?”

“How?”

“Yes, how? How’d God make everything?”

William Langley merely grunted, which Albert construed as a license to continue. “What if God’s colours are different? What if his green’s our yellow, and his blue our brown? What if God Himself’s a different colour from anything that ever was? A completely new colour, that only saints and angels see!”

“Blimey, lad, I don’t have time for these infernal questions. We need to be home for tea.”

So that Albert was compelled to construct his own solutions, causing him to flood with sweat, and begin to diminish visibly, developments which Lucy Langley, who was ever alert for palpable signs of the deterioration she always somehow seemed to expect, was quick to notice.

"No doubt it's a fever," she deduced, removing her hand from her son's clammy brow. "Why ever didn't you take his coat, Bill? This is no weather for shirt-sleeves."

An assertion to which William Langley, who realised that, as far as his wife was concerned, no weather conditions existed that were suitable for shirt-sleeves, elected not to respond.

2.

The streets near the Langley home in Liverpool were grey and imperturbable. They had almost certainly never changed. Albert was forced to exercise a good deal of creativity in order to achieve the sort of abandonment which, from a very early age, he had craved. Billy Sutton, a plump-faced two and a half year old who lived a couple of doors away with his father and elder sister (his mother having died giving birth to him) was the paradoxical target of many of his escape attempts.

The fact that Billy seemed to like Albert, and more significantly still to trust him, made the frisson to be derived from subverting his expectations all the sweeter. All it took was a poisoned pill concealed inside a cake. "Wanna play, Billy?"

Causing the infant's eyes to shimmer with hope. "Yes, play!" And he would wobble willingly and gleefully across the street to embrace his fortune.

Using a small thin tube of steel piping, Albert dug deep into the heart of the ants' nest, eliciting a highly amusing frenzy of chaos and consternation. The same tube could then be used to transport the ants on to various exposed parts of Billy's anatomy, causing the child to wriggle and chortle with glee. When the first bites struck home, Billy's face at first conveyed bemusement, as though a choice sweet he had been invited to suck bore an unfamiliar, unexpected flavour. Seconds later he would be frantically flapping his hands and stamping his feet, wailing all the while with hysterical confusion and terror. "Alby, Alby, no like!" All of which was but a prelude to the real epiphany, as the ants began to get into Billy's eyes, ears, mouth and hair, up his nose, and inside his clothing. Then he would collapse to the ground in despair, shrieking and howling with all the anguish of a lost soul.

Approaching the miracle of appeasement, Albert might perhaps have moaned, as cruelty surged, tsunami-like, inside his trousers. He loved the helpless skin which Billy's face had clearly seemed to proffer. Although devoid of blood there is nothing in any of the medical literature to insist an injury must be bloody; or even to imply that blood is always visible. And so he wallowed in his lover's hopeless pain which was, of course - if only metaphorically - his own.

Meanwhile, the blood in the celebrant's chalice began to trickle down across his hands, his eyes alert in sudden realisation of his plight. And the congregation collectively moaned, their joined flesh orgasmically enhanced, belief unleashed and rampant like an escaped bull.

"It's over now," insisted Jennifer. "He's gone. It was just an act of desperation, or of fear. Forgive me, sweetheart!"

Eliciting a holy baptism of sperm – a seminal emancipation. Albert's body grew unwieldy.

He became attentive then, and reassuring, picking Billy up and talking soothingly. He would tell his victim-lover's sister that he had found the child in tears beside a nest of angry ants. Her gratitude would then, in effect, be Albert's absolution, and he would return home, in time for tea, exonerated.

Days later, the same cycle of veneration and betrayal would recur, for Billy had yet to escape the asphyxiating yoke of trust.

In bed at night, Albert's darkened room consoled and understood, and he felt himself expand. Two furtive gleams of light transformed themselves into Billy's eyes, exposing his sumptuously vulnerable flesh, as he gazed across at Albert with ingenuous adoration.

"I'm awful glad we're friends, Alby."

And Albert shook with either terror or delight.

Hand in hand, they walked towards the centre of Coronation Park, to the boat lake, where the marble sky was oscillating gently. They reached the water's edge, where Albert tightened his grip on Billy's hand, before abruptly gathering him into his arms and hurling him as far as he was able out towards the centre of the lake.

We are all, Albert knew, the victims of each other's helplessness, as Billy splashed, and screamed, and gurgled, frightening a nearby group of ducks into reluctant, spluttering flight. An obviously well-heeled gentleman and lady might then have arrived, attracted by the commotion.

"I say, that child appears to be in difficulty," remarked the gentleman.

To which the lady, perhaps more in tune with the underlying nature of things than her partner, replied, "Oh, isn't he a darling?"

Meanwhile Albert, tense with speculation, and hidden from view by a happy accident of light, watched.

"I'd better dive in after him," resolved the gentleman, removing his overcoat.

"But Maurice dear, you'll ruin your clothing!"

The man referred to as Maurice paused, looking briefly uncertain, then said. "Of course, you're right my dear – these shoes alone cost twenty guineas."

"Let him drown, darling – it's for the best. I daresay his poor parents will welcome a reduction in their weekly food bill."

And, linking arms as though to formalise their conviction, they walked away.

Feeling an unexpected but quite agreeable warmth enveloping his loins, Albert returned to the water's edge, anticipating consummation. Billy's cries were getting weaker as his fate became less complicated, and Albert felt a sudden pang of jealousy, an overwhelming urge to suffer inexplicably at the hands of someone previously considered trustworthy. After spending a few moments acceding to such feelings he, too, moved off, thereby intentionally protecting himself from the sight of Billy

Sutton's final moments, and from the weight of blame to which it would undoubtedly have given rise.

3.

But the Time of Reckoning eventually arrived.

"I don't feel well enough to go to school today," said Albert.

But Lucy Langley, who had already embarked on other preoccupations, was oblivious. "Your uniform's laid out," she said. "Come through to breakfast when you've washed and dressed."

So his fate was sealed, free will no longer plausible.

The school bus, as always, was full to the brim with the condemned, most of whom stood or sat mutely, although a handful of the younger ones could still find reason to converse with one another. Only when Marlene boarded the bus at Elizabeth Field Shopping Centre was Albert able to construct the most hesitant of smiles - which, he liked to imagine, was fleetingly reciprocated before she clambered up the stairwell to the upper deck.

It was the last moment of pleasure on a day he would later look back on as one of the very worst in his life.

At shortly after nine o'clock, an artificially re-animated corpse with greedy, pock-mark eyes, and flesh the texture of desiccated tree bark, stood, or loomed, before the forty-two members of grade seven, trembling slightly with what Albert later learned to recognise as thinly controlled loathing. "My name," it croaked, so indistinctly that everyone in the room had to lean forward to decipher the words, "is Mother Christopher, and while you are in my class you will obey me instantly, and without question, or" – and its eyes shifted surreptitiously but meaningfully in the direction of the wall to its right, where a foot long white cane with a red tip lay straddled between a pair of hooks – "be prepared to suffer the consequences."

Just in front of Albert, a girl raised her hand, eliciting a smile, or perhaps a grimace, of gratification on the face of The Corpse. "Yes?" it breathed.

"Please, Mother, could you repeat that? I didn't quite catch it all."

The Corpse's trembling grew more violent. "Your name, my dear?" it sinuously enquired.

"Please, Mother, Leonora Wilkinson, Mother," quailed the girl, uncertainly, like a rabbit that suddenly suspects that the chasing stoat does not want to play after all.

"Leonora Wilkinson," mused The Corpse, rolling its tongue around the words with obvious relish; it might in actual fact have drooled. "Leonora Wilkinson – why, you are to be congratulated." And, hobbling away to its right, it plucked the fateful article from the wall, and, almost soothingly, invited Leonora to join it at the front of the classroom.

"With which hand do you write and draw, my dear?" asked the now uncontrollably tremulous figure of The Corpse.

Leonora pointed to her right hand.

"Then hold out the other one."

For Albert, the next few moments were a confused but seminal blur of movement, accompanied by a sequence of sounds to which he would all too soon become disquietingly accustomed.

"Just one, I think, to make a point," said The Corpse, and its ostensibly frail arm moved with whiplash swiftness and brutality. There was a faint swish followed by a strident thwacking noise, and Leonora Wlikinson's eleven year old conception of a warm, consoling world was instantaneously and irrevocably fractured. She returned to her seat, red-faced and tearful, caressing her wounded hand as if it were a broken-bodied pet.

"That," explained The Corpse, in a voice that was, if anything, even less audible than before, "should be a lesson to you all. You are to regard every word I utter as proceeding from the very mouth of God the Father Almighty, which means you must always, always, always PAY ATTENTION!" And the final two words were a Banshee howl to which Albert, in the days, weeks and months ahead, would repeatedly awaken, palpitating, perspiring and perplexed.

"What must you always do, Leonora Wilkinson?"

"P-pay attention, Mother."

"Indeed. Now fold your arms, face the front, and prepare to" – this to a sudden baring of teeth, as though in acknowledgement of some cruel and terrifying secret – "learn."

So that Albert, ready or not, was propelled headlong into a confusing, often seemingly contradictory morass of opinions, facts and ideas, most of which were forgotten almost as soon as they had been encountered. Perhaps the only genuinely important lesson he learned during this particular school year was not to antagonise the beleaguered, bitter, merciless woman who oversaw and, to a significant extent, shaped it. Almost from the start, he perfected a technique for effectively remaining invisible, thereby rendering himself immune from punishment. On the rare occasions that Mother Christopher actually became aware of him, there was never the merest hint of recognition. Indeed, Albert managed to pass through an entire year under The Corpse's tutelage without it ever managing to learn his name. He was 'laddy', 'you there', 'his nibs' – even, on one uproarious occasion, 'Charlie Chaplin' – but never himself, a fact which alternately appeased and irked him.

The other kids at school, Albert's fellow inmates, seemed almost universally to regard their cell-mate's invisibility with a mixture of suspicion and disdain. There was something feeble, almost cowardly about it, and as a result Albert found himself effectively ostracised.

He did not mind. For a while, he derived a measure of consolation from the unexpectedly fervent friendship of Leonora Wilkinson. On the day of her initiation, during playtime, Albert had spoken to her consolingly, and a bond of shared humiliation was initiated. Sometimes, if they managed to find a secluded corner of the playground, she would let him hold her hand – the very hand on which The Corpse-inflicted scar could still be detected. And once, on the day that Leonora announced that she would be returning to England soon with her parents, they had even kissed, with a somewhat cumbersome uncertainty that Albert nevertheless found wholly exhilarating, and that he would spend most of the remainder of his life endeavouring, and failing, to duplicate.

If his pleasure was minimally sullied by an intimation that he might somehow be betraying Marlene it was nevertheless, he somehow managed to convince himself, a useful life experience.

His only other friend was stolid, faithful Dafydd Gynne, who walked with a slight limp, and was deaf in one ear, and who therefore, like Albert, was in the view of the majority of his peers neither to be endured nor trusted. Unlike Albert, however, Dafydd was far from immune to persecution from teachers, attracting their ire not only for alleged misdeeds but sometimes for no discernible reason at all.

During playtimes and lunch breaks, while the other boys forgot their dignity in the relentless pursuit of footballs or each other, Albert and Dafydd remained cocooned in theirs beside the antiquated gum tree that supervised the most secluded corner of the playground. "We who are alike must share our persecution," Albert observed, one summer afternoon towards the end of that fatal, final year at Primary School.

Dafydd seemed to find this inference hilarious. His frail form was rolling on the grass with mirth, all dignity forgotten.

Albert sucked his teeth.

When Dafydd had reclaimed himself, he sat propped against the tree, wheezing slightly as he almost always did in the wake of any physical exertion. "When I grow up," he confided, "I think I'd like to be a martyr."

Giving Albert cause to look. He tried to breathe complacently. "Well...... that would seem to be the quickest way," he acknowledged, but his face was not quite convinced. "Perhaps, though –" His lips were cats assailing butterflies.

And Dafydd knew to undertake a silent vow of silence.

Albert resumed. "Perhaps we don't actually need to die in order to embrace a *kind* of martyrdom."

Consigning Dafydd to a further bout of mute deliberation.

Beneath the overarching branches of the tree their limp forms were somehow squashed. Coarse gleams of dead light were dappled over Dafydd's face. His pale skin began to flicker.

"There's really nothing left to know," said Albert. "This gum tree could confer redemption."

Perhaps it would.

Dafydd's face became a pallid jewel. There might have been the merest glimmer of derision. "You'd have to climb it first, though," he insisted.

Both now saw that this indeed was true. A martyrdom of words would not suffice.

In class, while sitting imperceptibly a couple of rows behind Dafydd, Albert loved the tender, untouched vulnerability of his friend's exposed neck – a neck which seemingly was bared to greet the hungry knife. Albert then imagined Dafydd's enormous, suddenly redundant head careering down the stairs and into darkness, vanishing forever. He shuddered cold from premonition, or from fright.

But Dafydd's face, which was still alive, turned round to probe him, revealing a kind of wordless indignation. He would not be stymied by compassion, it affirmed, which Albert, albeit unconsciously, interpreted as being tantamount to a statement of intent.

Time through time: the almost endless world was shrinking, as Albert seemed to grow - although in truth, perhaps, it was just a vacillation in the atmosphere. Such things are often hard to tell.

Then, as the future seemed to linger tantalisingly just out of reach, Albert achieved an apparent insight which would delude and sustain him ever after. Lying in the shade of the gum tree one sunlit summer morning, he and Dafydd combined in a fervent pursuit of the enlightenment to which both of them so earnestly aspired. "We must prostrate ourselves," said Albert, almost piously. "Our only chance is absolute submission."

As the rustling tree surrendered to the wind.

"Our martyrdom is here and now," he carried on. "We die, and are born again, each moment. We might as well endeavour to devour ourselves as try to comprehend eternity."

And he felt his breath expended and renewed.

"Each moment kills the one before."

Said Albert, unopposed.

So that Dafydd saw the universe as emerging out of thwarted possibilities. He rolled cold in grass, as an endless surge of nothingness perturbed his summered face. Cool red. His trousers torn by one of time's regurgitations, consigning him to immobility.

But Albert's eyes were racing. His hands, it seemed, had throttled truth, while excitement drooled like grease from sloppy lips. "Can you show me yesterday?" he almost yelled. "Can you pick it up and play with it and tear it into useless little shreds of crap like *this*?" And his fingers murdered skeins of unprotected grass.

As Dafydd mewed, or spluttered.

"Come on, then," insisted Albert. "Come on!"

Inducing Dafydd to retaliate. His threatened feet advanced towards the tree, which he briefly touched in veneration, then began to climb. "I'll show you, Albert Langley!" he declared, as only ever upwards he advanced. "I'll show you!" Enmeshed a tremulous baby in his adamantine mother's arms.

And Albert saw.

He saw the dirty, half-forgotten leaves which once had acted out a brief if not exactly unambitious scenario on Dafydd's willing face. He saw the bending of the unrepentant branches as they clashed against the wounded air. He saw the sky, now grown sullen, begin to weep as though in recollection of a loss.

And Albert watched as Dafydd's once for certain solid shape became a gash of technicolour helplessness recumbent on the bastard grass. He moved and almost leaped with uncontainable urgency, as the derelict remains of Dafydd Gynne were stroked and cooled by what was once the only stream of truth to penetrate eternity. His memories for once incapable of consoling him, he turned his misted eyes at sky in a vain attempt to cancel out the now indelible pre-eminence of blood.

It seemed to Albert's granted somewhat battered mind that some vast snake was sinking serried fangs into skin which looked deceptively like its own. There might have been a line between the sacred and the secular then, a line across which Dafydd, in a sudden, irresistible reverie of devotion, had plummeted.

The shouts and screams of others as they became aware of what had happened, and hence of their own mortality, seemed wholly inappropriate to Albert. They had surely missed the point, he thought, as he felt himself confined by harsh, unnecessary arms. The aftermath was a scene from a film, in which he, Albert Langley, was cast in the role of an ostensibly confused and sensitive eleven year old, whilst simultaneously manning the camera, observing. The actor-Albert felt impressed at his own virtuosity, and found the effect his feigned emotions had on others quite invigorating. The Albert-at-the camera, though, was much less easily convinced, and would, had time permitted, have liked to shoot the scene again.

At home he dutifully allowed his mother to console herself by wrapping him in her frantic arms. He told her not to worry, he was fine, he merely needed to be alone, but all this seemed to do was make her worse. Only after several hours of selflessness was he able to escape.

Dafydd Gynne's martyrdom was the first of many that Albert was to witness, but the only one that left him feeling envious. Although he had little doubt that it had not been preconceived, it nevertheless seemed both meticulously choreographed and brilliantly perpetrated, as though it had been rehearsed repeatedly for weeks. Had a God of justice and compassion existed, Albert had little doubt that he or she would have had little hesitation in conferring on Dafydd all the consolations and privileges of sanctity.

4.

Whenever Albert thought about Dafydd's death he was conscious that an immense waterfall of distressing feelings was being continually staunched by the strength of his will alone. By using the mundane and the innocuous as a kind of screen or curtain he was almost entirely able to protect himself from the horrors that lay beyond. Indeed, as time went on, he even began to forget the existence of these horrors.

Father Ballantine, a thickset, rather oppressed looking man who appeared to be perpetually on the verge of asphyxiation, was proving to be a most effective curtain. As he tugged instinctively at his dog-collar, presumably in an effort to reduce his feelings of constriction, he addressed Albert's mother almost deferentially. Her son had undergone a quite traumatic experience, the priest explained, and his lack of apparent concern about it was much more likely to be a symptom of shock than a manifestation of hardness of heart or callousness. "He just needs help in bringing his feelings to the fore," reasoned Father Ballantine, who imagined himself enlightened, and who had been known to quote from the likes of Montaigne, Voltaire and Jung during his sermons, "and support in dealing with them when they do."

"I'm sure you know best, Father," said Lucy Langley, who actually was. "But what exactly do you recommend?"

The priest grew quite resplendent then. "I'd like to take him personally under my wing," he proposed, "and give him the first hand benefits of my counsel." And he smiled as though to emphasise his magnanimity.

Lucy Langley looked across the room at Albert somewhat fearfully, but managed all the same to seem appeased. "Say 'thank-you' to Father Ballantine, love," she suggested, but Albert merely stared.

"How would you like to be an altar boy, Albert?" enquired the priest, with what he liked to assume was a kind of avuncular familiarity.

"I dunno," Albert said, alerting his mother to the level of disquiet he felt by grimacing almost surreptitiously.

"Aha, that's the boy!" laughed Father Ballantine. "I can see we'll get on famously!"

And so it was decided.

That Sunday morning, Albert entered the vestibule at St Thomas More's to undergo his initiation. He found the low ceiling, stern walls and minimal illumination quite consoling, but was almost instantly repelled by Father Ballantine's blithe façade of *bonhomie*. "Aha, the star of the show arrives!" the priest chortled. "All ready for the big debut, then, Albert?"

To which the initiate deigned to grunt.

"There's no need to worry now, laddy, Philip and James here'll do the tricky bits. Just watch and learn, my boy, watch and learn."

And the other, older boys were leering at him with disdain.

In the chapel it was cool and bright. The air seemed vibrant with either desperation or enthusiasm, as incomprehensible Latin praise rebounded from the consecrated walls.

Albert watched in a kind of stupor as the white emblem of sinlessness was raised, accompanied by heavenly chiming. There had been a time, in fact, when he had actually assumed that the tinkling bell accompanying the consecration of the host was being rung in heaven, presumably by an angel. Since then, however, the universe had become a lot less unpredictable, and his assumptions somewhat more so.

And so he watched without amazement as Father Ballantine was dangling from the glistening cup, his fingertips supposedly in touch with deliverance. The stains of sweat became ridiculous upon the priest's swaying, undulating brow, while the universe became a lolling ball of darkness around his bewildered, iridescent eyes.

After Mass, Albert hastened to immerse himself in silence. He was conscious of a nameless, visceral craving, centred deep down in the pit of his stomach, gnawing at him irresistibly, insatiably, compulsively. His starved, apocalyptic mouth was gobbling blindly, desperate for something tangible and reassuring.

And there was Father Ballantine, helpless feet swinging, pig-body dangling limply, a lifeless slab of meat condemned to hang and rot and fester.

So that Albert saw redemption as potentially disastrous, as a kind of snare - a veritable honey-trap, in fact - enticing, charismatic and deadly. He resolved never to let himself become beguiled like Father Ballantine, but to treat the persistently proffered cup with amused disdain, aware that to drink was to enter a kind of suspended animation.

5.

Coach Abbot had two daughters. Melanie, the elder of these, was the same age as Albert. She had shoulder length sandy brown hair which she usually wore in a single plait, freckled, tautly muscled arms, and an air of consummate, unfussy competence. She was the state record holder in her age group over a number of distances but this was not something she would ever see fit to mention, let alone boast about. Albert treated her with the same good natured *bonhomie* that he habitually bestowed on those of his male acquaintances whose status verged on, but did not quite arrive at, friendship. If the fact that she was female had any impact whatsoever on Albert it was scarcely perceptible to him, even less so than in the case of his sisters.

Melanie's younger sister Josephine appeared to have been calculatedly designed to embody all the feminine qualities her older sibling lacked. Had she been born in an earlier era, she might have been called coquettish. Almost from the first day they met, she and Albert conspired to pursue a relationship that was playfully, and in the main wordlessly, tactile. During breaks in training they would engage in mock wrestling bouts that typically ended with Josephine giggling and shrieking uncontrollably in the face of a relentless onslaught of tickling. Had Albert's dad been witness to Theresa engaging in similar activities with a boy of her acquaintance there is no doubt that he would have reacted with disbelieving horror, and immediately forced them to stop. Coach Abbot, however, gave no indication that he even noticed Albert's and Josephine's antics, a fact that both of them implicitly regarded as a license not only to continue, but to relish doing so, as if what they were engaging in was merely a standard feature of their education, like long division or the causes of the English Civil War.

6.

When Albert first saw the ship he was to call home for the next six weeks he was immediately reminded of Angela Tewksbury's words aboard a river Murray paddle steamer more than a year earlier. "Half close your eyes," Angela had said, "and you could imagine yourself aboard a boat sailing back to Ingerland." Albert's response had been both immediate and scathing - too scathing, he had quickly acknowledged, if only to himself. Now, it seemed, he was receiving his comeuppance, for although the *Castel Felice* was officially classed as an ocean liner she was, at barely a hundred and fifty metres in length and just twelve thousand tonnes, really little more than a large ferry. Indeed, if Albert were half to close his eyes it was possible to imagine her as a rather ramshackle, unprepossessing paddle steamer.

He was tempted to close his eyes fully, and wish the ship away, but he knew that when he opened them again, she would still be there, as would his equally unpretentious, equally unsatisfactory future.

7.

After five years in England Albert finally emerged from hibernation and began to embrace the possibility of a future in which he featured as an active participant rather than just an observer. The principal catalyst for this development was his move from Liverpool to Derbyshire to attend a teacher training college. He had no especial desire to teach, indeed was almost wholly bereft of desires of any kind, but within a few weeks of commencing his training course he had begun to exhibit definite signs of wanting to re-impose himself on the world.

In Alan Saunders he found the first true friend he had known since leaving Australia. A superficially dour cockney, Alan soon manifested himself as a genuinely kindred spirit, attending college merely because that was the way he had been pushed, and nursing a veritable multitude of trapped and trammelled emotions. Finding that they shared an interest in chess, Albert and Alan started a college chess club, which was how they came to meet Ruth. Tall, somewhat on the voluptuous side of plump, with intensely black hair and uneven but not unpleasing facial features, Ruth turned up at the club's inaugural meeting and announced that she would like to learn how to play the game. Between them, Alan and Albert devoted themselves wholeheartedly to this not exactly tortuous task, for Ruth soon showed herself to be an avid and capable learner, and she was soon holding her own or better in games against several of the club's weaker members.

Albert made numerous other acquaintances at this time. His room mates in his hall of residence were Jim Strowther, a naive, football-obsessed Yorkshireman, and Gordon McConie - always known as 'Jock' - a laid back, excessively garrulous Glaswegian whose outwardly cordial disposition disguised, and in some ways protected, a highly tortured and confused inner core. Inhabiting the same hall of residence were Damon Reilly, an ever-smiling, wholly fanatical fundamentalist Christian; Mike Salter, his room-mate, an equally fanatical hedonist; the perpetually ebullient, occasionally anarchic Belfast 'twins', Ian and Sean; and in the various classes which Albert attended there were numerous others, like fields of flowers, male and female, dull and bright, closed and open.

But in that initial term it was to Alan and, almost by extension, Ruth that he returned most often. After chess club as well at various other times the three of them would sit together in the college bar, sharing ideas, silences and laughter. "People will think we're a Bloomsbury trio," remarked Ruth, eliciting appreciative chuckles from both of the men, neither of whom had the slightest idea what she meant.

They soon found out, however. Towards the end of term the students in Albert's hall of residence hosted a party, which Ruth attended. Albert had never before enjoyed such affairs, but on this occasion things were different, perhaps in large part because he had never before drunk so profusely, and with such abandon. As the evening progressed he discovered with something that initially resembled perplexity, but quickly became acquiescent absorption, that he was discerning in Ruth a range of enticing characteristics of which, until now, he had been entirely oblivious. He noticed how the skin on her face was flawlessly smooth, how the face itself was paradoxically rendered more appealing by virtue of its idiosyncrasies, how artfully she moved and arranged her hands as she spoke, how vibrant and captivating her eyes were. He recalled how Alan had once maintained that a game of chess was much more analogous to sex than to warfare, a remark Albert had dismissed at the time as typical Alan blather, doubtless solely intended to provoke a reaction. Now, however, as he aimed increasingly protracted glances at Ruth, who somewhat ironically was engaged in a conversation of considerable apparent intensity with Alan, Albert felt persuaded to revise his opinion. Chess was, indeed, intrinsically, undeniably. outrageously sexual, and his failure to perceive this before had undoubtedly deprived him of much potential gratification.

After the party, the three of them tumbled, groped and fumbled their way down the steep hill pathway which led to Ruth's lodgings. When they got there Ruth, perhaps feeling that she ought to repay them for all their solicitude (including all the chess lessons), or more probably because she was simply too inebriated to think of any viable alternatives, invited them in 'for coffee'. That formality over with, they retired to Ruth's bedroom to enjoy a shared pursuit of freshly concocted challenges, shedding their clothing like confetti, and, at least in Albert's case, penetrating at least some of the mysteries which his reading of *What Every Catholic Boy Needs To Know About Puberty* more than half a decade earlier had scrupulously obscured. He watched in mingled horror and fascination as Alan and Ruth seemingly coalesced, their two frantic, heavily perspiring bodies surging and waning as though in time to some nameless, elemental rhythm. When Alan came there was an explosion of laughter and shrieking from the pair of them, while Albert felt himself go limp from trepidation. If the entire room had been ablaze with purifying purgatorial flame he could scarcely have felt more cowed or penitential.

"Oh, the poor little mite," remarked Ruth on seeing, and both she and Alan burst out laughing.

"This is not at all like any chess game I've ever played," said Albert, and he got up and began fumbling for his clothes.

"You can't go before you've come," insisted Ruth, which both she and Alan seemed to find hilarious.

Gently but firmly, Ruth grabbed hold of the nearest part of Albert and chortled with surprised pleasure. "Is that a foreskin?" she enquired, and, not waiting for an answer, engulfed him orally and started doing things with her tongue that Albert could never previously have even begun to imagine possible.

The rest was a recrimination-soaked welter of clumsiness, confusion, excitement and ecstasy. Albert felt both violated and inviolable, enlivened and preposterous, deflated and supreme. "Thanks for the coffee," he managed to say, before slumber overtook him.

Next day, feeling strung out, hung-over and passionless, he went through the motions of attending lectures and, at lunch time, went with his English group to a nearby pub, their tutor having promised to buy them all a Christmas drink. "I'll just have a half of bitter, thanks, Tom," said Albert. Mick Wilkins, the only other male in the group, asked for a lemonade and lime.

"Well, I did think the *men* in the group might have wanted pints," remarked Tom, with what seemed to Albert an unnecessary amount of irritation.

Sorry to disappoint you, Tom, thought Albert, but manhood isn't something I can properly aspire to, not today.

8.

Alan Saunders left college at the end of the autumn term. When Albert returned after the Christmas break he found a letter waiting for him in which Alan explained that he had never really wanted to be a teacher, and he had begun working at a garage as an apprentice car mechanic. He asked Albert to convey this news to Ruth, and also to let her have his address if she wanted it.

Ruth, however, proved difficult to track down. She never seemed to visit college hall for meals, she no longer came to the college bar, and Albert never encountered her at other times. Finally, three weeks into the term she turned up at a meeting of the chess club, and Albert seized his opportunity, telling her about Alan's departure, but all she offered in response to this was a palpably disinterested "Oh".

"I've got his address if you want it," said Albert.

Ruth looked genuinely mortified. "What?" she squeaked. "Why on earth do you think I'd want his address?"

Albert learned more from that single sentence than he did from an entire year's worth of college lectures.

Ruth, it seemed, was determined to view the previous term's impromptu *ménage a trois* as an aberration, as a wholly alcohol-induced calamity. Albert, who deep down actually regarded the affair in much the same way, was nevertheless confused and a little wounded at Ruth's resultant retreat into a spuriously cheerful kind of insouciance. There would be no more late night sojourns in the college bar; from now on their relations, if such they could be called, would be confined to intermittent games of chess, and if Albert derived a measure of frisson from the ease with which he tended to win these encounters it was negligible compared to what he knew was, if only in theory, available away from the chess board.

Artificial as his romp with Ruth - and Alan - had been, Albert longed for a repetition, or at any rate for something similar to fill what could only be described as a kind of inner void. He recalled the preposterous séance in which he had taken part back in 1969, when in answer to the question "What is my destiny?" the 'spirits' had seen fit to spell out 'I-N-S-I-D-E-D-I-E'. It was outrageous, of course, to think of according any credence to such things, but there was a part of his brain, a part over which he seemingly could not exert any control, that yearned for something more, something over and above the mundane and merely physical.

According to this vagrant segment of his mind, the universe itself was intelligent, proactive, even calculating, assiduously seeking to unsettle, disorientate and punish. What one needed to come up with in response was an adequate hide-away, a bolt-hole, or failing that a form of camouflage. And camouflage did not have to take tangible form. This was something Albert had learned early in life, although he would have been unable or unlikely to articulate it in quite that way. However, he was perfectly aware that by assuming a stoical demeanour he could avoid most of the unsavoury forms of interaction to which so many of his fellow students - particularly the males - tended to fall victim.

What he had not reckoned with, however, was the almost limitlessly persuasive power of delusions, even, as would emerge in Albert's case, delusions that were expressly and consciously acknowledged as such.

In early February Albert accepted an invitation from the perpetually happy Damon Reilly to attend a meeting of the college's Christian Union. Through both this meeting, and several subsequent ones, he was exposed to a whole new vocabulary, indeed an entirely different and unfamiliar way of looking at and interpreting everything. Damon's and his friends' brand of Christianity was very different from the Catholicism that had been instilled into Albert as a child and in which he was still, to an extent that might have surprised him had he realised, comprehensively enmeshed.

Damon himself had something of a paradoxical effect on Albert. His smile, which was worn almost constantly, somehow managed to be both irritating and infectious. The glory of the risen Christ oozed from his every pore, so that even his clothes and spectacles seemed awash with virtue. When Albert discovered that Damon was prone to ironing every item of clothing he owned, including his underpants and socks, he regarded the disclosure with equanimity, as just another visible aspect of a faith that was principally about appearances.

Essentially, Damon's clique harboured an unquestioning belief in an interventionist God, a miracle worker or, more accurately, a magician whose mighty spells were capable of subverting or even obliterating the laws of nature. This God actually inhabited his followers in invisible, ghostly form, and interacted directly with them in ways that they could understand and interpret. Most commonly these communications would be filtered via the Bible, which was regarded as being infused with divine, which is to say magical, powers. The magic stemmed from the fact that every word in the collection of writings that comprised the Bible had been telepathically (or, again, magically) transmitted to its authors by God.

On a conscious level, Albert found the supernatural elements of Damon's cult superficially alluring, but ultimately hollow and absurd. He was, he told himself, no longer easily deceived. Life was not a thing of magic or of romance, he realised. Most of life was gap-toothed, unkempt and malodorous. It did not strive for excellence or beauty; it merely was.

To the man forced to devote virtually every waking hour to acquiring the basic necessities of life, things like art, philosophy and the pursuit of personal salvation seldom, if ever, presented themselves for meaningful, active consideration. The examined life was a luxury most could not afford.

Ultimately therefore, at least inasmuch as he told himself, Albert saw behind the shiny outer carapace which Damon and his friends had so guilelessly constructed to the rotten, fetid, wholly insidious inner core. He regarded the maladroit bastardisation of Christianity that they embraced with utter contempt, as a contrivance both born of and characterised by naivety, wishful thinking and credulous mumbo jumbo. Later, other elements such as the ineradicable urge to power and the hyper-inflated sense of self would reveal themselves.

Paradoxically though, it was precisely these inherent weaknesses which rendered the college Christian Union attractive to Albert. Getting inside Ruth's pants had been, in every sense, a seminal event, and one he was anxious to repeat as soon as possible, with as many different women as he could manage. With what was for him an unusually high degree of sagacity he perceived that not only are some girls easier than others, but Christian girls - wide-eyed, gullible, sweet-natured, submissive, trusting as lambs - were easier than most. It was therefore quite ironic that the woman with whom Albert ultimately ended up boasted none of these traits.

9.

In an effort to advertise himself as an earnest and wholehearted student of the world, Albert Langley decided to grow a beard, but it made him seem inquisitorial rather than inquisitive.

During his frequent walks around the market town in which the college was located his grief, his bitterness, indeed almost all aspects of his malaise became temporarily submerged beneath a welter of mundane, but nonetheless importunate, preoccupations. Trite as it seemed, there was a sense in which escape of a metaphysical kind could be linked to a fleeting sense of physical freedom. Impending pain was rendered briefly unbelievable, or at any rate unlikely. All blinkered men-beasts feel themselves consoled by such delusions, for to think of self is to be capable of, indeed prefigured for, deceit.

10.

Given that he was deploying the majority of his physical and emotional resources endeavouring to further his academic reputation, college lecturer Gerry Collingham had little left for more workaday activities, such as cultivating meaningful social relationships. For a time, this had caused him considerable disquiet. His first marriage, for instance, had ended after less than two years, when his wife became aware that, beneath his veneer of scrupulous complaisance Gerry nursed wounds of such disabling severity as to render him untouchable. Faced with the prospect of being imprisoned for life with a man who neither knew nor cared about her, Mrs. C number one had quickly called time.

Not long afterwards, Gerry had "found Jesus", or, more accurately, professed that he had. The discovery wrought little change in his outward behaviour, but it did at least give him someone other than himself to blame for his ongoing failure to elicit any kind of admiration or affection from either his colleagues or his students. It was therefore somewhat surprising when he found himself the very obvious object of adulation of a young, pert, scrupulously neat bank clerk who, like Gerry, had found solace in the saviour's arms. They were married after a three month courtship following which they continued to delight themselves in one another, both in and out of bed, until the roseate glow of carnal infatuation had waned. It was at this point that Albert first encountered Gerry, who from the outset treated him with a disdain that was as inexplicable as it was palpable. Perhaps there was something in Albert's charmless naivety that excited in Gerry the perfectly understandable impulse to injure and disorientate. Or it could have been that Gerry was simply jealous of Albert's apparent, though wholly superficial, popularity with women. In endeavouring to undermine this at every turn, Gerry grew increasingly frustrated and bitter at what he regarded as his failure, little realising that what he was fighting was, in essence, only a mirage.

Gerry's significance to Albert was considerable. From Gerry's sanctimoniously framed injunctions to deprive oneself of all the baser human pleasures in pursuit of holiness Albert derived an acute awareness of his body's immense malleability and frailty. Needless to say, he had no actual desire to become holy, merely to achieve the appearance of holiness and it soon became apparent that he had, in Gerry, an excellent potential role model. The one mistake that Albert made was in imagining that Gerry's visible adherence to all the tenets and strictures of fundamentalist Christianity was rooted in an alert, sincere, unquestioning belief in their validity. Paradoxically, Gerry's thinly veiled hatred of Albert actually derived from an identical misconception.

When Jennifer first showed up at a Christian Union meeting Albert experienced the same familiar knotting sensation in his stomach that his initial encounters with the Indian Princess and Marlene Hirsch had generated. This time, however, older if not quite wiser, he recognised it for what it was - anticipation of the thrill of the chase.

Albert had probably seen women who were more beautiful than Jennifer, but not many, and none who showed such conspicuous, nonchalant awareness of their own beauty. Her most striking feature was her exquisitely curled mane of natural blonde hair that extended down as far as the small of her back. The fact that she was small and slim of stature somehow made the hair appear all the more majestic. She wore a serious, slightly haughty expression, and Albert would soon discover that she smiled only rarely. She was casually holding a saucer in her left hand and taking frequent small sips from the cup that she was holding in her right. Only an occasional slight raising of the eyebrows afforded evidence that she was actually listening to the man who was talking to her, in a fashion almost suggestive of supplication or fawning. That man was Gerry Collingham.

As one of the few college lecturers who professed to any kind of Christian faith, Gerry was sometimes invited to speak at Christian Union meetings. He had been doing precisely that this evening, taking as his theme the sin of lust. Student life, he had declared, was full of potential pitfalls for the unwary Christian, and far and away the most dangerous and numerous of these temptations had to do with sins of the flesh.

Sins such as he himself was manifestly perpetrating now with this eminently seductive stranger, thought Albert, and, resolving to do what he could to derail Gerry's ambitions, he went over to where they were standing and said, "Hi, I'm Al'," extending his hand to the girl, who took it briefly, limply. "I don't believe we've seen you here before."

"Or will again," she said, and almost smiled.

Gerry, tortuously masking his consternation at Albert's intrusion said, "I've been trying to persuade her that her Catholicism is no reason for her not to get involved in the Christian Union. Perhaps you'll have more success than I've had, given your background."

Albert winced, as much at Gerry's blindingly incandescent smile as in response to the words. Turning to the girl he told her, "I'm Catholic, too. Or was. I have the scars to prove it."

She stared at him with what he at first took for belligerence, but may in fact have been a kind of tacit sympathy. "You'll have to show me some time," she remarked and, having put her now empty cup and saucer down on a nearby table, added, "Excuse me" before escaping to the other side of the room.

Turning to Gerry, Albert said "I found your talk .... illuminating" to which Gerry might have sneered, but instead managed to say "I'm glad", as he set off in pursuit of his quarry, anxious no doubt to finish what he had started.

Despite her promise to the contrary, the girl continued to show up regularly at CU meetings. Over the ensuing weeks, Albert discovered that her name was Jennifer - never ever 'Jenny' - and that, like him, she hailed from Liverpool (not that you would know it from her Home Counties accent, which put Albert in mind of Angela Tewskbury). She had been brought up a Catholic, and still attended Mass each Sunday. She tolerated Albert's advances - for such they obviously were - but on the whole remained as taciturn and phlegmatic as on first acquaintance.

All around Albert there was an abundance of fruit, ripe for picking, but he devoted all his efforts and energies to the wholly futile task of trying to captivate and capture Jennifer. One day, without preamble or warning, she shocked and deflated Albert by revealing that she was "seeing" Gerry Collingham.

"But isn't he married?" was all that Albert could think to say.

"He's leaving her."

"There'll be a scandal!"

"Queen Victoria's dead, Al'."

"But he's a lecturer!"

"He's a man, and I'm a woman," said Jennifer, as if that explained it all.

Which, thought Albert, it probably did. And they were, he had to concede, as admirably suited a couple as it was possible for two such insular souls to permit themselves to be. To Albert, it merely exposed more vividly than ever the essential hypocrisy of Christianity, and of Christians.

When Damon, newly elected president of the CU, discovered what was going on he informed Jennifer that she would no longer be welcome at the group's meetings, but it was in truth a rather feeble, lackadaisical riposte. Jennifer actually laughed, and said, "You don't have the right or power to stop me".

"Nobody will have anything to do with you," threatened Damon.

"Nobody does anyway - except for Al', who clearly wants to fuck me."

"I really must ask you to refrain from using such language."

And Jennifer laughed again. "Let he who is without sin," she chanted merrily, and walked away.

Once again, however, Jennifer did the precise opposite of what she had intimated, and ceased attending the CU's meetings. Not long afterwards it was rumoured that she and Gerry had had a falling out, or more likely had simply grown tired of one another, with Gerry returning, ostensibly contrite and woe begotten, to his eight months pregnant wife whose outward show of forgiveness was tempered one assumes by a realisation that it was only a matter of time before history repeated itself.

Jennifer, meanwhile, had disappeared off the radar.

Two days before the end of the summer term there was a knock on the door of the dormitory that Albert shared with Jim and Gordon. Albert happened to be alone at the time so he shouted out "Come in!" whereupon Jennifer entered the room and, without preamble, said "Take me out somewhere, Al'."

Totally taken aback, all Albert could think of to say was, "You've had your hair cut."

"It was getting to be too much trouble," Jennifer said. "Are you coming?"

And Albert, neither really knowing nor caring whether it was a sensible thing to do, duly got up and went with her.

11.

"You make me wonder sometimes, Jennifer," said Albert.

"I make you wonder what?"

He laughed inexpertly. "Ah, nothing."

As they lay beside one another on the saturated grass, jointly awaiting something more decisive than the dank autumn stillness. Their condition was comparable to that of women on the verge of giving birth, their mutual flesh alive with expectation, or foreboding.

"Al' - look! A shooting star!"

The previously listless sky was animated, if only briefly - a harsh, defiant flicker, then extinction. Albert was momentarily transfixed, before being pulled, almost against his will, into a sitting position. “Let’s go,” he said, getting to his feet. “Here, give me your hand.”

But the gift was unforthcoming. “I’d rather keep it, really,” she replied.

He tried without success to seem unmoved. “It isn’t yours to keep,” he muttered.

“Isn’t mine?” Her eyes were quite absurd.

Albert sighed. “Let’s not get tangled up in philosophy. It only makes us irritable.”

“O Albert, really!”

“I mean it!”

The single viable response.

“Well, then.” She was never going to let herself be taken and so they remained, in essence, divided.

“I’d marry you tomorrow, Jennifer,” said Albert.

Jennifer recoiled. “You’d have to slay me first.”

“Perhaps.”

The pseudo-proposal was not as flippant or fantastic as it seemed. He was watching her for signs of vulnerability or weakness. Her firm flesh, he knew, was just a form of camouflage, but even his recognition of this fact did not enable him to penetrate.

“I’m going home,” he said.

“Okay.” She looked at him.

"Will you be coming?"

"May as well." Continuing to look.

"I'll get a taxi."

"If you must."

"Oh?"

"I'd really rather walk."

"Do you realise how far it is?"

"I need the exercise."

"Well, tell me if you're tired."

"I won't be. The exertion will do me good."

Albert sighed. "You're a living, walking paradox, did you know that?"

"I fail to see your logic."

"I wasn't being logical."

"Then what's the point of speaking?"

"It helps to clear the brain of junk." He laughed. He would not stop.

"Your metaphor is rather flimsy."

"I'm not surprised. I never was especially imaginative."

"I hope that's not intended as an excuse."

"Excuse? I wasn't aware of the accusation."

"You must be pretty dim then."

"I wouldn't care to argue."

"It's seldom advisable," she agreed.

"So you're certain you'd prefer to walk?"

"I'm wholly certain."

“The weather’s fair enough,” he conceded.

“I shouldn’t worry if it weren’t.”

“We’re walking then.”

“You’re free to take a taxi if you want.”

“I wouldn’t think of it.”

They set off, in the process perhaps coming as close to genuine unity of purpose as they would ever manage - much closer, certainly, than they would ever come during sex, which always developed into something of a battle, from which Jennifer, who felt and cared less, invariably emerged the victor.

They walked together in silence for fully half an hour before Jennifer produced a sigh of exasperation, and said “You really are absurd, you know?”

But Albert, rather than replying, sought temporary consolation by chewing on the inside of his lower lip, for he understood that, in the face of surging, overpowering lust, words were wholly useless.

So Jennifer relented, unfurling the secret alternate self that only occasionally, and then only ever very briefly, emerged. “I’d like to meet your parents some time, Albert” - an announcement that they would both later look back on as the first tacit acknowledgement that they were In A Relationship.

There were still hurdles to surmount, however. “I wonder sometimes if we’re suited, Jennifer,” said Albert. “We seem to argue such a lot.”

She raised her eyebrows slightly, but was silent.

“I sometimes get the feeling you disdain me,” Albert continued. And failed to smile.

“I see your point,” she said, and seemed to drink it down like undesired but needed medication.

“You agree then?”

But her only answer was another raising of the eyebrows, coupled with a brief sigh, or gasp.

“We’re almost there,” he said, referring in the main to the proximity of Jennifer’s lodgings.

“I’d invite you in for coffee” she ridiculously claimed, and swallowed deep with either confusion or despair. “You understand?” she rather needlessly added.

“I really wish I did,” responded Albert, who was nevertheless more in tune with the underlying nature of things than he realised.

“You’re trying to be self-effacing.”

“Yes, I know,” he conceded, and gave a small, almost apologetic chuckle. “I actually managed it once,” he endeavoured to amuse her by adding.

She did, in fact, give vent to something that resembled laughter, but her stolid, unblinking eyes provided what was probably a less disingenuous reaction. “You’ll have to write a book,” she suggested.

“I nearly have,” he laughed, “but aren’t we rather losing track of things?”

“I suppose we are,” she condescended. “But isn’t it inevitable?”

“All things are possible,” pronounced or quoted Albert. “That means that nothing’s quite inevitable - not even sunrise.”

"Now who's waxing philosophical?" she retorted, but Albert was defiant. "Philosophy's never left us," he insisted, his words a beam of light that exposed the looming vacant doorstep.

"Perhaps we need to think things over, Albert. It's all so desperately confusing!"

They were standing near the doorway waiting, he tentative but hopeful, she a tightly knotted ball of indecision and tension. "I really must have time," she said, less to Albert than to herself, and seeming suddenly vulnerable, indeed as unconvinced and frightened as a baby bird about to embark on its maiden flight.

Albert reached out then, desiring at least a cursory instance of physical contact, but Jennifer immediately moved beyond his reach and, finding her new surroundings congenial, decided to remain there.

12.

It was a dour, unmemorable courtship, almost completely lacking in animation or craving. They were both enmeshed in convention, which in Albert's case contorted itself, at least ostensibly, into full-blown religious observance, and there was nothing in the unremitting tedium of their relations to encourage either intimacy or lust. Perhaps if there had been, things might not have gone so incandescently awry.

Two sizeable glasses of whisky was all it took in Albert's case; in Jennifer's, a half bottle of cheap Portuguese wine. They returned to his digs besotted by a new level of connection, which as yet was only tangentially physical. After that, all it took was an accidental collision of enraptured flesh to ignite the touch paper.

It was then, whether from weakness or conviction, that they simultaneously capitulated, collapsing on the virginal bed like felled pheasants, writhing and giggling and fumbling with what ought to have been foreboding.

Eventually, once they had grown accustomed to the absurdity of their plight, Albert was moved to embrace her from behind, his loins coiled snake-like in readiness, prompting her to manoeuvre him into position with amused indifference. Squeezing gently, she began slowly to open and close her legs, simultaneously rocking slightly backwards and forwards. "Do you like that?" she said. "Is it good?" But it was all that Albert could do to remember his own identity.

Squeezing tighter, she began to moan, with either pleasure or despair, and Albert felt himself trapped. There is and can be no escape, he knew.

"Can you feel it, Albert?"

As they swayed in time to some implacable rhythm.

"You can have me, if you want," she lied, while defiantly, almost callously, tantalising him. "Would you like that? Would you like to fuck me now?"

As their flesh became submerged beneath their mutual, but in truth very different, aspirations. They were swaying more quickly then, a single, indivisible entity, trapped within a terror of their own devising. Jennifer grappled with Albert's hands, forcing them below her clothing, rubbing her breasts against them with an urgency that Albert found disquieting. "Be rough with me," she implored. "Hurt me, Albert."

For only in pain was absolution.

Albert then became her nemesis, as all doubts, all sense of uneasiness, became subordinated to his sudden will to conquer. "I am coming, Jennifer, I am coming!"

As nirvana burst with anti-climactic swiftness across his wayward loins.

"Oh fuck, oh fuck, oh fuck!"

So that their inter-connected flesh grew suddenly intolerable, causing Jennifer to withdraw and then constrict herself, becoming a kind of foetal ball, a taut manifestation of denial. She clutched herself for reassurance, but with a firmness that was almost brutal, and then remarked, "That was lovely, darling."

When Albert later confessed his mortal sin at confession, the priest was unperturbed. "Do you love her, Albert?" As though forgiveness hinged on the answer to this single, altogether subjective question.

"I think so, Father."

"Then marry her, my son, and spend your seed in the purity of God's grace."

And so it was arranged.

“What is it, Albert?” Jennifer asked later that day, as they were strolling, arm in arm, though separately cocooned, around the local park. “You haven’t been yourself all afternoon.”

An accusation that Albert, having learned the cost of liberty, received without surprise. “I suppose,” he shyly ventured, striking out at words which whistled past like tennis balls, “that is, I think that I’m in love with you, Jennifer.”

It was, in a sense, the true climax of their relationship, but if either of them knew this they gave no sign. Indeed, the only thing that Albert felt was slight disdain at the way in which his words had tried to appropriate control.

So this, thought Jennifer, recalling the fiery wetness of their sin-stained bed, is it. You could, she mused, have been a bit more subtle, Albert (though aspiring nonetheless to something masquerading as relief).

Relief constrained by silence.

And Albert clawed.

“Aren’t you going to say anything, then?”

His words, he felt, were etched in sallow timber.

She smiled.

“Convince me, sweetheart.”

As though provoking destiny from a position of obdurate security. Her comfort was, it seemed, incalculable.

“I would like to know how you feel,” he said, although immediately regretful.

Albert Langley was decidedly unnerved. Beneath a coy disguise of clothes his nakedness was blazing. His view of things became distorted by a vain and rather gratuitous filial love for this, his only body. And for Jennifer's, which stood released beside him.

She was staring from a mirror.

"Love is just a word," she seemed to say, reflecting similar thoughts which he himself had had. "Don't let your sentimentality beguile you."

Forcing desperation on his blinded eyes.

"I know what I believe," he lied, "and nothing you can say or do can change that."

His own mouth, he knew, was virtually autonomous, was clutching madly at the shreds of faith his own uncouth uncertainty had torn. A crumpled, thwarted, pseudo-resurrection. Putrefied. Inanimate.

"I won't argue," she said, suffused with melancholy detachment. "Words can seldom alter things."

And forcing him to flinch. "You're tearing me apart," he wailed. "You know that, don't you?"

But silence surged like gobs of spit. The world inverted, overturned..

Again.

So that after that, they met less often, but at the same time it was obvious that their confrontations were intensified, were coloured with a re-awakened eminence of passion, which perpetuated an illusory sense of compatibility. This confused things, and as time transpired, the overall illusion was vivified. Until, that is, the day that Albert made his fateful proposal.

Shortly afterwards, things began.

Sleeping together (legally, by now) in the same ubiquitous double bed, bodies squeezed helplessly against one another in a confusion of abhorrence and need, their lives became surreal. Albert, seeing the virile flesh exhibited upon her sallow body, worshipped her in cold, unmitigated relief. His own intrinsic ugliness provoked a blinding veil of fury in her taut, invincible eyes, so that Jennifer, beyond all question or retort, Began to Feel the Need.

"Albert, you are….. immense," she observed, one evening, in the shadow of their virgin's room.

But "No" he said. "You're quite mistaken, darling. It's merely the light which elongates."

So that Jennifer, rebuffed, was forced to flounder for resistance. "No, Albert, it's true – and it's not a flight of fancy, either. My mother, too, has noticed. She was only saying."

Albert gasped. "Well, then, it must be encroaching middle age – and your mother is a palpable one to talk!"

"Why, Albert, don't be horrible!" And she fixed her serried teeth like ice bergs.

Uncertain how, or why, she should protect her mother, towards whom she was in truth indifferent, Jennifer nevertheless felt constrained to manufacture irritation. Perhaps compassion goaded her; in any case, her seeming loyalty was startling. "Besides," she maintained, as though it mattered, "My mum's fine figure of a woman. Quite why society should set itself so stolidly against a couple of superfluous inches I will never know. Never."

Her firm, luxuriant bosom reinforcing.

"Why, then," he declared, "in that case, what are you complaining about?" And found his laugh of triumph almost meaningful.

"I am not," she said, emitting words with brusque conviction, endeavouring at authority, "complaining."

So that Albert in his nakedness was palsied.

"I see," he said, and his words were laced with tension. He was terrified.

Fumbling with his own eroded recollection.

So that she, in sudden desperation, tried to plummet deep inside the reflection of his hairy face, desirous of hiding. But deflected by an air of battered hope.

Unreasonable, she mused.

"You were always so unreasonable, Albert," she observed.

Not seeing the derision in his smile. Insensitive. She pulled, or lunged, at something numinous.

One Sunday afternoon, in the quietude of after dinner bliss, their bodies made a vain attempt at love in what was, for them, a somewhat adventurous location, the linoleum-covered floor of the rear parlour. Albert, repressed and stifled by this strange woman's sonorous breath, could easily have cried in anguish, yelled out in fear to fill the vacuum of his starving, attenuated hope, and yet, for reasons hard to justify if easy to define, did not. Instead, he languidly allowed himself to be transmuted into something like an object of love, lending himself almost aimlessly to Jennifer's, his wife's, incessant barrage of desire.

"Could we go a walk, do you think?" he asked, in a rare instant of freedom.

And oh, how she laughed! Her marble face became delirious. Albert, Albert, please, she said. In spite of which, her sullen, formless voice remained unused.

"Ah, grasp me not, the clawing desperate hands!" he cried.

Her deep assaults were virtuous. Deadly. Almost unavoidable.

"What in heaven's name do you take me for?" she said, through muffled breath. Her face became incompetently stagnant.

And oh the clawing desperate hands!

Whose mind inside that muffled breath conspiring?

So that Albert could have said, with warranted reserve, "Who are you?" but kept his vacuous, horrified jaws unopened, perhaps in muted deference to the Married State. (Who knows?) Instead, he complied with Jennifer's redundant, homicidal breathing.

Keep back, keep back, his murdered, enigmatic silence could have screamed, their tortured shells devouring distances.

"You remind me," Albert wished, his flaccid voice beseeching air. A frenzied, mindless eructation.

"Ah, yes, yes, yes," her tremulous mouth uncertain as it seemed.

Until, with inexorable cohesion, conception followed.

Like smoothened, unremitting turds.

Do drop.

Albert gave to her then. Gave to her his own deflected self.

"I am yours," he could have said, though softly, conscious all the time of other possibilities.

"Yes," her opened mouth declared. (Detached, it was, or seemed - detached in appearance, but servile still, corruptible.) So that "Yes" she said, but carried on, "Yet that is not all, my darling."

Her silent smile was suddenly evasive.

"I need you," said by thought-provoking lips. "I need you, Jennifer, I need you."

Repetition was, of course, inevitable. As inescapable as hatred.

And Jennifer was leering like a clown. "We need the sun," she said, "and air to breathe. And food to eat. And flowers, perhaps. Particularly roses. But as for me."

Her words became disastrous.

Albert then was made aware of Jennifer's, his wife's, unenviable position.

This made him fervent.

So that Jennifer was rendered crippled, even during after dinner walks.

As Albert's stabilising hand insisted on her arm.

And occasionally pulled.

It was then that Jennifer became confronted (though fleetingly) by the utter ludicrousness of things. Finding herself alive beside a stranger who had departed many months before.

A meaningless charade.

“O, Albert,” coughed her plying, empathetic lips to elusive, wished for air one afternoon when vacuum surged around like wasps. “Don’t you understand? Our love is just a game. We’re covering up. Distorting. All we’ve really done is hide the hate – the hate that, deep inside, is all that’s really there.”

For what is love, but blind, ridiculously convoluted hatred?

The atmosphere declared.

As this recognition dawned, Jennifer was lured to passionate consideration of her embryonic hope. Her intimation grew distended. Wanton lust became her predominantly unrequited preoccupation. Her body tore at Albert, anxious to destroy, to tear him down. But fear of blood repelled.

Had he only known.

Albert watched her passion soar. Felt her pointed, callous fingers rise to devastate him. Became resigned.

What is love? he cried. What is love beside this naked female body? Beside this bared inhuman flesh which drains my very being, denudes my very soul?

He felt himself uncaring.

Ah, what, indeed, is love?

Before her stark, insensible eyes.

Deflecting.

Remorse has but the pain unsure inside our fervid anguish crying.

Albert laughed.

“Well, then,” he said, “we must perforce redeem ourselves. Salvation they say, is a somewhat messy affair, involving nails. But why not see if we can find a less excruciating procedure?"

The crown of thorns inexorably descending.

"Albert, don't," she wailed - and so, in time, he came to see that she was actually virginal.

So proud to be a man, her husband. So proud to keep her tarnished flesh beside himself in deranged anticipation of paternity.

Oh, yes, he's got his daddy's ears.

The people came, and worshipped. But God in its unpolluted cot was (and seemed) oblivious. And even cried. Its flagrant tears indignant. And sexless in their terrified contempt.

"We'll call him Joseph," said his mother, hoping perhaps for a show. But Albert, dazed by importunity, declined all else but what he saw inside his son's as yet unseeing eyes.

They would grow together, he and he, compressed inside the music that was theirs and theirs alone.

But Jennifer, of course, was unaware.

Ensconced within a chorus of her own creation.

It was several days after the baptism that the palpable Mrs. Allcott – Jennifer's mother - announced her presence in the Langley vestibule. She was permeating powder, and her normally pallid lips were smeared with scarlet-tinted sweat.

"I have come, my love," she maintained, "to convey my heartiest congratulations. And to snatch, if at all convenient, a glimpse of the new arrival?"

She was obviously and tangibly constrained by a sense of her own undermined maternity.

So that Jennifer was laughing. "Of course, Mum," she agreed. "Though I'm afraid I can't promise anything enthusiastic on Joseph's part – except a touch of wind, perhaps. He is, you understand, as yet a closed flower."

And clutched him to her breast as if to emphasise her ownership.

"He has, as you will no doubt see, his father's turn of feature."

And Mrs. Allcott smiled, as women do, though not alert enough to realise. She rallied then, and said, "It's character, though, which makes a man. Don't you think so, darling?"

"Oh, yes," she chuckled. "It's character all right." And could have carried on.

"Of course," admitted Mrs. Allcott, "it is far too early yet to tell."

And nibbled at her mouth, which now resembled blood, her comfort grown disquieting.

She began to hate her daughter.

And Jennifer could understand.

"It was good of you to call, Mum," she decided. "I'm sure Al' will be pleased."

Her pursed lips were twisted furtively, concealing her disdain.

"When I tell him," she derided.

So that Mrs. Allcott smiled. "You'll give him my regards, I hope?" she ventured, rising. "And now, I'd best be off."

Impatient for the gentle purging of the outside air.

Having Seen.

That night, the pantomime continued, though still they failed to realise.

"My mother called," said Jennifer, "to have a look at Joseph."

(So my son is now to be placed on Public Exhibition, Albert mused.)

"That's nice," he said.

(And did she, perhaps, approve?)

Jennifer was blunt. "These things must be endured," she said.

And Albert not quite smirked. "Yes," he said, "I suppose we must be philosophical."

There was something slightly sinuous in his smile, something somehow insipid; but a lack of light precluded confirmation. He allowed himself to fantasise a bit, permitting Jennifer, his woman, to achieve a somewhat idealised bearing. And so their secret skins made love in feigned retaliation against the deep undying hatred which pervades. The damning darkness seemed symbolic then; their blinded eyes were counterfeiting visions, operating invidiously like drugs upon the candid, unrequited innocence of their souls. And this, indeed, was Albert's element (though Jennifer was silently reproving). He started then, with bewildered rapidity, to Find Himself. A most perplexing process, involving anti-social tendencies.

So that Jennifer was lost.

"Come back, my love," he could have said, indeed implored, but languages require a mutual frame of reference.

And Albert's wife remained conspicuously inaccessible.

So that time once more was rampant. In fact, so swift and unremitting that Albert missed the encroaching adolescence of his only son. The passage of time became a complicated blur, indistinguishable from shaving and the taste of bitter tea, and Albert soon became amazed at his own relentless, incorrigible inconsequence.

Each day after Albert departed for work, Jennifer attempted to convince herself that she was waiting with resigned anticipation for his eventual return. Indeed, as though to fortify herself in this conviction, she would often walk around Coronation Park, anxious, or so she claimed, to unearth memories of mutual importance, and to provide herself with licit scope for sentimental aspirations.

This was all a joke, of course, for like her mother, Jennifer had long ago been endowed with a fundamental capacity for Sight. So that while her skin became increasingly redundant, her mind grew gradually more alert.

It was around this time that Joseph Langley, Albert's son, despite having already reached his middle teens, began at last to arrive at something vaguely resembling self-awareness. As a direct result, he ceased to believe in the enigmatic, hairy man, his father, whose face had grown increasingly imponderable.

In the wake of his mother's surging, omnipresent forcefulness, her rising, virile breasts, the boy was quite distraught, discomfited. He lacked cohesion.

“My son will kill me, surely,” Mrs. Langley mused, and viewed the notion as an aid to re-established sanity.

Joseph Langley was a thin, decidedly unpretentious sort, with a slight harelip. Other than that, his most conspicuous features were his eyes, which never seemed to move, and which thereby rendered him reputedly simple-minded.

I could even care, his malformed mouth rejoined – though only ever at the breeze.

There was something about his manner which was quintessentially, almost grandiosely, self-effacing. Neighbours found him either trite (these were the superficial ones) or else obnoxious. “Joseph Langley,” they would prophesy, adopting somewhat rueful airs, “now there’s a weird one for you. It’s rare you meet a lad as rum as that one. He’ll be set for either glory or despair, you wait.”

But Joseph, for the moment, was content merely to effect a kind of laboured resilience, to hide his tender, fertile innards behind the ostensible candour of his enigmatic lip. This caused his mother, at least, to throb with speculation, and to wish – on more than one occasion explicitly – for the cold but yet familiar violation of her husband’s tantalising fingers.

But Albert wasn’t there, for one day he had surprised both Jennifer and himself by announcing “There’s a post I might apply for in Hong Kong. They need an English teacher at the British Council there.”

And Jennifer merely said “Do whatever you think best, dear” - which Albert elected to regard as both a blessing and a curse, or at any rate a kind of exoneration. He duly applied for the post, and was successful. "I'll be away two years" he told his wife, who either did not hear him, or felt herself constrained to silence by the prospect of freedom. To one another, Albert and Jennifer acknowledged that it was not really a trial separation, merely a breather, but only one of them actually believed this.

Toward the apparent culmination of his parents' war, which in essence never really ended, Joseph began, as his grandmother termed it, to 'open out'. The expression, indeed, became quite fashionable – much to Mrs. Allcott's gratification – but in the end her unfamiliarity with pleasure of this kind provoked her undoing. When they found her, eyes gaunt and breathless, grinning overbearingly like a mischievous chimp, it was obvious that Joseph had, to all intents and purposes, achieved his revenge, and the sun was now gigantic in the fervour of his omnipresent eyes. Despite his unrelenting weakness, he came at last to understand the paradoxical strength to which the poets all too frequently allude. This strength was balanced coyly on the summit of his cataclysmic upper lip. It danced like effervescent summer downpours, across then through the lenses of his spectacles, sweeping over his eyes, and finally causing him to gasp and sob as though reacting to a physical assault.

And his mother, Jennifer, became unusual in her solitude. Desiring to nurture and console, she was kept back by her own innate, and suddenly incontrovertible, potential to destroy.

I will, of course, be killed - or kill - she realised. But must, in spite of this, endeavour to protect him, for in so doing I reinforce myself.

As Joseph wailed. His solemn chin like jelly. “Help me, mother! This war has grown too personal.” And his arms were flapping wings attempting to remove him.

She laughed at that, became derisive. “You’re more like your father every day,” she said. “There’s nothing less personal than war.”

And Joseph felt the shame begin to fester.

Which shame became, in course of time, his pride.

“Mother,” he said, one spring time, in the soundless, omnipresent blooming of flowers, “I’d like you to meet a friend of mine – Malcolm Baxindale.”

Who was wanly staring.

“Malcolm wants to be a fighter pilot.”

Giving Jennifer recourse to seem impressed. “Why, how commendable – a wholly worthy ambition,” she allowed, starting, and then deciding not, to cough. “And certainly a job with prospects.”

To which Malcolm sneered. “It is the Arab scum,” he ventured, “who force us to persist.”

“You mean, I think, the more extreme among the Arabs?”

“Extremists, insurgents, terrorists, renegades – who cares? They’re vermin, aren’t they, pure and simple? Nuke ‘em all, I say.”

Consigning Jennifer to a tense thread of disillusionment. She looked at Joseph, her son, with sudden consternation. I must disown this man, she thought, his friends have grown obscene.

But Malcolm kept returning.

"Are you all right, Mrs. Langley?" he said on one occasion, when contempt had bred familiarity. "You seem a trifle pale."

Confounding her. "I don't get out much," she acknowledged, never having excelled at pretence.

So that "Ah," considered Malcolm, in a tone not far from triumph. "Well, then." And his eyes became her snares. He might have swelled before her, like a threatened toad. "We are quite alone," he teased.

For they were.

And Jennifer was tremulous, encroaching on acceptance.

"Well, then," he reminded her.

His frail, lascivious voice a noose.

It is a sin, she thought.

This thing.

A sin.

But still his voice was tightening. "Well then, Mrs. Langley."

So that when Albert finally returned from Hong Kong, Jennifer had undergone a metamorphosis.

"You've changed, my love," he said.

A fact to which she could not innocently admit. "It's you, my sweet, who've changed."

Which far from being a reprisal, effectively confirmed her guilt, denying Albert any vestige of encouragement or hope, a plight exacerbated by his son's conspicuous refusal to embrace his long imagined father's reappearance.

As far as Joseph Langley was concerned, his father was a needless inconvenience, a random and unnecessary insertion into an equation already rendered volatile by the suddenly bewildering behaviour of his mother.

"I detest him," Joseph said one Sunday afternoon to Malcolm, who was standing, at any rate in theory, beside him, open-mouthed.

"You have the right," said Malcolm, who presumably derived a form of vindication from his friend's despair.

But Joseph was unconvinced. "Perhaps," he said, as though soliciting proof.

And watched his friend preparing to retreat. "I'm off now, Joe," said Malcolm. "See you 'round."

But Joseph knew.

Shortly afterwards, he notified his mother, unwrapping his words like precious jewels. "Malcolm," he announced, or possibly conceded, "has gone."

To which Jennifer elected to appear oblivious. "Has he, dear? Oh, well, never mind. I'm sure there'll be others." And she gave a mirthless laugh. "These things leave gaps," she said, "which only time can fill."

He loved her then. And frowned. "Yes, mother." Preferring not to understand.

So that Malcolm really should have been forgotten – and no doubt would have been, were not reality so flagrant.

Confronting Albert in their sin-soaked bed, as Jennifer resisted reassurance. "What is it, love?"

She laughed, and said the darkness made her cold.

"Ah, yes, the bane of darkness." For Albert surely knew.

And Jennifer was fretful. "I do not want to die," she said. "I do not want to simply disappear, to cease – the thought is too intolerable."

Albert, though, was less concerned by this than by the surging tumult in his own abdomen, which alerted him to hidden possibilities. He watched his wife from a distance, as though through an inverted telescope.

And was suddenly alive with comprehension. "How long," he said, skin starved of sensation, voice constricted with denial, "have you known?"

She stared at him, as though eschewing acknowledgement. "How long? – who knows?" And might have laughed. "All my life, perhaps. Or since this morning. It's hard to say, and scarcely matters. It's simply something we must accept. It's the truth that now confronts us, Albert – it's reality."

He looked behind her, at the solid wall. "Whose is it?"

But remembrance was far too cloying for response. In a tacit sense she trembled slightly, but remained to all observable intents and purposes motionless.

"Whose, Jennifer? Whose?"

But this was going nowhere. "Don't press me, Albert, please. It's over now. He's gone. It was just an act of desperation, or of fear. Our lives collided briefly, that's all."

"Did you love him?"

But he realised at once that no answer was possible, and so was forced to take her in his arms, to re-assert his ownership with an ostensible ardour that was nevertheless entirely bereft of passion. They removed each other's clothes with almost perfunctory savagery, as though in so doing they were stripping away the calcified membrane in which the war, and Malcolm, had encased them. He entered her almost at once, engorged beyond logic, and came torrentially within a mere half dozen speculative thrusts. She gasped and groaned, immersed in a pleasure that was wholly independent of her physical circumstances. But smiled in any case, stretched out her body sinuously across the bed, away from him, and told him calmly, shamelessly, "I love it when you fuck me, Albert".

But Albert, along with his semen, had expended all sense of self-importance. "Why ever did you do it, Josie?" he demanded. "Did you think I wasn't coming back? Is that it?"

But she moved still further away, and turned her back on him, recalling Malcolm's unfussy, but deceptively fervent, ministrations, the prurient abandon of his questing hands, the cry of anguished surprise that always accompanied his orgasm. At last she murmured, "There are no reasons, Albert, only consequences" – and would never, no matter how determinedly or desperately he implored, say more.

In course of time the baby – a girl – arrived, giving rise to unanimous acclaim. Even Albert seemed appeased. After all, he laughed, who is to know?

There was little doubt that Joseph knew. He had learned to read the secret horror in his father's calculating eyes.

Causing Albert to quiver under siege.

This strange child, nominally his daughter, began to bring forth loud sounds of agitation at the slightest inconvenience. To Albert, the persistent tears seemed a pretence (he was unsure why). But Jennifer was anxious, even fretful. After all, her involvement with the child was more than merely nominal.

Joseph, after an enthusiastic start, began to seem uncaring. His twitching lip was imprecise. His eyes appeared retarded. Gazing deep inside his father's face, he began to discern, or to imagine, untold secrets of lithe, anonymous Chinese lovers. It was fun to watch his father's pain, and to contribute, too, if possible.

So that Joseph's quaking lip became sadistic.

Finally, however, the horror was upon them. Jennifer became disastrous in her wailing. And Joseph, too, was apparently unnerved. Only Albert, it seemed, was happy just to stare, his vibrant, spuriously tearful face a God of Judgement.

"It's for the best," he could have laughed, but Jennifer, perhaps not surprisingly, was conscious only of remembered longing, of the frail, emaciated corpse she might, in time, have loved.

She said, "I'm sure you're right," and became suffused with hatred. She was feeling pulverised.

I must escape, she saw, as her wet clothes embraced her flesh like sandwich-wrap.

"There'll be others," Albert said, although uncertain what or who.

So that Jennifer became appalled. "O, Albert!"

Flying in the face of desolation.

"O, Albert – darling!"

So that everything was finished.

For the days that remained, Albert stood, walked, sat, and breathed in predetermined rhythms that were only intermittently consoling. For the most part, he was uncontrollably distraught, beset by images of wanton desecration, or disease, or self-inflicted torment. When he arose, semi-miraculously, on what must have been the fifteenth or sixteenth day, it was to an environment completely bereft of warmth or material succour. The letter acted as a kind of jolt back into reality. It read:

Dear Albert,

I expect the notion of my writing like this will appear misplaced, but a letter is always somehow more personal than a face to face confrontation, don't you think?

I had to go. Please don't blame me for it, Albert. It was unavoidable. My feelings for you stay the same. I cannot love you any more than I can hate you. It is really quite beyond my means to change. Believe me, Albert, I have tried. Can you possibly understand, and, I hope, forgive me?

Albert, I know it was a betrayal, nothing more, and nothing less, but neither of us deserves the repercussions we have had to endure. I'm a victim just as much as you, believe me. We have both been scarred by different strands of the same cat-o-nine tails.

Now, Albert, I am away from you, and cannot hurt you any more. For such small mercies, let us be grateful.

Well, my erstwhile darling, any more would only be wasted ink and paper.

Farewell now

from

Jennifer

Albert laughed, a cold, rather emaciated laugh, which both belied and reinforced his feelings.

I am finished, he perceived.

And as for Jennifer……

He laughed again, less helplessly.

Ah, Jennifer!

So that everything was gone.

Her final words dissolved like flickering atoms as the paper littered the floor, and Albert believed himself thereby absolved and resurrected.

I am free! he laughed, though inwardly unnerved.

Upstairs, in the haunted cellar that became his night, Albert buried the final remnants of his yoke in the warm and sensual caress of his own tear-sprinkled hands.

13.

Albert is reading a book about a stranger who professes to love God, and so is almost completely self-absorbed. The stranger, whose name is Albert, inhabits a somewhat ill-defined realm that nevertheless contains enough familiar features to inform, if not perhaps entirely convince. The Albert in the book spends most of his time meticulously examining his own behaviour for symptoms of waywardness and decrepitude, which he spots incessantly, and parades before his imagined audience with spectacular, incalculable delight. There are other characters too, but none of these are real.

14.

It always starts the same. Albert is in some kind of desert, alongside an enormous stone monolith. His flesh feels firm and vibrant in a way it has not done for decades. A woman, whom he knows to be Marlene even though he has only ever previously seen her as a young girl, is lying in the sand a short distance away. Both she and Albert are completely naked.

After that, he is swept along like a twig in a raging stream, battered this way and that, colliding with rocks and other twigs, sometimes even being wedged hard against the bank for brief periods. Ultimately, though, the ending is inevitable, for as he has known for years, almost indeed since his consciousness first sparked into life, there is and can be no escape.

15.

The night air is cold and still. Stars litter the sky like pin-heads against a backdrop of velvet. Albert is aware of an infinitesimal, unnameable pain, teasing at the very borders of his consciousness, producing a sense of *déja vu* that undermines his equilibrium and prompts him to clasp himself tightly for reassurance.

Then he realises, or recalls, that the flesh he is embracing is not his own, and the pain intensifies, either surging up from somewhere deep within, or else assailing him from without, it is difficult to tell. He is either drowning in pain, or pain is suffusing his body with all the inexorable intensity of an orgasm. He remembers gunshot, and flashing lights, and thunderous explosions, and the harrowing screams of men who have seen.

And unfurls himself like a flower opening its petals upon the omnipresent sand.

The girl, looking very pale and cold and frightened in the still, stark shadows, crouches down beside him. “Then you’re not dead,” she infers.

To which he coughs, or gasps, or laughs. “Of course not.” As the pain, and its concomitant recollections, recede.

“You worried me.”

So that this time it is unmistakeably laughter which emerges, harsh, inevitable, insistent. He is rendered almost flaccid by it.

The girl sighs. “It’s not surprising,” she concedes. “This whole thing’s too outlandish.” And she begins scooping up handfuls of sand, allowing it to drain gradually through her fingers, in a desperate attempt to arrive at reassurance.

The girl’s name, he knows, is Marlene, but whether he has ever met her before is unclear.

Albert is suddenly inspired. “This sand,” he announces, “is a metaphor for what we’re going through”. And he gathers up a handful himself, squeezes tightly, then hurls it from him in disgust.

Marlene clambers angrily to her feet, and retreats toward the nearby rocks. Suddenly, almost certainly for the first time, Albert is aware of her nakedness, and is assailed by an overriding need for absolution. He hurries after her. “I’m sorry, Marlene, forgive me.” He catches up, and takes her by the arm. “I’m just as scared as you are, honestly.”

She removes her arm, but smiles. “These sands will turn us crazy,” she concedes. “Let’s rest.”

And so they lie.

Together on the all-pervading sand.

As Albert coyly watches from afar.

It is years, he says, or thinks, since I have lain prostrate beside a woman.

Feeling trapped.

Her cool skin cascades across him, though their bodies do not touch. The horror of his barless prison, meticulously constructed over years of self-neglect, appals and overwhelms him. There is and can be no escape.

Marlene nestles closer. "Albert?"

His borrowed body stretches, tightens. "Yes?"

"Do you think any of this is real?"

Soliciting his gaze. He allows himself to dwell upon the innocuous certainty of her features: her tranquil, almost furtive eyes, the somewhat unwieldy nose, the whimsical mouth. He takes in the smooth curves of her throat, and shoulder blades, and breasts, the slightly ponderous rotundity of her stomach, the weighty firmness of her buttocks, thighs and calves. He is marginally consoled by admiration, and impelled toward a kind of reawakening. He clasps her by the hand, and this time she does not resist. "Does this feel real?" he asks, and squeezes gently.

She replies by moving nearer. Albert, encouraged, resumes, "There is more to life than – than food and drink," he somewhat inexplicably decides. "There are thoughts, and appetites, and dreams."

"Is this a dream then?"

Albert laughs. "Do you want it to be?"

She moves away once more, and does not answer.

"Get some sleep," he says. "We'll talk again tomorrow."

Feeling trapped again, constricted, so that Jennifer is presented with an opportunity to retaliate. "Man shall not live by bread alone," she taunts. "You're shirking, Albert."

But he will not be undone. "Get thee behind me, Satan!"

"Albert, please, control yourself!"

As the fingers of the trap begin to tighten, steadily asphyxiating him. "Forgive me, Father, for I have sinned," he gasps.

And the celebrant's holy face is clean. "*Misereatur vestry omnipotens Deus*," he declares, "*et dimissis pecatis vestries, perducat vas ad vitam aeternam*."

But Albert remains distraught. Squalid earth is plastered on his helpless skin. "*Domine, Domine, non sum dignus, ut intre sub tectum meum, sed tantum dic verbo, et sanabitur anima mea! Domine, Domine, exaudi orationem meam*!"

But his conscience, defiled by the unintended lessening of his borrowed body's load, denies him consolation. "I am free," he wishes, whilst simultaneously constrained by hitherto unnoticed shackles.

The silence stings their opened wounds like salt, while the seemingly motionless desert floor is thwarting them. They are forced to grapple with the only tangible adversary within reach, cruelly scratching, pummelling and biting, as if to effect a kind of subjugation, or at very least a temporary reprieve.

She feels the supple, inextinguishable irony of ample, receptive thighs.

My thighs, she thinks.

And hidden underneath her frightful skin her own, inexorable destiny.

The future purged by surging sperm.

She pants.

Albert leaves her then, the body of this unimagined woman, her face, her breath so hideously real. Her lucid flesh untouchable, yet touched.

"O Jennifer!"

As remembrance squirms and fluctuates, intermittently persuasive and unassailable, although in actual fact there is nothing there but the naked wind.

"It's clear we must make plans," he says, but at the atmosphere. The girl is asleep. Her face a churning sea, revealing anguished dreams, reflecting the immense, incalculable weight of disappointment.

"How are you, Albert?"

"Disappointed."

Which, when all embellishment and artifice are stripped away – as indeed they have been – is only to be expected.

So that "Plans" he says, "we must make plans" - although the domineering sky is heedless.

"This whole affair's a memory."

And sleeps.

In silent, devastating waves.

Of pain.

His son's exasperating head refusing madly. "No, Dad, no. It won't do. Can't you see? Don't you understand? My heart would never be in it."

"People change," says Albert, his normally unpretentious face alert, "and so do things."

But Joseph is unyielding. "Some things," he insists, "never change."

So that Albert is unnerved, recalling similar discussions with his own father. He is inwardly gaping madly like a landed fish.

"I'm not cut out to be a warrior," says Joseph. And pretends to sigh. "I am not at all," he prods, with brandished sword, "the truculent type."

Which, as Albert sees it, is tantamount to betrayal. I might as well be dead, he thinks, his shrunken breath grown wholly, fundamentally superfluous.

And "Judas! Judas!" with ardent, unequivocal resolve.

My father now is dead, sees Joseph. And it is I, Joseph Langley, I alone, who have murdered him.

The pleasure held at arm's length, like a slightly unexpected gift.

And suddenly the air looks strange. The furniture is wobbly. My mother's face, he understands, is fretful. And hears a distant, fading voice retort.

This thing, this death, is like a storm, he thinks. Its aftermath a green, ineffable sky. As my father lies inert, untroubled, like a fallen twig afloat upon the green unnecessary river, swept beneath an endless, autocratic sea of green, the sky. So that I, too, am lost, he understands – a fragile stick confused between the ubiquitous sheets of greenness which surround.

A flimsy, brittle, inconclusive shard, with no recourse to resistance, let alone redemption.

As their wind-blown forms are gradually rendered unrecognisable.

In course of time, Albert duly finds the silver piled high beneath his son's bewildered corpse. He notices that resurrection, which by now for him has grown habitual, is trapped inside the body's unproductive eyes, effectively denying Albert scope for understanding, or for grief. Instead, he laughs, abandoning his body to a grim, relentless orgasm of hilarity.

To live and then to die, he sees. There is and can be nothing else. There is and can be no escape.

Next morning, Albert surreptitiously examines the smoothness of his partner's sleeping form with an overriding lust that is almost sexless. Her nakedness reminds him of the quiet vulnerability of his son's corpse. You could be dead, he provokes himself by thinking.

But she moves. Self-consciously, she covers herself, and then remembers. "Albert."

He fights a smile. "The same."

For perhaps the first time, her usually furtive eyes examine him. "You look imaginary," she decides.

And waits for something indefinable to astound her.

But Albert merely flinches. "I don't understand it either," he explains.

Eliciting a frail, uneasy silence.

Marlene eventually gets up, and moves out of sight behind the rocks, presumably to relieve herself. Moments later, she calls out. "Albert, quick! There's water!"

He clambers to his feet, and follows. Sure enough, she is laughing with renewed self-confidence, water dribbling maniacally down her chin. She splashes him playfully, and is suddenly, but briefly, transformed beyond his recognition. He allows himself to feel momentarily enticed as water, dank but cool, re-awakens his momentum. Kiss me, Marlene! he has to restrain himself from cackling.

Her face, he sees, is lean and parched, bereft of any kind of obvious beauty, but granted a certain allure by its exuberance. Experience has etched its mark upon her with the cruel indifference of a surgeon's knife, but there remains sufficient animation and fortitude there to captivate.

As she wipes her mouth with her hand, she decides it is time to test the water. "Are you – happy – Albert?" The uncomfortable word is a knife, balanced by the point of its blade on skin, its absurdity lessened by the possibility of blood.

And Albert is forced to remember that, for all her apparent equanimity and resilience, she is, after all, just a woman. "I might be happier if I understood," he decides. But failing not to smile.

"I think I begin to see," says Marlene, eyes reflecting swarming clouds, as she scans the distant corners of their shared world. "There's something more though, isn't there? I can feel it. I can sense it in the edges of your mouth. You can't deceive me, Albert. Don't you realise yet? Our nakedness is more than merely physical. This desert is –"

She pauses, gulps at air, and then, with either irritation or perplexity, shakes her head.

As Albert winces under siege. "Yes, Marlene?" he prompts, but far too eagerly. He realises straight away that the inspiration has dissolved, and he finds himself once more beside a rather dour, unprepossessing woman, who, appearing suddenly crestfallen and discomfited, is refusing to look him in the eye.

"What is it, Marlene?"

The gaunt air is murderous.

"Who are you, really?"

As his ears are filled with all the inexpressible silence of stone.

She shakes her head again, as though reacting to an inner voice, and begins to move away. "I need to be alone," she says.

So that Albert, yet again, is forced to endure the inescapable malaise of solitude as, unseen by human eyes, but incontrovertibly so for all that, the fringe between the distant sky and distant land dissolves.

16.

The golden sand is turning amber underneath the shadow of his outstretched hand, and pouring coldly through his undulating fingers, as Albert squats to safeguard his dignity, or else to seem unmoved. "I somehow don't believe all this," he ventures.

And the sky is once again a raging sea of fervent blue.

Marlene moves away towards the constant rocks. Her feet disturb the sand in time to the relentless churning of Albert's stomach, or his soul. She disappears from sight.

Albert decides to lie prostrate against the looming backdrop of the monolith, breathing long through nostrils suddenly rendered alert by reminiscence. He recalls the overwhelming smell of death at Mr. Ballantine's, the butcher's – a scent which is intermingled with the lurid perfume of the waiting herd, their lascivious eyes agleam, their denture stains diminished by saliva.

There once had been a huge and skinless pig with gaping eyes that might have swung if touched.

And persevering in the face of everything was Mr. Ballantine himself, his permanently purple hands defiant in response to providence. His father before him, too, had sliced and hacked at senseless flesh, until indeed the very day he died; while later on, when the slightly less commercial killing of the war had finally subsided, the Ballantine dynasty had extended into a third generation - a female one this time - which had likewise luxuriated in innocent blood, and learned to camouflage the truth in inoffensive parcels of pastry.

Albert rises to his feet. The eastern borders of the rocks are beginning to darken, indicating the onset of afternoon. He yawns. The girl can clearly be heard splashing playfully, or desperately, in the recently discovered spring, and Albert's thirst is re-awakened. Clambering up the nearby rock-face, he is astonished by the supple strength which courses through his body. If this is a dream, he thinks, then I do not want to wake.

The looming pig begins to sway, ridiculous and imperturbable. Albert chuckles.

"What's the joke?" asks Marlene, who is seemingly reduced in size, and who stares at him with something akin to recognition.

"Sorry – I was reminiscing." And, after scrambling down the moss covered rock-face to within a couple of feet of the spring, he crouches on his haunches, as though expectant. Marlene's face is disappointed. She too crouches down, stirs the water with her palm, then cups a glistening mouthful to her lips. That done, she tosses back her head, trailing moistened strands of hair behind her, and sighs. Her body suddenly seems immensely fragile as she kneels beside the tiny pool, which remains their only palpable defence, and Albert is correspondingly disabled by contrition.

A pock-mark melon of an eye is perched astride the distant mountain range. By way of self-defence, or in reaction to a sudden feeling of futility, Albert drops his gaze.

"The past won't help us now," says Marlene.

The endless sky endorsing.

But Albert disagrees: "There may be lessons to be learnt," he insists, and kneels beside the spring to wash. His smooth, surprising face confronts him with a mixture of uncertainty and pensiveness. This sallow, enigmatic body not his own. The firm, undeviating features; a crop of comfortable hair. The whole an antithesis.

As mirror, mirror, asking after fairness - no response. Our flesh the flawed reflection of a demigod.

While all the time the supple water tries to ooze.

Always greenness asks and makes appropriate replies to questions of the nature of the soul. A green walk in the still park. The floating actual leaves obscuring depth, emasculating danger. Down there once seen the drowning, frantic face of Billy Sutton - and Albert then had laughed. The leaves, of course, are brown against the murderous preponderance of green – too brown for living witnesses to truth, the green assassinators.

Immeasurable decay.

Has held in careless hands the needful parcel of her formulating flesh.

"My dad once brought me here when I was small. I was nearly choked by all the colours."

There is and can be no reply.

"I remember looking up and being almost floored by green on blue."

He laughs, at what is in actual fact quite a complicated joke. The railings intervene.

"The drakes are always easy to discern," he says, and points toward the distant shore. A speckled blur of red and blue against the mottled vegetation. The water only turning.

Jennifer removes her quite respectable mittened hand. Her wintry eyes are glazed against the possibility of yearning, or belief.

As Albert stamps his feet.

“It’s getting cold,” he says. He likes to see himself as subtle. There is colour even now alive inside his devious mind.

So parting hand in hand the senseless park lake remains.

His counterfeit eyes observe what might have been a dream, the unmolested mountains now a standing proof against alternative solutions.

“This one’ll live, I’ll wager.”

“Yep, I reckon so.”

“He’ll hardly be a target for the ladies, though.”

As laughter circumnavigates the spring. And Marlene, in prepossessing certainty, returns.

“What kind of lessons?” Asked with intermingled earnestness and mirth. The sand assaults his prying fingers underneath an illusory film of flatness, as a sudden wisp of wind invokes a recollection, or an insight. He fumbles weakly with the awkward button of an explanation. “Mistakes,” he says, “can sometimes be didactic.” And his coat flaps open in the searing wind, inviting Marlene to slash and tear with brutal teeth and harsh, malicious talons. The desert floor becomes subjectively stained by the fearsome flow of blood, as Albert metaphorically wails. “Philosophy,” he contends, “is useless. What we need are tangible plans.”

And Marlene remarks that even plans must have their covers wiped and pages scoured before they can approximate to fruition, so why the ceaseless talk? Was it not agreed to investigate the mountains?

So that Albert sighs. "Why, yes, indeed – the mountains. Something tells me they're the key."

"Indubitably."

"But what of food and water?"

The torrid air might howl. It is usually the unexpected arrow which penetrates, and their broken flesh has caused the heedless sands to flow with blood.

A yielded slab of lamb adopts a sacrificial posture underneath the strenuous, darkened hands of Mr. Ballantine. Albert, who has yet to learn to enter credit through the unconventional conduit of a lapse into the red, remains deceptively self-sufficient, dropping short; he cannot quite believe in solvency.

"Are you sure we wouldn't make it in a single all-out spurt?"

Impossible to determine; but hardly worth the risk.

"There must be something we can do."

The ever unarticulated urge to suicide.

"Perhaps we're meant to stay?"

Implying sentient surveillance.

"Or, there again, perhaps the test involves our getting out."

But Marlene, at this, is riotously contemptuous. "There is no test," she spits. "There's nothing, Albert – nothing but the wind and sand and sky."

Deceiving no-one. "Just who exactly," Albert wants to know, " are you attempting to convince?"

As endless golden waves of sand continue to proffer a kind of mute implicit scorn, and Albert, who would like to believe himself magnanimous, derives a meagre form of appeasement from the sight of inexplicable tremors forming in the small of Marlene's back. He gropes with almost wanton pleasure in the less immediately accessible regions of the underlying sand, encountering harsh, implacable granules which resist and intermittently abrade.

And then the clashing, strident reverberations of innumerable potential aftermaths resound against the desert floor with all the stern intensity of an earthquake, with Albert's firm, italicising hand implying something in the nature of a frenzied denial. There appears a stain of blood on Albert's tremulous, bitten lower lip, which nevertheless contributes to what he likes to feel is quite a valid recommendation.

"We might as well wait for a while," he ventures. "There's nothing to be gained by haste."

But Marlene remains disdainful. "We're not a team," she says, "so don't presume to tell me what to do."

Effectively emasculating him. "Would you prefer to go it alone?" he asks.

To which she laughs. "Do we have a choice?" And walks away.

Albert ventures to his feet. He focuses on the dimple in the small of Marlene's back until she disappears from view behind a clump of rocks, then turns to look away across the desert. With shaded eyes, he scans the distant line of blue, attempting to discern some previously unnoticed landmark or feature that might provoke intensity of purpose. He is mildly astonished by the apparent sense of perplexity which accompanies his failure. He resolves to circumnavigate the monolith of stone, which soon, he wryly muses, may find itself appropriately named.

He is, he calculates, walking north. The scant area of shrubbery which surrounds the spring soon lapses, but terse yellow grass remains, and is harsh upon his unaccustomed feet. To the left, angry rock emerges like an upturned fist, firm, intransigent and leering. Albert feels a sudden upsurge of intimidation, exposing and reaffirming his nakedness. He experiences an intense but senseless yearning after buttered toast and coffee, and it is only with considerable determination that he is able to stymie tears. At the northernmost extremity of rock, even the grass contrives to dissolve. Confronted by the ubiquitous antipathy of sand, which is intensified and reinforced by flailing whips of memories, Albert flounders to his knees. There is implicit loss and fear and desolation edging across his skin. He sinks below the inexplicable darkness of his burden with the uncomprehending terror of a scolded pup.

His mind distinguishes the faint but importunate tinkling of a bell, heralding divine intrusion: a tiny disc of concentrated effluence perpetuating deadness, as Mr. Ballantine, who has metamorphosed into a priest, is lifted bodily above the watching throngs, responding to the mild interminable summons of the mild interminable bell.

"Albert! Albert?"

The noise is slapping at his cheeks. He awakes to Marlene's confounded floating form. She is pounding at his flesh in seeming terror, crying out. "Albert, what happened?"

He resists the urge to speak, responding instead by means of protracted, convalescent breathing.

Marlene, having grappled clumsily with his wrist, presumably in search of a pulse, seems appeased. "I imagine you'll survive," she says, and rises to her feet.

Albert, deriving a momentary burst of impetus from dependence, says, "I didn't like the way you walked away from me just now". The ignored ground becoming tremulous.

Marlene laughs. "Then all my deportment classes were in vain." There seems to be a slant upon the horizon, which quickly levels out. She kneels beside him, whispering sullenly. "I can be rather selfish, can't I?"

And now her eyes are sparkling, so that Albert finds the sudden energy to stand. Even the dearth of grass no longer aggravates. "Why don't we see if we can find some grub?" he suggests. "Then we can agree on what to do next."

17.

Back at the spring once more, Albert splashes his face with water, while Marlene relaxes on the sand. Above the leering rocks the sky is callously brooding. The flavour of the atmosphere has calcified into something resembling an after dinner staleness, although the appetite remains, and Marlene salivates compulsively. Albert's paleness seems to lose itself in omnipresent rock.

The overwhelming sky a dome.

And now she sees the ram, eliciting a murmur of surprised hope, a starting gun which urges Albert into action. His scurrying feet produce a drum-roll of expectancy, his frantic hands unfurl. The air expended hard, then pulled in against the tightness of emaciated throat, retreating, while his weeping breath rejoices at the sight of sanguine, spurting blood.

An unfamiliar wave of brightness rises as, colliding resolutely with the rock, a merciless pre-eminence of brain becomes exposed. The dying embers float, as weeping might have fallen tears of ecstasy. Marlene clasps at Albert's weary hands, aghast yet gratified.

A nascent unity of purpose arises from their mutual devotion over roasted leg of mutton. Albert's unctuous lips are close to Marlene's. The damaged succulence inspires their stinted stomachs to a fertile roundness, and they laugh, or wheeze, as though released.

The darkened sky extends a heinous veil, implying admonition, articulated in a clamorous wail of wind. Albert mutters indecipherably, while Marlene's gleaming face is unabashed, her hostile teeth despising. She eats with irredeemable haste, gulping, gnawing, tearing. Voracious fingers strip the undefended bones. She soothes herself with violence, a heavy indignation stirring in her abdomen, stern tugs of passion pulling at her throat.

The sky a purple enmity.

"We'll have to find some shelter," Albert says, against the now forbidding backdrop.

Marlene is hopeful. "I think I saw some caves," she says.

So that running through the sympathetic gorge their legs become supreme. The exhilarated fervour of a rising coolness in the atmosphere infects them with abandonment as their gushing faces luxuriate in wind. It is good to stand beneath the unexpected sanctuary of caves, to laugh at one another's suddenly brightened faces as the sky ignites and belches forth a warning. Then clambering madly up the rock face, seeking refuge.

At the same time as Albert's eyes are suddenly invaded by remembrance, his outward presence settles back. A warm, alluring curl of sensuality enfolds his spine. There had been that all too brief interval of solace when he believed he had found a soulmate, only to discover that hidden behind Jennifer's winsome smile was a dagger, which she pulled on him just as he had turned his back to embrace a future free of doubt.

" – is time to go. Perhaps we'll never make it, but we surely have to try."

His perfect eye investigates. There are occasions when alternatives reinforce.

A sudden, piercing sense of loneliness invades him like a stab wound, compelling him to flinch. His strained, contorted face erupts.

"Are we, then, or aren't we?"

The woman's unenlightened cheeks are dour, and Albert, seeing that internal complication may be unavoidable, is induced to vomit on the desert floor. He edges closer to the brink. "I'm ready if you are."

For, despite being fixed in place by vicious nails, his outstretched arms have comprehended freedom.

"We'll go tomorrow, then," says Marlene.

The thunderous cacophony of rain resounding in endorsement.

"I wish you'd told me of this place before," says Albert, smiling feebly in an effort to disguise his petulance.

"It didn't seem important earlier." She dares him to demur.

But Albert merely grunts, a response which Marlene is content to interpret as acceptance. "The gorge is filling up," she remarks. "It's virtually a river."

"We might well have to stay here longer then," says Albert, presuming to hope, but Marlene, who has returned to the cave-way entrance, fails to hear.

So that Jennifer is breathing in his furtive eyes. The sudden warmth is overwhelming. "I want you, Albert - take me further."

Amidst the stifling smell of after dinner staleness. Too confusing. Causing him to suck his knuckles.

"Are you all right, my darling?"

"It's nothing."

As his rib-cage writhes in unexpected pain. I can not breathe, he thinks. I must escape.

But Jennifer is quite inexorable. "I need you, Albert." Affording him a sudden glimpse of purgatory, as he waits to be engulfed by surging hills of flame. There is hoped for screaming in his cramped, inoperative mouth.

"What keeps happening?" asks Marlene, her moist hand firm against his palpitating brow. Albert gasps, though whether from relief or pain even he is not quite able to decide. "We need each other, Marlene," he hears himself declare. The words are like a loose page re-inserted in a book; the glue may take some time to set, but ultimately the book will be restored, if not as good as new, at least sufficiently well for it to be read again.

Recalling verdant brightnesses in steaming jungle depths. The endlessness of two and three times tables, suddenly, and inexplicably, grown comprehensible. I get you now, he irreverently proclaims – to Sister Mary Vincent's amazed consternation.

Enlightenment, though, is blotting paper to the ink of pain; his anguished tears are actually alive with hope, so that Marlene becomes dismayed. This new, unwanted complication is disquieting.

"Stop it, Albert, please! We must be serious." Her face grown quite immense with fear.

I cannot bear this, Albert thinks, acutely aware of the sweat-saturated sand upon his back and buttocks, as the rain relentlessly persists.

"Albert, get a grip on yourself!"

And her words are like a dancing swarm of bees, to which Albert's flesh feels starkly vulnerable. He tries to reassure himself with careful hands, but in the face of such overwhelming odds the gesture is futile. "I can't stand it!" he sobs, conscious only of an omnipresent buzzing.

But then returns. "I'm – sorry," he concedes, releasing himself. Marlene's eyes relax, if only a trifle. She winces, though, and says, "There's no reason to feel sorry, Albert, it's entirely understandable. This whole situation's so…….unreal."

The final, stabbing word inflicts a gash in the spurious veneer of self-assurance that Albert has so meticulously concocted. He hugs his knees to his chest, as though to interpose a barrier between himself and some truth he has found to be distasteful. "What is reality?" he resents himself for asking.

Marlene replies: "It's what we find ourselves confronted by." And the still air endorses. "It's what the universe proclaims or asserts."

Persuading Albert to his feet. "I can't accept that, Marlene," he says. "Reality is sometimes surreptitious as a worm."

But "You don't have to be consciously aware of something to be confronted by it," Marlene insists. "Reality is tantamount to personhood. No matter what, you have to make some manner of response – it forces you."

As Albert stares across the desert, desperate for conviction.

"Reality," she postulates, in careful, measured syllables, "is not to be avoided."

But Albert's suddenly animated limbs are argumentative. He lunges ostentatiously to the floor, unleashing clouds of whiteness all around, and inducing Marlene to splutter, wanly: "I hope you understand me, Albert."

The conversation wavers. They have either flirted with a breakthrough, or are more enmeshed than ever in disharmony.

As Billy Sutton frantically screams, "Gerroff! Gerroff me! Nasty brutes!" – apparently believing himself assailed by ants, which might as well be Albert's investigative fingers.

I can not stop, thinks Albert, as the beauty of his partner's suffering flesh excites aroused anticipation in his own.

"Alby, Alby, help!"

His loins ablaze with mirth, as he realises that the frenzied waving of his victim-lover's ant-infested arms is his own path to freedom. Perhaps, in spite of everything he believes himself to have learned, escape is actually conceivable.

There, inside the cave, a nebulous trickle of light glimmers palely on the inner wall, as Albert whispers softly to himself. Could it be that their most enlightened course of action would entail an abnegation of the obvious? He laughs at what is really, once again, quite a serious joke. But Marlene, whose posture has grown ungainly, retains a prima donna's right to silence, and so their progress is, for the moment or forever, stopped.